AF507218

DEVOTED to HIS SWORD

FLORENCE A. BLISS

CITY OWL
PRESS

DEVOTED TO HIS SWORD
Swords of Chevalerie, Book 2

CITY OWL PRESS
www.cityowlpress.com

Cover Design by MiblArt. All stock photos licensed appropriately.

Edited by Jessica Shearer.

For information on subsidiary rights, please contact the publisher at info@cityowlpress.com.

Print Edition ISBN: 978-1-64898-570-6

Digital Edition ISBN: 978-1-64898-571-3

Printed in the United States of America

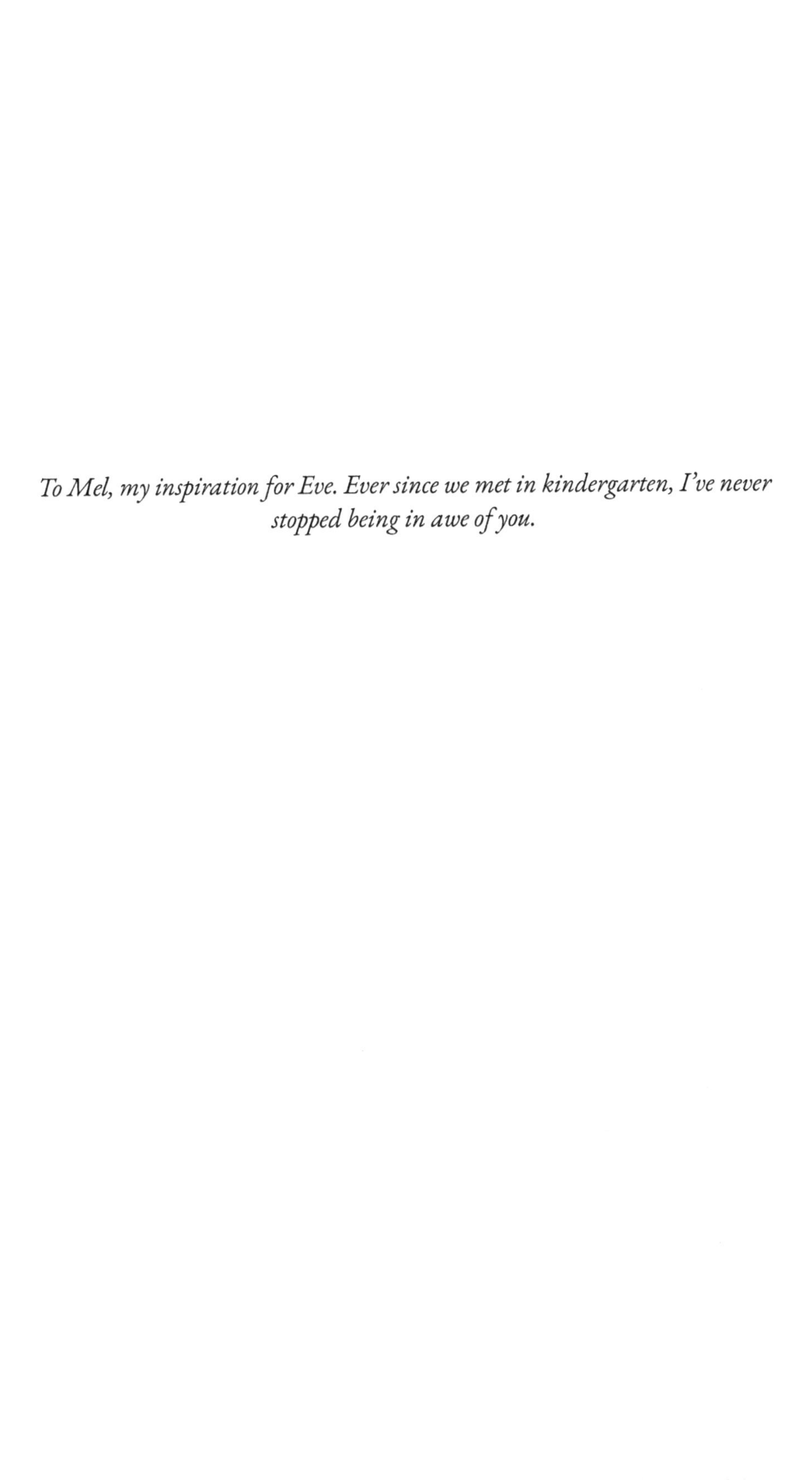

To Mel, my inspiration for Eve. Ever since we met in kindergarten, I've never stopped being in awe of you.

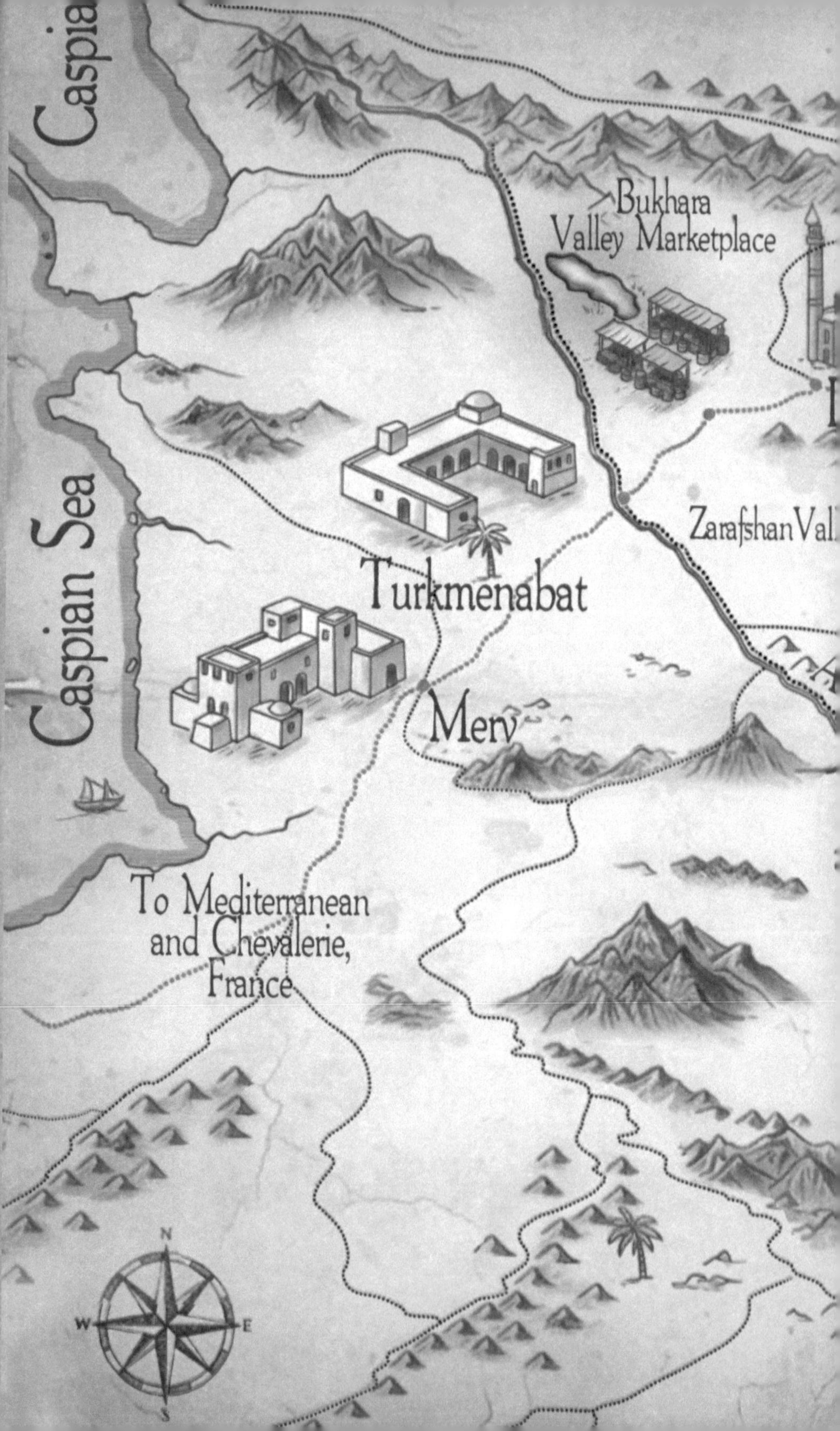

Caspian
Caspian Sea
Bukhara
Valley Marketplace
Zarafshan Val
Turkmenabat
Merv
To Mediterranean
and Chevalerie,
France
N
W
E
S

The Great Silk Road
1650s
Issyk Kul lake
nara
Samarkand
Kashgar
Darya River
Carth
Indus River

Chapter One

1655, MIDDLE EAST, EARLY SPRING

Michel du Chevalerie, first son of the Duke of Provence, France, leaned back against the outside wall of the whorehouse in the dusty city of Merv. The other men in his crew were inside, enjoying the activities, but Michel was impatient to get back on the road. Such stops had proven necessary to help the men keep their wits on this long journey across the old Silk Road. Michel preferred other ways to keep himself sharp. Instead of the indulgences inside, he took the time to make plans, organize his supplies, and just enjoy the moment of solitude and the peaceful clatter of the afternoon roads.

That is, until a woman fell through the canopy above him and right into his arms.

He'd heard the crack of wood just in time to look up and prepare himself to catch a bundle of flailing skirts, wild golden blonde hair, and silks from the canopy.

"What—?" he blurted as dust and debris pelted down, the peace and solitude dissolving. "How—?"

The bundle was tossing and righting herself in his arms, wriggling like a caught fish as he continued to spit confused questions at her. "Are you alright? How did you get up there?"

The woman managed to untangle herself from the canopy and get herself upright. Her feet hit the ground, her head came up and—

"*Mon Dieu*," Michel said, halting completely when he got his first look at her. Everything around him blurred away into nothing: the noises of the street, the dusty buildings, his own questions and confusion. Never had he seen eyes quite like hers—mottled green and brown, sharp and insistent. Never had he seen someone with her golden coloring and such striking features.

Never had the sight of a woman caused his thoughts to stop long enough to notice each thunderous beat of his heart.

But the woman, not seeming to slow or be affected in the least, grabbed him by the collar of his jacket, her eyes urging, beseeching, *commanding*. He could see that she wanted something from him, but the *what* and the *how* still made no sense.

"What do you need?" he implored. He understood nothing, but he certainly was curious.

She brought her finger to her lips and shushed him.

"Did you—?" He quickly lowered his voice to a whisper, going from concern to disbelief. "Did you shush me?"

She threw her hands up as she tucked herself away into the shadows of the alcove behind him.

Just then, he heard a commotion on the street. Among the din of wagon bells and bleating animals came a man's voice, shouting. Michel's head snapped back to her.

"Are you hiding?" he hissed, following her deeper into the alcove, protective on instinct. "Is someone after you?" he insisted. He looked at the broken canopy above him, thinking she could have been hiding on the rooftops before crashing down. He turned back to her. She wore a ragged peasant dress, covered in dust from the fall, with a streak that could easily be blood on her sleeve. He moved tentatively closer, now concerned he would frighten her. "Can you...speak?"

The woman made an exasperated sound, put her hands on Michel's shoulders, turned him around, and gave him a shove back out toward the street.

Michel was dumbfounded. So much for frightening her. He would have been amused by how casually this woman was ordering him around, but the thought that someone *was* coming for her kept him tense. With no chance to think or plan, and despite knowing how much trouble skirmishes out in the open could cause him, he couldn't ignore the situation.

His integrity would always win—if the woman needed help, he was going to help her.

The decision made to put himself between her and whatever she didn't want to get her, he placed his hand on the hilt of his sword, in readiness, and sidled back out onto the street. He gave her another look, his own finger up to his lips. She nodded back at him, and he believed the understanding passed that he wouldn't let anyone harm her.

Out on the street, chaos had stirred up the quiet afternoon. The lazy streams of farmers and merchants moving through the market had already been disrupted. Michel immediately saw the source of the commotion: a short, fat man with wiry hair and a bloody nose charging up the road. He was leading a donkey with a merchant cart, but abandoned it as he got closer to the whorehouse, huffing as he did.

Veronica, an elegant and shrewd woman in her fifties, and proprietress of the establishment, stood in the center of the busy street with her hand up for him to stop, her dark burgundy dress the only color of the otherwise sand-washed street.

"Do not come near me, Armin," she called, her voice booming over the rest of the market. She spoke French, as she was one of the many French expats in this area. "I don't want any of your stolen nonsense, and neither do my girls."

"Veronica, you can't believe what I discovered," the man said in broken but passable French. "For your business!" He hunched down to cough and catch his breath.

"You are a pest and a thief," she replied. She cocked an eyebrow and paused before lowering her voice. "What do you have?"

"She must be here somewhere," Armin spat, desperate, scanning the road. "I just had her."

"*Her*?" Veronica snapped. "You better be talking about a cow."

"You must see her," Armin said. He turned to Michel, looking past him.

"There!" he bellowed, pointing past Michel and directly at the woman. "She's there!"

Armin, still puffing, took a dash toward the alcove, but Michel caught him by the arm and hoisted him away. "Nope," Michel said.

"Let me go, *fis a putain*." The man sneered.

"Did he just call me a son of a bitch?" Michel said to Veronica, affronted, as the man struggled to get past him. "Does he know who I am?"

Veronica just shrugged.

Michel pushed the man back and settled his own posture, making it clear he wasn't getting past.

"I will call the guards. She's mine. Guards!" Armin blustered. "Guards!"

"Have you lost your mind?" Veronica said. By now, the scene had drawn a crowd. Women had perched at the windows above them. Men with carts in the street had halted. "Get out of here, Armin, before I have you arrested."

"I have carted her here all the way from Bukhara!" Armin spluttered. "She owes me!"

Michel still blocked the man from getting to the woman behind him, but he did turn to glance at her. She was flattened against the stone wall, eyes wide, an intense stare fixed on Michel. She expected help from him. Michel could feel it. It was in her demeanor, in her posture. What he could really do for her, he wasn't sure. As the first son of the Duke, and the proxy on whom trade between his country and the East rested, Michel deftly avoided trouble on these streets. His reputation was far too important to tarnish through insults and impractical fights. Especially now, when the King and Cardinal Mazarin had saddled him with new complications. But how could he step away and not help this woman escape this dirty little man?

He had two choices: beat the man bloody or just give him what he wanted.

Michel faced the man. "How much do you want for her?"

Veronica turned to Michel with huge eyes as Armin tilted his head. "Make me an offer," the man said, a grin showing his still bloodied teeth.

Michel, a professional at haggling on this route, slipped into form. "Let me be clear, I have no use for this woman on my travels. I will turn her loose as soon as I know she is safe from you." He folded his arms. He spoke in

French to keep the man at a disadvantage, though he could easily have done the barter in Mongolian. "Two silver *tanga*."

"Two silver *tanga*?" Armin squawked. "Look at her. Have you ever seen anyone so beautiful?" He threw up two fingers. "Two gold *tillā*."

Michel scoffed. "A waste of two *tillā*. Beauty has no utility where I'm going. The only reason I pay you at all, *Chi nohoinii gulug,* is to shut you up." He enjoyed enraging the man by calling him a son of a bitch in his own language.

Now Armin straightened his spine, clearly insulted by that. "She is Mongolian like me. Mongolian women are the strongest women you will ever know." Then he waved his hand to his bloody nose as proof of this.

"Beautiful or not, she is a peasant, and I don't have any fields for her to work. Besides, any man who could afford that price wouldn't want a peasant for a bride." He gave the man a disapproving stare, meant to cajole and intimidate. Then he turned to Veronica, without taking his eyes off Armin. "Veronica, would you pay that price?"

Veronica folded her arms. "Absolutely not. My girls are all here by choice."

Michel watched the calculations die on the man's face. He did love winning a good negotiation. "I tell you what, since she doesn't seem to be hurt, I will give you one gold *tillā* and one silver *tanga*." Then he stepped toward Armin, in his face, intimidating once more. "If I ever hear that you try something like this again on my route," he threatened, "I will find you. I'll cart you back to France and throw you in the *Bastille*." He stayed glaring at the man. "Veronica, you'll tell me if he ever tries something like this again?"

"Absolutely, I will."

Armin chewed his lip. Then he shoved out his hand. "Alright," he said. "One *tillā,* one *tanga*." He nodded at Michel. "And I will stay with selling pots and kettles." He gave a half-hearted laugh and shook his head. "She really was more trouble than she was worth."

In a moment, they finished up, and the little fat man turned away, tottering happily back up the street, his purse full of coin, no longer a squealing mess.

Michel was pleased with himself. He crossed his arms in satisfaction, glad he had been able to squash the problem, as the street returned to normal activity. As a Western man traveling into tribal territory to do business, he had to be very careful not to upset the balance or overstep any boundaries. He knew terrible things happened, but through his traveling and his presence, he always did his best to keep everything legitimate and safe for his kinsman, for anyone traveling these routes, including a woman who seemed very much on her own.

He turned back to the woman to *really* look at her. She was Mongol clearly, with the characteristic eyes and high cheekbones, but striking, dark, golden blond hair that made her all the more remarkable. She was several inches shorter than Michel, though still a tall woman. Despite the tattered attire—with the streak of blood which he was sure was from Armin's nose —she stood tall, healthy, supple, *strong*.

Michel gave her a bit of a grin, expecting some sign of gratitude, but she just stared at him with that same intensity, her brow furrowed, her eyes narrowed. She didn't look grateful at all.

She looked furious.

"How many times have you come through Merv, Michel?" Veronica balked at him. "And never once have you indulged in my girls. Yet, you pluck this rose right in front of me." She moved forward and took the woman's hand, pulling her into the sunlight. "I'm insulted."

"Veronica," he scoffed, waving her off. "You know me better than that." He moved closer to the woman. "What's your name, sweetheart?" he asked, his voice gentle. He repeated it in Mongolian. He didn't know if she understood anything he said. It was unlikely she spoke any French. Many of the traders and merchants in this region did, but the tribal nomads didn't.

Veronica fixed the woman's shawl over her shoulders with a motherly tenderness. "My, you are a pretty girl." Veronica then spoke to Michel. "What do you plan to do with her?"

"Me?" he asked. "I don't plan to do anything with her."

Veronica shrugged. "You bought her."

"I didn't buy her," Michel said, annoyed. "I just got her away from that idiot." He cocked his head and looked at the woman. "She sure looks mad."

"You just bought her," Veronica nagged. "Of course, she is mad."

Getting frustrated, he spoke, "Veronica, come now. I would never..." he trailed off, trying to make sense of what just happened. "I would never *buy* a woman." He folded his arms and assessed the woman in front of him. He switched to Mongolian since the woman hadn't responded to French. "*Tuslamj*," he said. "Help? Do you need help?" Though that was obvious. "What's your name?" He reached forward to touch her chin.

She narrowed her eyes at him, this new anger clearly on display. *Mon Dieu*, he thought, feeling pressure in his chest, not sure if it was just her lovely face or the fact that she seemed suddenly angry at him that caused him to perspire.

Veronica smacked his hand away from the woman and said something to her in a Mongolian dialect that Michel did not know. The woman spoke and shook her head. She had a low, sultry voice. Smooth. She stared at Michel, her eyes never leaving him.

"What did you say?" Michel asked.

"I asked her if she wanted to work here. For me."

Michel turned to Veronica, a sudden pit in his gut. "What did she say?"

Veronica gave him a discerning look. "She said she was going with you."

"With me?" Michel blinked. "She can't come with me." He turned back to the woman.

"You bought her." Veronica stepped back. "She says she's yours."

"Tell her I was just trying to help..." he trailed off, still looking into the woman's eyes, a strange, overwhelming feeling of desire to do her bidding came over him.

Michel suddenly felt the sting of his actions. What had he done? What would he do with her? Would word spread that he had purchased a woman at a whorehouse in the middle of Merv? Michel was traveling the old Silk Road, and the route funneled more than trade. There were enough eyes and mouths to carry this gossip back to his King and all the way to the great Khan in the East.

Just then, Gerald, one of the men in his party, exited the building and came over to them. "Ey, Michel," Gerald called, still tucking his shirt into his pants. "Who'd you find out here?" he said, eyeing the woman next to him. "She escape?" He tipped his head back to the entrance of the whorehouse and grinned.

"Back up, Gerald," Michel barked as he put his body in front of the woman, an instinct to shield her from this gawking man, who still reeked of sex and perfume. Michel turned again to Veronica. "Will you help her get home?"

"Where? Here?" Veronica said. "She doesn't live here. I would have seen her before."

Michel blinked, realizing he may have created quite a problem for himself. He was having a hard time pulling his eyes away from her, her gaze intense, speaking furious words that her mouth did not vocalize.

"Veronica?" Michel asked sweetly, hoping to charm her.

"No," the patroness said. "Not with me. Not if she doesn't work. I run a business, not a school for ladies."

Michel turned his head the other way and saw Gerald lift his eyebrows. "I wouldn't mind having a woman with us," Gerald said, grinning widely like he did.

Michel scowled at him. He looked at the woman who had clenched her jaw and ran his hand up the back of his neck. The urge to reach out to her, put his arm around her, or do something comforting was overwhelming, but he thought he might end up with a bloody nose like Armin if he tried. "Will you tell me where you're from?" he asked instead, softly, hoping to get something out of her. When she refused to answer, even with Veronica's translating, he sighed, feeling his heart palpitate at his own resignation. "I guess you're coming with me."

That morning had started with Michel declining to go into a whorehouse. Somehow, he had ended up with a woman in his lap anyway.

Chapter Two

Every two years, Michel took a journey through Eastern Europe into Western Asia. He kept to a meticulously planned route that took him across the Mediterranean, into Damascus, Bukhara, Samarkand, up to Kashgar, and then to the edges of the mountainous steppes north of Tibet. He had contacts in each of the major cities and friendly acquaintances in the little towns scattered between the cities. Some, like Veronica, were French expats who had built their livelihoods on the trade Michel funneled to them. Others were trusted locals, eager for business.

These contacts would arrange meetings with town merchants and officials, organize travel parties from one city to the next, prepare lodging, horses, wagons, and supplies, and communicate between each other on Michel's behalf. In the sixteen years he had been taking this journey–with his father at first but leading it on his own for some time now–Michel and his father had established a solid network of trade and a safe route for merchants.

This was, however, the first time Michel had ever done the route with a woman.

They had been traveling East of Merv for three days since he had brought her into his company. His current crew of twenty-five men was coming out of the high desert and into a flood channel of the Amu Darya River. The mountain runoff for spring was just starting, which cut the red sand and created pools of water to feed the blue-green desert bushes around them.

Michel glanced over at the perplexing woman, hoping to catch some expression on her face other than the irritation that had developed just before she joined his party. She had not said a word, nor had she as much as acknowledged him or anyone else, since he put her on a horse in Merv. He'd tried to talk with her, but there was no reason for her to know French, and she didn't respond to any of his Mongolian either. Veronica told him the dialect she'd spoken was from much further East—a dialect Michel did not know. Still, because his eyes rarely left her, he'd noticed her perk up during certain conversations. Directions, names of cities, where they were going, and where they would stay. She understood *something*, he'd determined. But otherwise, the woman seemed incapable or uninterested in even basic communication. She hardly ate. Never made a sound. When they camped each night, Michel put her in the small tent he used when traveling between cities, and he slept just outside, frustrated at his inability to communicate. He couldn't help her if he didn't know where she needed to go. And, more critically, these roads could be dangerous. He couldn't ignore his duties to keep her safe.

"Up ahead," Michel called to the crew. He indicated a thicket of low oleasters and tangled licorice roots where the men could take a rest and give the horses a chance to forage.

The high heat of the desert was a few months off, but it was still warm, and Michel looked forward to the cool water. Once they reached the little oasis, the woman hopped from her horse, as competent a mount as any of them, if not more so. It was no surprise given her heritage. Then she disappeared into the brush that obscured the bank. He laughed to himself. For someone who claimed Michel owned her, she certainly never waited for permission. He felt a pulse in his chest as he watched after her. He took a quick scan of the men to be sure everyone was accounted for before following her to the water.

He went through the low trees to see her sitting at the water's edge with her bare feet sliding in, her slippers next to her. She rubbed the red sand into her toes and rinsed them in the clear water. She did not look at him.

"*Bonjour?*" He spoke in French and then tried in Mongolian. "*Saim bai-noo?*" He watched her for a reaction. She had to understand something in nothing more than his body language or his good intent. He *had* gotten her safely away from Armin. He'd like to at least know that he had done the right thing by her.

She massaged her feet at the edge of the water as Michel came and sat next to her, careful to give her space. He felt the woman stiffen at his presence.

Michel draped his arms over his knees, his head turned her way.

"I wish you could communicate with me," he pressed. "I have this sense that I offended you by exchanging money for you. But I *tried* to have Veronica explain that you were free to go. I didn't mean to make you feel like I expected something." He pulled off his boots to rinse in the water as well, wishing she would see him as others knew him to be. "I hope to find someone who speaks the same dialect as you when we reach Turkmenabat," he said. "We'll figure it out. And I'll help to get you home." He paused, trying another tactic to pull some awareness out of her. "Though I sure do like looking at you. You are the prettiest woman I think I've ever seen."

The woman said nothing, still dipping her toes.

"I'm glad I was there to help you in Merv." She may not understand, but it made him feel better to say the words. "However you got yourself mixed up with that man, he was determined to get money out of you." He shook his head. She had to be a runaway, but from whatever terrible thing beyond Armin he may never know. He paused before giving her a grin. "*You* may not have liked it, but having you fall into my arms wasn't the worst thing that could have happened to me."

She was really just amazing. He rolled to his side, leaning on his elbow, unable to pull his eyes away.

"Maybe this is your life. Maybe looking like you do makes it easy to grift, and we just met on a day you got caught." He couldn't help teasing, eager to get a rise out of her, even though he didn't really think this was the case. "Maybe you swindled Armin. Maybe you swindled me, too. I guess I'll never know."

She stretched out her legs, the hem of her dress soaking into the water. He watched as it bled up her calf. He cleared his throat to corral his thoughts. "I have to be very careful around you. Especially now." He trailed off, pulling his eyes away from her, putting his focus back on the river.

"Before I came here, I met with Cardinal Mazarin." He catalogued his woes for her, pretending this was a real conversation. "Our king is still too young to rule, so the Cardinal makes the decisions regarding trade, tax, that kind of thing." Michel sighed. "He wants more money from the territories to offset his debt from the war with Spain. I promised to bring back new trade and new business to avoid the tax." He sat back up and crossed his arms over his knees, clenching his fists to relieve some tension. "If I succeed, he won't levy a tax. If I don't succeed, I fear it could lead to a civil war."

The water, trailing up toward her knee now, caught his attention again. He kept himself talking as a distraction. "Your people aren't the easiest to negotiate with," he grumbled. His eyes roamed over her. "It would be a great insult to the tribes if I were to harm you." He swallowed, his voice going lower. "I wouldn't harm you."

The woman turned to him. Her mottled eyes focused on him, sparkling with concentration. She seemed to listen.

With a heavy, frustrated sigh at all the accumulating unknowns, he stood up and walked out toward the water, pulling his tunic off and tossing it back on the sand. He leaned down, cupping water with his hands and washing it over his face and chest, the cold sting of it feeling good on his overheated skin. He turned back to see that she was watching him. He grinned at her, friendly, as he hooked his thumb in the belting of his pants.

Rather than smile back at him, the woman stood up suddenly and dove beneath the water.

Once again, amused by her unrelenting confidence, Michel returned to the shore and sat back down, watching her. When she emerged, Michel's mouth fell open, and his eyes went wide. The water poured off her, the thin material of her dress adhering to her skin, making the fabric nearly transparent. His heart thundered as she came toward him. The clinging fabric showed him everything—her breasts, her torso, the fabric dipping in a deep crevice between her thighs. She was no waif, and he suddenly forgot all his resolve. He forgot that there were men on the other side of the brush, that he had vowed to stay honorable.

She stood in front of him, watching him with intense concentration. Michel stared at her like an idiot. Water trailed from her hair and down her skin. She leaned forward, so her face was just before him, water beads splashing from her skin to his. He watched her as his heart stuttered. He felt a deep pull in his groin.

"Careful," he said. He didn't know if he was saying it to her or himself.

She looked into his eyes with that same commanding intensity, once again giving him that feeling that she wanted something from him. If he only knew what it was, he would do it. In that moment, she could ask anything of him. He didn't understand the pull she had on him, but for once in his life of planning and practicality, he didn't care.

"Siren," he whispered. He had no other name for her, and his desire made the word come out deep and thick.

She responded by reaching forward with her open palm and clacking his jaw closed with her fingertips.

She tipped her own chin up, stood, and left him to head back toward the horses.

Michel twisted around to watch her, lust, concern, and frustration a confusing whirlpool inside him. Her body was fully on display as the dress tattooed her skin. He realized that once she crossed through the bush, the other men would have the chance to see her like this. He trusted his men as workers, but that didn't mean he'd let them be alone with her or get a look at her like this.

"Stop," he commanded. Words, language didn't matter. His tone was clear.

She stalled and glanced back over her shoulder, her curiosity seemingly piqued. Michel jumped up, nearly tripping over his own feet as he'd become lightheaded from her attention. He picked up the tunic from the beach and jogged to her. He situated it and then dropped it over her head. Once he did, she let her arms find the sleeves.

Reluctant to let her go and return to the inattention he'd been getting from her, he thought to try to console her in some way. "There is something you want from me. That much I can understand. I would think that you just want to get home to where you are safe." He spoke in Mongolian because he thought it was the closest he could get to something she understood. He reached to take her hand, tentatively, holding just her fingertips. "I know you don't trust me. I understand that too. But I promise, if you give me some indication of what you need, I'll do my best to help you."

She stared at him a moment, then jerked out of his grasp. She turned, and Michel watched, the tunic giving her a shapeless form even as he continued to imagine the shape beneath it.

Mon Dieu, he thought. He was going to have to get her a more decent dress, if nothing more than to get those images of her wet and dripping out of his own head.

Several hours later, they entered the outlying markets of Turkmenabat, which were along the main shore of the Amu Darya River. As they passed through the streets, Michel made quick purchases to acquire the things he thought the woman would need, things she would like.

Michel would be staying in Turkmenabat for several days, switching out some of his crew and bolstering supplies. It was early evening by then, but before he could rest, he still had the laborious process of setting up camp and erecting the yurts that would house himself and the men. He made his way to the designated area just outside the town walls, alongside the river, where space had been cleared for his arrival.

Once he helped corral the horses, he sent word to his contact that he'd arrived and organized the site with the porters who had welcomed him. Then he fought the yurts, wrestling the felt onto the structures, all the while keeping his eye on the woman, who watched him back with keen disapproval. Once again, her irritation made him laugh. If only she could know him better. He certainly wasn't used to people regarding him as ineffectual.

She sat by the fire, and as the last yurt was placed, he took a moment to return to his own things, retrieving the items he had purchased. He approached her and held out the bundle.

"This is for you," he said, gesturing for her to take the gift.

She stared at him, suspicion in her brows.

"You do not make anything easy on me," he teased. He squatted next to her and laid out the items he had purchased for her. "A comb," he said. He kept his voice gentle. He hoped to please her with these gifts, to see some spark of interest. "Some things for your hair." He unwrapped the next package. "Some oils to clean?" He didn't know what they were, but a merchant said that women liked them. He looked at her as she reached forward to examine the little vials. "And this?" He handed her the oils and pulled the last pack open. He held up a dress for her. It was a simple off-white dress, made for travel, light. "I got you a night shift and, um, underthings too."

She nodded, and it was the most affirmation he'd had from her.

"I'll leave everything here for you." He indicated toward the river. "You can wash and change whenever you are ready."

She stood, taking the items in her arms, but before she left, she reached forward and took his hand. She squeezed it as she looked at him. She still did not smile, but she let him see that, for once, she was less annoyed with him. She turned and headed down to the riverbank.

He felt a bloom of pride as she went, the nagging desire to please her eased just somewhat. He sat by the fire, where she had been, and watched to see that no one followed her.

A short while later, the woman returned to camp. Her hair was set in two braids running across her scalp and down her back. She was wearing the dress he'd bought for her with her old garments over her arm. She walked across the camp into the center and then casually tossed the old garments onto the fire.

He still felt pride at earning one little sliver of her trust, but seeing her make use of the items that he had purchased and *chosen* for her triggered something else—deep and possessive—inside him.

Right now, the only thing he knew about her was that she was beautiful. He hoped he would get to learn more before he had to say goodbye.

Chapter Three

The next morning, she walked next to the Frenchman through the marketplace at Turkmenabat. He guided her with his hand on the small of her back. She accepted this light touch. He did not know her story. He did not know that she was called Eve. Still, he insisted on keeping her near. Eve could tell that he was trying to be kind, but in the four days since she had joined him, she had found no solace in this journey, no comfort in this company, only stark irritation with this man and what she had learned was his path directly back East—into the mountains from which she had escaped and toward the dangerous men who pursued her.

The man himself—*Michel*, she had learned—grated on her like no other. At first, he had seemed like a much better option than traveling with Armin. The party of Frenchmen that Michel led was cleaner, better equipped for travel, with more swords at hand. But Armin was simple and easy to manipulate; *Michel* had too much importance about himself. He was a noble who wore a sword that she was sure was all for show, cloaked in the protection of his country, used to people doing what he wanted simply because he was noble. She hated such pretense.

Her only armor, then, was to ignore him. Perhaps he would leave her alone, forget she was there, allow her to travel safely, cloaked in the same protection he was assured of. But the man babbled *relentlessly*, trying to get her attention as though he were a child, never giving her a moment to plan her next move. He didn't harm her, but he was terribly condescending. The way he had spoken about her value and then exchanged coins for her like she was livestock. The way he handed her basic necessities like they were treats.

She had thought she could manage her pride and use this party as a way to escape to France. But she was choking on her own choices, infuriated to find herself in this vulnerable position where she had to wait for him to finish his business before he would return West. If he only knew where she had come from. If only he knew what would be coming after her. Then he would turn back to the safety of his country immediately.

That, or abandon her at the first opportunity.

As much as she hated it, she did need help. And this man did seem willing to help her, if for nothing more than to fluff his own ego.

She shuffled to stay next to him in the busy marketplace, aware of the way Michel held her close, aware of the amount of heat and pressure each fingertip pressed into her skin as they jostled through the crowd, aware of his dark eyes and strong jaw. Of all the things that upset her, her unexpected attraction to him was the worst. For some inexplicable reason, every time she looked at the man, her skin quivered and her breath caught in her chest. She glanced at him now, feeling free to do so since, for once, his focus was not all over her. He was tall with thick, dark hair pulled back from his eyes, unkempt just at his neck. He wore breeches, a jacket over a shirt, and a sword on his belt, typical of Westerners. His clothes were worn from travel but finely made. He really was quite handsome.

She didn't understand her attraction. He may look strong, but he was still a spoiled noble, handing out coins and trinkets wherever he went to gain the goodwill of the locals. Where Eve had grown up, weakness had no purchase. Men and women both had enormous strength. A weak man would never inherit power simply through his lineage. Still, there was no logic to the flutters inside her when they met eyes. She had almost gasped out loud the day before at the river when he took his shirt off. He was broad and muscular, lean but strong. When she had seen the ridges leading down his stomach and dipping below his beltline, her belly flipped. Afraid she would make some kind of animal noise, she had no choice but to throw herself into the water.

Even now, being near him in the midst of hundreds of people, his was the only body she was aware of.

They came around a corner, the sun shining down from the hazy sky onto the clay stone buildings. Goats bleated among barrels of colorful spices. A herdsman walked a yak past them, the bell on the animal clanging as it stepped. Michel gripped the back of her dress, keeping her in his space. Eve cinched her shawl around her head, keeping her eyes cast down, knowing how she always stood out. Anyone looking for her could spot her coloring in an instant. Luckily, she was good at hiding.

He guided her to the edge of the market into an alleyway that led to ornately carved wooden doors that she assumed opened to the apartments of the wealthier vendors. A well-dressed man in his late fifties with a ring of short, light hair around his head and a cleanly cropped beard leaned against one of the doors. He smiled and opened his arms wide when he saw Michel.

"Michel!" he boomed, with the same accent Michel spoke. "How have you been, my friend! What news from home?"

"I am well, François. Busy as always," he said. "My father sends his regards."

The men shook hands, and Eve watched as they exchanged pleasantries.

"Come, come," François exclaimed. He nodded toward Eve with a questioning look.

"Yes, she is in my care." Michel laughed.

François gave her a kind smile with a nod of his head. "*Mademoiselle.*" He held out his hand to direct them inside. "Come in, please. Relax."

They followed François up a set of stairs while the men continued to chat and then down a hallway with carved wood embellishments that matched the entrance. The hallway opened into a large room with flowing curtains that led to an oversized balcony. Everything in the room showed wealth, from the gold-gilded chairs to the plush cushions. A well-dressed young valet shuffled in. François gave the young man instructions, and Eve watched as he went off to the kitchen. Michel indicated for her to sit on a silky green cushion as he relaxed into a chair.

Eve folded her knees beneath her and perched. She wasn't exactly sure why Michel had brought her with him, but she preferred to stay close. She could learn more about his plans this way. She could learn more about him.

Looking around at the finery, she suddenly realized one reason Michel could have brought her along. Here she was, dressed in clothing he had bought her. Cleaned with oils he had given her. Wouldn't caring for a "peasant" girl cultivate good favor? Make him seem all the more important in the eyes of another? After the way he had spoken about her...*well*, he had found a way to get some value out of her after all. Despite the gestures he made to appear kind to her, what he really had in her was another trinket to put on display.

The valet returned with a carafe of coffee on a tray and placed it on the low table between the men.

"Do you still take your coffee the same?" François asked.

"Two sugar cubes, if you have them." Michel nodded. "Did you receive my letter?"

"Yes, son, but I have no ideas for you. The markets are all tapped."

"I have an idea," Michel said, leaning forward.

"It seems you didn't come for any advice then." François chuckled at the younger man.

"I want to find a cashmere dealer."

Cashmere? she perked up, listening.

François leaned forward to take his cup. He held his head to the side and let out a long whistle through his teeth before taking a sip and setting the cup back down. "That's going to be difficult."

"It's the only solution," Michel affirmed. "What else can I bring home that France doesn't already have? That can bring in substantial revenue?"

François leaned all the way back into his deep chair and surveyed Michel as he stroked his chin. "Cinnamon?"

"Ah," Michel threw up his hand. "The Portuguese have a lock on spices, and it is too easy to trade with them already." Then he leaned in. "Consider it. Cashmere. What do you think?"

"Michel, yes, you would be a hero if you set up a line of cashmere. You know they keep the market very tight, though. The sources are well out of our reach, deep into the steppes." He held out his hands and shrugged. "I could perhaps get you a few rolls if you were willing to do some illicit trading."

"No," Michel asserted. "I can't do anything illegal. And I need a sustainable source."

"This is coming from Cardinal Mazarin?" François asked as he crossed one knee over the other.

This caught Eve's attention—a name she recognized. Michel had mentioned the Cardinal the day before at the river. She lowered her head to seem uninterested, though she continued listening closely.

"He is looking to cover the debt he incurred fighting Spain," Michel said. "He wants to keep it from the king."

"This is what happens when you appoint a king when he is a child." François went back to stroking his chin.

"I met with the Cardinal in Versailles," Michel continued. "Just before I began this journey. He said he would tax Chevalerie and the rest of the duchies if I am unable to provide a solution."

François laughed and shook his head. "Your father won't stand for it. That is exactly what he and I rebelled against in our day. Does he know of the Cardinal's intentions?"

Michel leaned forward and took his coffee. "No, of course not." He shook his head. "I am doing what I can now to avoid it." Michel sat back again with his cup. "You know my father. He'll wage war on Paris if he finds out about this."

François nodded. "I'm sorry I can't give you better news, son. I will send out correspondence and see if we can locate anything. I fear you will need some luck to find someone willing to work with you."

"Luck has nothing to do with it," Michel defended. "I will figure something out."

"I'm sure you will. You always do." François leaned forward to take his cup of coffee in his hands, then indicated toward Eve. "Now," he began. "What's going on here?"

"A man was trying to sell her at the whorehouse in Merv." Michel sat up straight, a proud look on his face. "I just couldn't let it happen."

His self-satisfaction caused her nostrils to flare before she was able to regain her control.

"Ah, Michel. You have a big heart." François smiled and eyed her in a curious way.

"What can I say?" Michel said. "I am here to maintain laws and safety for our merchants. I can't allow something like that to happen right on my route."

"You're right, you're right." François took a sip of his coffee. "Do you speak her language?" he asked, an eyebrow raised to Michel.

Michel shook his head. "When I rescued her, she spoke an eastern dialect I didn't recognize." He let out a long sigh. "I am hoping the translator you've arranged for me to take east can communicate with her."

"He's quite good," François conceded. "He spent time in Kashgar when his father was still working as a merchant. Picks up dialects fast." François cleared his throat. "He's young. Traveling with you will be good for him."

"I look forward to meeting him," Michel nodded. Then he turned his attention back to Eve. "I'd love to know where she came from. I'm guessing she has run away or perhaps got separated from her tribe." He glanced at her. "She is lucky she stumbled upon my route."

"You will cause yourself trouble trying to get her home," François said. "There are hundreds of hill tribes, and many of the people are hardly literate. They won't like seeing you with one of their own." He raised his eyebrows in a warning. "Be careful how you treat her, son."

Michel held his hand to his chest. "You know me, François," Michel said. "I know how to handle the tribes. I wouldn't do anything to offend them."

François gave him a tight smile and a nod before taking another sip of his coffee.

Michel continued, taking his own cup. "I have no other intentions, I promise you. This is my duty. I will help this girl return safely to her home." He looked at her and shook his head. "I just wish she spoke an educated language so we could communicate."

It was that final comment that made her explode.

"You disrespectful twat!" She jumped up, the cushions she sat on toppling, her fists balled, and her chest strained. Both men jumped, and Michel spilled his coffee down his front. "You think you saved me?" she spat. "I could have ridden that fat merchant's cart anywhere I wanted!"

"You speak French?" Michel sputtered, looking between her and the coffee he had spilled all over himself.

"Do I look too poor and stupid to speak your idiot language?"

"Did you...call me a twat?"

"You bought me because you wanted to avoid a fight. *And* you said I was a peasant who wasn't worth as much as a goat."

"I didn't—" He held up his hands, surprise in his expression. "I was just negotiating! I didn't mean it!"

She stomped over to him and grabbed a napkin from the tray. "Well, you got me for a great price. You own me now, so let me serve you."

She went to her knees and pressed the cloth into his chest. Michel sat stunned in his seat. She fumed even as she felt the heat coming from him seeping into her skin.

Perhaps she took a misstep in revealing that she understood every dumb word he said, but now at least she could take a more active role in getting him to do what she wanted. She couldn't take it—his words, him thinking she had no value, had no means by which to protect herself.

She'd never been subservient to a man before, but if she had to learn the role to get what she needed, then she would. Besides, this man—she realized as he sat there with a stupid, surprised look on his face—was not going to be difficult to manage.

If she could keep herself from strangling him.

Chapter Four

Ganbold. Warrior. Hunter. Ganbold. Warrior. Hunter.

Ganbold repeated the meditation chant in deep throaty tones as he crushed over the twigs and rocks in the dirt. Far from his mountains, he was on the hunt for the missing woman with light hair. She had disappeared from the edges of his tribe, just as she had become a part of it.

When he had learned of her crimes against his people, he had set out immediately. He did not wait for the Il-Khan or the elders to make any decisions, to organize or plan how they would bring her back. He was not interested in what Borjigin Khan—the leader of all the Il-Khans and their tribes—thought about his daughter disappearing. He hated the planning that went into journeys. When she ran away, Ganbold was the first one after her, determined to find her and be the one to return her. It would be his way back into the tribe.

As the daughter of the Khan, the woman coming into Ganbold's tribe was an enormous celebration for Ganbold's people. Her marriage to Ganbold's kinsman would create the alliance his tribe needed to be respected, to connect themselves with the tribe that ruled them all, and to get better wives for his people.

But Ganbold did not like her, did not like her tribe. Ganbold did not want the alliance.

Hundreds of years ago, during the rule of the great Genghis Khan, the woman's tribe and Ganbold's tribe were one. They were of the conquerors that pushed furthest west, swallowing up towns and cities in brutal glory, the people who looked like him and the people who looked like her. They had been the fiercest warriors the land had ever seen, their voices and songs alone enough to cause people to tremble. *These* were the ancestors of Ganbold. He knew he had come directly from those men who fought with fire in their fists. He was proud to come from these warriors.

But the ancestors divided, and there came a distinction between the tribes. The children who grew into the woman's tribe began to settle. They spent less time following the herds. They built monuments and palaces. They liked the soft touches of the Europeans they had conquered. Ganbold hated these changes. His people were put on the earth as warriors, and it angered the ancestors to see them become soft. Ganbold did not want this filthy influence in his tribe, the influence of the light-haired woman. Then she arrived. He watched as his tribe celebrated the woman—a woman who would fool his tribe, attack his tribe, and then run away.

Ganbold would find the woman and bring her back to stand for her crimes.

Ganbold. Warrior. Hunter.

He had been searching for close to three weeks. He went from the small villages that bordered the tribal territory to the larger cities beyond them. But with each step west, Ganbold struggled more to communicate, the tones of the many languages no longer making sense. It made the path to find the woman blurry. That is, until his ancestors guided him to a man who not only spoke his language but had seen a merchant hauling her off to a faraway city called Merv. Before he had left this man, Ganbold had him write the words *merchant* and *light-haired woman* in all the languages he knew on a parchment.

Armed with this parchment, his own intimidating stature, and a direction, Ganbold was able to track the merchant all the way to Merv. Ganbold knew not to attack him in the city. He needed to have him alone on the road, where no one would see Ganbold take the girl, and where she couldn't get away and find someone else to hide her.

Now, just outside of Merv, Ganbold waited. He had stalked the merchant leading his donkey and cart to an isolated section of road that wouldn't be disturbed. Ganbold got ahead of the merchant on a bend in the road. Ganbold thanked his ancestors, the fiercest ones, because only they would guide him. He would honor them by cutting a strip of her light hair from her head and wearing it like a pelt.

The clanging of the donkey's bell and the whistling of the merchant came up the road before Ganbold saw him. He stood waiting, eager. He knew how to make himself even more terrifying, like the ancestors had. He was tall, the largest in his clan, his black hair pulled up high in a warrior braid, his moustache full, and his beard long. He bared his teeth.

Like Ganbold expected, the merchant froze when he saw him. The whistling and clanging stopped.

The merchant spoke words that Ganbold did not understand. He waved his hands in what Ganbold thought was a greeting. He said a few more words, then tried the only language Ganbold understood.

"You speak a dialect of the Issyk Kul. You are far from your home, friend," the man said with a nervous cheer. "Are you seeking wares?"

"Woman," Ganbold ground out "With you." He pointed to the cart. "I want her."

The merchant squirmed. "She is not with me."

Irritation prickled. "Why not."

"I—I—," the man stuttered. "She was for the whorehouse. A man bought her outside the whorehouse."

Anger flashed through his body. Into his hands. "What man?"

"I do not know his name," the merchant said, his eyes big. "A Frenchman!" he said, like he just remembered. "Uh, he was tall." He raised his hand to show his height. "And French. He had dark hair."

"A Frenchman," Ganbold snarled. He did not like the woman, but he was enraged that a Frenchman would dare to buy one of his people. "Where do they go?"

"East is all I know," said the merchant. "Hey, you and me," he pointed to Ganbold's beard and then plucked at his own. "My mother was from the Issyk Kul. We are of the same lineage."

"We are not of the same lineage," Ganbold stated bluntly. "My kin don't sell a woman to a foreigner. The ancestors—they do not approve." Then he reached forward to take the man's neck.

Ganbold liked a stronger match. But the merchant's helpless gurgling as Ganbold dug in with angry hands was enough to pay his ancestors for their assistance, for now.

Ganbold. Warrior. Hunter.

Chapter Five

Michel tore after her, through the entrance of his yurt at the edge of town. He had completed arrangements with François and spent the next moments pursuing this unpredictable woman as she stormed back through the town to their lodging.

"Please stop for a minute," he said as she whizzed back and forth. He held back a grin. He couldn't help it. He knew she was upset, but the way she was taking charge had both alarmed and amused him.

She came around the iron stove at the center of the yurt to straighten the stools at the table, then set to work, noisily arranging a kettle of water on the fire. "I am your servant," she snapped. "I only answer to orders." Then she pointed to the stool at the table behind the stove. "Sit!" she demanded.

Michel, too perplexed to argue about exactly *who* was giving the orders, went to sit. Just as he did, she launched a cushion right under his ass. He threw his hands up, exasperated.

She had absolutely stunned him when she began screaming at him earlier. He had truly believed she didn't understand his language outside of a few words. But she had left him gaping like an idiot, while François had just laughed and laughed.

Now, in the yurt, Michel watched as she dedicated herself to this role of servant, rushing around, straightening and organizing his things. She arranged their shoes just outside the door, dragged a stool from the front of the yurt to the back, balled up his sleeping roll, and tossed it to the other side. He put his elbow on the table and stretched out to lean his head on his hand.

"Slow down," he teased. He knew how bad he must look to her. Especially considering some of the things he had said to her when he didn't think she understood. "Listen. *Listen*," he called as she zipped around. He wanted a conversation, but she wouldn't stop, so he just talked. "You're right, I gave Armin money to avoid a commotion," he said, sitting up straight again. "I just acted on impulse." He tracked her as she moved. "You *had* just fallen on top of me. I thought I was helping you." He paused, speaking solemnly. "I can see how some things I said could be insulting." She slowed just long enough to give him an annoyed look.

"Ha, 'could be insulting,'" she scoffed. She leaned down to pick up the bed at the corner. She jerked it away from the wall, and it groaned across the floor.

"What are you doing?" he asked.

"The bed is on the wrong side."

"Sit down," he said, going to the structure. "I'll move it." He lifted the frame and paused. "Where do you want it?"

"East wall," she directed, her arm pointing to where his sleeping roll had been.

"Why did you hide the fact that you speak French?" he grunted as he dragged the heavy bed frame to the other side. He halted in sudden realization. "Do you speak standard Mongolian, too?"

"Of course I speak Mongolian." She gave him a look of pure disbelief. "I am Mongolian."

"Then why," he grunted again, getting the bed where she wanted it, "did you pretend you didn't understand me?" He placed the bed and scooted it against the wall with his knee. Then he watched her as she came over to straighten the blanket.

She stopped to look at him from the other side of the bed. "I'll tell you." She folded her arms in challenge. "But first, agree to take me to France."

"To France?" he balked. For a second, Michel thought of his mother's reaction if he returned to Chevalerie palace with a tribal girl in tow. Or Cardinal Mazarin's response if he thought Michel was treating this journey like a holiday. No, he couldn't bring her back to France. He was to be the future Duke. No one could know that he had engaged in such a transaction or compromised a tribal woman, even if it had been with good intentions. Michel looked at the woman and shook his head, unable to agree. "I will take you to your people," he said. "I will keep you safe until then."

"No," she said.

"No?" he asked, his eyes coming up in surprise.

"I will be your servant." It was a declaration.

Michel shook his head slowly. "I don't need a servant."

"Well, you have one now." She took up the blanket and shook it out with a snap. "Plus, you *do* need a servant. You live like an animal."

"I do not—" he began, but she cut him off.

"You don't even know how to set up a yurt. You anger my ancestors."

"It's fine…" he trailed off, looking around at the scattering of furniture and the supplies she had pulled out to reorganize.

"France," she said. "I will go with you to France." She looked at him over her shoulder. "As your servant."

"For someone who hasn't spoken for four days," he said, coming around the bed, toward her, "you sure have a lot of demands."

"I didn't tell you I spoke French because I wanted to avoid this argument." She waved her hand back and forth between them.

"You thought if you didn't speak, and I couldn't figure out what to do with you," he looked at her, in his own disbelief, "that I'd just take you all the way to France?"

She stopped then. She turned to face him, and her voice went soft. Her hands came together in front of her, in a gesture of self-preservation. "I need to get to France," she stated, a glint of fear shimmering through her eyes. "It was the best plan I could come up with." Then she glared at him once more, her resentment returning. "I, too, was acting on impulse."

He leaned back against the table, trying to assess everything despite her sudden softness and distress, which stirred a deep protective instinct inside him. He folded his arms. He still had too many questions—where she had come from, why she wanted to go to France, why she was *still* so mad at him —but he didn't want to give her a reason to stop talking again by asking the wrong thing.

He tried a different approach. "I insulted you. I see that. I'm sorry. I truly didn't mean the things I said to Armin." He tilted his head, still watching her. "Why don't you tell me something about yourself? So I can stop making wrong assumptions," he said, coaxing. "We can start there."

"No," she said, her eyes promising new challenges.

She went to move away, but he took her elbow to hold her in place, her dismissive attitude sparking his own irritation. "We're still going to have a problem communicating if you are going to be this disagreeable all the time."

She pulled her arm away and turned to face him, close, eyes lit with furious heat. "What would you like to know, *Master*?"

"How about your name, *Siren*?" His patience did wane.

She bit into her bottom lip hard enough that he could see the indentation from her teeth when she released it. Then she took a breath and spoke. "Eve," she whispered.

"Eve," he repeated. He liked the way her name felt in his mouth. He couldn't help the feeling of triumph that she capitulated, even as he noted the control she exhibited. She had to know that she had no power over him, to insist as she had. He looked down at her. The fact that this woman had fallen under his care struck him again. Suddenly, it felt like a much larger responsibility than he had anticipated. "Why don't you want to go home?" he asked, his voice soft, leading.

"That," she said, turning away once more, the acquiescence gone, "is none of your concern."

Michel trailed her with slow steps. "If you want me to take you all the way to France, it sure as hell is my concern."

She didn't answer, but she turned to him again. He saw it, that same control come over her, like she fought an urge to be reckless, to smack him or tell him to bite his own tail. He could see her thinking, figuring. He realized then that she was a very smart woman and not just a beautiful one.

He liked her.

Then something changed in her, suddenly, like a storm. Michel felt it instantly, her edges turning to curves. Truly, she had a siren's call, and his body responded to it before he could control himself. The pressure in his chest, the tightening in his gut, a twist of lust going right down into his groin. Her body was looser now. He was aware of her shape, her scent—

black currant, an orchard of citrus—in a way that invited too many problems.

She stood in front of him, looking up, her dark golden hair rippling in streams down her body. She pawed her hands across his chest, each touch sending a little jolt. He watched her, aware his breath had quickened.

"Why did you buy me?" she said, still watching, words soft. She invaded his space, took it over.

"I didn't really buy you," he said, swallowing.

She bit her lip, lightly this time, enticing. "You knew what you were doing," she sighed. "You say you just wanted to help, but you knew what exchanging money with that man would do. That it would bind me to you. You had to know."

"I wanted your safety. I didn't want to have to kill a man in the street to get it," Michel said, his own voice softer.

She paused, pressing closer, letting her body lean into his. "Did you want me, Michel?"

He felt that dangerous muddling again, looking at her, hearing her say his name. She was undeniably beautiful. "I wanted to help you."

"That's not why you bought me," she purred.

She was right, he knew. Though he wanted to argue and claim his intentions had been pure, she had addled his brain upon first sight. Right now, feeling her soft heat against him, all he could think about was what it would feel like to throw her down and enjoy her on the bed beside them. He wouldn't. It would be hell to stop himself from thinking it, though.

He took the opportunity to touch her, even as he warned himself against it, and he trailed a finger down her arm, still watching her. She had a draw, a pull he couldn't resist.

When his fingers reached her hand, she gripped it, pulling it up before her. Her eyes, green and brown, a swirling mixture of East and West, were still on him. She rubbed her thumbs into his palm, holding his hand between them. Then she parted her lips.

All he could see were her lips. He wanted to kiss her. Was dying to kiss her.

He dropped his head, his resolve flying away, but Eve moved instead, opening her mouth and angling his hand. She took the tip of his finger, touching it with her tongue. Then she drew his finger into her mouth. With his other hand, Michel reached up to grab the back of her hair, holding her in place, his heart either frozen or beating so fast he couldn't track it. Eve gasped and then closed her lips around his finger, letting it slip over her tongue.

A flash of heat engulfed him from the inside out, centering on where her mouth held him. His brows came together, and his own mouth fell open as he watched his finger sink to the back of her throat. It didn't matter that he towered above her, that he had the strength or the title. He knew, in that moment, that there wasn't much that would keep him from giving this woman whatever she wanted.

Suddenly, a sharp pain shot through him, causing him to release her body and hop into the air. He cursed at the pain before he even knew what had happened. He grabbed his hand and saw his wet finger with red tooth marks all down the side. He looked at Eve, who had backed up a step. She was standing in place, her face flushed, hair in a mess from where he had held her, a breathless smirk on her face.

"To be clear, I will not be that kind of servant, *Monsieur*," she said, crossing her arms. "But I will be happy to fold your towels." She glanced at him, her words weighted. "At least, until we reach France." She turned to his travel bag and dumped out the contents. She returned to organizing his things.

For the second time that day, he stood there gaping. *What the hell just happened*, he thought, massaging his throbbing finger.

***

She probably shouldn't have done that.

Later that evening, she was still thinking about it. Eve lay on the bed in the yurt, turned away from her keeper, with the taste of his skin still on her lips. *What had she let happen?*

She toyed with a rag in her hand, but she kept her body still, not wanting to invite any more interaction from Michel now that they had finally stopped bickering long enough to settle down for sleep. She had allowed an intimacy between them, one she didn't trust. Yes, she felt she could safely control this man. He had a gentle nature, and she didn't fear that he would demand anything of her.

The problem was going to be controlling herself around him.

Growing up with six older brothers, Eve was never surprised by the fits of men, and she considered herself quite proficient in being able to gently prod their egos into doing what she wanted. In fact, she'd never been at a loss for someone to do her bidding her whole life. She outwitted them easily, and her father always commented on how she may have been the youngest, but she had always been the one in charge.

Things changed for her when her brothers began to marry. First, Dzhambul, her eldest brother, was married, and he was closely followed by Esen, the second eldest. The next three did the same in succession. When she had been taken from her home, her last brother was preparing for his wedding. As her brothers entered into courtships and marriage vows, she had seen them each controlled, in a way, by the woman they married. She noted how these strong, intelligent men whom she loved and respected would be angry, despondent, irrational—and how one trip to the bedroom would restore their senses. Though she knew her brothers would never stop loving or caring for her, Eve quickly recognized that her own position in their lives had diminished, and their wives held a very different kind of power over them.

Eve had filed this information away. She knew one day she would be a wife—it was her duty to her family and tribe—though she never wished for that moment to come any sooner than necessary. So, on days when the men warred or planned, she spent much of her time listening to her elder sisters-in-law talk of the things they did to her brothers. They would speak in hushed tones, though they would talk in a way to ensure each would hear, trying to outdo each other without crossing the line. Men may have their challenges to assert dominance, but so do women.

Through their twittering, Eve began to understand the way certain intimacies could sway a man. She had never needed this weapon before. Her own intuition and cleverness were enough to get what she wanted out of people. Then suddenly she found herself alone and running for her life, with none of the protections she had become accustomed to, with danger close behind her, in the care of a Frenchman who didn't want to bring her to France.

When the Frenchman denied her request to go with him to France, she decided to experiment. She changed her body. She changed her tone. She changed her *tactic*. Michel changed, too, in an instant. She felt his desire fill the room, flames of it pressing on her from all directions, from his body against hers, his hand in hers, his other hand in her hair. He may have been trying to control himself, but his want for her was obvious. What upset her, however, was how quickly her body responded. His desire called to hers, causing her edges to fray and for strange, debilitating tremors to run through her body. In that second, Eve realized that she might not have all the control.

So, she bit him. And everything stopped.

The quiet of the night had settled around the yurt. Eve continued to wring the rag between her fingers as she lay in the bed, the one he had moved for her earlier. She still felt the tingles of his touch on her—on the places of her skin he had held. The room was warm from the stove at the center, but she wished she had a blanket to pull over her for comfort. Tomorrow, she decided, she would have him take her to the market to purchase essentials: blankets, tea leaves, some decent items to cook with, and a rug for the comfort of their feet. She had confidence that he would allow her what she wanted now that they were communicating. She would use her practiced ways to guide this man toward her goals. If anything happened to threaten her position in this company, or if he decided to leave her behind, she suspected she had a new weapon to use on him.

Until she had to use this weapon again, however, she would keep it a secret that she liked the way he had tasted on her tongue.

Chapter Six

The next morning, as Michel was tending to the horses, he knew he needed to talk to Eve. She had woken him up from his bedroll on the floor by poking him in the side with her toe and demanding that he take her to the market. Now he was waiting in the cool morning air for her to emerge from the yurt so they could walk into town together.

Michel, never one to leave things to chance, had decided last night about what he was going to do with her. No, he couldn't have an angry, insulted tribal woman on his route with him. The longer he traveled with her, the more he exposed himself to the eyes of those who would revile him for being so bold. His ability to safely travel and maintain a steady route for the other French merchants rested completely on his actions and reputation. He had to show respect to the people and their customs at all times. He had to live up to the standards his father, a man who never once faltered or failed, had set when he maintained these routes.

What to do about Eve? Purchased servant? No. He would be condemned, and more importantly, he didn't like thinking of himself that way.

A hired maid? Perhaps.

He *could* hire someone to make and break a camp. A woman made sense. A Mongolian woman made even more sense because of their nomadic upbringing. It was the best he could come up with in the moment, so he was going to go with it. Though he still hoped to find her people, he didn't have any reason to keep her confined or miserable. Besides, she was determined to stay with him, so what could he do? Lock her in the yurt and sneak away in the night? He might even be able to enjoy having her around. *If*, he thought with a laugh, *if* he could keep her from biting him again.

It sure would make everything easier if she weren't so goddamned beautiful.

Their camp sat at the edge of the city in the reddish-brown dirt that led back to the desert. The horses were foraging on patches of flat grass while he refreshed their water. Michel looked up when she came out of the yurt. She straightened the mat at the front and slipped on her shoes.

"Eve," he called, as he smoothed a hand over the back of a dun-colored mare. "Come here, please."

She glared at him, then came through the camp, past several men sipping coffee by the fire, until she stood before him.

"I cannot keep you as a servant," he began.

"But—" she started.

He held up his hand. "Wait. I have a proposition."

She clamped her mouth shut and watched him.

"I will hire you. You can help tend the horses, make and break camps. Organize...whatever needs organizing."

"Or?" she ventured.

"Or you can leave right now. I'm sure I can book you passage to your home if you tell me where. But if you stay, you will work, and I will pay you."

She turned up her chin. "Why?"

"Because I truly do want to help you. I owe you that." He shrugged. He poured another bucket of water into the trough, careful not to spill. "It won't look so bad for me if I truly have hired you."

She continued to glare, one eyebrow hitched, her golden hair falling over her shoulders. The horse whinnied loudly beside him.

He laughed away some of the unease he felt at the position he had put them both in. "I do want to help you."

He set the bucket down. He had the urge to reach out and take her hand, to level some softness or understanding between them, but he didn't.

"When I saw you," he cleared his throat. "You're right—you took me by surprise." He wiped his hands down the front of his pants. Now here came the hard part. "I'd like you to understand," he said, deciding exactly how much he should share with her, "I'm not here on holiday." He let his heel grind into the dirt. "I'm here so France has a presence. So the men who trade can do so safely. So that my country remains connected to this part of the world." He shifted his weight and folded his arms in front of him. "I have to be above reproach because if I insult any of the locals, the tribes could cut us off, forbid our travel in the area. That will upset the Cardinal, which will hurt my family and my people." He tilted his head, hoping she understood. "If you wish to travel with me, I can't let that jeopardize my objectives."

She looked at him, eyes narrowed. "Which means?"

"I can't have people think I've taken you." He paused to clear his throat. "For, um, my pleasure." He looked down and then up at her from under his brows. "If you want to travel with me, I ask that you help me so it doesn't look like I've coerced you. People talk. Gossip spreads faster than I can ride." The horse knickered, and Michel stroked her mane. "You are under no obligation to me. I know that I wasn't particularly respectful at first. But," he gave her a grin, one he hoped was charming, "I wouldn't mind having you around, if you'd like to stay. You're a lot nicer to look at than these men. Smarter too."

She reached out to place her hand on the mare's snout. The horse quieted. She watched Michel carefully. "You will take me to France?"

Michel ground his jaw. "I don't want to promise you something I can't fulfill. I'm not done with my business. It might get rough, still. But, if you work, keep me organized with the men that join, help us live less like animals, as you said..." He smirked at her. "My hope is that you will decide that you want to return to your people. But you are welcome to stay as long as you are comfortable."

She surveyed him. After a moment, she nodded. "Alright," she said. "That works." She moved to turn away, then she addressed him again. "The yurt," she said. "I would like my own yurt."

"No," Michel said, flipping the reins of the horse from one hand to the other. "I know a lot of these men very well, but some of the others are new on this route. I don't know how they'll respond to an unattended woman."

He tilted his head and looked at her. "You keep the bed. I will continue to sleep on the floor." Then he lowered his voice, softened it. "Last night, you made it clear I needed to keep my distance." He felt suddenly humbled, remembering the lesson she taught him when she bit his finger. "I'll respect that." He paused, looking for the words. "But you also showed me that you're not helpless. You wouldn't be here if you had a better option." He studied her face. "I think you may need me more than you want to admit."

She took a breath and looked away, past him, across the open desert. She brought her hands together before her. "I understand," she replied, her voice soft, steady. Michel noticed that she twisted her fingers together.

Before he could wonder again about her past—there was so much more than she was telling him that he saw in little flashes on her face—she turned on her heels, her inscrutable countenance back.

"Come," she said. "I would like to buy some fresh vegetables for your dinner tonight." Without looking to see if he would follow, she started on the path toward the market.

Michel tucked away the horse's reins and jogged across the camp to follow her.

As a girl growing up on the banks of the Issyk-Kul lake, Eve was joyous. She loved riding horses across the plains as the wind attacked her. She loved praising the warriors of her tribe with the songs and dances of her people. She loved the history of her ancestors and everything she could learn about the world. She was a proud addition to her culture. Having been the first girl in her lineage for many, many generations, she was exalted as a princess. Even her father, who was so shrewd in his dealings and never afraid of war, conceded to her a special love and protection. Wherever she went, she was treated as a flower, given to the people by the ancestors themselves.

But her threads were long and winding. She realized at an early age that the plains she loved did not hold the stimulation her mind needed. Eve refused suitors and potential matches over and over because she was too busy learning everything she could. She knew she caused trouble for her father. She just never quite understood how to hone her energy, and a marriage would certainly stop her from figuring it out.

She thought of the irony of her choices, how her refusal to marry had led her to this moment as the Turkmenabat market surged with early morning energy. The long strip of stalls cast tall shadows across the dirt road in the rising sun. Merchants called back and forth. Dogs nipped at their feet as they walked. Farmers laid out their produce, fishermen opened their brimming baskets, spilling river fish onto their carts.

"Hey lady!" shouted a local as they walked by. "Fresh chicken!" he said and a burst of feathers squawked and tumbled out of his hands.

Eve smiled and continued down the path, taking note of the stalls she wished to visit. She had accepted Michel's offer to be his maid, so now she had a focus for this journey. She needed several items for the camp: cookware, medicinal herbs, cushions, and blankets. If she was to organize this journey, she would do so correctly. Michel followed her obediently as they passed through the market.

"There," she said, pointing to a stall filled with brightly colored rugs. "Come," she said to him.

"Do we need a rug?" he complained.

"Yes, Michel," she said over her shoulder, "or do you wish to subject your guests' feet to the bare floor of your yurt?"

"I just let them keep their shoes on."

She stopped in the middle of the road to turn to him, aghast. "*Inside* your *yurt*?" This man truly was an animal.

Michel looked taken aback. He stuttered, his hand going to rub the back of his neck. "I...well..."

"A rug," she said, turning back around and approaching the stall.

She laughed to herself once she knew he couldn't see her face. This Frenchman, she thought, would make her insane. The French were known for their sophistication and beauty throughout the world, but he might as well have been a bear in a cave.

Eve had French blood. It's what gave her her unique coloring. She was as proud of this heritage as much as all the other things that made her up. The Western Mongols had mixed readily with Europeans since their great conquest centuries ago, but Eve's French blood was much more recent. It was her grandmother on her father's side, Cecile, who brought France to Eve's family.

Eve had grown up loving Grandmother's stories of her home and her adventure coming to the Issyk Kul, of how Grandmother fell in love with

Grandfather in such a faraway and exotic place. It was through these stories that France became a world beyond, the most exciting place Eve could ever imagine—filled with kings' courts and balls, politics and universities, the greatest scientists, philosophers, and thinkers of the time.

Eve had always dreamed, in a wistful sort of way, of life in a place like France, with so many more options for her tapestry of life. She never expected the need to escape there, however.

Now here she was with a traveling Frenchman who lived in a yurt with no rug. *Absurd,* she thought as she selected an acceptable size and pattern from the choices at the stall. She didn't know if Michel could protect her. She didn't know if he would keep her safe. All she knew was that being on this path with him was better than the fate that would have remained if she had stayed with the tribe that had kidnapped her. The tribe she had run from.

After making the purchase, she walked over to a nearby vegetable stand, with Michel close by her side, balancing the rug in his arms. After their conversation that morning and seeing how he tried to oblige her, a little flame of affection for him caused her to choose the very best vegetables that night for his stew. She truly didn't know how far the warriors of the tribe who stole her would come, or how violent they would be if they found her. The thing that worried her most, however, the thing that kept her chest tight, was the growing attraction she felt to the stupid Frenchman who had become her keeper.

Chapter Seven

Michel's crew remained in Turkmenabat for a week. In that time, he worked with François to complete their business, gathered the men with whom he would travel on the next stretch of road, and built a tentative truce with Eve, now that she agreed to be his hired hand. He *loved* having Eve around. She furnished the yurt with cushions and blankets to make it comfortable. She made delicious food that filled him with warmth. She packed and organized so efficiently that it could take days off his travel time. Despite the fact that she stayed reserved and didn't talk much more about herself, she gave him a peace of mind he didn't usually have on these adventures.

They'd left Turkmenabat early that morning. It would be a trek through open terrain and across several villages to get to Bukhara, an imperial city deep in the Zarefshan River Valley. They were a heavy procession of carts for the collapsed yurts, wagons for the supplies they would need between towns, livestock, horses, and the crew itself, which was made up of porters hired to help move the goods and tradesmen who wanted the added security. These men were used to travel, but many waited for Michel's protection to go to the furthest cities. Though the roads could be dangerous, Michel traveled with the sanction of France, which offered a certain assurance. It was a great responsibility, but Michel enjoyed the journey and prided himself on having the tactical precision to balance the travel and the trade and keep the routes safe. Every decision, every step, every transaction, Michel made with his home and its prosperity in mind.

However, despite all the planning and preparation, Michel could feel something off with the men. That night, as they settled the camp, he scanned the grassy area. Eve sat by the fire, working to mend a tear in Michel's pants. The men were scattered around, sitting on their bedrolls, some still eating their dinner, some engaged in a game of cards. Gerald was heckling the new recruits. Michel had worked with some of these men before. The rest were all vetted through François. There was tension brewing with this group, and Michel hadn't figured it out yet. All through their travel that day, Michel kept a close watch over them, trying to pick off trouble before it began.

He took another pass over the men. When he was unable to spot anything out of place, he went to sit with Eve at the fire.

Eve didn't look up as he came near, but she spoke. "You put a lot of tears in your pants," she complained.

"I appreciate your help." He smiled, even though she wasn't looking at him. He shuffled through his rucksack to pull out his writing utensil and the bound book he carried with him. He was distracted by the tension in the air, but he needed to notate his progress. He set the book out in front of him and went back to his bag, looking for his pen knife.

"I'm sure it was here," he muttered, shuffling the contents of the bag.

"What can't you find?"

"My pen knife," he said, arm deep in his satchel.

"Will this work?" She pulled a small dagger from some fold of her skirt, holding it out for him.

"Why do you have that?" he asked, looking up.

She shrugged. "Protection."

"Protection," he repeated, irritated that she thought she would have to protect herself. From whom? *Him*? He reached forward to take the knife from her. "Thank you," he said, deciding not to dwell and taking the small dagger to the goose quill. He scraped the dried ink from the nib.

She nodded toward his book. "What do you have there?"

"It's my travel log," he said. "Cardinal Mazarin likes to see the details of the journey. To know how each penny is spent." He angled the quill, inspecting it, and ran the knife along the other side. "I am not so good at organizing in this way. I like to hold the information in my head." He tilted his head with a grin. "Unfortunately, others can't use it then."

"What do you record?" she asked, looking up from her mending. Her eyes went from the stitch she was pulling to the book at his feet.

"What materials we transport, the names of the men that travel with us," he said. "Which merchants I deal with in each market. What we purchase, what we gift."

He tilted his head and raised an eyebrow. "Every time I pay a lady's debt or buy a rug for my yurt." He gave her a wink, and she gave him half a smile in return. Then he turned back to the tools in his hands. "It's all terribly boring."

"I will do it," Eve said, going back to the stitching.

"You'll—you want to do my books?" Michel asked.

"Yes, I am good at those tasks." She looked up at him, a tease in her eyes. "Unless you still think I am too poor and stupid to read and write." She shrugged. "Perhaps I will just draw genitalia in your notebook."

His eyes widened, and he let out a surprised laugh. Then he gave her a wry grin. "I don't believe the Cardinal has that sense of humor," he said. "You might get me beheaded." He picked up the book and tossed it to her feet. "I'll choose to trust you."

Eve set the mending down beside her to take up the book. She flipped the bound pages. "There is nothing in here," she said.

"I told you I keep it in my head."

She shook her head and tssk'd. "You disappoint your king."

With every word she spoke, he was more transfixed. The firelight flickered in her hair. Her laughter twinkled in the breeze. *Who was missing this woman*, he wondered, because it would be impossible that she could disappear and no one would be looking for her.

"Where do you come from, Eve?" Michel said, taking the chance to learn more.

She smiled. "The East."

"I know that," he said. "Tell me about your family."

"I have six older brothers. I was the last child."

"Six older brothers?" he asked with a whistle. "What was that like growing up?"

"They each protected me," she said, still smiling. "I caused them all grief. Now their wives and children cause them grief." She pressed her lips. "They would tear your arms off and beat you with your bones if they knew you purchased me."

"Perhaps," he sputtered, "perhaps, if they knew I was attempting to help—"

"My father prefers a cleaner execution," she cut him off. "He is very conservative. You traveling with me without an escort? He would have you killed on sight."

"Uh," Michel stammered, eyes wide.

Eve laughed and looked at Michel. She set the book down next to her and resumed the mending. "Tell me about you. Brothers? Sisters?"

Michel blinked a few times, shaking her last statements out of his head. "I have two brothers. I am the oldest."

"Of course you are," she jested.

"Why do you say that?"

"You like to be in charge."

"You are the youngest, and you like to be in charge," he pointed out.

Eve gave him a wink as she snapped the thread.

Michel continued. "Serge is my middle brother. He captains the ship that takes me through the Mediterranean when I come East." He shifted and stretched his legs out. "My youngest brother is Philippe. He was supposed to take this journey with me, but he was married just a few months ago."

Eve nodded. "He did not want to leave his wife."

"Couldn't tear him away." Michel grinned. "He helps maintain the region, Chevalerie, my home. His wife, Alex, is a swordfighter," he said, looking for something to interest Eve.

She looked up, surprised. "A woman swordfighter?"

"She's very talented," he continued. "She trained with many of the same masters that my brothers and I did."

Eve gave him a strange look, a smirk, then turned back to the mending.

"What's that look?" he asked.

"You trained with that sword?" she teased. "It's not just a toy?"

"What—" he started. "Of course—" he stuttered. Then he moved to catch her eye. "Do you think I don't know how to use my sword?"

"I know very little about you. Though Westerners, *nobles*," she said, "are known to wear weapons merely as part of the costume." She gave him a once-over, her amusement on display.

His mouth dropped open. "I've been training since I was two years old," he said, offended. "With masters from all over the continent." He straightened his back. "I've won competitions..." he trailed off.

Eve just grinned at him and shrugged.

"Alright, alright," he said. He didn't know if she was just teasing him or truly believed he was a bumbler with his weapon, but he had to admit he enjoyed the playfulness of the conversation. He had nothing to prove, he reminded himself, and he laughed as he observed her.

Her golden hair was braided to the side. Her posture was straight and proper as always. He thought of what it would feel like to have her in Chevalerie, in his home. To introduce her to his family, to walk with her through the gardens. To let her see him spar and to stun her with his skill. He let out an amused grunt at the thought of surprising her once more.

She paused her stitching and looked over at him, her expression bright and open. He realized she was ready to share more of herself with him, that some bridge of trust had been built over the last few days. Then, before he could decide how to move forward, he heard a noise, a scuffle, behind him. The moment between him and Eve evaporated like beads of water in a hot pan, and Michel was on his feet. "Excuse me," he said to her before darting out into the camp, his frustration forming in his chest at having to pull himself away.

Just in the center, where the men had been playing cards, a large, bearded man named Iman, whom Michel had known for many years, towered above Terence, a spindly blond-haired French boy of only fourteen or fifteen who was the translator François had recommended.

Though Michel had been reluctant to take on someone so young, he had relented, knowing he still needed help communicating in the furthest reaches east. Plus, when he saw the gangly, scruffy boy, Michel couldn't help it. He had wanted to help the kid with a job.

And now he had to get himself between Terence and Iman before Iman beat the boy to death.

"You sneak!" Iman fumed, his hands around the boy's neck. "You cheat!"

Michel ripped Iman off Terence and then threw the boy back. Michel faced Iman as Iman charged, blindly trying to get through Michel to Terence. Iman slammed into Michel, but Michel braced and shoulder-checked him, knocking Iman back. Iman stumbled at the impact and fell on his ass.

"That little shit cheated me!" Iman fumed.

Michel, hulking between the two, turned to Terence.

"I did not!" the youth yelled, his voice still cracking with adolescence.

"You don't get carte blanche in piquet four times without a cheat!" Iman jumped up, his posture threatening to jump over Michel to get to Terence again.

"Stop," Michel growled at Iman. The man halted but still vibrated with anger. Michel turned back to Terence. "Whose deck is it?"

"Mine," Terence shrugged.

Michel glared at him. "Pick up the cards," he yelled. Then to Iman, "What was the wager?"

"A silver ring and my compass," Iman said.

Michel tallied a conversion in his head and took coins from his belt. He tossed the coins to Terence. "The wager is paid. I don't want to see you playing cards again."

The boy nodded, but Michel caught a snicker in his expression. Michel snatched him off his feet and lifted him nose to nose. "Do you understand what I said?" Michel snapped.

This time, Terence seemed cowed. "Yes, *Monsieur* Michel. Yes."

Michel set him down and helped him pick up the scattered cards. Then, like they were children, he yelled, "Enough drinking! Go to bed!"

Iman grumbled but seemed satisfied now that his debt was canceled. Terence scurried about picking up the cards. It was Terence, Michel realized, who was causing the tension among the men. A cocky young man who would steal from the men he traveled with. Not good.

After a moment of fizzling energy and some jeers from the others—taunting Iman for losing at cards and Terence for getting yelled at—the men quieted. Satisfied that the two had gone off to their own spaces, Michel felt the tension in the campground dissipate. Michel turned and made his way back to the fire near his tent, ticking this addendum to the mental list of things he would have to give attention to.

But just as he thought he would have to keep a closer eye on Terence, he looked up to see that Eve's eyes were stormy, and they were all over him.

Chapter Eight

The next morning, Michel woke up just as the sky was turning from black to gray-blue. He breathed in the smell of the dwindling fire while his eyes focused. He smelled coffee and turned to see Eve preparing a mug near the fire.

Eve had slept in the small tent he usually used when they traveled, and he had slept right at the entrance. He realized she must have had to step over him to get out. He stretched and sat up with his legs folded in front of him. He watched Eve moving around the fire. He thought again of how she had looked at him the night before, and he wondered what it would take to captivate her in such a way again.

The rest of the men, he saw, were mostly still asleep, though some were stirring on their bedrolls at the smell of the coffee. Iman snored loudly, and Terence was up, shuffling through his things. Michel turned his attention back to Eve as she rose from the fire and came toward him.

"Good morning," she said as she approached. She handed him the cup.

"This is for me?" he asked, accepting the warm porcelain cup in his hands.

She nodded. "Two sugar cubes, correct?"

"Yes," he said. "Thank you. And you?" he asked, looking up at her as he took a sip.

"I prefer tea." She smiled. "Don't take long. I am almost ready for your shave. I am just preparing the hot towels." She indicated to a cushion she had set up with his shaving materials laid out next to it.

"Shave?" He glanced wearily at the tools as he stroked his fingers down his cheeks. "I can do that myself," he said. He would typically get a shave while in the towns, but didn't mind the growth when they traveled between cities.

She grinned mischievously. "Do you not trust me?"

"I don't know," he said, looking between her and the blades she had laid out. "You have shown you don't mind causing me pain."

Eve just gave him a playful shrug and went back to preparing the towels.

A short while later, he was sitting on the cushion with Eve kneeling in front of him. He was learning that he couldn't dissuade her once she had decided on something. Having her this close, though, the proximity was suddenly pressing on him in a way that was making him uncomfortable. The closeness, though he enjoyed having her near, her scent in his nose, made him concerned he would do something stupid once more: grab onto her, touch her in a way he shouldn't. It would be a bad move to lose control now, especially when she held a blade to his throat.

Kneeling before him, Eve scooped the cream he used for shaving out of a small pot and leaned forward to spread it over his stubble. Her eyes narrowed and focused as she did. He watched her, enjoying the chance to see her up close, her skin so smooth and her pink lips pouting in concentration. The feel of her hands on his cheeks was stimulating and soothing at the same time. He allowed himself to enjoy the sensation.

Then she leaned over to wipe her hands on a towel and take the sharp blade, which she held by the bone handle with the Chevalier crest on it. He thought for a minute about how she had managed to find his personal effects and realized that she had been into all his things. He would have laughed if he wasn't having to keep such tight control over himself, having never shared his privacy with a woman like this. Never had he had a woman in his space for so long, never had he entrusted any part of his life to someone he dallied with.

He couldn't hide anything from Eve. She took control wherever she went.

She held the blade up against the top of his cheekbone, and he had a startle of anxiety run through him. He didn't think she would hurt him intentionally, at this point, but... maybe?

"Have you done this much?" he asked, his voice raised.

"Never," she replied as she slid the blade along the contours of his face.

She wiped the blade and came at him again. "Don't worry, Michel," she said, tipping his chin up so he could look into her eyes. "I am good at everything I do." She paused to give him a wink.

Michel chuckled, relaxing a little.

"Still," she commanded. She took another pass down his jawline as he obediently froze in place.

Moments later, Michel was rubbing his clean-shaven face while he urged the rest of the men up from their bedrolls. As he set about the last preparations to resume their travel, he watched Eve from the corner of his eye as she cleaned up his shaving supplies. He had never had a better travel companion, he decided.

About four hours into their journey that day, they came upon a small outpost in the grassy desert oasis of the Bukhara valley. The area was known to host a rougher lot, and though Eve had never been this far, she had known to avoid it when she was running away. Michel told her they would not be staying here, but he liked to go through the bazaars and meet with merchants. Eve knew Michel was on the lookout for cashmere trade, but she also knew that type of trade did not filter through this region. The trade was simpler here: dried foods, fresh kills, and gold embroidery done in the monasteries. Still, it was a good place to find curiosities and have a midday rest.

The men with whom they traveled spread out for their own business, while Eve followed Michel obediently, carrying his bag, which contained little gold coins stamped with the seal from his home and other novelties that he gave to the merchants. She found him to be frivolous with money, but in an affable sense. Like his title, he used his coin to avoid trouble. It wasn't really the way of her people, but she conceded the validity of his methods. And it seemed to keep everyone happy.

The market was set up in a large open square surrounded by squat semipermanent buildings. Stalls and patio covers stretched across the square in rows. Many of the merchants knew Michel, and they greeted him warmly. As they moved through the space, Eve noticed a group of pretty women without headscarves outside the door of an otherwise normal-looking building. One of the women snaked out and entangled her limbs with Michel's.

Eve froze and looked at the woman, enraged by her actions. For a split second, Eve wanted to punch her right in the nose, just like she had done to Armin when he had tried to loop a rope around her arms and drag her to the whorehouse in Merv. Then Michel pulled his arms away and declined what the woman was offering, leaving Eve with balled up fists and confusion in her chest.

Eve paused in the wake of her unexpected jealousy and shook out her hands. She had never known such a feeling before. It caused the strangest sensation to want to be closer to that man. To put her own arms where the woman's had been. *That wouldn't be appropriate at all*, she thought, moving once more, still surprised by her reaction. He had every right to go with that woman if he had desired to do so, even if it would irritate her. She had to admit, much deeper feelings of attraction to him had snapped free in her last night, seeing him insert himself between the man and the boy in their fight, his display of easy strength and power. Attraction had already been there, simmering inside her, but it roared to life when she realized he was not utterly weak, with only the protection of his country keeping him alive. She stole a glance at him then, while they walked, so handsome and always so proud. He charmed as he went, warm to the people around him, completely oblivious to the feelings stirred up inside her.

Silly Frenchman, she thought.

They came to a stall, and Michel talked to the merchant before them. Eve surveyed the crowd. Other than the ladies at the brothel, there were few women, and the ones about were modestly attired with long dresses and covered hair. The warmth of the afternoon hung around her, though she did not drop the shawl around her head.

She tinkered with a pretty stone on the table. The merchant leaned across to her.

"Do you like it, lady?" he asked with a friendly, toothless grin. "You have it," he said.

"No," she smiled. "I will pay you—"

She halted mid-sentence. Behind the merchant, through his stall and across the tiled walkway, she saw someone who made her insides seize.

It was Ganbold, there in the square, a warrior from the tribe that had kidnapped her. He stood a full head above the crowd and seemed to be scanning the people. She knew instantly that he had to be after her. Her people and the connected tribes did not come this far West normally. The herds that fed them preferred the sloping valley to the East of her home, so his presence was not by chance. She'd known the closer she got to her territory, the more likely it was to see the markings of the tribe from which she had escaped, but *Ganbold*? She panicked. That meant there was no desire for her well-being. She was being hunted. Ganbold was known among her people, among all the tribes, as a fearsome warrior, a man with steel in his fists. He was enormous, and no man who fought him ever survived. In her homeland, he was a legend.

Her body took over before her mind could catch up. She had to get away. She backed up and smashed into Michel. In doing so, she dropped the bag and scattered the trinkets. She sank to the ground in a panic to scoop them up.

"Here, let me help you," Michel said, coming down beside her.

She looked at him. She didn't mean to show him the dread she knew was in her face—he still could leave her stranded, these were not his problems— but the terror had overwhelmed her, and she knew it showed.

Michel seemed to understand the change in her immediately. "What's wrong?" he asked, looking around, trying to identify what caused her change in demeanor.

Eve sputtered. She couldn't speak.

He lowered his voice. "Eve, do you see someone you know?"

She blinked at him, still unable to form any words.

"Is someone after you?" he asked. His words were measured.

"Um, uh," she replied, nodding her head when words failed her.

He placed his hand under her chin and tilted her head up to him as they sat there, squatted amongst the people. "You have my protection, Eve. You are not alone."

When he said it, she saw his own warrior flash. She did not think he was just a silly noble, but she still didn't know if his power could tether her, that she could indeed rely on him for protection. His eyes said she could. Overcome with the need for relief, she collapsed against him.

"Let's go," he said, his arm around her. "We are done here."

He helped her stand. He wrapped his arm around her as she ducked into his chest, her shawl tightly covering her. She knew he paused to look around again, and she wondered if his eyes had landed on Ganbold. He kept her tucked into him, hustling her out of the marketplace, the scent of him filled her nose—leather, spice, and something soothing that was only him.

Despite her fear and distress at seeing Ganbold, it was Michel's scent she dwelled on as they rode away from the outpost.

Later that night, Michel lay on his bedroll, outside Eve's tent, unable to fall asleep, even though the rest of the camp had settled. He had done this route through the area before, many times, but tonight it had been difficult to find a place he believed to be safe to camp. He hiked them further into the crevasses of the mountain range so they couldn't be approached without warning. Now he lay on an uneven slope just outside of Eve's tent, with rocks knifing into his back.

That wasn't why he couldn't sleep, however. Michel had set out on this journey with one goal: to access the rich cashmere market of the closed-off tribal communities to appease the Cardinal. To do this, he would need to travel further East than he ever had before, deep into the Tian Shan mountains, past the typical reach of Europeans. Up until Bukhara, European merchants were welcome. Past Bukhara, they were merely tolerated. Michel always stretched his travels to the very end of France's reach, but he understood the limitations in where he would be able to safely travel. He hoped to find someone who just happened to be like him, out of their usual range, looking to find a contact to expand their trade.

It would be like finding a grain of rice in a bucket of beans.

He moved his arm behind his head and stared up into the night sky. The fire crackled nearby, illuminating the sleeping bodies around. He was still fully dressed, sword just next to him, unease in his chest. For the moment, however, it wasn't cashmere he cared about. As soon as he'd seen that huge man in the marketplace, larger than anyone there, he realized that Eve had more complex secrets than he had imagined. He also realized, in that same instant, he would rip that man apart if he tried to hurt her. The thought melded with a purpose he began to understand had already been cast deep inside him, though he didn't know exactly when it had happened: he would protect this woman with all that he had.

But Michel couldn't instigate a fight with a tribal man. An aggressive Frenchman would incite the tribes, destabilize the trade line, and undermine Michel's mission to travel into forbidden territory. How much danger were they really in? When he questioned Eve, she did not respond and shook her head with a stubborn frown. Michel didn't think she had expected to see that man. Her fear was confirmation that she was indeed running from something.

He needed more information. The only option he could see was to tease these secrets out of her as best as he could. That and hire some extra guards to travel with them. Thankfully, Michel didn't believe the man had seen her, though how closely the man pursued her, Michel didn't know. Had it been by chance that they came upon the same market? Or had they just barely escaped?

Michel heard her stir inside the tent and wondered if she was also lying awake. His instinct was to crawl in beside her. He wanted to soothe her, and to feel soothed by her as well. Feelings brewed inside him that he couldn't quite explain. How had he gone from helping a woman get out of trouble to inviting trouble into his own mission? Michel had enjoyed many women in his life, but he had never felt so enraptured by any one of them. His heart was for his country. His loyalty belonged to his country. Eve however, drew his thoughts and motives like no one ever had before.

She had indeed entranced him, and he wanted more. Her banter, her authority, her touch, her lips. Even her problems, if it meant getting closer. He wanted it all.

Except that bite to the finger, he thought, laughing to himself as he finally drifted off to sleep.

Chapter Nine

The next day, they were traveling through a grassy area that cut through the Zarafshan mountains. The narrow valley opened to the warm sun cresting the naked, sand-gray mountain tops. The long, spring grass moved like the sea in the breeze, and Michel was glad the day was temperate. He knew this passage. If the weather was not right, strong winds would scream in their ears and cut like razor blades across their cheeks. This day, however, was warm and pleasant with nothing more than a soft breeze, which fluttered the manes of the horses and, Michel had noticed, the edges of Eve's hair as well.

The crew of nearly thirty would reach Bukhara proper by evening, an important city that connected the lower towns to the arid high plains villages. At the moment, Michel and Eve were riding their horses side by side while the rest of the men had relaxed the line and spread out in the valley around them, each horse picking its favorite way through the fertile desert grasses. Michel kept looking over at her, but she was only staring ahead. He had so many questions, so many details missing that he needed to know. He couldn't plan, couldn't prepare if he didn't have all the information. As their horses carried them through the valley, Michel watched her, trying to figure it all out.

"Why are you watching me?" she asked, after his staring had apparently become obvious. She smiled as she said it, though she did not turn to look at him.

"I am interested in learning more about you," Michel said, leaning toward her.

"You don't need to know any more about me," she said, the breeze twisting her hair behind her. "You know all you need to know."

"You misunderstand," he said, angling his horse closer. "I *want* to know more about you."

She laughed, glancing at him, her eyes glinting. "Okay," she said. "What do you know so far?"

"Well," he began thoughtfully. He needed a place to begin with her, some conversation line that would allow him better access to her citadel of secrets. "You are very beautiful. Your looks are unique. This has made you stand out in a way that you don't like," he paused. "But you aren't one to pass on an advantage." He watched her, trying to gauge how well she thought he described her, hoping that if he did well, she would let him know more. "You are good with organization. You *can* read and write," he teased. "You also have six older brothers who will beat me to death if they ever meet me."

She grinned at that. "What else?"

"You control your emotions very well," he remarked, slipping into a teasing tone. "That or you don't have any emotions besides irritation with handsome Frenchmen."

"More like *arrogant* Frenchmen," she teased. Then she held up a finger in explanation. "Discipline is part of my culture. Ill-timed emotions are considered a weakness." She nodded back to him. "Irritation with Frenchmen is just one emotion I'm comfortable sharing." She smirked. "Keep going."

Michel continued, encouraged. "You pass yourself off as a commoner, but you clearly come from a higher position."

"Why do you say that?" she asked, her eyes meeting his again.

"I see how you interact with the men. And with *me*." He looked at her, guiding his horse into her line of sight. "You have authority. You aren't a peasant." He paused and adjusted the reins around his hands. He lowered the tone of his voice, taking the opportunity. "You are running from something. I want to know what that is."

"Hmmm," was all she said, turning her head back to the road.

He sat back on his saddle. *Too soon*, he thought. But though she did not elaborate, her body language did not close off, so he kept going, if nothing else, just to keep her talking.

"You are also incredibly smart," Michel said, trying a different approach. "Perhaps even as smart as I am." He couldn't stop the grin as he said it. He did like teasing her.

"As smart as you?" she echoed. "That does not seem a difficult accomplishment." Now she smirked at him.

He laughed. "Alright." They were coming up on a gushing stream, and the passageway turned rockier. The horses took their steps more carefully, but the brisk pace continued. Michel checked back over the men to be sure the rocks hadn't disrupted any of the carts, then returned to his conversation, still trying to build momentum, to just keep her talking. "I am impressed that you speak so well," he said.

"You mean French?" she asked.

"Yes." He nodded. "I hear hardly any accent at all."

"I have always had a gift for languages."

"You speak other languages?"

"Yes," she replied. "And you?"

Michel typically kept his knowledge close to his chest, but he wanted to astound her, dazzle her. "I speak five languages," he boasted.

"Oh," was all she replied.

Michel continued, holding out his hand to tick them off. "English, French of course, Latin, Spanish, Mongolian. Some Turkic."

"You don't really speak Mongolian," she said, her green eyes playful.

The comment struck him in the chest. Of all the insults she'd thrown at him, playful or not, this barb stung. "Indeed, I do," he insisted. "I speak it. I speak it well. You have seen me interact with the tradesmen."

"Yes, but they barely speak it either," she laughed. "You communicate well enough, but you don't speak it."

"If I communicate, then I believe I speak it," he said resolutely as his horse picked over a large rock.

Eve shrugged and turned away, a small smile on her lips. Then she continued, "For example," she said. "You use the phrase *mal mini* incorrectly."

"No, I don't," he said. "It's 'your animals.' I say it to trade the herd animals."

"Yes, *mal mini* refers to animals. But you don't use it correctly." She cocked her head at him. "It's an insult."

"An insult?" Michel blustered, a window suddenly blowing open in his brain. "How?"

"I don't know *how*." She shrugged. "It's idiomatic. The words are what you say, but we use it to call someone a dirty animal if they are acting poorly."

"So, I have been calling all the merchants along the road dirty herd animals?"

"Yes, you have," she said, grinning. "They don't care. You have good products, and you are generous. They will trade with you no matter what you call them, and then they will laugh at you later."

They were silent for a moment, Michel feeling stupid. This wasn't his intention for the conversation. They were coming to the end of the open valley with low cliffs now in view, and he had learned nothing more about her, only that he was an idiot. "So how many languages do you speak?" he asked.

"I don't know," she replied.

"How can you not know? That is silly."

"I learn languages easily," she continued. "I hear a language, and I find myself speaking it not long after."

"That sounds like you speak dialects, not languages."

"I speak the languages you mention. I read and write in all the romance languages. I speak many dialects, too."

"I wasn't counting dialects," Michel said. He tallied in his head. "I speak seven French dialects."

"Seven," she mocked.

"And you?"

"There are twelve in my region alone and many more beyond that. I haven't found one I couldn't learn."

Michel watched her, blinking stupidly. He spoke five languages, seven dialects, and had absolutely nothing in his head to say.

"I think," she said, "you perhaps miss being the only intellectual around." She grinned at him as she pulled her hair back over her shoulder.

"I may not be the smartest one here. I don't care." He shrugged his shoulders. Then he turned to her again. "I am someone without any secrets." He, at least, could take this as a chance to change the trajectory of their conversation.

Eve looked down, her face becoming cloudy again.

"Why don't you tell me?" Michel urged, soft again, his voice coaxing. "You don't have to tell me everything. If you tell me something, then I can be better prepared."

"I am your hired hand," she asserted. "You don't need to help me."

"The girl in the market needed help. If that gigantic man comes after you again, you are going to need more help. If you don't prepare me, Eve, you may end up needing more than I can give."

She was quiet for a long time. He waited. He wanted her to work out whatever was in her head. In whatever language she was doing it.

Finally, she spoke. "You want to know why I am running?"

"Yes," he said, giving no more words so the conversation wouldn't change again.

"I am running, Michel." She paused and looked out across the road that was soon to be swallowed up by the cliffs. "I am running because I murdered my husband."

Chapter Ten

Ganbold. Warrior. Hunter.

Ganbold was huffing through a little village somewhere north of the Tian Shen mountains. After killing the merchant who had sold her, Ganbold had continued along the same road. He thought he was close to the woman when he reached the Bukhara outpost. People had seen the blonde woman with the Frenchman there, but Ganbold could not be sure which way they went after. He had a choice—he could take the northern or southern route. Ganbold, knowing that the northern trail would lead into the mountains, chose to go south. A Frenchman would surely choose the easier path.

Ganbold was wrong. No one saw the woman along the route he chose. He lost their trail.

This made Ganbold very angry—anger in his eyes, in his chest. Ganbold poured tea into the ground as an offering, asking the ancestors why they favored the murderous woman over him, a warrior. Their voices did not answer him. Ganbold turned his path then and cut his own way through the mountains that separated him from the northern route he should have chosen. The ancestors may be laughing at him, but he would change their minds when they saw how determined he was.

Ganbold. Warrior. Hunter. Ganbold. Warrior. Hunter.

Ganbold did not know the name of the village he'd entered that afternoon, but he found the marketplace at its center. He stood at the edge, scanning the stalls, looking for someone who may speak his language. This land had been of his people many generations ago. Now it was Ganbold who was the outsider. It angered him that his people, the people of his great ancestors, had bartered it away for comforts. Comforts that led his people to become lazy and weak. Comforts that made women think they deserved more than their husbands chose to give them.

As Ganbold moved his eyes over the little square, he thought of the crime of the woman. Ganbold had watched the wedding from where he slept outside the camp. He watched later as the woman entered the yurt with the other wives. He watched when the wives left and then her new husband, Ganbold's kinsman Bataar, entered. The pair would not emerge until the morning, and Ganbold had turned away, disgusted at the union.

The evening of the wedding, Ganbold did not return to his sleeping mat. Instead, he slept on the ground with no blanket or warmth, wanting to see the couple emerge in the morning. He woke before the sun and circled around the back of the wedding yurt, looking for the best angle to see the pain in the woman's face, as was common in the new brides. He waited there for many hours, but they did not come out of the yurt.

At first, Ganbold could hear the laughter from the neighbors, joking that the new couple was exhausted from their activities in the night. Waiting, Ganbold paced. As morning became late morning, he walked through the high grasses to burn off his energy. His only solace in this union would be to see that Bataar had taught her that she was subject to him, that she would not influence this tribe. At almost midday, Ganbold discovered a small piece of fabric that had caught on a tree stump. He picked it up and examined it, just as he heard a scream peal across the plains.

Ganbold shot up to see Bataar's first wife at the entrance of the yurt. Her screams called the other wives, who went into hysterics as well. Ganbold watched as, one by one, the elders entered, as well as the Il-khan. Someone had died, he understood. Someone else was missing. At first, the words he heard did not make sense, and Ganbold thought Bataar had killed his bride. Ganbold felt pride—in his chest, in his cheeks—for his tribesman who refused this woman from the soft tribe. But why would Bataar run away and not share the decision with his tribe?

Then he saw the elders carry the body of Bataar out of the yurt and heard the confusion as they searched for the woman, worried for her *safety*. Ganbold looked down at his hand and realized the fabric he held was from her wedding deel. The woman had killed Bataar and escaped while the tribe slept. Anger shook Ganbold's body—his feet, his fists, his chest, his shoulders.

He ran in the direction of where he had found the fabric to follow her path before the tribal leaders fully understood what had happened.

Now Ganbold was very far from his home, in a place that should still belong to the tribes but no longer did. He walked through the marketplace, listening to the ugly rhythms of words he did not understand. Finally, he stopped at a stall with a man who looked very scared to talk to him. "Woman," Ganbold choked out the word.

The scared man said some words. Ganbold shook his head.

"Brothel?" asked the skinny man again, this time the language enough like his own that Ganbold understood.

"No," Ganbold said. "Woman. Light hair. Tribal like me." He tapped his face.

The man quaked before him, saying more words in the language Ganbold knew. "Yes, yes, I saw that woman."

"When?"

"Three days? Yes," he said. "Three days ago."

"Where did she go?"

He said more nonsense. Then Ganbold understood a word: "Samarkand."

Ganbold grunted and turned away. The ancestors favored him once more by guiding him to this information.

Michel and his crew traveled the next few days without incident. Though he felt that they had escaped any immediate danger, he would rest easier when they got off the open road and reached Bukhara, where he could speak with his contacts and reconnoiter. He hoped that seeing that man had been a fluke. He feared, however, that whatever was coming for Eve would be bigger than he could handle quietly.

She had said she had murdered her husband and then said no more. Leaving Michel with questions overflowing.

In his years of business and politics, he had learned that he had to trust his instincts about people. He knew tribal politics to be rudimentary, physical, brutal. He did not know Eve well, but he did not believe she would do something unfounded. He so badly wanted to understand her.

And, of course, he knew how angry the tribes would be if they knew he was harboring her.

But he had committed to her. He wouldn't turn her away at the first confidence she gave him. Though this new knowledge of her certainly did not ease his mind.

The crew would reach Bukhara later that evening. The landscape had already begun changing as they had gone deeper into the river valley. Ancient earthquakes had carved steep hills into the area, while the river provided the arid desert with enough moisture to cover the ground in thick, green underbrush. Now, they were coming through a rocky passage which cut a wedge between two hills. The men had slowed. Michel turned scenarios in his mind while listening to snatches of conversation echoing up the high rocky walls. A wheel may need replacing soon. A story of a girl at home. A missing pipe. A song.

Michel hulked in his saddle. He was still agitated, every new sound causing him to think they were under attack. The horses' hooves crunched through the slate. Another man behind him laughed and said he'd lost a razor too.

Michel thought for a moment, keying in more closely to their conversations. It had also been a while since he'd seen his pen knife, he thought.

"*Goddammit*," he growled suddenly. He nudged and called his horse to stop before climbing off. Behind him, the men bottlenecked, coming to abrupt stops of their own. Eve looked on as he stalked back down the line.

Michel locked onto Terence. The youth's hazel eyes grew wide as he sat up straighter on his horse. Michel approached him, grabbed the boy by the shirt, and jerked him off the horse.

"*Monsieur*!" Terence cried. "What—what have I done?"

Michel didn't respond, but tipped Terence up by the back of his pants until he was almost upside down. From his pockets tumbled a selection of items: a compass, a ring, a scattering of coins. Michel let Terence right himself, but he didn't let the boy go. Michel reached for the saddlebag that carried Terence's knapsack. Michel dumped it as well.

"My razor!" shouted the man who, moments before, had been complaining. Several of the others murmured as they began to see their own materials, patting themselves down for confirmation that things had gone missing.

Michel dropped Terence in a heap, and the boy scrambled up. He held up his hands, "I don't know..." he started. "I didn't..."

Michel pointed at him. "You're done."

Terence froze. "You're not gonna leave me here?"

Michel grabbed him by the back of his shirt again and threw him over the saddle of his horse. "Not here," Michel said. He stroked the muzzle of the horse with one hand and then led the horse to the front of the procession. "When we arrive in Bukhara, I will arrange your return to France. You are too young to be this far from home."

"*Monsieur*, please," he sputtered, "I'm useful. I'm strong. I can speak dialects the rest of you can't—"

"I don't want to hear anymore. I don't have time for this," Michel said. He tethered the horses. "Keep your mouth shut, or I'll kick you off the horse, and you can find your own way home."

Terence—now covered in reddish dirt from being dropped in the road, his cropped hair a mess—closed his mouth, but Michel saw his eyes blacken with anger.

"I don't intend to strand you, boy, but don't press me," Michel said, hoisting himself on his saddle, irritation, anger, and frustration warring inside of him.

The party entered Bukhara in the late afternoon, just before the dinner hour. Eve had not been through Bukhara, but as it had been settled by a Mongolian Khan less than a century ago, there were people here who shared her same lineage. Bukhara housed massive buildings made of pale brickwork that blazed yellow in the last rays of the day's sunlight. Huge mosques and temples with domed roofs covered in turquoise tiles towered over shaded streets that cut between the thick, tall walls. Enormous rectangular iwans pushed far above the courtyard walls that contained them, showing off intricate and colored tile work. As they walked through the streets, Eve felt as tiny as a fly on the tail of a camel amongst the structures. It seemed a city built for giants.

Michel led them through the city to the northwestern corner, just outside another massive, earthen building—the city's citadel—with walls that seemed to stretch to the clouds. Here, they would set up their yurts and housing since this would be their base for a stretch of time. Once Michel spoke with the town officials, he turned to the men and hollered at them to start setting up the campground.

Eve stepped forward and put her hand on his forearm. He stopped yelling to look down at her hand and then to her eyes.

"It's my job," she said. "I will oversee the camp preparations." Then she nodded toward Terence, who was kicking rocks into the wall. "You have other things to take care of."

He held her eyes for a moment, then nodded and indicated with his hand that she should go ahead.

Satisfied, Eve called out to the men, who were already unloading their materials. "Look at me, please," her voice rose above them as she cut through the space. The others paused the preparation of their own spaces—some setting up yurts, others preferring their tents—to look at her. "We will have one main campfire at the center," she called out, turning her body to make eye contact with each man. "It will be where I am standing," she called out. "Iman," she leveled her eyes on him, "please find the stones and the starters in the wagons and bring them to me now."

Iman hesitated for a moment before nodding. "My lady," he said as he moved to retrieve the materials.

Eve continued. "We will eat together, and you will be one with us for as long as you continue on this journey." She looked at Iman. "This will help to squash any disagreements." She nodded at the resolution. "Those of you departing here, please see me before leaving. If you are awaiting a payment, I will take care of that as well."

By now, the men stood still, awaiting her next instructions. Eve put her hands on her hips. "Get to it," she called out. "You don't eat until your yurt is set up." She toed a circle in the dirt where the cooking pit would be. "Make sure the entrance faces south, or you will most certainly do it again."

Across the space, at the edge of their camp, far from the center where she stood, was Michel, standing with Terence. Michel watched her with amusement on his face, and for some reason, it caused her insides to flutter.

Chapter Eleven

In just a few hours, camp had been set up, yurts placed correctly, and everyone was settled. Eve had been to the marketplace, and she had purchased vegetables and grains, cooked dinner, and fed the men. She also had organized the yurt she would share with Michel, setting up the space as was traditional, taking great care with his things. Now, she stood at the central campfire, surveying the men, the darkness separating the camp from the greater part of the city, while their firelight illuminated the massive wall behind them. It was the first time in a long time that Eve felt satisfied with the work she had accomplished.

She had not, however, finished her duties for the evening.

She leaned toward the fire and rotated a log as she waited for a pot of water to boil. The feelings she had been avoiding were coming up. Intimacies were blooming between her and Michel that she feared but enjoyed at the same time. She lived now with a heat swelling inside her that she wasn't quite sure what to do with or how to soothe. The only thing that seemed to make it better was being near him, even though proximity also made the feeling glow warmer.

The truth was, she wouldn't mind having his hands on her again.

It was also probably the reason she let slip why she had run away. She felt too close to him. Eve had sworn never to speak of what had happened, the circumstances that led up to the murder of the man who had forced her to wed. She believed that by keeping the information hidden, she wouldn't put anyone else in danger. Her hope had always been to get to France uneventfully without causing any more problems. Yet she had connected herself to a man who was heading in the opposite direction, closer to those looking for her. Then they had seen Ganbold, and she knew there would be more coming for her. She also knew she owed Michel an explanation, but she didn't know what information would be helpful and what would be harmful. Until she could unravel everything in her mind, she would not say anything else.

She did need someone to trust, though. Since the moment she had been stolen from her own lands, she had been destabilized in such a way that nothing she did seemed right. She didn't have her family, she didn't have her home, she didn't have the pillars of comfort she had relied on all her life. She wanted badly to rely on Michel, to trust him. It would make her current position much easier. She also wished she could dive into the feelings that he made her feel—safe and unhinged at the same time.

She didn't know if she would be a fool for doing so.

The pot of water steamed over the fire, so she carefully dipped and rolled several towels and put them in her basket. She took a last glance over the settled camp before she went to the yurt, removing her shoes before she entered. The coals glowed hot at the stove in the center, creating a sensual warmth in the space. On the low table behind the stove sat a lantern which filled the enclosure with a soft light. Michel had traveled with only one bed, and she had set that up on the eastern edge of the space for herself. For Michel, she created a bed out of soft blankets on the western side of the yurt. She felt pride in having set the yurt up correctly.

Eve began the preparation for their evening tea, then she prepared herself and dressed in her nighttime shift. It was a clingy linen that buttoned snugly around her waist. No man had seen her dressed in such a way, she knew, but such were the circumstances, and she would not sleep in full dress. Once she had prepared herself, she completed the tea, then moved to the area she had arranged for Michel. Soon, she heard his voice come into focus from the camp as he barked the last orders at the men for the night. *Always so surly with the men,* she thought, bringing her hands up to her lips in a laugh.

She opened the door of the yurt, called his name, then kneeled beside the stool and waited to serve her master, a man she had begun to enjoy being bound to.

The evening was cool and, when he opened the door, she felt the wind swirl the air before being pulled upwards through the open space at the apex of the yurt. Michel stepped through the entrance and stopped. He watched her wide-eyed.

"What is this for?" he asked.

Eve, her hands rested calmly on her thighs, explained, "I will wash you now and prepare you for sleep."

He took a tentative step toward her. "This is not necessary," he said. "You have done a lot today, I don't need—"

"Hush," she said. She nodded toward the stool. "Sit."

He hesitated a moment, then came further into the yurt.

She stopped him. "Sword and boots," she instructed.

He removed his sword belt and then his boots and placed everything by the door. He stepped forward and sat on the low chair. His eyes never left hers.

She moved her own body so that she kneeled directly in front of him, watching him as she did. She relaxed her posture, soft and calm. His was the opposite—rigid and restless. She rose to her knees, this new affection drawing her closer. "Relax," she said, moving closer to whisper into his ear.

Michel breathed deeply through his nose, and she watched his muscles ripple under his clothing. The night air felt cool, but heat flamed from his body—heat of his own desire, branded into his skin. She had known the want of men before. She had seen desire in their eyes when they had looked at her. This was different. His desire for her came off him so strongly that it penetrated her skin, sank into her deep, and braided down her own want.

She touched him then, aware suddenly that if this man chose to take her, she could do nothing to stop him. Part of her wondered exactly what that would feel like, but it wasn't something Michel would do without permission. She knew his character. She could take as much of him as she wanted without worry. She leaned down to dip her hands into the bowl with warm water and cleansing oils, then ran her fingers through his hair. She inhaled his scent deeply, musky and yet sweet, wanting to pull this part of him into her. Michel ground his jaw, his eyes stalking her as she ran her fingers through his hair again, this time to pull it back and knot it on the top of his head.

"Eve," he said. His hands gripped the stool beneath him, but he leaned into her. "It's difficult not to touch you."

"Where would you like to touch me?" she said, the words playful, drifting with the closeness.

"Here," he angled his head into the crook of her neck, "with my lips," he said, his words dusting against her skin.

A course of goosebumps ran down her spine. "No," she said, "you may not."

"Okay," he said. He moved his head to the other side and tucked into her neck there. "What about here?" he asked, letting his lips brush her skin.

Eve shivered as goosebumps exploded down her back once more. She felt Michel smile at her reaction to him. "No," she said, now breathless. "Not there."

"Then where?" he asked, still whispering against her skin.

"Nowhere, Michel," she said, wedging her hand between them, pushing him back with her fingertips, enjoying the power she held over him very, very much.

"*Siren*," he said, drawing the word out in frustration as he fell back in the chair.

The way he looked at her, with his brow angry and his want so clearly on display, she couldn't help but respond. She felt tremors traveling up her thighs and coming together deep inside her. It was a new sensation, and she didn't want it to stop. She smiled.

"Hands to yourself while I work," she ordered. She pulled her bottom lip between her teeth, and Michel let out a low growl in response, his eyes darkened with desire.

She reached up to undo his shirt, watching his eyes as she pulled the laces from their holes. He had leaned back, with his arms still gripping the sides of the chair, thick muscles straining. She pushed his shirt back over his shoulders, taking the opportunity to lean close again and explore him with her hands. She liked the feel of his skin—smooth, supple leather over iron muscles. She liked his reactions even more when she touched his bare flesh. He breathed heavily, jerked at every stroke of her fingers, and made low noises deep in his chest.

Once his shirt was off, she took the wet towel and ran it over his naked chest, following each trail of water with her eyes. She lifted his arms and washed over each muscle, from his hands down his side. Then she went across the ridges of his abs as low as she could travel until she was stopped by the belting of his pants. She cared for every piece of his skin before dropping the towel back in the basin. She watched him now and reached toward his pants.

"Eve." He jumped and grabbed her hand to stop her.

"Hands back," she demanded.

Michel gripped her a moment before releasing her and dropping his hands, still breathing through his nose, clenching his jaw.

Eve undid his pants. "Up," she said.

Michel lifted his bottom, and she pulled off his pants, leaving him covered only by his undergarments, a thin material that came to just above his knees. Michel reached forward to cover himself, to the muscle that let his intentions be known. Eve was quick to place another towel over his most intimate spot. Michel accepted it, but let out a long, labored sigh as she continued to work.

She did enjoy teasing him.

She continued his cleansing. She ran her cloth over each leg, taking away the dirt and sweat from the day. When she had finished with the water, she took a cream for his skin and ran it over the same parts she had cleaned, this time starting from the bottom and going to the top: first his legs, then his torso, and across his back, the smooth cream allowing her to massage deep into his skin. At the end, she rubbed her hands over his cheeks, darkened with stubble. She held his face in her hands and looked into his dark eyes, glowing with want, as she pressed her body close to his. "All done," she said, her lips parted with a smile.

Suddenly, Michel's arm grabbed around her waist, his hand spread across the small of her back, holding her tightly, aggressively. Eve dropped her arms in surprise. Then, his other hand was in her hair. He gripped her by the nape of the neck, and his hungry lips were on hers. The tremors that had been running through her tore across her body, causing her to moan against him. His grip tightened, holding her body to his.

She had never felt anything like it, both inside and out. His lips on hers caused everything to sparkle: all the places they touched, new places deep inside her, and the air around them. He parted his lips and took hers again, connecting and melding them together. Part of it felt perfectly right, a physical display of all the intimacies they were sharing, while the other part caused her heart to boom in warning that she shouldn't hook herself deeper into this man, for his safety, for her own. Then he opened her mouth as he tilted her back, and the only thing she could think was that she wanted to taste all of him. She felt his tongue, and she met it with her own, not knowing what to do other than follow her instinct and his gentle instructions.

Heat poured from him into her—or her into him, she didn't know—and it caused her head to swim, her body to cling to him, and for an exciting heat to throb down between her legs. The sensations thrilled her. At the same time, the rush of new feelings startled her, alarmed her, made her world spin. Suddenly, she feared tipping over into an abyss where she didn't have control anymore. So, she did the only thing she knew to do when a man took more than he was allowed. She pushed him back and smacked him across the face as hard as she could.

"Ah," he grunted as he squinted, his hand coming up to his face. "I'm sorry, I shouldn't have—"

That was all she needed to cage her control once more. Before she could think of anything else, Eve grabbed him around the shoulders and kissed him herself. She met his lips again, his body still just as hard. His hands flew to her once more, grabbing and pulling at her greedily. She loved this. She had never experienced a desire like this, boiling inside her, turning her blood to steam. How did his lips on hers make her stomach tremble and her inner thighs ache? She thrust her tongue into his mouth, and Michel met it with his own. He took control of the kiss again and now held her strongly, kissing her intensely, his lips and tongue soft but insistent, dominating against hers.

His hands ran up the back of her as he pulled her to her feet. Then he moved one up across her breast, while she felt the other unraveling the lacing up the side of her shift. With heavy steps, he backed her up and Eve realized he was leading her to the bed. Amazed by how quickly she forgot everything and let the sensations take her over, she panicked. This was a dangerous fire that had to be tamed. So, she pushed him back again. And with the force of all the passion coursing through her, she smacked him a second time.

This time, when he stopped, she turned away. She leaned down to collect the bowl of water and the rest of the items she had laid out.

"You should sleep now. You have important business in the morning."

She glanced up at him. His expression was incredulous, but humbled, eyes still dark with lust, his hand on the place where she had smacked him. Eve clicked her tongue and turned in a huff. Though she had admonished him, she couldn't stop smiling as she realized his scent was still clinging to her skin.

Chapter Twelve

Borjigin Khan, emperor of the Chagatai Khanate, direct descendant of Genghis Khan, vector of control for all the western tribes, smoldered as he sat in his throne room. His daughter had gone missing. His brash, irreverent, beautiful daughter, who could move a man with her smile and a mountain with her wit, had disappeared.

His only daughter.

Six sons and then her. Three generations of only boys and then her. A joy beyond comparison. Her given name was Enebish, but everyone called her Eve because, as his mother had noted, she was their first.

For some decades, it was seen as a gift, the blessing of so many boys. His family, the ruling family of all tribes in the horde, always had fearsome warriors. Eventually, though, the people started to wonder when there would be a girl. Had there been dark dealings? Had there been some kind of curse? It made alliances difficult because there were no jewels to offer the sons of other powerful tribes. Mostly, though, after the fleet of brothers, uncles, and sons, it made everyone wonder: when would they be blessed with a girl?

Then, when his wife fell pregnant the seventh time, Borjigin knew before anyone else. He felt his daughter's spirit come into the room while he lay in bed with his sleeping wife. He smelled citrus and honey and heard the tinkling of bells. He knew this was his daughter. He announced to his people that his wife was carrying a girl. He never once considered that he was wrong.

When she was born, Borjigin held her in awe. The golden hair that he had, the mottled eyes that he had. None of his boys had the same complexion as him, but when he held his daughter in his arms, he beheld his own image.

He watched down the corridor of the throne room, across the stones that had been smoothed by thousands of feet, and out the massive doors, three stories high, as he waited for his leader of guards, Khuyag, to return with information. It was from this position that Borjigin did most of the business as Khan, where his family and clan had watched him carry out decisions, deliver justice, and enact executions. Though nothing else—no decision made, no war begun—had ever weighed on him like the worry he felt for his daughter.

The girl had never stopped amazing him. Everything she did was with joy, poise, and intelligence. She excelled at women's tasks. She commanded as confidently as any khan or il-khan he had ever known. She read every book in their home, so finally, Borjigin had to agree to let her study with scholars in the nearby cities. Had she been born a boy, Borjigin knew she would be the only one of his children to rival his oldest son for succession as leader of the khanate.

Borjigin had known this early about his daughter: despite her gender, she needed to conquer. The calling flowed like her blood.

Then the unthinkable happened. She was kidnapped by a lesser tribe, ambushed in the fields. The kidnapping had not been realized for several hours, and it took additional time to determine which tribe had taken her. Borjigin's first instinct was to bring war to that tribe. However, he knew they would have wasted no time and that Eve would have already been wed to the man who claimed her, so it was futile. A marriage was sacred by the *Yassa*, no matter how it came about. Besides, stealing a bride was a tolerated practice while destroying a clan to take a man's wife was not.

In fact, she could already be with his child, Borjigin thought in his darkest place. That, too, would need to be given special consideration.

Borjigin, tormented by the customs, wept for his beautiful daughter, who had never shown interest in marriage, who could have been a leader of men if Borjigin had just found the right match for her. Despair clawed at him and did not abate until Borjigin's wife reminded him that hope could remain. A wife could be in a powerful position. Now that the issue had been forced for their child, perhaps her influence would help the young tribe flourish. Borjigin's hope grew wings inside him, fighting the animal of despair. Perhaps his daughter could find solace in leading once more.

He called on the ancestors in prayer, offering tea and milk. He touched his forehead and spoke to the spirits of the land and the eternal sky. He asked them all to help this marriage be happy, because if it wasn't, he would storm the tribe and take her home despite the customs. Marriage should bring joy, like his own had for nearly forty years. Though Borjigin wanted to strip the flesh from the man who took her, he would be patient and swallow the warring beasts inside him. Perhaps the ancestors had chosen this path for Eve and knew what was good for her better than he did.

But he soon learned that joy was not to be. Through circumstances he did not understand, his precious daughter had disappeared. The man she had married had been murdered. The clans were in an uproar.

For the first time in his life, Borjigin had no idea what had happened, and it involved someone he loved so deeply.

Borjigin thrummed his fingers impatiently against the arm of the high-backed chair. His throne faced high doors that opened to the south, which, to his people, represented the beginning of the world. To his left was the East, considered the feminine world. But Eve had not gone East, where they had searched at first. He should have known his daughter better. She went West, like the conquerors had.

Coming from the hallway leading into the great hall, he heard persistent footsteps approaching. It would be Khuyag, his head guard, advisor, and trusted friend of many years. The man approached and held his arms out. Borjigin placed his arms over Khuyag's, and they held the traditional greeting. "I bring you news," Khuyag said.

"Speak now."

"You were correct to send lookouts to the West."

"They have seen her?"

"No, but there's been word of a light-colored tribal woman as far West as Turkmenabat."

"We must send our fastest riders."

Khuyag dropped his head. "There has been another sighting, Khan."

Borjigin tensed. "Who seeks her?"

Khuyag paused, his head lowered to the ground. "It is Ganbold."

Borjigin bellowed into the room. His cries echoed against the walls and the finery. All of it meant nothing if he could not protect his precious child.

Ganbold. A punishment sent to the earth by the Gods. It was Ganbold who pursued Borjigin's precious daughter?

"Launch the guards. Launch the ships. I will flay anyone who touches her," Borjigin said, choking his words through his rage.

"It is done, Borjigin Khan," Khuyag said, running out of the room.

Borjigin bellowed again. He hoped the ancestors heard him because he would burn down heaven and take them each prisoner to find her.

Chapter Thirteen

Michel was agitated. Having settled his initial business for his arrival in Bukhara, he had taken a small group to travel to a nearby market town, a few hours away, known for textiles. His primary contact, Johann, was away, and Michel was too impatient to wait around. Michel had hoped he could find some information on the cashmere trade in the little market town, but he had no success. No cashmere, and no one had any information for a Frenchman.

Now, on their return to Bukhara, he was irritated that he wasted the day and upset with himself for exposing Eve. It seems she went more or less unnoticed in the large cities, but in the smaller towns, she stood out more. In small towns, information could rage without words. He saw it happening, looks getting passed, tucked-away whispers, blazing through the market. He regretted bringing her instantly.

He couldn't have left her alone in Bukhara, either, now that he knew the danger surrounding her. *Ah,* he thought, *this woman,* that kiss still on his lips. They were riding through a dusty road that wove through a series of smooth hills. The hills were grassy in areas and desert-like in others. Red sand ran in layers over the curves of the earth. This stretch was typically safe, but Michel knew skirmishes could erupt anywhere, and the way the people in the town had ogled Eve had put him on edge. Still, they were nearly back to Bukhara, and with the sun burning his back and his duties nagging his mind, all he wanted to do was think about how to get Eve's lips on his once again.

The evening before, when she undressed him and touched his skin, he didn't know how to keep his hands off her. She had to know that she was teasing him. She was a bold woman to touch a man like she had, and for a second, Michel thought she wanted him to undress her in the same way. Then she smacked him, kissed him, and smacked him again, leaving him stunned, dazed, and filled with a need to corral her and kiss her until she begged him to continue. This woman had too many secrets. She was also filling him with a consuming desire he had never known before. If only he could figure out what it would take to get more of her.

Off in the distance, Michel heard the collective bleating of a herd of goats. They were traveling a road along a tall cliff on one side with hills out across the other direction. A breeze dashed across their ranks and fluttered Eve's skirts, outlining the perfect shape of her backside. Michel shifted on his saddle with a groan. Eve turned to him then, looking at him over her shoulder. For just a second, he allowed the want he felt for her to filter through his eyes.

The look on his face must have startled her because she blinked back a look of surprise. "What is on your mind, Michel?" she asked.

Michel watched her for a moment, then gave her a sidelong grin. "I think you know exactly what's on my mind, Eve." He let his voice rumble toward her.

Eve turned her head and gave a small cough. Michel thought he may have seen a blush. He just continued watching her, amused. He liked taking the chance to put her off balance as she had certainly done to him.

Eve turned back to him, clearly trying to shift the subject. "You know Genghis Khan is responsible for populating these hills," she said to him, with a teacherly authority.

Michel just watched, letting her talk, letting his eyes roam her body.

"He had hundreds of wives. They say thousands of children," she continued. "He was so prolific that it is forbidden to marry within your own tribe for fear of being related." She adjusted her skirt over her knee. "Arrangements must be made outside of the tribe, and even then, the families must produce elaborate family trees to be sure there are no relatives in common."

"Does that happen?" Michel asked. Her story had managed to interest him, pulling him from thoughts of getting his hands up her skirts. "Are your tribes that closely related?"

"Sometimes," she mused. "Now it is more out of custom. It is also another reason that wife-stealing among tribes is still tolerated."

"Wife...stealing?" Michel looked at her. Now his dirty thoughts were dashed. He tapped his horse to get up next to her.

Eve's eyes grew big, and she turned away.

Michel paused for a second, his brain quickly tying strands of thought together, things she had said here and there. "Is that what happened to you?" Michel asked, suddenly realizing what would cause this woman to run away.

He saw her shoulders rise and fall as she took a breath. If she had not meant to let him in on this secret, she was holding her composure well.

She looked at him from the side. "Yes," she said. "I was taken from my clan." She turned and met his eyes. "Stolen," she said before looking back to the road.

Michel was quiet. The thought enraged him. He had heard of the practice but didn't realize it still happened. The tribes could be brutal, and here he was spending his life trying to ingratiate himself with people who let such a thing persist. Then, worse than the sudden anger, he felt a tremendous wave of guilt at the thoughts he had been having about her minutes ago. He'd been thinking of her lustfully, of all the ways he could enjoy her body, not considering what she could have been through. He would have to take a step back, he thought, cursing himself. Now the smacks when he had kissed her made a lot more sense.

"I'm really sorry that happened to you," he said after a moment, unable to come up with something better. "I'm also sorry," he looked over at her, "if I have done anything that has made you uncomfortable."

She gave him a smile. "You can trust that I will let you know if you make me uncomfortable."

A warmth grew inside him again, hoping she meant that, that he hadn't crossed any lines he couldn't recover from. He tried to think of something else to say, to continue the line of conversation and pull more out of her, but some far-off noise caused his soldier's instinct to steal his focus. He held up a finger to Eve, then shot a quick command to the men behind them. He saw Eve press her lips and stiffen as she watched.

The rumble of horse hooves thundered toward them, just seconds before the swarm of men came over the hills. Fifteen or so of them. He had eleven with him who would fight. Michel jumped from his horse and led the animal to the side. These were not warhorses they traveled on, so they would fight on foot. He knew these fights, always the toll on these roads, assertions of dominance by the tribes while he traveled their land, to remind Michel he was a visitor, to test his worth. The Mongols would never do business with a weak man.

He knew the rules. No fatalities. Just a show of strength.

Michel turned to Eve in a rush, pulling his sword from his belt. "Do not dismount your horse," he said. "It should be over quickly." He guided her horse so she had the cliff at her back. "Stay where you are. I won't let them get you."

Eve nodded, her eyes locked on his in understanding. The thunder was loud now, in their ears, in the ground below them.

Michel and his fighting men formed an impromptu line. He drew his sword, and his men followed, several with pikes and lances. It was by no means a military formation, but it would deter the horses and get the men on the ground. Michel scanned the line. From the end, Iman nodded at him, and Michel nodded back. Michel steadied himself, his sword ready before him.

The men on horses charged down the slope, and just before they crashed into Michel's line, a bearded man who looked to be the leader pulled his horse back and shouted something in a dialect Michel didn't understand. The men behind him adjusted, spreading out, rather than charging directly. It was different, Michel thought. Definitely different.

Shit, he thought.

The bearded man charged Michel. Michel braced as the man swung his blade. It came down on Michel's sword with a clang that echoed through the hills. The rider turned the horse and came back toward Michel. Michel steadied himself, and when the horse came near, he leapt in its path, causing the horse to take a step off balance. Michel spun fully around and hooked the rider behind the knee to yank him down from his mount. The rest of the men engaged around him. These hill tribes fought differently, more bodily, less sword than in his home, but Michel adjusted well. He body checked another man who had dismounted and come for him, throwing the man to the ground. Michel pivoted with a skid, ready for more.

A young warrior who screamed between swipes of his blade came at Michel. His blade nicked Michel's shoulder and tore through his jacket into his skin. Michel responded by swinging low to take the fighter off his feet. The man landed with a thud, then turned his body to rise again. Michel put his boot to the man's ass and shoved him to the ground. Michel did not fight to injure, just subdue. But the eyes of these warriors kept darting, not all of them engaged. It was because of Eve. He knew it was because of Eve.

The bearded leader shouted more orders, then came for Michel. He swung his blade from above. Michel dodged it and delivered a sideswipe with his own sword that doubled the man over. Michel righted himself just to see someone streak behind him toward Eve. This man, tall and fast, had his arm around her waist in a flash as he tried to drag her from her horse. Eve hardly had the chance to let out a yelp before Michel was on top of the man. One hand to the throat took him down, forcing him to release Eve. Michel shoved him to the ground and reared back to punch the man square in the face. Blood burst from his nose, pouring into the man's beard. Then Michel's hands were around the man's neck again, and he was squeezing. He could kill him for touching her, he thought, his vision glazed in red.

"*Michel!*" Eve's sharp voice cut through his haze.

In a wave of realization, Michel released the man. He scrambled out from under Michel just as their leader called for retreat. A last moment of chaos fizzled in clanks of blades and shouts of men as both sides took their final hits. Then the tribesmen were back up on their horses, riding away just as quickly as they had descended.

Michel watched them disappear back over the hill. He breathed heavily, still feeling the energy coursing in him, causing his hands to shake. The savagery he'd felt startled him. But Eve was his ward now. It was his job to keep her safe. That was his only explanation.

He wiped the sweat from his forehead, then touched the cut on his arm. It bled, but the wound was superficial. He stretched uncomfortably and winced.

"Are you okay?" he said, turning to Eve. "Were you hurt?"

"I'm okay," she said. She appeared shaken, but otherwise intact. "You're bleeding, Michel. Let me help you." She made to dismount her horse.

"No, not now," he said. "Let's get back to Bukhara." He took a moment to settle his horse, to check in with the rest of the men, and secure their position once more. Then, before remounting his horse, he put his hands on his knees to catch his breath. He watched over the mountain, naked once more.

It was in that moment that Michel realized he might not be able to do the business he had come for and be able to protect Eve at the same time. He hoped he didn't have to make a difficult decision.

He turned to her. Her expression caused him to lose his breath and stand up straight. Her eyes were wide, and her lips were parted. He had the feeling that if he went to her now and took her in his arms, she wouldn't smack him or bite him this time.

He walked to her, took her hand, and kissed it. He could do no more in the moment, but with her fingers in his, and their eyes connected, he knew that if he were forced to make a decision...it wouldn't be a difficult decision to make.

Chapter Fourteen

Her hand, where he kissed it, still tingled.

The rest of her flooded with gratitude as they fled the scene where they had been attacked.

Michel had said it was common for such attacks. That the hill tribes didn't like intruders but would concede to let them pass after a good tussle. She believed that to be true. *This* attack, however, meant something more.

The tribes had been alerted that she was missing.

Individual tribes and clans roamed the region, carving out different slices of territory as they went. They still intermingled. She knew how the lands, the clans, and the affiliations worked. She also knew her father would be looking for her, but her father would use intelligence and his own guards or kin to find her. He wouldn't trust another tribe to capture her. No, it would be the tribe that had kidnapped her that alerted the hill tribes. They would share her disappearance and perhaps the tale of her husband's murder to rouse the outer tribes to bring her back. Perhaps they offered a ransom. Perhaps they wanted her dead by the time she was returned, so they had no blame. The fact that she was the daughter of the Khan afforded her some protection, but the clans were fierce and independent and would have their own feelings about a woman who escaped a marriage. Her father may be

Khan, but there were old laws her people followed. Such laws did not favor a woman who killed her husband, whether she had wanted the marriage or not.

Eve loved her home. She loved her people. The Issyk Kul was her heart, her life, her garden. But she couldn't deny the things that forced her to escape.

And now, there was a Frenchman at the center of her world.

They came up to the outer borders of Bukhara, slowing the horses as the road narrowed into the reaches of the city. Her horse was near his again, and she felt herself wanting his closeness, feeling more reliant on him by the second. She did not know if he understood when they said to *kill the men and seize the woman*. She thought it would be a slaughter, that she would be taken, that it would all be over. She had seen some fight in Michel among men that were like him, but those attacking were *her* people, the most ferocious warriors the land had ever known.

Michel fought savagely to protect her. He took two, even three men at a time, and then still had his eye on her. He smashed the face of the one who attacked her before the man had even closed his grip on her. Eve had to call Michel off before he ripped the man to shreds.

She hadn't expected it.

But, *yes*, it did impress her. The feeling of having a protector again, after having been alone, stolen, attacked, and sold, caused the quilt of her emotions to unfold and unfurl, with threads of affection reaching for the man who had put himself between her and the danger that threatened to lay her bare.

Now, as they came into Bukhara's walls, she wanted to show the Frenchman her gratitude.

A few hours later, Eve sat on the floor of the yurt, knees beneath her, ready to prepare Michel for sleep like she had done the night before. When they had come into town, Eve had insisted that the men go to the bathhouses to clean the fighting from their bodies. Eve had done so as well, and upon return to their camp, she was refreshed as she prepared a quick dinner for the men and a medicine broth for those with cuts and scrapes. Now, she waited for Michel, listening to notes of his voice outside the yurt while he discussed the attacks with the town officials.

Many feelings stirred inside her. Gratitude, yes, she could identify and understand that one. A desire to be near him, yes, that too, though she had already been feeling that. Relief. Affection. Attraction. These emotions felt very connected to her body, her lips, her lower belly, the insides of her thighs, other places deep inside her. She could not understand where the emotions ended and the physical sensations began, though they all seemed to be telling her to touch him.

She straightened the towels on the mat beside her. The feelings throbbed through her along with a new one: fear that Michel would decide she was not worth the effort. That fear just served to sharpen the other emotions, to make her needier, and to make it all the more important that she express her gratitude to him right now.

She heard his voice outside the tent as the cadence changed, signaling that the town officials were leaving. She stirred the broth she had made for him one last time and adjusted her shift around her waist. She bit her lip to hold it all back, but his voice had caused her to flush. She took breaths to calm herself, the flutters in her belly making it hard to be patient to have him near her.

He came in and stood at the entrance, watching her as he pulled off his boots. "I have washed already. You don't need to do this tonight."

"A cleansing towel before bed will give you settled sleep," she said. "And you must drink this broth to help heal your wound." She indicated to the seat with her head as she took the bowl in her hands. "Come," she said, holding the bowl up for him to take.

Michel finished removing his trappings and came over to her. "It's just a scrape," he said. "It's not bad." He sat and took the medicine and leaned back in the low chair while he watched her. He raised the bowl to his lips. Then he grimaced and pulled back. "This smells terrible."

"Drink it in one gulp," she replied, kneeling before him, eager for him to finish so she could touch his skin.

He gave her a wary look but complied. "Yuck," he said. "That's more painful than the cut." He set the bowl down and smiled at her. "I do appreciate it, though, how you take care of me," he said. He let his eyes run over her. Then he cleared his throat and looked away.

"I'm happy it pleases you," she said, scooting up between his legs. She leaned up until they were nearly eye to eye, with Michel just a bit taller in this position, pressing herself into his chest. He breathed in through his nose at their closeness. Part of her wanted to just give herself over, to see what it was that Michel would do to her, to experience the things that she had heard other women whisper. She had never had these signals from her body, these urges to touch and to please. The new sensations shook her. She didn't like not being in control of her body. So she would take control of his.

She took the towel and dipped it in the basin. She ran her fingers through his hair and then washed the warm water over his forehead and his cheeks. His lips parted, and she knew his desire to have her, the smolder in his eyes casting spells in her belly.

"Eve," he ground out. He gripped her biceps, letting his thumbs run over her naked skin. "It's difficult to be this close to you without trying to kiss you."

Her body responded, arching against him. She wanted to let him devour her and to use her in whatever way he wanted. All she did was lean forward and whisper back, "Not yet," against his lips.

Michel held her a moment longer, then sank back with a growl.

In that moment, she realized that she loved to tease this man. She unhooked the buttons of his shirt and pushed it back over his shoulders, drawing it off and holding it before her. She watched him as she brought it to her nose, inhaling his scent deeply, like an incense, an intoxicant. Taking those traces of him into her body—deep and raw—caused her to close her eyes and do it again. She could suffocate in his smell, she thought, breathing him into her. When she opened her eyes again, Michel was gripping the stool, every muscle straining as he tried to hold himself back. Eve bit her lip.

"I didn't know," she said, suddenly overcome.

"Know what?"

She met his eyes. "You are a warrior, Michel."

Still gripping the seat of his chair, he leaned closer. She felt the heat from him. "Did you really think that I'm just a pretty Frenchman with a title and nothing more?"

She nodded, solemn. "Yes," she said. "Exactly."

Michel laughed. "And now?" he asked, smiling, shifting his body, closer still, not touching.

"Remove your pants," she said.

Michel blinked, her words sobering him. Then he stood and obeyed, undoing the belting and snapping out of the hooks. He dropped them and stepped out, leaving just his undergarments. She took his pants and folded them, placing them along with his shirt off to the side. As he sat down, Michel reached for another towel to cover himself. Eve stopped him.

"No," she said.

"No?" he asked, as Eve took the towel away from him. His want was very evident in the thin fabric of his undergarments. Eve looked up at him, a thrill inside her.

She took the moistened cloth again and ran it up each leg, outside first, then inside. She ran the rag up his body again and pressed into him as she did. She felt his throbbing want between them, pressed into her belly. Michel leaned over her, breathing quickly, as she looked up at him. The intensity in his eyes was different. She used her tongue to wet her lips. Then she leaned forward to wet his lips with her own.

Now Michel's hand was in her hair, while his other arm, strong and demanding, was around her. He arched over her, into her, crushing her to him as the kiss came furiously. Eve let him control her. She felt his body desperate, but his kisses were focused, breaking sensations free like firecrackers all over her body. She threw her arms around his neck and sank into him, wanting to indulge in all the feelings he could give her.

She let the kiss continue for just a moment, but it wasn't enough. She pushed him away with a devilish grin, letting desire billow through her in a way she had never experienced before.

Michel groaned but let himself fall back in the chair, "Eve, *mon dieu*, I don't know what you want from me."

"Shhhh," she said, touching her finger to his lips, cutting him off.

She moved down to put her lips to the center of his chest. She placed a kiss and then continued, tracing the depression between his stomach muscles with her tongue. She kissed again at his navel and tucked her fingers into the waistband of his undergarment. She felt him, hard, and she continued to move her kisses, hearing him suck in a breath as she did.

She felt the tension in his body. He moved, roiled beneath her. She continued to trail down lower.

Then she ran her tongue along his skin, across the line of fabric until she reached the center. She dipped her tongue just below to taste the tip of his length tucked in his waistband.

"*Siren*," he hissed, a strained growl inside of him. His hands gripped the stool below him as his hips jerked up toward her.

The taste of him was magical. Salty sweet desire. She'd been diving into his scent, but his *taste* was a whole new discovery. In an instant, Eve had his undergarments unlaced, and he was completely exposed to her, open, vulnerable. Michel had frozen in place as she pulled the fabric away, her curiosity for this muscle coming through. It strained, hard and proud, certainly bigger than she expected. She placed the tip of her finger at the head and drew it down across satin skin until she reached the base, which caused Michel to shudder and pulse. She looked up at him, knowing the door she'd be opening. Michel let out a breath and ran his fingers through his hair, his muscles twitching as he did. "Holy shit," was all he said.

Loving his reactions, she let her hands explore. She ran her palm up the length again and wrapped her hand around it as best she could, her other hand reaching below to feel the softer weights. She had never touched a man like this, but she had heard little stories here and there, things men said, things women whispered. Michel continued to grip the chair and groan, and she knew this strong, throbbing muscle was a man's weakness. At one point, she had thought to exploit him, to exploit *this*, but the sight of him, his abdominal muscles crunched as he struggled to keep himself down, his furrowed brow, the strain in his jaw muscles, the low growling in his throat, everything, caused electric sensations to run through her. She didn't know for sure if she was still doing this just to express her gratitude or if it was her own desire she needed to soothe. *Her* desire, which she felt throbbing on the inside, swirled down her thighs, bled across her skin, and tickled over her breasts. This wasn't just about giving. Eve wanted more of him. And, she knew, if she had ever wanted to control this man before, she was his god now.

Holding his thick length with one hand, she leaned in and ran her tongue from the bottom to the top, pausing to taste the bead of liquid at the tip. She wet her lips with her tongue, dragging his taste across them. She pressed her lips back over his skin, now slick with his want. Then, just as she opened to take the broad head into her mouth, Michel released his grip on the chair and grabbed her by the nape of her neck, pulling her head back by

her hair. "Eve," he choked out. He swallowed. "You wouldn't hurt me...
please don't..."

She stared at him a moment, unsure what he was trying to say. Then she
realized...

He was afraid she would bite his dick off.

Eve, her head still pulled back, just smiled at him mischievously. Then
she leaned in and took his length into her mouth, Michel groaning, with fear
or pleasure or a mix of both as she did.

It was a strange sensation at first. As she took him across her tongue and
back further into her throat, it felt like she would lose everything in her
stomach. She relaxed her muscles, working to figure it out, and took him as
deeply into her as she could. Her senses were overwhelmed with him now.
His sweet scent and taste a hundred times more intense here. She pulled
back and eased him across her tongue. And as soon as she pulled away, she
wanted the sensation of being filled by him again. She went down once
more, this time using her hand on his shaft, her saliva and his fluids mixing
in a delicious, slick mess. She had never felt a muscle like this. It was smooth
and velvety across the skin but hard as steel underneath. Even if she had
wanted to bite him, she thought, it would break her teeth if she tried.

She found a rhythm, breathing through her nose and opening her
mouth wide enough to take him all. Her jaw and her throat ached, but it
was delightful soreness that laced into the other parts of her body that ached
for him. She felt him trying to be passive, fighting against himself, to allow
her a chance to please him. One hand still gripped the chair, the other
hovered above her. She felt the balance of gentleness and savagery in him,
and she knew she was dancing right across the edge.

Michel's breath came quick and tortured. His abs flexed as his hips
moved up to meet her lips. His sounds of pleasure filled the space. It wasn't
long before Michel gripped her by the hair again. "Eve," he said, his fingers
pulling roughly against her scalp. His voice cracked, and he swallowed. "I'm
going to...I'm going to..."

Eve just let the devil shine through her eyes in response. She pressed her
lips on him again and let her throat contract around him. Michel's hips
jerked, and he cried out. He pushed himself off the chair, his hips coming up
to meet her. He gripped the back of her head and thrust into her mouth. Eve
felt completely choked by him now, and if she had wanted to pull away, she

realized she couldn't. She sucked him more deeply into her, letting him force her open. Then she felt it, pulsating streams of him pouring into her, down her throat as he gasped out her name. It surprised her, the sensation and the energy with which his liquid flowed. She let her body guide her, and she swallowed him into her. She continued sucking through every moan and every jerk of his hips.

What a sensation, she thought.

Finally, his grip on her lessened, and she pulled back to look up at him, letting his still throbbing muscle slap back against his stomach as she gasped in her first full breath. She was wet and sticky all over, it seemed, as she wiped her mouth. Michel stared at her intently, in a crazed daze. He ran his fingers through her hair, panting. Then he grabbed her by the arms and pulled them both up to stand. He gripped her and held her tightly. He reached up to run his thumb across her lips while she watched his torpid eyes. They held one another like that, staring at each other, tangled emotions between them. Then, suddenly, the moment broke, and his hands were pushing wildly up her skirts.

He wanted to undress her, Eve understood. He wanted to repay the favor.

"Stop," she said, leaning her head back as he tried to kiss her, his hands still everywhere.

He moved against her, his strong arms wrapping around her back. "But—'

"No," she said. "That was for you. To show you gratitude for fighting earlier." She looked into his eyes. "For protecting me."

"But—" he said, trying again to wrap his arms around her. "Eve," he asserted.

"No," she repeated. She pushed back against his chest. He let her go. She leaned down to take his clothes from the floor. She handed them to him. "Here you are," she said. Then, without another word, she turned away.

Once again, she had to turn away quickly. Because if she let him see her face, he would see the desire and excitement tearing apart her seams. The lust she could no longer deny or attempt to hide. She had pleased him, that was for sure. It only unlocked the absolute desperation this man caused inside of her. She wasn't sure she was ready for him to see the delighted grin she wore or the flush that stung her cheeks.

Michel was destroyed. Across the tent, Eve slept on the bed with her back to him. He was lying on his bedroll, the bed she had made for him, turned to face her. He lay in disbelief, watching her body move with each sleeping breath she took, still not quite believing what just happened.

What she had done to him had been *incredible*. Instead of calming the fire inside him, though, it only enraged it even more. He had gone from having a spark of need for her, a spark he could control, to an inferno. He wanted to crawl across the room and slip under the blanket and feel her body against his. He wanted to brush her hair out of her face when she turned. He wanted to kiss her neck and then enter her dreams. He wanted to be next to her for as long as she would let him. His body had gotten just a taste. And now, he feared, he was about to form an obsession that would break apart all the armor he had forged to keep himself good and legitimate and decent, if only for the chance to get his hands on her again.

When had she decided to do that? Part of him wanted to believe that she was overcome with desire, but he was starting to know better. He was not too stupid to understand why he was being rewarded. Eve, it seemed, wanted his protection guaranteed.

Laying there, watching her, he realized suddenly that she had been grooming him. She had known there were men looking for her. She had known that she would bring danger. All the while she was his maid, she had been turning him into her guard. Eve had been manipulating him since the moment they met. To think, he had worried that he compromised her. In truth, he was the one in danger.

He cracked a grin then. And started to laugh. He'd never been affected by a woman like this. He'd had liaisons, he'd had affairs, but he had never gotten so involved he couldn't get out when it was no longer convenient. Michel's loyalty had always been to his family, his king, and his position. Somehow, Eve had put herself at the top of that list.

He had found a true treasure in the sand, and now he had to fight to protect it. Whatever it was that she wanted from him, she had won. But it wasn't her gratitude he wanted. He wanted her affection. He only hoped he would have the chance to show her some of his affection as well.

As he began to doze off, he folded his arms and laughed and laughed. He closed his eyes, still grinning to himself. How easy it had been for her to take advantage of him, but he didn't mind in the least. She had made him into her puppet. But for her, he mused, it would be an honor.

Perhaps it had been the wrong tactic to treat her like something so delicate. So, he decided, tomorrow he was going to take more.

She could handle it.

Chapter Fifteen

That next morning, Michel received word that his trade contact, Johann, had returned to Bukhara. Michel set out right away to meet with him. Johann hailed as a merchant who specialized in dyes and virgin silks, but his true passion came from the curiosities he collected on his travels. He also collected gossip and knew secrets that reached across the continents. Michel had known him for many years and felt comfortable asking him candid questions.

Michel had insisted that Eve stay by his side and go with him to meet Johann. Part of him didn't want to leave her for fear of her safety, part of him wanted to introduce her to his friend, and part of him just didn't want to spend a second away from her, especially after last night. He shook his head again, thinking about it as they walked through the alleyways that led to Johann's apartment. In one hand, he held a gift for Johann—his tithe— but with the other, Michel held onto the back of Eve's dress possessively, prepared to leap out at anyone who looked at her. Luckily, the walk was uneventful, and in a moment, he was knocking on Johann's door.

"Michel!" Johann said, pulling open the door. The short man had neat white hair and a long white beard. The coloring had made him always seem old to Michel, even though he was probably only a few years older than Michel's father. Johann held his arms wide. "My friend!"

Michel smiled to see the man and gave him a hug. "Good to see you, Johann," he said. "I hope your travels were profitable."

"They always are." Johann leaned back with a wink. He turned his attention to Eve, then. "Now, who is this lovely lady?"

Michel spoke up. "This is Eve. I have hired her to help me with my books. Keep me organized."

Johann took her hand in both of his and gave her a warm smile, looking at her over his gold spectacles. "It's nice to meet you, *mademoiselle.*"

"You as well." She smiled.

"Hmmm," Johann tittered, retreating into his apartment. He held out his hand. "Please, come inside."

Johann's apartment was small and cluttered with curios from all over the world. The doorway led them through a narrow hallway with shelves crowded with all kinds of things: pots and pans, tools, springs, china, pocket watches, spectacles, buttons, dolls, utensils, magnifiers, glass disks, and scores of other knick-knacks with no obvious purpose. Michel remembered his first visit here with his father, when he had been fifteen. He'd spent hours examining the unique items. Now, however, Michel had too many other things on his mind to enjoy Johann's oddities.

Johann led them to his sitting area at the end of the hallway. It was a small room crowded with wardrobes and mismatched chairs, a cluttered workbench, and uneven stacks of books and parchments in little towers across the floor. One high window was open and gave the room light. Johann swiped a pile of gears off the settee so Eve could sit, and then he picked up the side of a bench to slide a collection of spoons into a basket, clanking and rattling as they went. Johann smiled proudly and held out his hand for Michel to sit.

"Johann, somehow it is always more crowded in here than the previous time," Michel said as he sat down.

Johann grinned. "You know me, Michel," he said as he cleared a spot on his workbench. "Now what do you bring me?" His expression, shining with excitement.

"Bold of you to assume this box is for you," Michel grinned at the man.

"*Ho*, Michel, don't toy with me." He held out his hands. "Give it here."

Michel handed over the package, and Johann put it on his worktable. "Okay, okay," he said, observing the weight and size of the box, perhaps just big enough for a pair of fancy boots, as he unwrapped the fabric covering it. "Ah," he said, a giddy note in his voice as the covering fell away. "It is lovely." He ran his hands over the gold-leafed etching, over the dials and windows with numbers. "What is it?"

"It's a Pascaline. An adding machine," Michel said. "They are wildly popular in Paris."

"An *adding* machine!" Johann clapped his hands together with glee. "My, my, my." He twiddled the dial. "I can add...I can add anything I want!"

Michel enjoyed watching his friend play with his new toy, but he was eager for his reward. "Now, Johann, what is the news? I need information."

"Yes, yes," Johann said. "What would you like to know?" He twisted a knob, and the box made a click. "Ooh!" he chortled.

"We were attacked in the hills."

Johann scoffed, not looking up. "You are always attacked in the hills," he said, playing coy.

Michel glanced at Eve and met her eyes. She looked down. "Yes," he said, "but this was different."

Johann spoke but did not turn his attention from the Pascaline. "The horde is looking for someone." He pulled his hand down his long beard. "A woman." He adjusted his glasses. "An odd-looking woman." He glanced at Eve, then Michel, over his spectacles. "Perhaps one traveling with a Frenchman." He raised his eyebrows and turned back to the adding machine.

"Why are they looking for her?" Michel asked evenly.

"Her tribe wants her for retribution. It is said," he cleared his throat, his voice dipping low, almost as a mumble, "it is said she killed her husband."

Michel sat still. "And what will they do with her if they find her?" He turned to Eve. She looked back at him, with secrets in her eyes.

"That I do not know, Michel," he said. "But," he drew the word out as he fiddled with the machine. "The tribes know better than to disrupt the trade routes. The woman is lucky she has found a Frenchman to travel with. We French are safe in this part of the world, if we don't step out of place," he said, accentuating the *if*. He ran his fingers over the little windows that displayed numbers. "Eight plus seven," he muttered to himself. "Let's see." He adjusted a few dials. "Too far East, the French have no influence. The inner clans care not for such connections." He clicked something into place. "Fifteen! My goodness! It's correct!"

Michel gave him a small smile, thinking how these inner clans had been the exact ones he had hoped to woo. What a fool. "I'm glad it works," he said to Johann.

Johann turned in his spot to face Michel and Eve then. "Listen, my friend, you are safe in the walls of the cities. You are safe if you stick to the well-traveled roads. The tribes don't want to start trouble with France. Or with you. But you, young lady," he turned to Eve and took her hand before continuing, "You stay covered when you are out. Gossip travels faster than horses." He gave her hand a pat before releasing it. Then he addressed Michel, "The tribes are mostly on their northern treks with the herds right now. It is unlikely you will have many encounters like you did coming into town, if you stay clever." He paused. "I would complete your business promptly and not linger. You understand that angering the horde will destabilize the entire line. It will put a lot of men out of business between here and France. And lives..." He gave a grim nod. "Lives could be lost." He turned back to his table. "I wouldn't want to be the man who causes Cardinal Mazarin any trouble."

Michel looked at Eve, whose eyes were downcast. "Well, Johann." Michel sighed, already feeling defeated. "That brings me to my next question. Any chance you have found a contact for cashmere?"

Johann grinned. "Actually, my friend," he chirped, still twisting knobs on his machine. "Yes. I believe I have found someone who will be willing to trade with you."

Eve listened to Michel and Johann talk as she stared out the window. Despite Johann's warning, Michel had shifted back to business and talked with excitement about the potential deal. She wanted Michel to achieve his goal. She understood his objectives. Eve had selfishly placed herself in his path, never thinking about the trouble she would bring him. She had seen him as a way to get to France, to escape. He didn't need to know more about her or her past.

But she had begun to rely on him. She had begun to want to be near him.

Her focus had changed.

It had all happened so fast, these changes to her life. Just three months earlier, Eve had been standing on the arid plains of her homeland, surrounded by the beautiful colors that would always live in her dreams. The wind howled that day. It blocked everything else out and let her mind work. As she tended the goats in the pasture, she knew she was at a crossroads in her life. There was nothing better than the cold of dawn and the screaming wind to help her focus her energy.

The last of her brothers, Yul, had announced his engagement, and the tribe celebrated this wonderful union. She had felt nothing but happiness at the pairing, but it meant, once again, eyes were on her. Who would Eve marry? She was twenty-five. Most women her age were married, already mothers. Eve had refused every suitor she had ever been offered. She just had no interest.

It wasn't that marriage was distasteful to her, but she wanted to ensure her own union would give her a chance to continue to grow. Her father had always allowed her to participate in strategizing for the tribes, but he was unique in his ways. Eve knew she would not be satisfied if a marriage took away her voice, and it was very likely this would be the case. An ability to influence, a desire to help her people prosper, lived inside her. A wrong decision about her future would silence her. She always thought about France in such moments, wondering how her life would have been different if Grandfather had stayed with Cecile in France instead of the other way around.

Those were her thoughts as she had gazed out across the hills that were her home, among the noisy bleating from the goats, the soothing cries of the wind, the dancing grey-green grasses, when she had heard a noise that didn't match. She turned to see three men on horses, not far from her. She ran immediately, knowing she would never get away in time, hoping someone would help her. She sprinted, heart pumping, legs darting. For a second, the wind at her back made her think she would get away.

Then a hand had gone over her mouth, and she was swept onto the back of a horse.

From that moment, nothing had been the same. Somehow, months later, she had found herself a world away, sitting in a cozy little hovel, next to a man who had saved her from being stolen once more. But in doing so, she feared, this very man was on the verge of stealing her heart.

Chapter Sixteen

Ganbold. Warrior. Hunter.

Ganbold had traveled to Samarkand. He did not find her.

He found a few people who could speak his words or read his parchment. He had learned to say *Frenchman* and *woman* in common Mongolian. It helped, but no one had seen them.

The man who told him to come to Samarkand had lied to him. Or maybe Ganbold had just not understood. He felt anger in his fists as he sat in the square, deciding where to go next.

The ancestors did not make the path to find this woman easy. He did this to honor them. To honor the old ways. The true ways.

Travel was more difficult than Ganbold had expected. No language made it hard to negotiate a ride, to understand routes. He had spent his life with his tribe. The only times he had come in contact with westerners, he had been with others, with the il-khan and the elders who could speak more than their tribal language. Alone, he had little money, no horse, and almost no communication. But he was a good nomad and could live easily from the land. He could not make any more errors. Others would be searching for her by now. His next route had to be correct, or he would surely lose the chance to be the one to bring the woman home. He looked to the sky, begging for guidance.

The afternoon sun beat down as he sat in a busy square at the edge of Samarkand, a place of large buildings with rounded roofs, very different from the cities closer to his home. Ganbold, with distaste in his mouth about going further West, decided he would backtrack. There were hundreds of routes in this area, going through outposts, towns, and villages. The woman and the Frenchman could have gone over the hills, across the mountain ranges. Ganbold felt fury that the people in this city could not talk to him. He would already have the woman by the hair if they had not mingled with the westerners and lost their ancient language.

He thought of the pride he would feel in his chest when he brought the woman to his tribe. He thought of the relief he would feel when he was allowed back around his tribal hearth. He thought of the pleasure he would feel when he took the woman he wanted for his wife. Ganbold had not been permitted to marry her before, because they were of the same tribe and were in danger of having close relations. The last time he had gone to her yurt, her father was waiting. The girl had rushed between Ganbold and his father, and she had been struck.

That was the last time Ganbold saw her. He escaped through the window because there was so much screaming. The Il-khan shamed him for the attack and sent him out of the tribe.

Sadness at the loss of his tribe and his woman was brewing inside him when, suddenly, he heard the throaty language of a Frenchman there in the square. Ganbold's eyes snapped to the source: a tall man with a shorter blond companion.

The woman! The ancestors had blessed him.

The figure was cloaked, but the light hair betrayed her. Relief and excitement surged. Ganbold hunched and stalked the pair through the crowd. They moved through the square, past a tavern, on the road that led out of town. He would like to attack now, but the people would not allow an open war with a Westerner, and they might even protest the woman being taken. No, he had to catch them on the roads, away from others. So, he prowled, letting the pair get further down the road that led into the rustling trees of the plains.

Hunter.

As they reached the outer limits of the town, away from the crowds, the man and his companion came into better view. Ganbold saw that the blond companion was not a woman, but a boy, tall but thin, just on the verge of becoming a man. Ganbold felt frustration in his shoulders, across his back, and tightening up his neck. He wanted something in his hands to squeeze.

Then Ganbold got a very good idea. Since he could not find the correct Frenchman to kill, he would start to kill all the Frenchmen he found. All the travelers and all the merchants. There were rules from his clan that controlled how his people acted with the Westerners, but Ganbold didn't want to mind them. As long as he could do it away from the eyes of the townspeople, no one would know. The ancestors did not give him the woman yet, but they gave him this idea. He would use them to find the Frenchman, to find the murderer woman, so he could bring his trophy home.

Warrior.

Moments later, the pair stopped for a drink. The trees along this stretch were sparse, but Ganbold stayed hidden in the high grasses off the road. When they paused, Ganbold approached.

He heard the blistering gibberish as he came near. The pair jumped when they finally noticed Ganbold.

"Hello," the man said, a word Ganbold knew, before trailing off into words Ganbold didn't know.

"I seek a woman," Ganbold said in his own language.

The man stared. He did not understand.

Ganbold grunted. He moved closer with his hands out to terrify, a tactic used by those of his lineage.

The man reached for the sword on his hip and spoke words to the boy. The boy said something back to him.

The man shouted at Ganbold and held out his sword.

Ganbold.

Ganbold had a sword, but he preferred to use his hands. He moved to lunge, baring teeth.

"You scared us," the boy said, his voice high with fright. "We are going to rejoin our company."

Ganbold stopped short, hands still outstretched. The words were not perfect for his language, but they were close. He understood. "You speak my language," Ganbold began. "How?"

The boy shrugged. "I am a translator. I'm good with languages."

The older man next to him spoke words to the boy. He indicated toward Ganbold.

The boy nodded. "He says to tell you that there are more of us just down the road."

"More Frenchmen?" Ganbold asked.

The boy hesitated. "Yes," he said. "Twelve. A merchant convoy returning to France. We don't want trouble."

Twelve Frenchmen would be easy for Ganbold to kill with his strength and the spirits of the land and sky on his side. But he wanted information first. "I want to find a Frenchman and a woman," Ganbold said. "Hair like yours, tribal like me."

The boy glanced at the man beside him. They exchanged words. Then the boy spoke to Ganbold. "No," he said. "They are not with our group."

Ganbold felt anger in his chest. He crouched to lunge.

"I know them," the boy shouted, holding his hand out as both he and the man stepped back.

Ganbold paused, waiting for the boy to continue.

"I-I traveled with them."

Ganbold took a step toward the boy. The man stepped back, holding out his blade. It shook. The boy stayed.

"Where are they?" Ganbold snarled, his words infused with his hatred.

The boy glanced at the other man again, then back to Ganbold. "What will you give me if I tell you?"

Ganbold grinned. "I don't kill you."

"And him?" the boy asked.

Ganbold just kept grinning.

The boy swallowed. "Bukhara," he said. "They are in Bukhara. They will travel to Samarkand within the week." The boy turned and said something to the man. The man smiled and dropped his guard. He nodded at Ganbold.

Ganbold had all he needed, so he leapt at the man, snatching forward. He ripped the sword out of his hand, grabbed his arm, and put his other hand to his throat. Ganbold squeezed, holding his grip tight just for a moment longer to watch the man's eyes blaze in a panic, his free arm flailing. Then he applied enough pressure to stop his breathing. The man collapsed, and Ganbold went down with him, holding him in the dirt. Ganbold didn't know what he heard break first, the man's neck or his arm, but in moments, Ganbold was breaking bones like brittle twigs.

When he knew the man was dead, Ganbold remembered the boy. He looked over and saw him, wide-eyed, staring back. Ganbold moved toward him.

"You-you said you wouldn't kill me," the boy yelled.

"You come with me now," Ganbold said, thanking the ancestors for this gift of someone who could speak the languages that Ganbold could not.

"Where are we going?"

"First, to your group of Frenchmen."

Ganbold. Warrior. Hunter.

Chapter Seventeen

Michel and Eve had spent the better part of the morning with Johann, enjoying his oddities once the business had been completed. As Michel and Eve walked back to camp, Michel felt some relief that he had a tangible contact for the cashmere. He would meet with the man, secure the deal, and then he could focus on what he wanted to focus on: *Eve*. He worried about the complications of those looking for her, but Johann was right. If he stayed on the roads and stayed smart, it was unlikely he would be attacked. Plus, he could handle a fight here or there. It may be a good way to take out some of the frustration he felt in his body from being near her and having to resist. He looked over at her then and started whistling a tune at his good humor. She just shook her head at him and laughed.

They wove through the maze-like alleyways between the buildings. As most families were now having lunch to avoid the high heat of the day, the shaded walkways were empty other than the smells of food cooking in the apartments. Cloves and spices. Onions and oil. Eve looked back at him, and he raised his eyebrows at her, still whistling.

"Will we be leaving right away? To meet this contact?" Eve asked, smiling at his good mood.

"A few more days," he said. "I have business to finish here, and then I still have other important men I have to meet with on the way."

"Why is this cashmere so important to you?" she asked.

"France has been at war with Spain for years. I fought in the war, and so did my brothers." He moved slightly closer to her, letting the backs of his knuckles brush her dress. "The war has mostly ended but there is debt. Cardinal Mazarin plans to levy a high tax on the regions, but I," he let a finger brush her hand, his mind trailing away before coming back to his thoughts, "I promised to secure new, profitable trade." Michel shrugged. "Cashmere." He scoffed. "The Cardinal agreed not to enact the tax if I did."

"If you don't succeed?"

"My father is a powerful, beloved Duke," he said. "He will organize and go to war with Paris over it." He glanced at her. "He could raise an army overnight."

Eve nodded, stepping in line with him, allowing her arm to touch his.

"Cashmere is tightly held. No one has ever secured a stable line. I would be the first," he said, turning into her, enjoying the proximity. "I hope this friend of Johann will be my answer."

"My family has a herd of wonderful goats," she glanced up to him. "Many of the tribal people weave cashmere."

"Perhaps if you ever tell me where you are from," Michel teased, "then we could trade directly." He circled behind her as they walked, his eyes on her like he wished his hands to be.

"Oh no," she said, looking directly ahead, ignoring his movements as he worked to get closer. "The elders of my people would hate you."

"Why?" Michel asked, intrigued. "I'm respectful. I bring good business. What have I done that's so bad?" He hooked his finger in the back of her dress and pulled her to a stop. He whispered into her ear, "Except for a few of the things I've done to you."

She turned and pushed him off, grinning as she did so.

He let her get a few steps ahead, then continued stalking her. "Really," he said. "Why wouldn't they trade with me?"

"They don't like Westerners. Plus, it is far, and the trade routes can get messy. There would be loss."

"That is why I patrol."

She rolled her eyes. "Michel, you really think you are more important than you are." She laughed, teasing him.

Michel stopped in the center of the walkway and held out his hands. "I think I am just as important as I think I am." He grinned. Then he jogged up to her again and grabbed her arm. He couldn't help it. He couldn't help pawing at her. He turned her around to face him and shuffled her to the wall. "What do you think of me?" He pressed himself against her.

For a second, she looked surprised, but her body never stiffened against him and he leaned into her, already feeling his blood shift.

"I am your servant," she said, her voice going breathy. "You shouldn't care so much what I think of you."

He watched her for a moment, tilting his head to look into her eyes. "After what happened last night, Siren," he said, the memories of her causing changes to crash through his body, "how could I not care?"

She tilted her chin up to him. "What happened last night?"

He watched her lips. "When you..." He couldn't find the right words, words that wouldn't be vulgar. "When you, uh..."

She whispered, leaning up to nip at his bottom lip. "When I what, Michel?"

He cracked a half smile. "When you took me in your mouth," he said.

"Oh, yes," she said. "*That.*" Her eyes sparkled.

"Yes," he growled. "That." And his lips were on her, hard against her. All of him was hard against her. What was he doing kissing her out here where anyone could see? He just couldn't help it. Any attention from her, any chance to touch her, he couldn't stop himself. What in the world was he going to do with her? Eve was not the kind of woman that he would be able to move on from. Just standing in the street, tasting her lips, feeling her yield to him while he stroked his hand through her hair made him forget everything in the world. Her lips, her scent, her body, her words, made him understand addiction. As soon as he dealt with this cashmere nonsense, he was going to figure this out. His duties mattered less and less. He just wanted to make Eve a permanent part of his life.

He pulled back to look at her. A needy whimper escaped her lips, and it almost caused him to push his way up her skirts in the middle of the alley. He groaned, feeling weak, blurry from the kiss. He wanted to take so much more, but he also didn't know what she had endured in the past, before she had escaped her situation. "Listen," he said, the warm desert air now separating their bodies and the soft desire building between them. "I want you to know...you don't have to do that."

She looked at him but didn't say anything.

"I mean, I loved it," he said. "Your mouth." He reached up to draw a line down her jaw with his thumb. "On me." Then he shook his head again as his body wanted to remember. "I know why you did it."

She continued to watch him. "Why did I do it?" Her voice was teasing still, but he recognized the sober note to it.

"You think I'm going to abandon you." He gripped her side as he said it. He wanted to pull her to him again but didn't because he wanted her to see his sincerity. He continued, his voice low. "I'm not, Eve," he said. "I don't care who is coming after you, or what you did. I'm not going to leave you behind."

She watched him with a serious expression on her face and nodded. "Thank you, Michel," she whispered.

He wanted to kiss her again, to keep kissing her, but he feared he would sink into her lips, here on the street, and never be able to stop. So, he took her hand and pulled her back to the alley. They continued to walk, hands together. "If you should decide to reward me again, though..." he looked at her playfully. "I will take any scraps you throw my way."

She laughed at this. Then she looked at him and shrugged. "I guess you'd better keep your blade sharp then," she said, still smiling.

He stopped, causing her to pause and look at him. He brought her hand up to his lips and placed a kiss in her palm. "You're going to need to tell me more, though. Soon, I hope."

"Yes," she conceded. "You are right." Then she took a big breath and let out a sigh. "I just don't want anyone else to get hurt."

Michel nodded at her. "I understand, but I can't protect you if I don't know who's coming."

She nodded. "I know." Then she looked up and gave him a smirk. "I sure am worth the trouble, though, aren't I?"

He held his arms out, his hands open, and he smiled at her. "Absolutely," he promised, sure of the words.

Chapter Eighteen

Borjigin marched across the camp of the tribe that had taken his daughter. His two eldest sons and his advisor, Khuyag, were behind him. Borjigin hated this tribe. They were petty and difficult, clinging to the old traditions with an obsession that threatened the existence of his people. Of all the far-reaching tribes Borjigin commanded as Khan, this one angered him the most.

But before war, one must yell.

They followed a short man who scampered, seeming to fear upsetting the Khan as he took them to the il-khan's yurt. This tribe was still fully nomadic, but their camp had settled for the spring. Borjigin noted the family yurts and the center camp area where they would have gathered for the fated wedding celebration that caused his daughter's disappearance. Borjigin could hardly control the simmering anger he felt at her treatment.

When they reached the yurt at the center of the camp, the short man called out to the leader inside. Once he was acknowledged, the man held the heavy felt door for Borjigin.

"*Nokhoi khori*," he said, spitting out the traditional formality of calling off the dogs when entering a home. Borjigin alone entered, thinking he would love it if the il-khan set dogs on him. It would give him the opportunity to release his violent energy.

"Borjigin Khan, I am honored to have you in my ger," Timicin, the tribe's il-kahn, said, his words carefully reverent.

Borjigin allowed the traditional greeting as they gripped each other's forearms.

"You've come far. Sit. Drink," Timicin said. He offered *suutei tsai* tea with both hands.

Borjigin glared at the man as he accepted the cup and took a small sip out of tradition, though he wanted to spit on the floor. He had known Timicin most of his life. He was a vicious leader with a sharp tongue, but he knew his place.

"I am sorry we must meet under these circumstances," Timicin said. He stroked his long, black and silver beard as he sat down. "I had hoped to meet again in celebration of the connection between our tribes."

"You have caused my daughter to go missing," Borjigin said, taking his seat. His voice even, body still. The only way he could control himself was to control everything.

He held out his hands, as if to hold Borjigin's anger at bay. "Your daughter has killed the man who was her husband. A warrior of my tribe. By the *Yassa*, I could attack rather than sit with you in my yurt."

"You attack me? After taking my daughter and letting her become lost?" Borjigin glowered. "Do so, Timicin. I beg you to give me respite."

Timicin dropped his gaze. Borjigin knew Timicin would bark like a small, angry dog, but when challenged with real power, would always back down.

Borjigin breathed in and released, letting his nostrils flare, letting the act settle him. He spoke, "The ancestors did not support her kidnapping, or she would be here now."

"Your daughter was alone in the field, a clear signal she was available to be taken," Timicin said, barking again.

"Are you saying this is her *fault*?"

"My Bataar has led hundreds of raids against the Kazakhs. He saw her in a display of availability and decided she would be his wife. How can it be that your daughter does not know these ways? That she was not taught to acquiesce in the presence of a warrior?"

"My daughter has been taught to never kneel to someone beneath her. A thousand Bataars do not equal one of her," he said through his teeth.

"He was my greatest fighter," Timicin said with affront. "This was meant to be an incredible union. Your influence with my power. Our tribes aligned. Our people as one. We could conquer anyone." He shook his head. "Bataar's other wives and children are beside themselves with grief."

Borjigin, brows furrowed, conceded on this point. "I am sorry for them," he said. "Does he have a brother?"

"Two. They have taken on the wives." Timicin shifted. "You must understand, Borjigin, your daughter pierced him with a knife and disappeared. We believe that she took his life while he put his spirit inside her. You must understand," he repeated, the dog exposing his belly, "as il-khan I cannot ignore this crime." He shook his head. "What a terrible thing to do to a warrior. A husband."

Borjigin gritted his teeth at the thought of the scenario.

"For taking his life, you must pay me reparations," Timicin said. "On her behalf."

The violent energy crested inside Borjigin. He released it with a powerful burst, allowing one fist to pound down on the table. The earth shook at his anger. Perhaps the heavens, too.

Timicin weathered it, looking down.

Borjigin calmed himself. He was a father, but he still was the Khan, bound to many laws and even more people, all of whom relied on his judgment. "I will discuss that when she has been found."

Timicin nodded. "I understand."

"Tell me this, Timicin," Borjigin continued. "What of Ganbold?"

"Ganbold was thrown from the tribe months ago," Timicin continued. "I did not send Ganbold after her. I would never."

"Why is he trailing her? Does he want her for his bride?"

"No. Ganbold is single-minded." He sighed and sat back down. "He had been obsessed with a daughter of our tribe. He bungled an attempt to get to her while she was sleeping and badly injured the girl. He is too dangerous when it comes to women." Timicin brought his hands together, looking contrite. "I believe Ganbold is looking for your daughter to win his way back into the tribe, as a tribute. But he is not wise, Borjigin," he said, his voice supplicant. "He is not efficient. I don't believe he will get very far."

The men sat quietly for a moment. Then Timicin spoke, "I am a father too. Every daughter I marry to another tribe is difficult in its own way. This situation." He paused. "It is beyond comprehension. I put out the word immediately that she should not be harmed. The tribes will respect her. They know she is your daughter."

Borjigin smoldered and breathed heavily through his nose. He had no solace from this meeting. "If by some chance you locate her before I do, by hellfire Timicin, bring her directly to me or I will flatten you, the ancestors," he breathed in deeply, "and everyone in between."

Chapter Nineteen

After Eve had been kidnapped—knocked off her feet, bound, and gagged—she had been brought directly to the yurt of the first wife of the man who would marry her, a man named Bataar. He had three other wives: two older than Eve, and one who looked much too young to be married. The girl was scared and timid like a sable mouse, but Eve quickly detected the angry restlessness about her. It made Eve's stomach clench in dread. The wives took over, preparing Eve for the wedding—she was stripped, bathed, and dressed in a wedding deel. There was no time for Eve to process what had happened and what her new life would be. She had no time for regret. She had no time for tears.

The older wives worked with a serious intensity, ignoring Eve in unison when she asked question after question. *Does Bataar seek counsel in his wives? Are there women among your tribal elders? Is he kind to your children?* The youngest wife followed in the steps of the older two but with a defiant lack of luster, making every effort, it seemed, to be invisible. When Eve caught the young woman's eye, the only reaction Eve got from the girl was an apologetic frown. Despite Eve's own distress, Eve's heart hurt for the girl. These were the things that she disliked about her people. That there were still tribes that would force a marriage on a woman, and in this case, a very young one, who clearly didn't want to be in it.

The wives finished their ministrations and hustled Eve to the ceremonial grounds. The tribe had gathered and Eve was jostled to stand next to the man who would be her husband. Just her height, Bataar had long hair, mostly silver, tied back for the wedding. He looked much older than her. In fact, as their marriage was spoken into existence, she realized he had sons looking on that were near her age. Bataar did not have a pleasant presence. He seemed to have no desire to soothe her fear. Despite her calm exterior, she was terrified and mournful. She glanced at him, trying to understand this man who would be her husband. He did not look at her as the tribe elder spoke words to form their union.

After the ceremony, a small feast had been put together by the wives. It was no great celebration. She was a fourth wife. This was no reason to inconvenience anyone. No one seemed to care much that a woman's life had ended. She was led to a table and seated beside her new husband. He did not speak or talk to her, but before she sat, he squeezed her bottom roughly, letting her know his intentions. Inside, Eve cried.

Time held no meaning for her. The next thing Eve knew, she was sitting on the bed in the dark in the marital yurt that she would share with her new husband for the night. The yurt was filled with plush cushions and blankets and trunks containing other plush things, she assumed, whatever a new couple wanted to be cozy. Eve just stared at the door. She wondered if she would have any more opportunities in her life after this. A wife could be lauded, respected in the clan. She could become a tribal leader. She could advise the il-khan. She could help protect other women from this same scenario. All her options would depend on this new husband.

Those thoughts had woven themselves into a pattern in her mind when her new husband entered the yurt. He flung back the flap and entered with a swagger steeped in drunkenness. Eve, frightened, jumped up. For a second, she hoped he would calm her, to make some kind of connection. All he did was grunt once and say, "Turn."

Eve, still in a daze, didn't know what he meant. She turned in a circle to face him once more. The gruff man responded by chuckling low, then grabbing her arm and pulling her into a sour kiss.

"No," she hissed. She planted her feet and pushed him off. This couldn't be what the ancestors wanted for her, for any woman. If this man were to be her husband, he would learn to respect her now.

He came toward her, and she pushed him back again. "You will take more care with me," she insisted.

He grabbed her again and flung her around, dismissing her demand. She fell onto the bedding, struggling against him as he lifted her skirts, cursing this man and this union. Her mind went wild, combing for tactics to get away, but the rustling sound of him opening his pants and the smell of beer coming off him dulled her courage.

That's when she heard the sound of flesh snapping. The gurgle of blood.

Eve flew around to see the youngest wife behind her husband with a blade buried in his neck. She must have crawled out of a trunk and then climbed on top to carve into his skin while he was focused on Eve. The young woman jerked and thrust the blade in the same way she would bleed a goat, causing Bataar's blood to spurt and splatter. He reached forward to grab at Eve, but she jerked back, still not sure what she was watching. The girl leaned and pressed the blade in as deeply as she could, her face wild and unflinching. Baatar fell to his knees with a thud.

Blood poured in a dark river from his lips, his neck, and his nose as he fell facedown. The girl stepped back. She made eye contact with Eve and held her finger to her lips.

Eve's first reaction was a pure stream of relief. But she quickly realized that the tribe would see the girl's attack as an injustice, rather than a punishment.

"What have you done?" Eve whispered harshly to the girl as she found her words. She was shaken and upset and unable to understand the many crimes of the day. "What does this accomplish?"

"I could not bear to be with this man for another second," the girl whispered back, equally as harsh. "Him taking you was my chance to get away. You must help me."

"What do you wish to do, little sister?" Eve said, still careful of her volume. "How can you expect to escape this crime?"

The young woman looked up to Eve. "I plan to blame it on you."

"Me?" Eve asked. "But why?"

"I am in love with Bataar's brother. Now I will be able to marry him.

They will think it is you who killed Bataar. I will be free of this terrible man."

"What of me? What am I to do?"

"You can return to your family," the girl pleaded. Her silken black hair flowed over her deel, which hung off her small frame, making her look innocent despite her crime. She came down from the chair and took careful steps around the growing pool of blood. "You are from the white bone tribe, the daughter of Borjigin Khan. He will protect you."

"Little sister," Eve rasped, shaking her head in shock as the moist smell of blood filled the air, filled her nose. "You have just caused a war. My father will be expected to return me here. If he does not, our tribes will fight. My brothers will have to fight. The man you want to be your husband will have to fight. Only the ancestors know who among them will perish."

"How does it feel," the girl spat, "that killing a warrior will start a war, but stealing a woman is celebrated?"

"It has been done for centuries," Eve trailed off, confused and not sure what to argue.

"You must run away, and all will be well. Please," the girl begged. "Please allow me this happiness."

"What are you asking of me?" Eve asked. Disbelief still made it hard to think, to understand. "You want me to take the blame for this murder?"

"If they think I did it, I will be killed." She shuddered, and her eyes grew bigger than the moon. "You have protection, elder sister. You are the daughter of the great Borjigin. You have nothing to fear." She grabbed Eve's hands and sank to the ground. "Please," she heaved and wept. "Please, you must." She put her face in Eve's hands. "Please, he tried every day to put a child in me, but I threw myself onto the rocks to kill any life that grew inside me." Still on her knees, she pulled up her deel, exposing her skin, revealing the heavy pattern of bruising across her legs and torso. "He didn't see the difference between the bruises he gave me and the ones I gave myself." She looked up at Eve. "I was stolen too. I have saved you. I have saved you from this man. You did not want to marry him, did you?"

"Of course not." Eve dropped to her knees, taking the girl's hands once more. "It is terrible to be forced to marry, but sometimes the ancestors decide such things."

"No, it can't be." The girl sobbed, dropping her head. "The ancestors don't want this unhappiness. I did this for you, too," she cried. "You don't know what it is like to be married. It is a terrible thing if you do not love the man." She looked up again, her eyes glistening. "But I do love a man! I love Bataar's brother! He is gentle when we make love. All that needs to happen is you must escape, and I will be given to him. That is all!"

"Shhh," said Eve. "Hush, girl." She pulled the quietly sobbing girl into her arms and stroked her hair, working everything out in her mind. Perhaps this was the best course of action, what was meant to happen. Perhaps this terrible situation had been designed by the ancestors, and this silly girl who thought only of herself had been given divine guidance all to force something from Eve. "I will go," Eve said finally.

"You will?" the girl whimpered.

"Yes," Eve affirmed, standing up quickly, looking around for whatever she could take with her that would help her journey.

"I have this for you," the girl said, her tears ceasing. She handed Eve a sack of supplies. "And your clothing." The girl produced the deel Eve had been wearing that morning. Eve looked at it, knowing which of her loved ones and kin had stitched each thread as she realized she would never have a chance to see them again. It was all brought on by her own pride. She had always been too good to take a husband, too good to sit and mend. Now her punishment was to be torn from her tribe, a thread thrashed from its tapestry. If she returned and claimed the murder to protect the girl, there would be war. If she returned and blamed the girl, the girl would be executed, and Eve would still be expected to marry the brother of Bataar, or there would be war. Eve knew no way out.

"How can I escape?" she asked as she stripped the wedding deel and put on her own garment.

"I have cut a strip in the fabric of the yurt and broken the lattice. It is how I entered. You can follow the moon east."

"I will go west." Eve looked down at the man. She felt for his pulse. It was no longer beating. She placed the wedding deel over him, then she said the prayer of her people, to send his spirit to those of his lineage who loved him. It was terrible to lose a life, any life, especially that of a warrior. But she felt little remorse for this man who did not honor his wives. When she completed the prayer, she reached down and ripped the knife from his neck, sprouting a new, weaker fount of blood. She wiped her bloodied hand on the marriage deel that covered him.

"Go," said Eve to the girl. "Get home safely. I provide you no more assistance."

The girl nodded and slipped through the slice in the fabric of the yurt. Eve exited after her. The cold air of the night came as a shock after the wet heat of the blood-soaked air in the yurt. The wind acted as her ally and blew strongly enough to cover her sounds. Eve had tears in her eyes, but she was too angry and mournful of her previous life to let them fall. *That silly girl*, Eve thought. Eve did not know if the girl was full of darkness or full of light, but perhaps she was an instrument to bring balance to that tribe. With nothing left to do, and her own war inside, Eve ran, leaving the young tribe to their own turmoil. She ran, with only the moon and the night to comfort her.

Chapter Twenty

Ganbold. Warrior. Hunter. Ganbold. Warrior. Hunter.

Finding the boy had been a gift from the ancestors.

The boy spoke Ganbold's language, French, and some others. Travel became much easier. Finding Frenchmen became much easier. Ganbold wanted to kill all the Frenchmen he encountered. With the boy, he could lure them out, away from protection.

The boy was useful at speaking languages, but stupid in travel. He could not hunt or start a fire. He complained. Ganbold had to feed him.

Ganbold and the boy traveled back toward Bukhara, where the boy had left the Frenchman and the woman. They arrived to find that the company had left just a day before, but people knew the route they would take. This was the closest Ganbold had been to them, and he rejoiced. With the boy in tow, Ganbold marched them back out of town.

Now he sat in the market of a town called Kalif, waiting. The boy was hidden along the alleyways, and Ganbold alone was exposed, sitting as he did to avoid causing commotion. His full height caused terror. As it should. These people were weak. They should fear Ganbold, especially with his favor from the ancestors.

The Frenchman and the woman should be here, too, Ganbold thought, in this market. All the people told the boy they would be here. Ganbold felt anger in his eyes and in his shoulders. Did they lie? He would kill every one of them to win his way back into his tribe. Then he had a thought that made him furious. Did the boy lie to him?

Just as Ganbold thought to go shake the boy to test his loyalty and then squeeze his throat, he saw a streak of yellow hair. Ganbold had to adjust his eyes to be sure it wasn't just sunlight. He saw it again—the yellow hair—as the woman fixed the scarf around her head. Then, the Frenchman, beside her.

Ganbold came alert, suddenly, fists clenching in anticipation of having one throat in each. Then he saw the Frenchman lean into the woman and whisper something that made her look at him and laugh. The gesture caused the rage inside his fists to spread to the rest of his body.

Ganbold stood, and those near him jumped back in panic. Ganbold walked fast across the square toward the woman, splitting a river in the crowd. He knew he shouldn't attack here. He should follow and catch them alone on the roads. But his anger controlled his hands, his feet, his spirit. He was going to grab her yellow hair with his left hand and kill the tall Frenchman with his right.

Ganbold locked eyes with the woman as he came for her. The woman jumped and grabbed the arm of the Frenchman. The Frenchman looked around in surprise at her urgency. When he saw Ganbold, he pushed her back behind him. Ganbold wanted to see the man's fear. Feel his fear. Ganbold waited for the wave of terror to wash over the man.

Fear did not show itself.

There was no panic in his expression. Ganbold narrowed his eyes and grinned. He would enjoy this fight even more now.

Ganbold swatted a person to the side and then another as he closed the distance. The Frenchman drew his sword.

Ganbold came with all his strength. He attacked the man from above with his thick blade, but the man did not crumble like he should. Instead, he took Ganbold's blade with his sword and ducked low, knocking Ganbold across the flank. Screams came around them then. Ganbold came down again on the man. The Frenchman caught the blade again and pushed Ganbold off.

Now, this man and his sword were angering Ganbold. *Fight like a man with hands*, Ganbold thought. He would need to remove the blade, but the

Frenchman was fast. He swung around, cutting a slice across Ganbold's chest. Ganbold looked down, surprised to see blood on his body. Then came the hilt of the tall man's blade to the side of Ganbold's head.

A sharp buzzing sound sliced through Ganbold's head as pain cracked across his skull. Ganbold was dazed. He blinked, his eyelids moving separately, one opening and then the other. He shook his head, clearing his vision enough to see the man retreating with the woman. He smiled, the sounds and screams around him blending with his own monstrous roar.

Ganbold would enjoy killing that Frenchman. Very much.

Michel had them on their horses and galloping away in no time. He had planned to stay the night there in Kalif and then continue in the morning. However, with that man so close, he worried about being attacked in their sleep. So, he recalibrated, checked his maps for a more direct route, pulled his reluctant men from the whorehouse, and set them on the direct road to Samarkand. Now was not the time to be seen fighting a tribal man in the middle of the marketplace. He thought this with lead in his gut.

Michel had only fought defensively. He hoped that's what the gossip would pick up: that he had been attacked. That man had enormous strength, and it was clear that he intended to gut Michel right there in the dirt. Instead, Michel had knocked him on the head so he and Eve could get away. Michel didn't want to think about what the man would do to Eve if he got his hands on her.

The crew came to a bend in the river as the setting sun striped the hazy sky in gold and pink. They'd been running for hours and still had a few to go to reach Samarkand. They could camp here, by the river, but Michel preferred to travel into the night rather than risk being attacked while they slept. As they came to the water's edge, Michel pulled his horse to a stop, dismounted, and helped Eve down as the rest of the crew stretched out and ambled to the river to cool off.

He watched as Eve took a moment to pat down the horses and give them treats before he walked a few paces upstream. He took off his boots and rolled up his pants before wading into the water among the cattails. He pulled off his shirt and tossed it to the bank. He spilled water onto the back of his neck and splashed his face. When he looked up, Eve was standing at the water's edge.

"Eve," he began. They hadn't spoken much on the ride. Michel was lost in planning, and Eve, as always, was quiet on the subject of her pursuers.

She looked at him. For the first time ever, he saw her truly humbled. It shook him.

"Eve, you have to tell me what's going on." He came to the edge of the water where she stood. "You want me to protect you. I can't do it if I don't know who is coming after you."

She looked down. "I don't really know," she said. "I didn't realize they would send him after me."

"Do you know that man? He was the one who scared you before."

She nodded. "His name is Ganbold. He is from the tribe of the man I married." She shook her head. "You should not have fought him. He could have hurt you. Badly." Then she looked at him, raw feelings in her eyes. "But he didn't."

Michel went toward her and took her hand. "No," he said. "You don't have to worry about that."

She breathed out to finish her sentence. "I'm sorry, Michel," Eve said. "To have brought this burden to you."

"Your safety is not a burden," he said. He touched her cheek, aware of the heaviness of her grief. He wanted to take it from her, to swallow up any fear she had. He let out a deep sigh. "If I had known of this trouble when I bought you..." He tilted his head, at least wanting to make her smile again. "I would have asked for a discount."

She furrowed her brow and allowed a small laugh. "You did!" she said. She smacked him across the chest, accepting his playfulness, this reprieve. "You *did* negotiate."

"Well," he said, letting the grin form. "I should have gotten you for much cheaper."

She scoffed and rolled her eyes at him.

"Listen," he continued, his voice softening, soothing. "You're going to have to give me the full story. Not right this second, but soon."

She nodded. "I know."

"Because, *Siren*," he said. He reached forward to touch her arm. As soon as he made contact, he wanted more, and his hands went to her waist. He gripped her. "I have other things I want to think about when it comes to you."

She bit her lip. "Like what?"

He continued, feeling his voice rumble low in his chest, "If I've figured you out like I think I have, then that means I may have a reward coming. For fighting off that brute earlier."

He smirked, still playful, "Not required, of course, but happily accepted." He pulled her closer and he felt the laces of her dress against his bare chest. One of the men may see them. He didn't care. Let the world know his claim to this woman.

She put her hands on his chest and ran them lower, tracing his muscles with her fingertips down the tight diagonals until she was stopped by his belt. She sank her fingers under the fabric and gripped his beltline. "Yes," she said, leaning up to whisper against his lips. "You do."

Michel groaned, his body ready to buckle at her touch. He took in a sharp breath and gripped her arms, pushing her back. "Then let's ride fast, or I will try and have you out here." Before he left, he gripped the back of her head and pulled her close, taking the chance to taste her lips, sweet and plump—cherries, currants, wonderful things. Then he pulled away and grinned at her before jogging back up the bank to yell at the men to hurry themselves. He knew she watched him as he did. It made his desire ache even harder.

Chapter Twenty-One

They reached Samarkand a few hours later. Michel had rushed a man ahead to alert town officials of his early arrival. He wanted to set up their yurts inside city limits, and he was pleased to see that space had been cleared for them. He didn't want to be near the edges of town where they would be more vulnerable.

Eve took over the camp preparations. Michel sent notes to his contacts, but it was late, so he didn't expect to hear anything that evening. With nothing else to do, he set up the area inside his yurt, washed, and tried to help Eve prepare the dinner, which just made her balk at him because he got in her way. He couldn't leave her alone. He didn't care if he ate. He didn't care if the fire was set up. He'd never wanted a woman with such intensity, and he never let desire get in the way of his responsibilities. He couldn't think of anything other than her. He found himself pacing around her, stalking her, like a damn hyena.

Then, when he felt like he might not make it another second without touching her, she dusted her hands and turned to come toward him. He reached out, ready to drag her to him, into their yurt.

Then a voice gave him pause.

"Hello there!" said a man. It was Harod, a Frenchman and important merchant in the town, coming to make his acquaintance.

Michel dragged his gaze from Eve, with great reluctance, his body already protesting his duty to greet this man.

"I'm sorry I did not come sooner," Harod said. "You arrived right at supper." He was a portly man with red cheeks and a permanent grin. He held his belly at the mention of supper.

Michel greeted the man by shaking his hand. "Thank you, Harod, for the quick preparations this evening. I know you were not expecting us so soon." Eve stepped closer, and Michel put his hand on the small of her back to bring her near. "This is Eve," he said. "She is accompanying me on this journey."

"Is she?" Harod said with a knowing smile. "My lady." He nodded, his eyes going to her. Then he looked back at Michel and indicated toward the yurt. "Is this yours?"

"Yes," said Michel. "Please. Let's go in."

They removed their shoes. The rest of the camp was settling down. It was quiet and cool. Many of the men were still sitting around the fire, enjoying drinks from their flasks, satiated by the dinner Eve had prepared. Michel held the flap open for Harod and waited until Eve entered as well. She let her body brush up against his as she passed, causing a pulsating tremor to run through him, urging him to end this meeting with Harod as quickly as possible.

They moved to the table at the back of the yurt. Eve began making tea for them. "Harod," Michel said. "How can I be of service? I hadn't thought to see you until morning."

"Yes, it is late," Harod said. "But my friend, I have to admit, I was eager to see you alive."

"Alive?" Michel asked. "Has the gossip of my fight this morning beaten me here?"

"Another fight this morning?" he asked, giving Michel a wide-eyed look. "No, I thought perhaps you were a part of the group of Frenchmen who were slaughtered a few days ago." He continued, always eager for gossip. "Who did you fight this morning?"

Michel stared at him. "Harod," he said, too many questions forming. "What of this group of Frenchmen? I know nothing about it."

Eve came over and laid out a portion of nuts and bread with jam. She sat on a chair next to Michel.

"Oh yes. Terrible," he lamented, though Michel could tell he was delighted to tell the story.

Harod took a scoop of nuts and continued. "Twelve French merchants, just outside the city limits. Just ripped to shreds." He cracked a pistachio open and popped it into his mouth. "A porter that got away said it was a beast of a man that took two at a time as they tried to fight him off. He didn't even use a sword!" Harod said, almost bouncing in his seat.

Michel stole a glance at Eve, who looked grim at the news. "Why were they attacked?"

"No one knows." Harod shrugged. "We had men out there for hours to clear away the bodies." He spread some jam across a chunk of bread. "The bodies that the animals didn't get to."

Michel's mind reeled. He had thought the man sought Eve, but maybe he was coming for Michel himself. And why had he killed the others? Michel's presence, the relationships he cultivated, these things kept the region secure. An open wage for war right now would not only mean that he and every other Frenchman were in danger, but it could dismantle his entire operation.

"Now," Harod said, breaking into Michel's thoughts. "Tell me of the fight you had this morning. Don't tell me it was the same man," he said excitedly, his eyes darting between Michel and Eve as he stuffed the bread behind his lips.

"It was nothing," Michel said flatly, not wanting to add more lines to this story. "A scuffle. Nothing more."

"Oh," Harod said, looking disappointed. Then he perked back up. "If I were you, Michel, I'd be very careful. At least until we know what this man wants." He finished off his bread and licked a spot of jam that had dribbled onto his sleeve. Then he looked at Eve. "Is it a brave man who escorts you, young lady? Is he capable of keeping you safe?" He said it in a teasing tone, but Eve did not wear a playful expression.

She looked from Harod to Michel. "I know no man more capable," she said, "than this one who sits beside me."

Despite the weight he felt inside him, Michel felt his heart spike, and the temperature of the yurt seemed to rise sharply. The words Harod had spoken dissipated in the lake of desire that surged inside him. These were problems and things to think about later. He reached for Eve's hand, the touch causing him to forget every one of his responsibilities and think only of her.

Harod stood, jostling the table as he did. He took the rest of his tea in one gulp. "I will be going," he said. "Leave you to the rest of your evening."

Perhaps the man had picked up on the energy shift, but Michel didn't care if he was being rude. He barely noticed the final salutations as he hustled Harod out.

Once the man was gone and the door to their yurt was sealed, he turned to her. Eve stood in the same place, her hands at her sides. She watched him with her mottled green eyes that glowed in the lamplight. Her loose hair flowed down over her shoulders, and she bit at her lip.

He went for her. Nothing would stop him now.

Chapter Twenty-Two

She saw him coming toward her, a dangerous smile on his face. Eve felt her body react in a way she had never experienced before. There was intent in his eyes, and before he even touched her, she knew she was in trouble, in a wonderful way. She sucked in a breath. So many places on her body wanted attention, she couldn't keep track of it all. A quiver ran through her center and down the inside of her thighs, and as he got closer, she wanted his taste and scent to fill her again. Her statement to Harod had been true. When she had seen Michel fight Ganbold, that monster of a man, she knew one thing: she had chosen the only one who could protect her.

In a second, he was on her. One hand gripped her hair, and one hand landed on her waist. He dragged her to him and claimed her lips against his. Eve opened her mouth for him. His soft lips were the only things soft about his body. She tasted his tongue, drawing the essence of him into her. She threw her arms around his neck, ready to show him not only her gratitude, but also her own acute need to be closer.

Michel kissed her in a way that she understood only because it matched the desperation she felt inside. She continued to meet his tongue greedily, wanting to please him, but at the same time eager to experience. Eve had never felt these sweet feelings in her body, the delicious twisting in her stomach, the heat in her center. She had no frame of reference for these things. She knew in that moment that she would give him everything. She no longer felt she had to convince him to keep her. No, now, she just wanted more of him.

She pulled back with a gasp, breaking the kiss. She looked into his eyes, which burned. She bit her lip through a smile. Then she moved, to sink to her knees, to drop to the floor before him. To take him in her mouth the way she had done before.

But just as she moved and her hands grabbed for his waistband, he caught her and pulled back up.

"No," he said.

"No?" she asked.

He grinned at her, taking another kiss from her lips. "My reward. I decide."

When he pulled back, she whispered, "I am your servant."

He groaned as he picked her up, putting his arms around her, under her bottom, moving her to the table where cups of tea still sat. He set her down, his body covering hers, his feet still on the ground. She wrapped her arms around him, and his lips were on hers again. She tasted him with her tongue and felt him grip roughly at the fabric of her dress. She had never been willing to yield to a man before, but with him, there was no choice. She wanted to submit.

His hands came up her skirts. Past her knees and onto her thighs. His hands on her bare flesh caused her insides to go wild. At one point, she had thought to use the promise of sex to keep Michel in line, but he was doing things to her she hadn't anticipated. She hadn't anticipated wanting him this badly. She hadn't anticipated losing her own control.

Her belting had disappeared. Her dress was up over her head. All while his lips were on hers, his hands everywhere, making it impossible for her to track how he undressed her so quickly. Suddenly, she had nothing on but the undershift. The thin material clung to her fevered skin. He pulled it up, and it bunched around her waist so he could settle his body between her legs, and she felt the hard length in his pants. Then his own shirt was off, and he pressed against her. A pleasure she'd never felt before shot through her body, causing her head to fall back. "Michel," she gasped.

"Yes," he said. "Say my name just like that."

Then his lips were on hers before she could say it again. His warm hands moved across her body. He reached into her shift, pulling it down over her shoulders, and gripped her breasts. The contact caused her to jerk before pressing herself into his hands. She heard him moan as he trailed kisses down her neck to let his mouth join his hands at her breasts.

She realized this was what it felt like to be wanted, adored, and taken all at once. He kissed her flesh and then went for her nipple, grazing it with his teeth. Eve reared back and cried out at the new sensation. He still pressed into her, between her legs, and her body rocked against him, seeking something more from the contact.

But he shifted his body away, leaving cold air between them. Eve shrieked and tried to pull him back to her, her breasts wanting more, the place lower wanting more.

"Wait, wait," Michel laughed, trying to appease her.

Before she could protest any more, his hands were gripping her bloomers, pulling them down. For just a second, she sobered, realizing she was to lose her virginity to him, that his mark would be left on her. Being a virgin was not something she cherished. She had always thought of it as both a duty and a burden, something for men to enjoy. Having been married, albeit briefly, it was no longer expected, but she regretted that Michel did not know. She regretted that she had to live her life with secrets. In that instant, she wanted to share the moment with him, for him to understand that this was not something she had ever thought to want, but with him, it was different. She tried to make a word, to have a thought come out of her mouth, to express to him in some way both her affection and her gratitude for having found him. But all the words and thoughts jumbled together into a moan as he continued to place kisses down her belly.

Then his tongue circled her navel, and she felt her breath coming out of her in sharp gasps as he continued moving lower. He settled down on his knees in front of her, his tongue tracing further. It felt like fire across her skin, but still she watched and wondered what in the world he was doing, and then, *Oh! Oh my goodness!*

His head was between her legs, his tongue and lips on her. She looked down in shock at the scene. The muscles flexing in his back. His wild head of hair moving. His hands gripping her thighs. She couldn't believe it, even as the delicious sensations caused her to enjoy her body more than she ever had before.

It was so intimate and so intense. She let the feeling wash over her, as it built toward something she didn't know. Cries and moans escaped her lips while Michel explored parts of her unknown until this very moment. At the center was a point she could feel that wanted his attention, even though he seemed to avoid it. She wondered why, as the attention to the outer parts made her body scream for more. She grabbed at his hair. She arched enough to break her back and bucked her hips toward him. She wanted something. The center of her wanted something from him, but he wouldn't give it.

"Michel," she said. "Michel," she begged.

"Yes, yes," he whispered against her. "Just like that."

Hearing his name seemed to double his efforts, and suddenly he was on her, on the spot that wanted him most. She felt his lips and tongue right at her center, and new sensations swept through her. Her head swam, and she cried out. This powerful man in her service, serving her pleasure. She had tamed this brutal creature. And now he was down between her legs...

More, she thought, *more, more.*

Then it hit her.

She had heard, of course, of orgasms. Though she had never focused so much on that part of her body or expected that some man would give her pleasure. But when she felt it break her open and rip her inside out, she never had thought to have such a thing. Doubled by the fact that she was riding the mouth of a man who had come into her life when she had been at her most vulnerable. This pleasure could only exist through him.

The powerful wave left her groaning, gasping, gripping him. Michel pressed a hand into her belly to hold her down as he continued to suck at her center, causing the sensation to go on and on until it was nearly unbearable. Then he slowed and was kissing the outsides again, all the sweet spots that still trembled. Then he was kissing her thighs, then her belly, and back up to her breasts. She clung to him. She wouldn't let him go.

As he started kissing her breasts again, it was something inside her body that begged for attention. It was different—a sweet, deliberate ache that wanted more contact with him. She urged him forward as he kissed her breasts and came up to her neck. He fumbled with his pants, and Eve yanked at his shirt. *More*, she wanted. *Hurry*, she urged. She waited impatiently for him to situate himself so she could experience all of him. Her body was screaming on the inside to be touched and caressed. *More*, she thought, *more, more, more.*

Michel had never experienced anything like what had just happened. She was so wild, so unbridled. He never let a moment take him over, but this... this he couldn't control. With her writhing body still beneath him, he struggled to break out of his pants as Eve's hands were all over him. Then they went to his cheeks. He stilled enough to look into her eyes. There were things she wanted to say in those eyes, he knew, but instead of speaking, Eve leaned forward to take his bottom lip between hers and run her tongue across his mouth. He realized she was tasting herself on him. The thought took him over again, and he was back to ripping and pulling at his pants, in a frenzy and a panic he had never before felt. Never had he wanted a woman like he wanted her. Her body pulled him close. He swore to himself to give her everything he could.

Suddenly, at the entrance to his yurt, he heard his name. Once, he ignored it. Twice, he paused.

"Michel," the man called a third time.

"What is it?" Michel demanded, turning his head to yell toward the door.

"We need your assistance."

"Can it wait?"

The voice paused. "No, *monsieur*, it cannot."

"*Merde*," Michel mumbled to himself.

He leaned in once to press his forehead against Eve's while he gripped the hair at the back of her head. "Don't move," he said through his teeth.

Eve blinked back at him obsequiously, gently repositioning her garments to cover herself.

Still grumbling, Michel fixed himself and tore through the entrance of the tent. "What?" he shouted.

Then it all came into focus. There was a rush at the end of the camp, and the noises of shouting men that he had ignored. He realized they had been calling for him for some time, but he...his focus had been elsewhere.

At the center of camp, there was a cluster of men around someone, all near the fire. When Michel approached, he saw a figure huddled by the fire, wrapped in a blanket. Irritated, he didn't understand why this couldn't wait until morning.

"Good sir," Michel said. "What is it you require?"

The figure turned to face Michel, and when he saw the battered face and the swollen, purple eye, Michel understood. "Terence," he said.

"*Monsieur*," Terence said. "I know you sent me away, but..." he choked on a grimace. "I don't have any other way to get home," he swallowed. "The merchant I traveled with was killed. They all were."

"You were with the party that was attacked?" Michel asked, moving to sit near the boy. Michel looked up to Iman, who was nearby. "Can we get him something to drink?"

Iman nodded and turned to retrieve a cup.

"The man you placed me with, in Bukhara, *Monsieur* Stefan. We joined a merchant party. They were completing travels and headed back to France. But we were ambushed by a giant." Iman handed him the cup, and Terence accepted. "I tried to help," Terence continued. "I don't really know how to use a sword, but I am good with a dagger."

"How is it that one man took out so many?" Michel asked.

Terence looked at him, wide-eyed. "He is a monster, *Monsieur*. A nightmare." He blinked. "He killed a few before we knew there was someone upon us. Then he took the rest out as they tried to fight him off. He pulled their bones apart like they were chickens." Terence sat up straighter. "I-I jumped on his back to try to hold him off, but he caught me and pounded me unconscious." He swallowed. "I woke up some time later. Everyone around me was dead." He looked up at Michel again. "I have been keeping to the shadows here, hoping to find another group going to France. Then I heard your party was arriving."

"Have you seen him again?" Michel asked, fearing the man would appear suddenly.

"No," Terence said, shaking his head. "He disappeared." He looked at Michel earnestly. "Can I stay with you, Michel? I won't cause any more trouble, I swear it. I just want to get home. I hate it here." He groaned and put his head to his knees.

Michel stared at him, grinding his jaw in thought. He didn't need any extra considerations right now, but he couldn't leave the boy like this. Not with Ganbold coming for them all like a storm. He did not trust the boy, but he already knew he would concede. Michel let out a long sigh. "Stay where I can see you, Terence," Michel said. "I do not have the energy to babysit you."

"Yes. I promise," Terence said, looking up, looking hopeful.

Then Michel continued, "Now I'm going to need you to start from the beginning and tell me everything you can remember about this interaction."

Chapter Twenty-Three

From the yurt's flap, Eve watched Michel speak with Terence. She heard them talking about his master and the others, who had been ripped apart by Ganbold. She felt terrible. Her fault, all of it. All she had meant to do was get away to protect the girl, to avoid a confrontation between her tribe and the young tribe that took her. But look at the deaths in her wake.

A light breeze came to calm her skin, which still flamed for Michel. Seeing him, his tall frame hunched by the fire in concentration, and seeing Terence, worry on his face, she looked to the sky, hoping for a sign that she had not chosen the wrong path. Should she have gone to her family and let her father sort this all out? She was not a warrior like her father or her brothers. In this way, she had thought to protect the ones she loved.

Now she feared she would destroy another life: Michel's. Even if she didn't get him killed, she was certainly on the brink of destroying any deals he hoped to make. As much as she wanted more of that man, he didn't deserve for her problems to take over his. She would tell him her whole story. Then he could decide for himself if he wished to leave her.

Even though the thought of being separated from him now made her heart hurt like a dagger had been stabbed into it.

She turned back inside the yurt to collect herself. She saw the table where, seconds ago, Michel had been ready to take her, and she had been ready to give herself to him. It was a mess—chairs tipped, tea spilled. She put her hand to her lips, as the last strands of her desire threaded through her. It wasn't appropriate, these feelings at this moment, but her body still ached deeply for him. She would have to deal with those thoughts another time.

She straightened the space and cleaned the spilled drinks. Then she set to work at the small hearth. She pulled out her cache of herbs and dried roots, choosing the combination she needed, and set to work on a calming tea for Terence. While the tea brewed, she straightened herself. It was her fault, she knew, that these men were being attacked. If she had only committed to something in her life, chosen a direction, she could have saved so many.

The girl from the young tribe, though. She would not have found her peace.

Eve finished the tea by adding a crystal of sugar to the kettle. She exited the yurt and came to the fire to sit beside Michel. She handed Terence a cup, and she handed one to Michel as well. Michel had been speaking, but when he saw Eve, he lost his words and just watched her.

She smiled. Whatever happened, she would not stop loving the way she affected him and caused him to forget everything he was doing.

Michel shook himself and turned back to the boy. "Did you have any indication of where he was headed?"

The boy huddled over his tea and shook his head. "He never said a word." He swallowed. "He didn't seem to want anything. Just to kill us."

"We will continue to hope that he has had his fill and will be gone."

"Have you eaten?" Eve asked the boy.

"No, *madame*," he said, glancing between her and Michel.

"*Mademoiselle*," she corrected, with a smile.

He nodded at the mistake as the fire continued to crackle and the men drifted into silence. The boy sipped his tea, and Eve poured cups for those who wanted some. She smiled to herself. He had called her *Madame*, which meant he thought of her as Michel's wife. Terence hadn't joined their party until after she and Michel started getting along. He must have assumed she was on this journey with her husband. She pocketed away the warm feeling it gave her, despite the cool of the night and the timbre of her thoughts.

The next morning, they awoke with the sun. Michel watched over the camp, the coffee Eve had prepared for him in hand, while he waited for the rest of the men to be fully awake. Despite his hope to return to Eve the night before and spend the remainder of the evening in her bed, enjoying each other, he could not leave Terence unattended. He didn't trust the boy, and Terence had had his fingers in at least half the men's items before Michel had booted him the first time, so Michel didn't trust the men to leave him alone either. Reluctantly, Michel put Terence in his yurt. Very reluctantly. Despite how badly he wanted to pick up with Eve, Michel didn't need another murder in the night.

A brisk wind whipped through the camp, and Michel went to sit by the fire, closer to where Eve prepared breakfast. After a moment, Eve dusted her hands, took her cup of tea, and sat near him. The closeness roused him again, having never quite calmed after getting a taste of her the night before. Her skirts brushed his leg. He wondered just what he had to do to have her lying vulnerable before him once more. Then Eve spoke.

"Michel," she began, her chin jutting out.

"Yes?" he urged. It always amused him when she talked to him like a teacher talking to a student.

"I feel you should know something about me."

Michel turned to face her now. "I've been waiting to know anything about you."

She tucked her chin in and looked down at her hands. "I have never been with a man. Like last night."

For a second, he felt a swell of pride inside him, thinking she meant her enjoyment. With that, however, came another stab of guilt at taking from her, for his own pleasure. Eve kept going before he could dwell.

"What I mean to say is..." She paused. "I never consummated the marriage with the man who was my husband." She looked down. "We were only married for a few hours. He died...just before..."

Michel watched her for a long moment. He reached forward to peel one of the hands from the cup she was holding and take it in his. "You were just defending yourself," he said gently, making the connection. "You should never have been forced."

"It is not unheard of what happened to me," she said. "Being stolen. It *is* unheard of what happened to him. I'll be in a lot of trouble if anyone from his tribe finds me."

She sighed then. When she didn't continue, Michel spoke.

"I don't condemn you," Michel continued, leaning forward. "If that's what you think."

He thought he saw relief in her expression. "I just want you to know," she continued, "that I'm not a widow. In the usual sense."

"Ah," Michel said. "I see." He gave her hand a playful squeeze. "You are telling me to keep my hands to myself."

"No," she said. He saw her smiling now, even though she still looked away from him. "I like your hands." Her voice came softly. "And other things." She bit her bottom lip. "One good thing that came from being kidnapped is that now I can decide when the time is right. I have that control over my body."

"I, uh," Michel said, giving her a nudge. "I hope to be notified when you make that decision."

She laughed. Then she looked up to him, her eyes sparkling. "You should know, I never felt that kind of desire, none of it, until I met you."

What a wonder to have come across this person, Michel thought. He felt pride come back at her words, that he had given her desire, given her *anything*. But more so, he felt fortunate that he had been the one to find her. He could have lived his whole life and never known her. He would kiss her right now. He didn't care. But just as he started to move, she continued speaking.

"I'm going to tell you my story now, Michel, if you would hear it. Then you can decide if I am worth the trouble or not."

"That decision had been made already. But please," he coaxed, "share this story with me."

She looked around. "Can we have the yurt? For privacy?"

Michel grinned. "I will take pleasure in tossing Terence out. Let Iman watch over him for a while."

She rose, and he followed. His problems were not solved, his work was not finished, but he felt hope filling his chest that soon he would be able to focus all of his attention on Eve. Because he knew, no matter what she told him, she was the only woman he would ever want again.

Chapter Twenty-Four

Borjigin paced his chambers. The search for his daughter floundered. His men had turned up no information other than a jade necklace she had sold in Carth, the deel she had discarded in an alley, and hundreds of roads she could have taken. Borjigin suspected she had gone toward France. How far could she have gotten on her own without being sighted? He had a constant stream of messengers going to and from his scouts, but it was difficult and slow to communicate at such a distance.

He had to decide how to act: how to find his daughter, how to deal with Timicin. He needed counsel. His wife provided comfort. His father had provided guidance. But in times of deepest contemplation, it was his ninety-year-old mother, Celine, who provided Borjigin with a different perspective. Especially when it came to Eve.

He walked through the halls of the large manor—crafted by his father in the style of the French palaces—and took the steps to her chamber. Celine and her culture had been very influential on his father, his family, and the clan. The great man had done everything to make Celine feel at home. He built not only the manor but the city where many clans settled when they weren't with the herds. He insisted his sons and their sons spoke French, so she could always have conversations in her native language. Borjigin's father was also the first in their line to marry only one woman. Borjigin, too, married only one woman. These were blessed unions. Borjigin couldn't imagine another way.

Celine had flourished, and, likewise, she had embraced the culture. Though she'd been born French and had the look of a westerner, for all intents and purposes, she was a Mongolian woman.

Borjigin knocked on her heavy wooden door, and when she called him in, he entered his mother's chambers. The furnishings of the room were of their eastern heritage—orange-colored trunks and drawers, an intricate box daybed with brightly patterned blankets—though the finely carved wooden structure of the building itself was in the Western style. Mother sat on a cushioned seat by the fire, mending the waistband on one of her deels. Her white hair was braided down her back. Only light wrinkles showed in her face. Her mind continued to be as sharp as ever.

"Mother," Borjigin spoke, "you do not have to do the mending." He came to sit on the traditional rug on the floor before her. The room was lit by the fire, the last light of day coming through the windows. "One of the boys' wives can do it."

"No, no," she said. "It keeps my fingers nimble. It's good for me." She smiled, stitching along the pattern. "Now tell me, what do you come here to discuss?"

"You know of the tragedy with Eve."

"Yes," she said. Borjigin could see her expression darken, pain coloring her light eyes, the color of his and Eve's.

"I have sent guards. I have sent the fastest horses," he said. "We have infiltrated the West as though we were conquering. Still, I cannot locate her." He paused. "And there are other complications."

"Yes?" She looked up at him from her mending.

"The one they call Ganbold is after her."

She pursed her lips. "Has Timicin called him off?"

"Timicin says he did not send him out."

"Borjigin, son." She pulled a thread taut. Outside came sounds of the pasture, bleats from the herds, clanging of bells. "I know you do not wish to hear what I am going to say," she continued. "I have been saying it for years."

"It is archaic, I know, to steal a bride." He sighed heavily. "I just didn't think it could happen to our family. To *her*."

"It is *horrifying*. But men continue to do it." Mother gave him a stare, the air darkening around her.

"It goes back to the ancients. Some of the greatest unions in our lineage were formed this way."

She scoffed. She cut him off with a raised hand. "It is a young tribe practice. The young tribes wish to force the alliances rather than earn them."

"It is difficult to deter, Mother. It is seen as a way to balance the tribes." He took a breath in through his nose, calibrating. "I must consider all the clans and their practices, not just what we want. Besides," he continued, "many women consider it to be an honor to be stolen, I've been told."

She looked at him, aghast. "By *whom*? The men who stole them?" She clicked her tongue. "My, my, Borjigin, I thought you to be much wiser than this."

He settled back, thinking of the politics of it all. "It will ignite war among the tribes if I move to punish the offense."

"We are not afraid of war," she said, plunging the needle back into her deel. "Sometimes only conflict can restore balance."

He nodded. "Yes. War is not always avoidable." Borjigin sighed and rubbed his forehead. "Regardless, whatever I do now does not bring Eve home to us."

His mother softened. She looped the thread and tied a knot. "Eve can survive in any land, in any season," she asserted. She took her small knife, a tremor of age settling long enough for her to cut the thread. "I don't agree that it is her fault for being kidnapped, but she was living a life with no direction, a thread left to be tied." She held the string in her hands up as evidence. "As your daughter, she has the responsibility to contribute to the tribe through an alliance or some other commitment. Her refusal brought this notice."

"I agree," he said, feeling his own spirit very heavy.

"I believe that if she has managed to evade everyone for this long, including Ganbold..." She paused to press her lips together. "Then she has found a protector. You know as well as I do that Ganbold is a bull and will not stop."

She placed the needle in the pin cushion and adjusted the garment to catch the light. "If Ganbold is the closest to her, focus on him. He is strong, but not smart. He will not cover his presence well, not like Eve." She struggled once to tie a knot but got it on the second pass. "Let his two eyes stay on her, but put a thousand eyes on him." She snapped the thread.

"I hope we find her before darkness does," Borjigin said, his thoughts wandering west, out the window.

"You have raised Eve to be a leader of men. She will not stop leading them now, son," she said as she dropped her mending and took Borjigin's hand. "I believe she is safe. As safe as she can be."

Chapter Twenty-Five

They remained in Samarkand for several uneventful days. Michel had business to finish, new porters and guards to hire. Some of the merchants who traveled with him disbanded, scared off by the stories of Terence. Those who remained were long-time companions or the gruffest of travelers.

He received confirmation that the cashmere dealer would be waiting at their next stop in Kashgar. Johann had arranged it. Harod had stopped gossiping long enough to organize everything. Michel felt much appreciation toward these men for their help. He wished he could think it was all his own doing, that these were his friends and contacts. He knew it was their allegiance to his father that afforded Michel their assistance. Still, he had business to complete, so he would use what he could.

Eve had told him her story. Of being kidnapped, of the girl who had hidden in the yurt to kill the husband, of having to leave, and thinking only of France. Eve had more emotion in her eyes than he had ever seen before. He took her in his arms, promising he would keep her safe from anyone who came after her. Then, before he could taste her lips once more, Terence had screamed into the yurt that he wanted breakfast.

Eve had laughed, and Michel had growled. He really didn't like that boy.

Now, he sat alone at the table at the back of the yurt, looking over a stack of maps, planning their routes. Eve was just outside, finishing preparations for the evening meal. The rest of the camp was empty. Michel had allowed Terence to accompany Iman and a few others to the bathhouse. The others spent the afternoon in town. Everyone was due back before dinner.

It would be nice if his father were here, Michel thought. That man never wavered. Michel strived to be as good and competent as his father. But now, especially now, he realized what it would mean to be discovered with Eve by the tribes before he completed this business—Eve, a woman hunted, a woman wanted for a crime against her tribe, whether it was merited or not. He would lose all the goodwill his father had established.

Once, when Michel was twelve years old, he had been playing in the palace garden at Chevalier with his two younger brothers and several other boys after their swordsmanship class. He had lived a carefree, though structured, life. As the future Duke, he had lessons and rules of decorum. He enjoyed his swordsmanship lessons the best, but loved learning about history and politics. The great world leaders fascinated him. Michel aspired to be one himself, one day. At that time, though, the only ones he had to order around were his brothers, who never listened.

That evening in the garden, they ran and shouted and played, climbing the large tree that overlooked the city. His middle brother, Serge, climbed further than anyone else, even though Michel called to him not to get so high. Serge had kept going as Michel turned to toss his littlest brother, Philippe, into the dirt. That was when Serge fell from the tree with a thud. Horrified, Michel skidded to his brother's side and saw the broken clavicle among gashes across his face and neck. The other boys descended onto them. Michel had ordered them back, trying to assess the damage to Serge, to decide what he could do to help. Someone bumped into Michel's back, knocking him forward. Someone else stepped on Serge's hand. Michel yelled at everyone, but they didn't listen. Nobody listened.

It was chaos. Michel tried to organize, to help Serge, whose eyes were rolling in pain, to settle the other boys and calm his little brother, who sucked in his bottom lip with a sob. Michel was the oldest, the most responsible. He should have been able to handle it, but he was caught in a whirlwind and couldn't do anything to control the situation.

Then his father arrived on quick, steady steps, and everything changed.

Everyone calmed, including Michel. He felt profound relief, knowing his father would take over. He also felt a deep shame that he had not been one bit useful. How would he command one day if no one listened? How would he lead if he had nothing worth contributing? He thought about this moment more often than he probably should.

Now, as he worked out a plan on his map, he knew he was a different person. More in control, more in charge. It frustrated him, though, that he remembered that feeling of relief so vividly. That he still sometimes wished for his father to show up and fix everything.

Just then, Eve entered the yurt. Michel reacted to her presence immediately, taking in her fresh scent, which calmed his torpid thoughts.

"What are you doing over there?" She had a basket of figs with her. She took one and began to peel it with her knife.

"I am figuring things out in my mind," he said. "Planning relaxes me." One thing that did not relax him was the fact that having Terence rejoin the party had meant he'd had no more opportunities to get close to this woman. His eyes flicked to the door, suddenly, wondering how much time they would have alone.

"What have you planned, great one?" she teased.

He scoffed. "I think it's going to work out," he said. "We'll take a direct route to Kashgar from here and meet with the cashmere dealer. Then we can go home. Once we are out of the immediate area, we should avoid any more trouble."

"What of the Frenchmen being killed?" She kept her eyes on the knife as she worked it around the fig.

"I will have to come back," he said, watching her. "Immediately. But I will get you to France first." He paused. "Your safety is my priority now."

Eve finished by slicing the fruit and putting it on a plate. "Will you come back alone?"

"No," he said. "My father will need to come with me to reestablish his presence. We'll have our army, too."

She wrung her fingers together. "So, it seems I have moved war from one place to another." She kept her eyes down as she set the fruit on the table beside him.

"We will not come in to destroy. It's more diplomacy than anything."

He reached out and ran the back of his knuckles down her arm. "I can't leave things as they are now, though."

She leaned on the table next to him. "What if this man does not wish to trade cashmere with you? You have no guarantees."

"Well, Eve," he said with a smile. He took a slice of the fig she had splayed out for him and bit into it. "I'm pretty good at charming people into working with me." He grinned now. "You should know."

"You think you charmed me?" She shifted to give him a look from the side.

"Of course I have," he said, chewing.

"Have you thought that perhaps I charmed you?"

He swallowed. "You didn't just charm me, Siren," he said. "You bewitched me. Thoroughly."

She grinned at him. Mischief in her eyes.

"But," he continued. "You *were* pretty lucky that you happened to run into me." He narrowed his eyes. "If you hadn't found me, that short merchant might still be chasing you around Merv."

She gave a playful nod. "It was indeed very lucky, looking to go to France, that I was purchased by a Frenchman."

"Yes," he said, nodding.

"The ancestors must have favored me," she teased.

"Yes," he agreed, a new suspicion changing the tone of his voice.

"How incredibly fortuitous," she said. She shrugged and stood to leave.

He reached out and grabbed her arm, dragging her back to him. "What are you telling me?"

"Michel." She looked at him daftly. "You know me to be quite shrewd, do you not?"

"Yes," he said. He felt like he was trying to solve a puzzle that was missing pieces.

"It was all my doing," she said. "All of it. Meeting in Merv, Armin trying to sell me," she lowered her voice, "falling into your arms." She drew a finger down along his collar, down his chest. "You must have been quite desperate for a woman's attention. You did not hesitate to buy me. As fast as a prized hog at market."

He stared at her, incredulous, still gripping her arm. "But how," he stuttered. "But...how?"

"I started in Carth. I listened for talk of French travelers. I learned who you were, your route. Despite your cockiness, people do actually know you in this region." She shrugged. "It's easy to get information when you speak as many languages as I do." She fluttered her eyelashes at him, a feigned innocence. "Then it was just a matter of tricking the little pig man into thinking he should sell me at the brothel where I knew your crew would end up." She bit her lip and looked at him slyly, seeming to enjoy finally telling him her scheme. "Getting the timing right was tricky. I really had to confuse that silly merchant to get us there at the right moment. But I did it." Then she moved forward to whisper in his ear. "There you were, standing outside. Utterly bewildered. Like a camel seeing thorns."

Michel stared at her, his mouth hanging open. "But..." he said and trailed off.

"It's true." She shrugged. "You don't have to believe me if it hurts your ego."

He blinked. "You planned our meeting?"

"Darling," she said. She reached out to take a piece of the fruit and place it in his open mouth. "You had no chance once I decided you would be the one to take me to France." She smoothed her finger over his bottom lip, grinning as she did.

He stared at her with the fig in his mouth. "You," he said. "You," he repeated as he swallowed. He wasn't used to being so outsmarted. She really had been using him from the beginning. It made him mad, at himself, that he had been so blinded. Mad at her for being more quick-witted than him.

It also turned him the fuck on.

He grabbed her under her rump, and she fell over his shoulders with a shriek. He stomped over to the bed and dropped her on it. He had no time, he knew, to properly dash all her plans, to turn her inside out and teach her a few things, things men with experience could teach women who thought they knew everything. The others would return, Terence would return. But Michel couldn't help himself in that moment, and provoking her was all he could think about.

As soon as her body hit the cushion of her bed, he was on top of her, nudging between her legs as he pulled her skirts up to her waist. She seemed startled by his attack, but was already panting and grabbing at his shoulders, pulling him to her. He leaned in to kiss her, a furious and greedy kiss as his hand struggled with her clothing. He was aching himself, inside his pants, but, for the moment, he was in control enough to stay in control of her.

He settled his weight so he could get his hand into her bloomers, and when he managed to find his way in, Eve arched up with a groan. Her soft skin went slick immediately at his touch, soaking his fingers. He loved that he had this effect on her, any effect on her. *This woman.* He kissed her mouth again as he canvased her delicate skin, teasing her, opening her up, calculating the best ways to use his calloused fingers to make her shudder.

Eve's head went back, and she groaned again. Michel pressed at the most sensitive spot and watched a tremor pass through her, ending on a moan from her lips. He smiled watching her, rubbing her firmly now, aware that his time was limited, wanting to make her say his name again before they would be interrupted. Wanting Eve to know that he had plans himself, ones that she couldn't predict. Or escape.

He changed his angle, feeling toward her opening. He sank his middle finger into her, followed by another. He knew this would be a new sensation for her, but he also wanted to shock and scandalize her. She gasped, and her eyes opened wide, finding his. She looked angry and wild at the same time, lustful and irritated. But he pressed in deep, and her body moved like he hoped she would move one day when they would be fully connected.

This was just a taste.

"You said you liked my hands. Was this part of your plan, Siren?" he asked against her ear.

Eve groaned. "Never," she sputtered, "I never knew..."

"Should I stop?" he teased, lessening the pressure of his hand.

"No!" she shrieked, grabbing onto him, her nails cutting through his shirt and into his shoulders.

He grinned as he kissed a trail to her neck, not wanting to muffle the sounds she was making. He curled his fingers on the inside and pressed his thumb on the outside of her, and she lost her words, except for his name, which she gasped over and over. He worked his hand, feeling the muscles burn in his arm in the most delightful way. A growl grew low in his chest. He leaned into her, over her, catching her panting moans on his lips, working his hand in the absolute best way that he could. And then she broke apart.

Her breath came out, and he felt her contract, her body lifting off the bed and crashing into his. He grabbed her mouth again with his, but her body was too uncoordinated to kiss him back, so he just held her and watched her while he let her ride out the last waves of release on his hand, the bed beneath them flooded.

In the next moment, her eyes snapped open. She glared at him, still letting her nails prick his skin.

"Sorry," he crooned, teasing. "You should know, I have some plans too."

She laughed. He grinned. Then they were kissing again, her body still soft and shuddering beneath him. His hand brushed over the smooth skin on her stomach now, still caressing, still intimate. He never wanted to leave this bed or her arms or the softness and wonder between them. Soon, though, too soon, he heard the sounds of the men returning, and he knew it would have to end for now.

"For now," he said, the thought on his lips. "That's all." He kissed her nose and then her forehead. "For now."

He rose off the bed and adjusted his clothing and his body. Then he took her hand to pull her up, and his heart felt full as he did.

No, this had not been part of her plan, Eve thought. But what a wonderful surprise the things he did to her had been.

She let him pull her up to sitting, her body still aching from the way he had just touched her. She tucked her knees under herself and watched him as he fixed his own clothing, a grin on his face.

That smirk, she thought, again feeling the desire to smack him, to kiss him, do something. He deserved to smirk, though. He had put her in her place. Though she had enjoyed being the one who had smirked at him minutes ago when she confessed how easy it had been to draw him in.

Everything she had told him before he threw her on her back had been true.

After she had run away, she had traveled west. The little sack of supplies the girl had given her contained all the things Eve had on her when she'd been kidnapped, including the jade necklace she'd worn. Seeing the necklace had surprised her at first, but the girl's intentions had nothing to do with money. Eve had sold what she could, discarded her tribal clothing for a simple dress, and traveled between towns and camps quickly. She took little time to rest and booked passages where she could, knowing that she had to put distance between herself and the tribe of her dead husband.

She knew the nomadic lifestyle. She was built to travel long distances, ride horses, and live under the sky. She could forage, cook, stay clean and healthy, and charm or outwit anyone who came her way. Yes, there were dangerous men, but Eve could navigate that problem. She knew men. She knew how to play with their egos, ingratiate herself, stir protective instincts, and pit them against each other if it came to her own safety.

It had taken a week to reach Carth, a major city on the trade routes. There, she went unnoticed and could interact with people who were not of the tribes. She had spent most of her time in the tavern waiting to hear gossip of travelers. It wasn't long before she had heard open speak of the Frenchman who came through the region every few years. The one who brought profit and gifts. The man was well-liked, well-respected. Eve had decided to find him.

She learned his expected route. All she had to do was find someone to get her there...and that's when she saw the fat little merchant wander into the tavern.

A fake twisted ankle on his route later, and the merchant was at her side, helping her to stand.

"I am lucky you have stumbled upon me," Eve had said to the man in the dialect she'd heard him using. "I am on my own, and no one knows I have run away." She gripped her ankle and looked up at him mournfully. "I do not speak the educated languages here, and most people will not help me. I'm lucky to find someone who understands me," she had said, surveying his expression as she did. "I may have never been found."

"Yes, sit down here on my cart," he said, watching her curiously.

"You hear such terrible stories of girls who are alone," she said as she let the man help her hobble to his little cart stuffed with wares. "I hear the brothel in Merv will buy a girl right from the back of a cart! Like pottery! Can you believe it?"

"They will buy girls at the brothel?" His bushy eyebrows went up.

"Oh, yes," Eve had confirmed. "For quite a bit of money, too."

And that was really all she needed to say.

Now she was here, in the yurt with Michel, the man who had been her target, her passage to France, and her freedom from crimes left behind. She had planned it all, yes. She had gotten lucky, too, just like Michel had said. More than lucky, really, because not only had she found the man she was looking for, she had found a man who was good. She sat on the bed, her knees tucked beneath her. She watched him swagger around the yurt, casting grins her way, still proud of himself.

He had been right. She felt the most marvelous sensation, like all her seams were falling apart and then weaving back together. Now with Michel as part of the pattern.

No, she had not planned for this. Never in her life.

Eve had fallen in love.

Chapter Twenty-Six

Ganbold paced at his camp outside Samarkand. The boy had said he would come as soon as he could get away. Ganbold had waited two days for contact with the boy. He started to think the boy had been lying to him. Ganbold knew he was with the Frenchman inside the city. He started thinking he should go into the city and just kill the Frenchman *and* the boy there.

Yet, the ancestors had told him to wait. He was still there pacing when he saw the boy come into view.

"Hallo," the boy greeted.

Ganbold snapped out and punched him between the eyes.

"What was that for?" the boy asked, grabbing his face and stumbling back.

"I wait too long."

"I couldn't just walk out of camp," Terence yelled. "He's making me sleep in his yurt and everything." He sniffed and wiped a streak of blood across his cheek. "I hate that guy."

Ganbold laughed. It made him like the boy a little, even though he was French. "What is their plan?"

"They leave for Kashgar in the morning. They are taking the route through the southern pass." The boy winced and stepped back. "He's hired twenty guards."

"Twenty," Ganbold grunted.

"You aren't angry?"

"You get the woman and man alone. Lead them to me." He glared at the boy. "Twenty guards are your problem, not mine."

The boy shuffled. "And of me? You'll really let me take the coin?"

"I have no use for his riches. When I kill the Frenchman, you take what you want and return to your country. Tell them of the warrior who killed him to take a Mongolian woman back to her tribe." He glared. "But if you take a wrong step and defy me..." He held up both his fists, letting the fear fill up the boy's face. "You understand the pain I will cause you."

The boy stepped back, eyes wide. He swallowed and nodded.

"I stay southeast of the party at all times," Ganbold said. "Any chance you get, lead them to me." Then he glared at the boy. "Don't make me wait." He tilted his head. "Go."

The boy scampered off.

Ganbold felt happy in his arms and legs. He would have the woman soon.

Ganbold. Warrior. Hunter.

Michel still grinned when he exited the yurt a short while later. That woman was ruining him in the best way possible. All his thoughts hovered on her, her body, her lips. He was proud of himself for not letting it get in the way of his business. Michel was handling everything well, something else to feel smug about.

He adjusted the felt at the door of the yurt, the good feelings stirring inside him.

The men were mostly back, tending their own spaces. Michel nodded and acknowledged them as they came near. They would be departing for Kashgar in the morning, taking a route that would allow them to sleep in or near towns so they would not be exposed in the night.

Then something struck Michel, an arrow to his thoughts. He scanned the men, not finding who he was looking for.

Where was Terence?

Michel stomped to the center of camp. "Iman," he called. The man turned to Michel. "Terence?" Michel asked, hands out with the question.

Iman swung his head around. "Um," he said.

The others began looking as well.

Aben, a newer addition to the group, spoke up, "He was at the baths." He looked around. "Wasn't he?"

There was a moment of searching to see if he'd been asleep in a tent or was rifling through someone's things. It wasn't long, however, before Michel spotted him, across the way, shuffling back to the camp.

Michel stomped over to the boy and saw immediately that something had happened. Michel grabbed his chin to angle the boy's face up to him. He saw bruises edging around his eye, along his cheekbone, on top of the old ones, and crusted blood in his nose. "What happened?" Michel demanded.

"I fell," Terence retorted, his arms hanging limply at his sides.

Michel turned the boy's head to examine the other side. "You fell?"

"I slipped and knocked my head at the baths."

Michel just grunted at him. Now what with this kid, he thought. "Be more careful," Michel insisted, releasing his chin. Terence jerked back with a glare.

Eve had come out then and approached them. She too took Terence's chin, but with a gentler hand. "Come with me, Terence," she said. "We'll put some salve on the scrapes."

Terence trudged away behind her, and Michel saw the heaviness in the boy. He didn't know what Terence was up to, or who had given him the punch to the head that Terence claimed to be from a fall. Michel just hoped to get him back to the safety of his family without further incident.

Still, he knew that boy was only going to cause them trouble.

The next day, they were on the road again. It was midday, and they were coming up on a road cut alongside a hill that sloped down into a shallow ravine blanketed by thorny bushes.

"Eve," Terence called to her from the horse. "Come with me to see those rocks." He pointed up ahead of their path.

"Terence, if we leave the convoy now, Michel will have a heart attack," she laughed. "Besides, no horse would go through that thistle."

Terence groaned loudly and trotted up ahead.

Michel slowed his horse to wait for her as Terence rushed past. "Looks like I'm not the only one who makes him mad."

"He is my little friend," she said, still amused.

"It's kind of you to care for him." Michel raised his eyebrows. "He does not like me."

"You're mean to him," she said. "But he deserves it. Iman's right. He *is* a little shit."

Terence had kept close to her since he had rejoined their party. She cared for him as a sister would. She had so many older brothers that it was enjoyable to feel the tug of attention from a younger brother for once. It was obvious Terence was lonely and needed someone to show him some warmth.

Truly, her mind and heart had only one focus at the moment. Now that she realized the feelings she had for Michel, she didn't know what it meant for her future. She had wanted to go to France and perhaps find work as a nanny or a tutor, but her heart had tangled itself around Michel in a knot she couldn't unravel. What was she to do? Confess her feelings like a heartsick girl looking for a husband, hoping he felt the same? He had promised to keep her safe, but then what?

She watched him, tall and proud in his saddle, feeling the heat in her belly just from being near, wanting his hands on her once more. She had never been so vulnerable with a man. She had told Michel her secrets. It was a great sensation of relief to have an ally after months of being on her own. The only thing she kept to herself was the specifics of her family. Michel didn't need the added stress of knowing he was transporting the Khan's daughter.

They rode further down a narrow passage among high boulders and rock. Up ahead, a fallen tree trunk blocked the road. Terence was urging his horse down the slope, but the horse whinnied and refused.

"What is he doing?" Michel grumbled. Then, louder, he called out, "Terence! Wait there."

"We should go around," Terence called back. "You, me, and Eve. We can check for a better route." Then he jerked the reins of the horse, trying to control it.

"He's going to fall," Michel insisted, tensing. "Terence, stop!"

Just then, Terence yanked on the reins again. This time, the horse went up on its back legs, knocking Terence off, right into the bushes and down the slope.

Eve gasped, and Michel swore. "Christ," Michel muttered as he sped up to get to the boy.

Eve caught up seconds later with the others coming up behind. Michel dismounted and stomped into the bushes. He reached in and pulled out a lump of Terence.

"Terence, you silly boy, what are you thinking?" Eve asked as she dismounted. She plucked thistles off his jacket

Terence coughed and groaned. "I thought we could find an easier route." He grimaced as Eve plucked stickers from his hair. "That log is too heavy. We'll never move it."

Michel brushed his pants off and walked over to the log. With a big breath, he hefted it up and moved it enough to allow the passage of the horses. "Terence," he said, shaking his head at the boy. "You make me truly hope that when I have children one day, they will all be girls."

Chapter Twenty-Seven

After a few tense nights of travel in which Michel hardly slept in his vigilance to keep watch, they finally arrived in Kashgar late in the afternoon, relieved to have made it with no trouble. Kashgar was an ancient city, marked by the architecture of the cultures that had inhabited it at different times. The Chinese, the Turks, and the Mongols all left their stamp, creating a diverse landscape of buildings in a city built around protecting itself from outsiders.

Michel's contact here, Renault, was a man who had fought with his father in France many years ago. He had since married, had a family, and built a profitable business here in Kashgar. Renault would also be hosting the meeting with the cashmere dealer. Just as they settled the camp, Renault arrived.

"Good friend," Michel called out from the entrance to his yurt. "You find us worse for wear."

Renault approached. He was a lean man with a regal look, chestnut hair, and a full, neat mustache. "It is good to see you, Michel." He shook Michel's hand. "You are safe in our walls."

"I have never been happier to arrive here unharmed," Michel said with a laugh. Eve approached. Michel put his hand on the small of her back. "This is Eve. She is traveling with me back to Chevalerie."

Renault nodded and took her hand in his. "My lady, I see that Michel has found himself a lovely companion for this trip."

"I certainly have made it more interesting for him," she said, smiling.

Just then, a cat yowled and ran through their feet. Seconds later, Terence came tearing through. He knocked into Michel, causing Michel to step back. Michel swiped out to grab him, but the boy was too fast.

"Terence!" Eve shouted. "Leave the cat be!" She turned to the men. "Excuse me," she said, going after him.

"You have your hands full," Renault chuckled.

"You have no idea." Michel grinned, dusting himself off.

"I have spoken with Malik, the cashmere dealer," Renault said, lowering his voice. "He is looking forward to meeting you. I am just waiting to hear when he will arrive."

"He is amenable to the deal?" Michel asked, pulling the rug flat at the entrance to the yurt.

"You know I sponsor anything you and your father wish." He gave Michel a nod of approval. "Malik is very guarded, but I believe with the support of Johann and myself, he will be agreeable, yes."

Michel felt tension dissipate across his shoulders, a storm of relief washing off him. "I truly hope so," he said. "I have always loved the adventure of these travels, but to be honest, old friend, I am more than eager to return home."

"The cashmere market is a viable investment and will benefit us all. Greatly." He glanced toward Eve. "I see you have taken on this very beautiful ward. May I speak frankly?"

Michel felt a prickling sensation of anger. Still, he nodded for Renault to continue.

"I would hate to see something happen to you, Michel. Perhaps you've taken on some unnecessary complications?" He raised his eyebrows as his eyes followed Eve while she chased Terence around the camp. "I wouldn't want any extra considerations to disrupt this deal." He folded his arms. "We stand to lose too much."

Michel took a breath and chose his words carefully. "Renault, let me worry about her. Them both." He ground his jaw to keep from telling Renault to mind his damn business. "You just get the dealer here, and I will do the rest."

"Fair enough," Renault conceded. "Should we go in? We can talk specifics."

Michel nodded, though now he was irritated. "Yes." He held the flap open. Renault entered. Michel looked back at Eve, seeing her hair catching the last light of the day. She had wrangled Terence, and they were sitting at the fire now, preparing dinner. Michel could no longer imagine this journey without her, couldn't leave her. He was...*mon dieu*, what was he? He shook his head clear before entering the yurt. All he knew was that he wouldn't be able to let her go.

Eve placed the heavy pan in the fire. Then she placed an onion on a plank and put it in Terence's lap. She handed him her knife. "Do you know how to cut that?" she asked.

"I think so," he said. "I used to help my mom cut the vegetables."

Eve smiled. "Let me know if you need help." She tossed a piece of suet into the pan and used a wooden spoon to move it around. After a moment, she spoke. "Do you miss your family?" she asked. "You are quite young to be traveling so far from home."

"I miss my mom," he said. "She died a few years ago. From a fever." He shrugged, his little chops striking a rhythm against the plank of wood.

"I'm very sorry to hear that." She glanced over, feeling sorrow for him.

"I don't miss my dad."

"No?"

"He yells at me. A lot. He used to be a merchant here, and he'd take me with him. He fell off his horse when he was drinking once and hurt his leg. Then my mom died, so he stayed home in France with my two little brothers and sent me back here to make us money."

"Ah," said Eve. "You are working for your family. There is honor in that."

"I don't know," Terence said, pushing his hair out of his face with the back of his hand. "He wants to buy our own piece of land so we don't have to be tenants. But he wastes most of the money. He gambles." He was silent for a moment, then continued. "I do it for my mom. And my brothers." He looked down, feathers ruffled. "I don't want to return home until I have enough to help them."

"I understand that," she said. "I, too, am on this journey for the people I love."

He looked up at her. "Really?" he cocked his head. "I thought because you were going to marry Michel or something."

She laughed softly. "No. That was not my plan."

"You needed money?" Terence asked.

She shook her head. "No, not money. I was like you, though. I didn't want to leave, but I had to."

Terence finished the onions. He handed the board to her. Eve took it and swiped the pieces into the pan. They popped and sizzled with the suet.

"I just want to get back to France." He sagged with the words. "I'll find work there."

"Let's hope for easy going. Once Michel finishes this deal, he will be ready to return. We are lucky that we have attached ourselves to a man who is able to get us there."

Terence looked at her with big eyes. Then he dropped his head in a soundless sob.

"I don't want to die, Eve," he said, putting his head down.

"You won't," she said. Eve reached forward and put her arm around him. She pulled him into a hug.

"I might die," he said. Then he glanced up at her. "You, too."

She rubbed circles into his back. "Terence, you can't think like that. Michel has promised you his protection. You will have it, just like me. You'll see your family again. And they will be so happy to see you."

Terence sniffled and took a breath. "I hope so," he said. He pulled back.

"To fight these feelings, you must be grateful for what you have. Focus on those you love. All your actions must be to protect those you care about. That is your duty."

He sniffed and nodded. She looked at him curiously, wondering about this boy, turning his phrases and tone in her head. Then she heard the noises of Michel and Renault exiting the yurt. They spoke a few more words and said their goodbyes. Eve caught Michel's eye, and he gave her a nod, which she knew to mean everything was going well. She felt light. Despite the despondent boy next to her, she hoped Michel's dealings and this journey would end soon, and then they could leave this place. She would be happy to be moving further away from the source of trouble rather than further into its nest.

A few hours later, Michel lay on his back on a mat just at the edge of their camp. He watched the stars with his belly full of another delicious meal from Eve. He felt content.

He caught her scent before he saw her, and warmth went through him.

She sat next to him. "Are you relaxing?" she asked, teasing.

Michel laughed. "Sometimes I do it," he said. "Watch the stars with me. It's peaceful."

"Do you feel better now?" She reclined beside him, her head near his.

"We'll be headed to France soon." He paused. "What do you hope to happen when you are there?"

"I thought to try to find work," she said. "Things have changed."

"What has changed?" he asked, feeling his heart beat in his chest, in his ears.

She didn't respond right away, but he felt her body shift. "Have you had many women, Michel?"

"Had?" he asked, amused. "You mean…"

"You know what I mean," she tutted. "Don't make me say it."

"I have no idea what you mean." He grinned. "I'd really like to hear you say it."

She let out a sound of exasperation. Then she turned on her side to face him. He did the same.

"You are very handsome," she said. "I thought so the first second I saw you."

"I thought you disliked me," he teased, savoring the closeness.

"I did, but I also thought you were handsome." She blinked as she searched his face. "I felt things in my body that I had never felt before I saw you. I imagine other women would too." She reached out to brush a finger on his lips. "How many women have you been with?"

"Why do you want to know that?" He had been no angel in the past, but he hadn't caused any scandals. He leaned a little closer.

"In my tribe, it is rare to be with anyone before you are married." She looked up at him. "The men, too."

"Would that bother you?" He hovered closer to her. "If I had been with someone already?"

"I don't know," she said. "How many?"

He gave her a half smile as he looked from her eyes to her lips and back to her eyes. "More than a few."

She moved closer, her knees touching his. "Did you love any of them?"

"No. Not one," he murmured. He didn't really know what she wanted from this conversation, but he was happy to keep it going. "What do you think about that?"

"I don't know," she said. She put her hand to his chest, working her fingers into the opening of his shirt. "Thinking of you with another woman...it makes me jealous. In a way, it makes me want you even more."

Michel let out a groan. "Eve," he said. They faced each other, the air warm between them. "I've never wanted to be with anyone the way I want to be with you." He knew she could take his meaning in a few different ways, but he was searching her, testing.

She blinked at him. "I've never wanted anyone else to have me."

He found himself pushing her back so he could hover above her. He didn't know if she meant for him to have her love or her body or both like he wanted, but at this point, he would take anything she offered. He searched her face, her mottled eyes. "Give me a little more time. A few more days. Once I finish this deal, get us further away, make sure we are safe, then I promise..." He pressed his forehead to hers. "I promise, I will devote myself to you."

"Yes, Michel," she whispered. "That is what I want."

He fought his body, which wanted to sink down and kiss her. He would have her here in the open, he didn't care, but it wouldn't be fair to her, for anything to be rushed. He pulled back, still looking at her. He held out his hand and helped her sit up. They watched each other until Eve broke the silence.

"I'm going to go to sleep now, Michel." She rolled her lips and wet them. "I just want you to know...I'll be dreaming you are there beside me."

Michel smiled. "If I can sleep through Terence's snoring, I will be dreaming of you, too."

Eve laughed and gave him a sudden kiss before pulling away. Michel watched her enter the yurt. He couldn't believe everything had worked out. Just a few more days. That's all he needed.

Chapter Twenty-Eight

The next morning, when Michel woke up on his bedroll in the yurt, he still had a smile on his face. He had dedicated his entire life to his position, his duty, his kingdom. He'd plan to marry only when it befitted his station. Now, though, he couldn't imagine being with anyone other than Eve. He didn't care that she wasn't titled or bringing any other connections. She was smart and beautiful, commanding and confident, everything he could want.

He couldn't wait to get her home.

A short while later, he was with her at the fire. They were teasing each other as they prepared breakfast. She tossed a persimmon at him. He snatched it from the air and grinned at her, just as he saw Renault coming into camp.

"It's Renault," he said, standing up, composing himself. Eve did as well, turning to watch the man approach.

Renault looked odd. Rushed. Michel folded his arms, already preparing for whatever could have gone wrong.

"What's the news?" Michel said as Renault approached.

"Michel," he greeted. "Mademoiselle." He nodded. "I received post late last night." He smoothed his hands over his legs. "I'm very sorry, Michel. Malik has declined to do business with you."

"But he was amenable just yesterday," Michel argued, his fists clenching in frustration. "What happened? Are you sure he knows who I am? Who my father is?"

"He does not wish to get involved with the French for the moment. He is particular with whom he trades." He paused, looking between Michel and Eve. "He does not want any violence."

"I don't bring violence." Michel sputtered. "This problem with the attacks is temporary. Once I get home, I will return with reinforcements and be able to clean up the routes once more."

"He doesn't care." Renault hedged, his mustache bristling around the words. "He is nervous and in no hurry to make any new deals."

"He just needs to meet me," Michel insisted. "To see that it is safe to work with me."

"Michel, you misunderstand—"

"We'll stay here, give him a few days to think about it." He was pacing now, heavy strides, nervous energy compelling him to move.

Renault shook his head, his voice faltering, his face growing red. "It's not a matter of a few days. He doesn't want to anger the tribes." He held his hands out. "Perhaps try again the next time you are here." He gave a quick glance at Eve. "When you have fewer considerations."

Michel took a step forward into Renault's space, pushing him back. "What did you say?" he snapped.

Renault stood up straighter, trying to come closer to Michel's height, even as the older man took another step back. "This could have been our legacy." He pointed a finger. "You've turned the tribes against us." His voice turning sour, his face bitter. "Everyone knows she's the reason those men were killed."

"You dirty—" Michel pushed his sleeves up, lunging toward the man. He was going to knock his teeth out.

"Michel. *Michel!*" Eve said, and she was beside him, hand in front of him. "Don't do more damage."

Michel took a quick breath through his nose, his jaw clenched. "You'd better get out of my sight, Renault."

"There's one other thing," Renault said, backing up, quieter but still cold, his eyes darting. "Before I go. They, uh, want you out by nightfall, the town officials."

"What?" Michel thundered. "After everything I've done to bring business to Kashgar? I will pull out every market this town has."

"They've already halted all commerce," he said. "They don't want to work with you. They will only continue if your father comes to reestablish himself." He held out his hands in apology. "I'm sorry, Michel. It's done."

Michel froze, hearing Renault's words. He couldn't *lose* Kashgar. That would decimate the entire connection. "I'm going to meet with Malik myself," he announced without another thought. "We're going right now." He started grabbing at supplies. "I'll convince him."

"You can't—" Renault began.

"Give me a day. You owe me that."

Renault held out his hands to the camp. "Who's going, Michel?"

Michel looked up to see the glances between the men, and he understood the voices of their thoughts. They would not accompany Michel, not many of them at least. This had become dangerous and complicated work, and many of them were just tradesmen. There was no benefit in helping Michel to protect Eve and secure a line of cashmere.

"Renault, get me ten guards," Michel demanded, turning to his hasty preparation. "And whoever else is brave enough to join us. We'll be up to see Malik and back by nightfall."

"I think you're on a fool's errand," Renault sighed. "But alright. I'll get you the guards."

"We'll be ready to leave in an hour." He nodded to Eve. "Let's go."

Chapter Twenty-Nine

Ganbold. Warrior. Hunter.

He watched as the boy tore through the trees. Ganbold stood up with excited anticipation.

"They're moving," the boy gasped. "Northeast. To a trapper's cottage. We'll be very few."

"I know the cottage," he affirmed, giving one sharp nod. "I passed the land."

"There is a stream," the boy rasped, still catching his breath. "I can get her to follow me. Michel will follow her."

"*Chi bol baatar,*" Ganbold acknowledged. "You are a warrior."

The boy stared and then gave a satisfied smile.

"Go, now," Ganbold ordered.

The boy nodded, scampering off.

Ganbold stood, feet spread, hands fisted at his hips. He heard the voices of the ancestors singing for him. He thought of returning to his tribe with the shame of the woman and the head of the Frenchman. Perhaps he would make her carry it.

And then, Ganbold would be given his bride. He would hold her once more.

"I will be ready," Ganbold said to himself as he watched the horizon.

A few hours later, they traveled the road to Malik's home. Eve had learned that Malik was tribal, so she convinced Michel to let her come. She could help him make the deal, she was sure of it. The company had been reduced to the bare minimum. Michel, Eve, the few guards Michel had been able to gather, and Terence, who insisted he not be left back with the others. Renault had given Michel specific instructions on where to find the hermit. They traveled through a sparse sweetgum tree forest to reach the cottage. The tall sweetgums, mixed with flowering pistachio trees and wineberry bushes, created a shady green trail, sweet with the scent of flower buds.

Eve could see that Michel moved on pure anger and desperation at this point, insulted and humbled. All his plans had collapsed. She wished she could ease him, that she could somehow use her influence as the Khan's daughter to ensure Michel's success, but out here, this far from her home, she was not sure if she had value in that way. Still, she had her own charisma, and Michel's now too. Together, how could Malik deny the connection?

They were coming up to a slope which dipped down into a stream that thrashed through the rocks. Terence had been whining that he needed to relieve himself for some time. Finally, Michel threw his hands up.

He pulled the reins on his horse. "Take your rest," he called to the party. "Five minutes!"

Michel came over and helped Eve down off her horse, while Terence scampered down to the stream. "I'll fill the water sacks," she said, pulling them from the saddlebags.

She stepped carefully down the slope to reach the stream. Terence had already gone up aways. "Terence," she called. "Finish up, then stay where I can see you."

She sank the containers into the cold water. She looked back over her shoulder to see the boy wandering down the stream.

On the trail above her, Michel spoke with one of the guards as he watched her, instructing the man to go up ahead to check for problems.

Down the way, Terence was still slipping along with the stream. Eve saw his back as he wove into the trees, disappearing. "Terence!" she called again, annoyed that he was dawdling.

"I'm just here!" he called.

"Terence, come back, I wish to return." She'd lost her visual of him. She listened for the rustling of his feet in the brush or his call to her, but she heard nothing. She set the water sack aside and took a few steps downstream. "Terence?" she called again. She felt needles of worry.

"Eve!" came her name, this time with urgency.

She called out to the boy again. She looked up over the hill to see if Michel was coming yet. She was arrested in what to do: go after Terence or stay and wait for Michel. Then she heard Terence call her name again, his voice desperate and afraid.

He had fallen, she thought. She would need to get to him. Her body moved to run to him, but she turned to call to Michel. She feared being far from him, despite the worry she felt for Terence. That silly boy was a constant danger to himself.

"Michel!" she called again, hoping her voice carried. She forced herself to wait until she saw Michel come over the crest of the slope. "Terence is calling," she yelled back. "I believe he has fallen." She ran down the path, toward Terence's cries.

Michel shouted behind her, but Eve was sure Terence was just over the next ledge. She had *just* had her eyes on him. She came upon the ridge and looked through the trees, but she did not see him.

She called his name again. She didn't go further now and instead waited for Michel to catch up to her. When he did, he grabbed her arm. "Eve, we can't be out here, this far from the guards."

"Yes, I know," she said. "Terence was just here." She trailed off. "He could be hurt." Then she heard Terence's voice call her name again. She jumped to run, but Michel grabbed her arm and pulled her back.

"Stop," he said. He drew his sword and edged forward. "What was he doing?"

"I don't know," she replied, feeling frantic, prickles of fear running down her back. Fear for Terence, fear for the sudden oddity to the situation. "He was at the stream, and then he was gone."

"Terence," Michel called out. "Come out right now." When there was no response, he turned to Eve and said with even words, "We are going to go back to rejoin the men. We cannot be out here chasing him through the forest."

"You're right," she agreed. She didn't want to leave Terence, but something was off.

"I'll come back with a few of the guards," Michel replied.

Eve nodded and went to turn, but then she saw something that made her freeze in her place. Just around the slope of the earth, past a few tall sweetgums, she saw Terence.

Standing next to Ganbold.

The sight ignited the prickles down her neck, making them burn with fire. At first, she thought that Terence had been captured. Then she saw the boy look down as he shuffled his feet. She understood. Terence had decided to place his loyalty with the wrong man.

"Terence," Michel said. "Get over here."

Terence shook his head.

Michel's sword was out and at the ready. His stance changed. She knew he would fight, despite this effectively ending any chance left he had with Malik and the tribes.

"Eve, confirm for me," Michel said to her. His voice was steady. "Is Terence an ally?"

"No, it appears he is not." She shook her head. Terence's betrayal gripped her, though somehow, she still felt for the boy.

Panic gripped her. This fight would be too much. Darkness came into her from the edges of her feelings. She didn't want this to happen. She wanted Michel to make his deal and for them to return together to France. They had been so close.

Michel made to move forward. Eve reached out and touched his arm.

"Michel," she said. She wanted to tell him not to fight, to run. To get away, leave her to her fate because she understood now that she couldn't escape it. But all she was able to sputter out was, "Don't...don't let him get his hands on you."

"I won't, Eve," he said, solemnly.

Chapter Thirty

Michel stepped out to engage Ganbold. He kept his eyes on both the monster Ganbold and the chaotic form of Terence, mad at himself for taking Terence on, for letting this boy infiltrate his plans. Up ahead, Ganbold swung his blade menacingly, grinning his red gummed smile.

This would destroy the relationships with the tribe. Done. No more negotiating. Michel knew in no uncertain terms that to kill a man from the tribes would be waging war. He couldn't avoid the fight any longer. Not with Eve under his protection.

They were too far to get back to the guards for help in time. The fight would be over before anyone could be alerted. Michel felt a focus come over him then. He felt it in his limbs, his hands. This would happen now. He would fight this man. He also knew that he would win.

Michel edged into the clearing, his eye flicking between Terence and Ganbold. He felt Eve's presence behind him. The two would have to come through Michel before they could get to her. He didn't know what they had planned or what Terence thought to do, so he waited, tensed, at the ready for one of them to make a move.

"C'mon, fucker," he spat.

Suddenly, Ganbold grunted something out. Terence darted to the side as

Ganbold came at Michel. Michel saw the glint of the knife in Terence's hand, just as Ganbold's heavy sword cut the air. Instead of engaging his blade, like Ganbold seemed to expect, Michel darted to the side and grabbed Terence by his shirt. With a swift motion, he launched the boy into Ganbold, causing Terence to roll to the ground and Ganbold to stumble over the boy's gangling limbs. Ganbold pushed the boy off. Michel understood their tactic then: Terence would try to secure Eve while Ganbold took on Michel.

Terence sprawled in a pile. While he worked to straighten himself out, Ganbold came at Michel, his thick blade slicing down at him. Michel took the blade against the edge of his sword and pushed Ganbold back, just in time to see Terence launch himself at Eve. Michel spun around, catching the boy in the stomach with the flat of the blade. The impact caused Terence to topple over with a winded release of breath. Michel repositioned himself again, between them and Eve.

"Frenchman," Ganbold taunted.

The giant swung his blade in a diagonal, first from his right, then from his left, a zip in the air. Michel leapt back, calculating an entry point. He made a precise jab with his sword. Ganbold went into a defensive stance, giving Michel an opening. Michel launched a furious attack, advancing again and again. *Clang, clang, clang.* Ganbold deflected only a few of Michel's attacks with his blade. The rest of the blows he absorbed into his leathers, with hardly a grimace in recognition.

They clashed, Michel darting, Ganbold swinging. Michel had a strategy and understood Ganbold as an opponent. Ganbold had no grace or great skill, just staggering strength. Michel outclassed him easily, but with Terence slinking about, Michel had to keep his attention split.

Then, Michel caught sight of Terence charging Eve. Before he could react, Terence had her around the waist, tackling her to the ground. The boy grunted as they went down. Michel turned to get to her just as Ganbold's blade came down on him. Michel caught the blade with his own, but instead of pushing back against the force, Michel released his weight, causing Ganbold to lose balance and trip to the ground.

It gave Michel a second. He darted back to pull a struggling Terence off Eve. Immediately, he saw red on her hands and her dress. "There's blood." He panicked. "There's blood."

"I got his arm," she said, revealing the dirtied knife in her hand. "I'm fine."

"*Michel*," she shrieked his name as a furious Ganbold rushed them, a snarling bear.

Ganbold swung his blade. Michel turned to take the heavy strike against his sword, the strength behind it causing him to buckle at the knee. Ganbold pushed and knocked him flat. Michel splayed across the ground but rolled, just missing a pommel hammer strike to his head.

He darted around, seeing Terence holding his bloodied arm. "Terence," he commanded. "Run back to the guards. Get help. Help *Eve*," he said, hoping to appeal to some sense of honor left in the boy. Ganbold swung his splitting blade again, stealing Michel's attention. Michel jumped back, thrusting his sword upward, making a point of contact on his flank, just above Ganbold's hip. With a sinking twist that took all his strength and nearly pulled Michel's arm out of its socket, Michel's blade snapped into Ganbold's skin.

Ganbold grimaced and came back with a growl, blood pouring down his leg. He threw his blade to the side and came at Michel like a boulder coming down a mountain. He got Michel around the waist and slammed him against a tree, hard enough to make the pointed leaves shudder. Michel lost his breath completely. The edges of his vision went black. Ganbold threw Michel to the ground.

Michel blinked, his thoughts shaken and foggy, his sword knocked from his hand, a sound ringing in his ears. He saw Eve at the edge of the clearing with her hands up to her mouth. She called his name. Then he saw Ganbold turn to look at Eve with that terrible smile on his face, with Terence orbiting him. Michel knew he could not protect her from either one of them if he were the one who ended up dead.

"Ganbold," Michel called, getting to his feet. He felt a heavy pull inside him—angst for Eve, remorse and betrayal at Terence, energy seeping from him. But he took strong, determined steps, anchoring himself. He and Ganbold squared off, Michel low to the ground, hands out, ready to grapple the beast into the dirt. He stepped to the side, rotating their positions, getting himself in front of Eve. Just then, before he could lunge at Ganbold, an arm came around his neck, and a knife was dragged down his side. Sharp, splitting pain. Blood coating his tunic.

"Die, just *die*," he heard Terence grind the warm, strangled words in his ear.

For a second, Michel thought Terence had gotten him, given Michel his death. Then Michel realized the cut was superficial. Terence's knife had hit Michel's rib, but the boy did not have the strength to break through Michel's bones. The boy ripped the blade back, tearing Michel's skin, delivering another shock of pain. Michel angled, trying to grab him. He didn't want to kill Terence, but how could he fight Ganbold with Terence clinging to his back? Ahead, Ganbold advanced. Michel arched painfully, trying to get the boy off him before Ganbold was on him again.

Then he heard a cry. A warm gush of blood soaked onto his back.

He turned to see Eve, wild and dangerous, her hand in Terence's hair and her blade buried in his neck. Michel stuttered at the sight, a convulsing Terence in Eve's arms. Terence's body being peeled off Michel.

"Michel," Eve commanded. "Ganbold is injured. Focus. Go."

All Michel could do was obey. He turned back to Ganbold, ready to finish this fight.

The brute came at Michel. This time, Michel ducked low and caught him around the shins. Michel picked him up and toppled the big man, his side screaming in pain as he did. Ganbold went face down into the dirt, and Michel was on him, his knee to the injury at Ganbold's hip. Michel yanked Ganbold's arm back using his own body as leverage, pressing until he heard the wet, splintering crack of bone. Ganbold bellowed into the woods.

Michel reached for his dagger as Ganbold lifted himself with his good arm and his own tremendous strength. He got his knees under his body and pushed up, knocking Michel back. Before Michel could right himself, Ganbold caught him around the waist, taking him to the ground. Ganbold got his good hand around Michel's neck, shoved him to the ground, and squeezed, his terrible smile dripping blood down his chin.

Michel's vision started to go, but he had his dagger tight in his hand. In a final calculation, he pushed Ganbold up just enough to get the blade between them. Then he pierced Ganbold just under the sternum—a deadly zone—in a deep, bloody, and soon-to-be-fatal wound.

Ganbold roared. His grip went around Michel's neck even tighter, and Michel thought it had been futile. Michel twisted the blade with his last burst of strength. Ganbold made a high-pitched animal sound before Michel finally felt the man's strength diminish.

Unlike Terence, Michel knew the strength required to kill a man.

Michel rolled with Ganbold until he was over the man, and angled his blade to Ganbold's heart. He pressed in, feeling first the release of the chest plate, then the snap of the skin, the crack of ribs, and finally the ease into the muscle. Blood spilled out of Ganbold's lips. Michel did not let up on the pressure even as Ganbold stopped thrashing under him.

Michel's mind was muddled. All he could think was that the man would rise. That is, until Eve was next to him. *It's okay now, Michel.* She seemed to say. *He's dead,* she crooned. *They both are.* She put her hands over his, still gripping the dagger. Slowly, Michel released his fingers, wet with blood. He stood up and took a step back, stumbled, and landed in the dirt on his ass. The storm of energy dissipated. New wounds identified themselves. His vision swam. His head went light. He stared at Ganbold's body, still afraid he would come after them. He saw Terence's body and thought it would rise. Michel ached in so many places, and somewhere far off, he knew his wounds needed attention. He couldn't move. His body wouldn't let him.

Then Eve was with him again. Her softness blew cool wind on the flames of his skin. She had her hands on him, checking him. He winced and pulled back, but she worked quickly, ripping strips of fabric from her skirt to tie off the worst wounds.

When he could focus on her face, he saw that she looked panicked still, even as she worked.

"Eve," he said, looking for words to console her. All that came out was, "Are they dead?"

She made an affirming sound and nodded.

"Terence?"

"I had no idea," she shook her head. "I never thought…"

"I didn't pay close enough attention," Michel said.

"Shhh," she soothed. She garnered up a smile and touched his cheek.

"You killed him," he said stupidly. "He almost got me."

"Michel," she said. Her face showed emotion, though her voice stayed steady. "You are mine to protect, just as I am yours."

Ganbold lay there looking up at the sky through the canopy of trees. He didn't know where his mind hovered, but he couldn't move. Pain beat a distant throb in his body. He heard voices: one of the woman, another of the Frenchman. He heard the wind. Everything felt far away. His mind and body were no longer working together. He was a warrior. There was no shame in being beaten by another warrior. He had done all he could to win his way back into his tribe by finding the woman and bringing her home. He had failed at that. Now he felt his life seeping into the dirt beneath him.

He thought of the shepherd's daughter. He felt her call, her voice, one of a thousand who called to him, in a thousand different languages. There was anger in her voice, as with many other voices, but as he began to understand better, the anger resolved, and the tones all began to match. He felt something aligning within him, in a way that promised soon there would be sense to it all.

He saw the light-haired woman come before him. She thought he was dead already, but Ganbold knew he was not yet. Or maybe he already passed to the other realm, and he saw her with something other than eyes. The woman reached forward to put her hand on his chest. She whispered the prayer of the ancestors over him, to hasten his return to them.

He wished for her to know that he thanked her for the kindness.

Then there was a glow that welcomed him.

Ganbold. Warrior. Hunter.

Chapter Thirty-One

Eve took it slow going back. Michel was able-bodied enough to walk, though he was bleeding and in pain. When they finally came upon the resting guards, she called out. Seeing her struggling with Michel, they rushed to help.

Michel was dazed from receiving a few good strikes to the head. He bled from his flank where Terence had gotten him. The men got him on his horse, and Eve directed them back to Kashgar. Michel grimaced as they rode, arm tucked into his side, struggling to stay conscious.

They arrived in Kashgar within the hour. Many of the others remained, having not yet departed in their own direction. Eve gave quick explanations. They helped get him off the horse, into the yurt, and onto the bed. The men who had been closest to them hovered about. She felt their guilt at not having been there, but she had no time to soothe anyone else. Eve gave them tasks. She needed water, towels, herbs, and other supplies. She needed to alert Renault. Once they all knew what their duties were, she shooed everyone out.

Michel sat on the bed with his legs bent and his arms resting on his knees. He watched her with a faraway look on his face, blood still seeping through his shirt. She turned to her box of medicines and chose the tea leaves. A mixture to ease the pain and help him rest. She put the kettle on the fire.

"Eve," he muttered, his words insistent yet disconnected. "Are you safe now?"

"Yes, I am," she said. "I am safe."

"Terence?"

"The boy's loyalty was misplaced." She poured hot water over the tea leaves. "He chose the wrong master."

"You killed him," Michel said, voice detached. "You are a warrior."

Eve came to him then and touched his cheek. She leaned in and touched her lips to his. "Hush," she said before going back to the steeping concoction.

One by one, the men returned with the things she had requested. She laid out her supplies, towels, and bandages. She kneeled before Michel as he continued to watch her with glazed eyes. "Eve," he said, bringing his hands up to touch her.

She smiled, but it lacked humor. "No," she said softly. "Now we take care of you."

She undid his breastplate. When she inspected it, she saw the deep cuts that had been left in it, and she shivered thinking about the fight. She had watched her brothers spar. She had heard stories from wars. She had never seen a fight to the death like that before. It was...terrible, and she wished none of it had happened. She wished, too, that she had not had to take the life of Terence. The sadness of his death rested in her. She felt no guilt, however. If it had to be Terence or Michel, *well*, Michel had earned her loyalty long ago. She eased his tattered, bloody shirt open and over his shoulders. He grimaced.

She cataloged the wounds across his chest. She had a needling desire to press against him, to feel his muscles and strength against her cheek, her body. She wanted to feel his protection and cry out her own heartache. She couldn't. It was her turn to take care of him. The blood ran freely from his side, onto his pants, onto the bed. She pressed a towel against it.

She left him for the stove to prepare a salve and pour the tea. She took the cup to Michel.

"It smells awful," he rasped.

"Drink it," she said. "It will make what comes next easier."

Michel looked at her warily and gulped down the tea.

"Now lie on your back."

He grumbled and obeyed, running his hand through his hair. He closed his eyes and let her continue her ministrations.

She cleaned the wound on his side. The flesh had been peeled from the bone of his rib. She pressed the skin down and laid out the rest of her tools. Then she drew a hand down his torso, looking him over as his muscles relaxed. The tea was doing its job.

Iman entered, with a few others behind him. "It's ready," he said. She felt the heat from the iron he held.

Michel's eyes opened, and he jerked up. "Are you going to—" he asked, looking at her wildly. "Is that for—" he couldn't get a full question out.

"Open your mouth," she said. She rolled a dry towel to place in his mouth.

Michel looked at her, wide-eyed. "Have you ever done this before?"

Eve responded by anchoring the towel in his teeth. "Michel," she soothed. "Don't you know by now that I am good at everything I do?" She gave him half a grin. "Now, quit talking and bite down. You've lost too much blood to argue."

Before he could make another protest, Eve took the iron from Iman and ordered two of them to hold his arms while Iman and Gerald braced his legs. In another second, she pressed the iron to his wound with a sizzle, and the meaty smell of burning blood and flesh permeated the yurt.

Michel yelled inside his throat, against the towel, as every muscle in his body spasmed. Then, in a whoosh of energy, the tension left his body as he passed out. *Good*, she thought, seeing the effects of the tea and the pain working with the instincts of his body. She changed the position of the cautery to get the rest of the jagged cut. His skin hissed as it burned.

She took a few more passes, checking the wound as she did, but she was able to finish as the iron cooled. Satisfied, she handed it back to Iman. The men hung around nervously, but now she just needed Michel to rest while she continued working on him. "Thank you," she said to them. "I will call on you if I need more assistance."

"I will be here, Eve," said Iman. "However I can help."

She smiled at him. "Thank you, Iman." She looked at the others. "Now out," she said, giving them all a weak smile in thanks.

Michel rested calmly. Finally. She took her first breath then. She set out to clean the rest of him, the rest of the wounds, and the sweat from his hair. She removed his boots and torn pants, leaving on just his undergarments. She cared for every scrape. She touched every inch of skin. She worked carefully, reverently. She knew what this fight had meant for him. Michel was not a killer. He was a politician. It would cause him problems in his home, in his kingdom.

She had caused these wounds, too. She washed his face with warm water and looked at the hard lines of his cheeks, softened with sleep. *My God*, she thought, feeling things inside her that she didn't know quite how to deal with. She wanted to worship him, to show him all her gratitude. At the same time, she wanted more from him too, a demand that threaded through each vein, knotting in her heart. She wanted him to guard her, adore her. She never wanted to be separated. At one point, Michel had called her lucky for finding him, and she had teased him.

It was true. Every moment near him was a blessing.

Outside of the yurt, the camp stirred with noise. She heard the voices of the men she knew and then the voice of Renault. After a moment, he called at her door. Eve rose to pull it open.

"Goodness," Renault said, coming to Michel's bedside. "Is it true he fought that enormous man?"

"I have not known you long, Renault," she said, still wiping a cloth across Michel's brow. "But you have known Michel for many years. Do you need to ask me that question?"

Renault shook his head, eyes still on Michel.

"I trust we have your sponsorship to stay now that the threat is over?"

"*Mademoiselle*, that is not my decision."

"Surely you can speak to the town officials on his behalf." She turned to look at him. "He has eliminated the threat. There is no more concern."

Renault stood in silence.

"*Monsieur*," Eve prompted, a sharpness to her voice, surprised he had not immediately agreed to be of assistance.

"My lady," he blurted. "I, too, am a Frenchman in a foreign land. I cannot press the issue."

Eve steeled her posture. She had not anticipated having no support, for a warrior deserved to be rewarded, lauded. She thought to finally use her position, her ties to her father, to secure a safe spot for Michel. And she was about to leverage it when Renault continued.

"You can go south to Carth," he proposed. "I will arrange a safe house for you there."

Eve pulled back and considered. "Yes," she said. "I know Carth." She nodded. "That will be acceptable." Then she rattled off a list of things she would need.

He turned to leave. She stopped him by calling his name. He turned to her.

"You should know," she said, her voice accusatory. "Michel may have taken me on, but his dedication to this route and his obligations never wavered. I don't think you could find someone more loyal." She turned back to Michel. "I hope you communicate that to whoever wants to know."

"I will, my lady," he said, slipping out the door.

Chapter Thirty-Two

Several hours later, Eve had completed arrangements with Renault, settled the camp, and made a stew for those who needed food along with a complex healing broth for Michel. The men had calmed, telling stories of Michel fighting the monster. Eve did not attempt to tamp down their gossip. Let the legend spread that Ganbold had been felled.

They held a little memorial for Terence, too. He had been annoying to most of them, but these were men who tallied losses. They wanted to say goodbye.

In the end, Iman said it best: "You were a little fuck, Terence. But you kept us entertained." He nodded his head. "We hope you have found your peace." They shared a drink. Eve included.

By then, evening had come. Michel had slept fitfully throughout the day, calling out for her, still fighting in the space between dreams and wake. She sat next to him on the bed and nudged him. "Michel," she whispered, running her hands down his chest, still using her fingertips to check for trauma. "You need to drink something."

Michel stirred and opened his eyes with a start. "*Eve,*" he muttered.

"I'm here." She stroked his cheek.

He blinked, coming fully awake for the first time since they had returned to their yurt. He pushed up, looking down at his bandage and then back to Eve.

"You took care of me," he said, giving her a smile.

"I should say that to you." She reached forward to touch his chest. Michel grabbed her hand and held it, pulling her toward him.

She sucked in a breath, her body responding, his heat seeping into her. But she pulled back. "You must drink if you wish to recover," she said. "Lean forward. Be careful."

Michel released her hand and lifted himself as Eve propped cushions behind him. Eve retrieved the bowl of broth and then sat on the bed, holding it out for him. "This will make it easier to rest."

Michel drank, watching her over the rim. He handed it back when he finished.

"Are you in pain?" she asked. She ran her hand over the skin of his chest, his arms, seeking contact. Feelings of gratitude and affection, need and desire, ballooned inside her, and she didn't know how to navigate them. So, she sat there, kneeling beside him, though she wanted nothing more than to feel his skin against hers, to affirm his spirit hadn't dissolved like she had witnessed happen to two others just that morning.

"The pain's tolerable." He stretched, giving a wince as he did.

"Michel." She took his hand. "We must leave here," she said. "Renault cannot guarantee us lodging. He has secured a place for us in Carth, instead."

Michel's expression turned dark. "His livelihood is because of me. Everything he has." He wiped his hand down his face, the disappointment evident. Then he shook his head, changing focus. "We must make some kind of arrangement for the bodies."

"Iman offered to take Terence's body back to France." She bowed her head. "And Ganbold..." She pressed her lips. "Died a warrior's death. The forest will feast on him. He will return to the earth. It is the most respectful way." She squeezed Michel's hand. "I truly don't know if his death means I am free from that tribe or they will come after me tenfold." She looked down. "I do know that it was him or me."

Michel leaned up, his other hand coming to her cheek. "Do you feel safe? With him gone?"

She smiled, knowing one emotion in her stayed pure, untainted. "To be truthful," she continued, "I have felt safe since the moment you bought me in Merv."

He pulled her to him. She leaned into his chest like she had wanted to earlier. As her cheek touched his skin, she borrowed his strength. She felt, for the first time, an overwhelming need to cry. It surprised her, because until that moment, she had never thought about tears. They flooded now. All of them. Tears saved from the shock of being stolen and losing her family. Tears for Michel's pain, tears for Terence. They all came at once, and they soaked her cheeks, Michel's chest, her dress, and the bed. The grief came as a rush of rain.

Michel held her and stroked her back. At some point, he tipped her head up and began kissing her cheeks, damming up the rivulets of tears. She didn't know how long they stayed like that—her tears writing all the words she ever wanted to say and Michel accepting each one on his glistening lips. When she felt her cheek begin to dry, she pulled back and looked at him. She touched her hands to his face. She ran her thumb over his lips. Michel just gave her a smile.

She needed something more.

Then she was up on her knees, between his legs. Holding his cheeks, she kissed him with sudden, delirious desperation. Michel startled at first, then wrapped his arms around her, adjusting himself to her kiss. She tasted the salt of her tears on his lips and felt his desire and urgency break through to meet her own. She opened her lips and took his tongue against hers. She drew him into her, wanting nothing more than to be full of him.

The space inside her that had been taken up by grief flooded with desire. Throbbing waves went through her, down her thighs, across her breasts. She changed her position and lifted her shift enough to straddle his lap, sinking down onto his lap.

She heard a moan deep in his throat. At first, it thrilled her, but then she remembered his injury. "Have I hurt you?" She pulled back suddenly, looking over his injuries.

"No," he laughed, keeping a firm grip on her hips.

"No?" she said, this time teasing. She rocked her body forward, sliding herself across his length.

Michel groaned and pushed up between her legs. The hardness of him pressed against the sensitive spot between her legs, separated from him by just a few layers of fabric. It caused her to gasp and brace herself with her hands on his chest.

"Should I stop?" she teased. "We can wait until you are healed."

Michel's eyes snapped onto her, and he gripped the back of her head. "Eve, I could have lost a leg today, and this would still be the only thing I wanted."

She grinned and pressed against him, her lips against his. "You deserve everything you want."

"*Everything* I want?" he rasped, nuzzling into her neck, his hands running along her thighs. "Are you sure?"

She made an affirmative noise, his breath tickling her skin.

"Take off your dress," he said, and his want thickened the words.

She reached down to pull her shift up over her head.

"*Mon Dieu*," he hissed between his teeth. With one hand around her back, the other came up to grip her breast.

Eve's body trembled at the sensation, and she leaned in to feel more. His lips came down, his tongue tracing patterns. Then his teeth were on her flesh, pulling and sucking the nubbed skin into his mouth, while his hands squeezed her other breast possessively. Eve groaned and rocked her body against his even more firmly, the feelings he created in her breasts making the spot between her legs beg for more friction.

"Yes," she said. She felt that wonderful feeling again that brewed between her legs and made her stomach go tight. She slid herself up the thick rod of him, believing that she could orgasm from just this contact. She shifted her body to get up higher, climbing him, claiming him...and kneed him right in his wounded side.

"Ah," Michel made a sound and jerked as he released her breast from his mouth.

Eve froze. "I'm sorry," she gasped. "Did I hurt you?" She shifted to check his bandages.

Michel grabbed her arm, pulling her back in place. "No," he said. "A little." He laughed. "Eve," he spoke, turning serious again, commanding. "Take these off."

"Yes," she said, her breath gone, unable to deny him or herself.

She raised herself up. He pulled down her drawers, slipping them past her knees.

His hands came up her body, then moved up her thighs, up her backside. He wrapped an arm around her, lifting her to pull down his own undergarments.

He struggled with them, but he couldn't balance her and lift himself with his injury. "Help." He chuckled. "I need help."

Eve grinned. "I can do that."

She stripped him, getting all their remaining clothing off. She'd waited too long to share this with him, this piece of her, all of her pieces. She spread her legs over him again, her body aching for contact, and she felt the press of him against her slippery skin, the slick contact causing her to gasp. He pulled her in to kiss her. She whimpered as he humped up to slide against her.

"*Mon Dieu*," he said, the words deep. Then he paused, sobering. "Eve," he whispered, pulling back. "Is this alright? I don't want that you feel obligated—"

"Michel," she put her hands on his cheeks. "I've never wanted anything more. This is my choice, and I'm grateful for it."

She kissed him, and his arms were around her. There was nothing left to argue.

She was ready for more, though she wasn't sure what came next. She looked down to where they touched, the pressure building enough to break her, not quite knowing how to connect them. She knew there should be more to it, but she didn't know what to do. Would it enter her by itself? Could he move the thing on its own?

Before she could question the ways of coupling anymore, Michel grabbed himself with his hand, positioned her, and thrust upward, in a move that said he was unable to wait any longer. Eve gasped with surprise and pleasure as her body jerked involuntarily. She had thought to feel more pain, but there was only a sharp spike and then nothing but pure pleasure. Her head fell back, her skin sparked with desire, her breath came in hungry gasps, and her hands gripped her breasts. She couldn't imagine a better feeling.

Then Michel pulled her down onto him, thrusting upwards again, and

Eve realized he hadn't even been fully inside her. This time, the pleasure repeated, compounded. She gasped and caught herself on his chest. And when Michel thrust up the third time, he hit a spot inside her, so deep she didn't even know it existed, and the orgasm took her instantly. It caused her to cry out and convulse, leaving her almost unable to control her movements.

After a moment, she blinked awareness back, and she looked at Michel, her body still writhing, grinding against him.

Michel, breathless himself, smiled and ran his hands up her back, pulling her close. "You made that too easy," he teased, brushing her lips with his, drawing her hair back over her shoulders. "I didn't have to do anything."

She laughed, her body curling around his, demanding the closeness. "You've done everything." She took his lips as she continued to roll against him. Even after the orgasm, she wanted more. After weeks of arguing, teasing, dancing around each other, running, coming closer but staying apart, they were connected. The pleasure was so thick in her, she didn't know what to do with it all, from the tips of her breasts, which he plucked as his hands passed over them, to all the places inside her that shivered against him. She lived because of him. He lived because of her. They had given and taken from each other. She felt full, fulfilled, balanced in a way she had never known. "Now," she said, "take what you want from me."

Michel's face changed, dark with lust. His lips parted, and his eyes burned into hers. He wrapped an arm around her waist then flipped Eve onto her back in one swift motion. She jolted, surprised he could still move her with his injury. She spread for him, needing him as deep as her body would allow.

"Michel," she whispered, still rolling her hips against him, unable to stop her body now, the feel of him just too good. "Don't hurt yourself." She arched at another pleasurable spasm inside her. "If you're okay, though, please don't stop."

"I'll never stop." He leaned into her until there was no space between them.

They were entangled. Eve's arms around his neck. Lips, tongues together, his scent all around her. Michel's hips driving into her as they found a rhythm together. He pushed one of her legs out and up, spreading her as he settled her leg around his waist. Michel's pace increased, and though she worried about him, the thought was lost as he stroked against that place inside her once more.

She lost control of her body, her movements. It was all Michel. Their rhythm was changing, less thoughtful, more erratic, every sensation running through her body and centering on where they were joined. Sweat slicked her body now, his body too. He thrust into her forcefully enough to slam the bed into the supports of the yurt. The whole structure shook, and for a second, she worried it would collapse on them. Then he hit that spot inside her again and then again, and she didn't care if the world fell in on them because she knew Michel would protect her, wherever they ended up.

Michel pushed himself up, changing his angle. It caused her to groan as she felt another new sensation. She looked between them, wanting to watch him enter her. But her eye caught a red streak across her torso, his blood seeping through the covering.

"You're bleeding again." She gasped, hands on his chest.

"It's okay," he said in a rush. "I'm fine."

"Maybe we should..." She gasped as he hit that good spot again. "Stop."

Michel only laughed. He grabbed her hands then and pinned them above her, holding her down while he kissed her. Then he gripped her wrists with one hand and shifted the other hand between their bodies. His eyes, dark and erotic, whispered his devotion to her, even as he stripped her of all control. Eve strained her body to feel him against her again, worried about his wound but still aching to touch his muscles flexing above her. She felt his thumb firmly stroking at her apex. Between this attention to her outside and the unrelenting assault on her inside, Eve went wild.

Michel continued, taking as much of her as he could, his moans punctuating his movements, until he put his forehead to hers and slammed into her one last time, finally holding himself inside her, just where she wanted him. Her body, so sensitive, reacted to having all of him. Blooming and exploding, she turned to jelly, the feelings rocketing inside her, ripping the orgasm through her. The power of it caused her to cry out his name, over and over, the only word she could think of.

Then she felt the sharp loss of him as he pulled back suddenly. She cried out again, protesting, wanting to continue to ride him, but she understood as she watched him lose himself across her belly with his own animal noise of pleasure.

He collapsed on top of her, his stamina having been siphoned away. She wrapped her arms around him, accepting his weight, kissing his cheeks, his neck, as Michel slumped into her. She was covered in him, filled with him. The mess of sweat and blood and his seed was slick between them. Michel brought one hand up to stroke her arm, tender, even as she felt his consciousness leaving him. With a little effort, she was able to get one leg free while he remained on top of her. She would have to clean them up and fix his bandage. For the moment, though, she'd let him rest. He tucked his head into the crook of her neck, and she felt him submit to sleep while she continued to hold him, rub her hands over his skin, and whisper soothing words into his ear.

That was the first night they slept together in the same bed. Still touching, naked skin, Michel gripping her possessively. A few times, she woke to him clutching her and kissing her as he became hard between the legs again, and she would laugh and tell him, *No.* "No, Michel, you *must* rest." Michel would groan, only to fall back asleep. The sedative tea she had given him was still working, just not enough to completely tame his desire.

Eve didn't want to think too much about what was to come. She needed to get him to the safe house so he could recuperate. Then they needed to get to France, still undetected. Now responsible for the deaths of two warriors from the same tribe, they would come for her eventually. They would not let such a woman live, though it would take time for them to reach her as Ganbold had. Her father would also be looking for her. He would never stop. Once they reached France, she would send communication to him so he knew she was safe.

And when they reached France? She'd had thoughts of finding work before. Now, though, all she wanted was to be with Michel. His wife. A wife to a husband like him would be full of possibilities. One thing she knew: Michel had dedicated himself to his position, and he wouldn't marry her purely for desire. If only she could tell him her status. That their union would be lauded across the continent. It was the one thing she had kept secret, because if he did know this information, he would feel obligated to return her home. A man of his position couldn't steal a wife.

His wife, she thought of the possibility, a feeling of warmth coming through her, causing her to snuggle more deeply into him as he slept.

Chapter Thirty-Three

The next morning, the small crew prepared to move. Only a few of the most loyal remained to help get Michel to Carth along with the remaining guards. True to his word, Renault helped by storing their materials and arranging an apartment. Michel knew that he and Eve would be on their own for a while, and he hoped they would avoid trouble.

Iman and Gerald helped Michel onto the horse before returning to their own mounts. Eve hovered. Michel enjoyed her concern a great deal. She had mended him and brought him back to life the night before. All he wanted was to heal quickly so he could get inside her again. He grinned as she fussed over him, trying to settle him as best she could on the horse.

He tucked his arm to his side in painful protection of his wound. With his other hand, he reached out to brush a strand of hair from her forehead.

She looked up at him. "You stop that," she teased.

"Stop what?" he growled, knowing exactly what she meant.

"You need your body to recover. Don't think about anything that will divert your blood from healing."

He laughed. "That will be very difficult," he whispered to her. "Now that I know what you feel like wrapped around me. It's no longer just in my mind." The want for her flamed through his body. "I plan to stare at you and divert my blood the whole way there."

"Michel," she said with a warning tone, but he could see her flush.

A short while later, they were traveling the road to Carth. The pain surprised him as every step of the horse ripped at his skin. Last night, he had hardly noticed. Even if he had, nothing had been more important than connecting with Eve. Now, though, pain made him woozy while fear of an attack kept him anxious. He kept nodding off, only to snap awake in a panic. In this moment, he didn't think he could do much to stave off any attacks. He felt marooned, isolated with a very precious treasure. His reputation no longer helped him. His position gave no more protection. Somehow, he would make it back to Chevalerie with Eve, but his legacy would be in complete shambles. He didn't care, though. Take his position. He just wanted her.

His body ached with the memory of her. They'd come together finally. The way she had looked spread open on top of him, the way she had felt when he took her beneath him. He'd never felt that kind of fervor before. Then again, everything was different with Eve. He hoped she didn't think that one time was all he would need. He laughed to himself at the thought as he watched her up ahead.

He also didn't understand how he managed to be rigid and broken at the same time. He winced from the pain in his side along with his straining erection as his horse took a trot over a slope, jostling him in the saddle. He made a noise that got Eve's attention, and she pulled her horse around, worry in her expression.

"I'm fine." He laughed. "I just want to get there."

She gave him another look and then adjusted her horse. He knew he would never release her. Not even a chance. The only thing he wanted was to get her home and put a fortress between her and anyone who would come for her. He would spend his life fighting to protect her. And with every slice of pain that cut his body, so did a throb of adoration for her. The only thing he cared to fight for was the ability to stay by her side. If, of course, she would have him.

The city of Carth boomed along the Indus River. Eve knew Carth. It had been her first stop when she ran away. A large eastern trade city, its population hovered around several hundred thousand. The people were a mix of many cultures: Mongolians, Middle Easterners, Chinese, nomads, and permanent residents. Merchants as far away as India and the Eastern coast of the African states frequented the city. The many hues of people made it easy to hide.

Known for its constant stream of political upheaval, fighting over which faction claimed the city as its own persisted. Still, the merchants and working people in the city soldiered on, despite the tides of war, continuing the palate of trade that rested within the city walls. It could be a dangerous city for one who strayed into dark corners, but with some smarts and planning, one could easily go unnoticed.

Renault had arranged a small apartment tucked into a busy strip of commerce patronized by an elderly man, his daughter, and her husband. Upon meeting, Eve liked them right away, which was a relief because they would have no other comrades here. The elderly man seemed happy to assist them, as friends of Renault's, and swore no one in the city would threaten his properties due to his strong reputation.

They brought the horses into the small courtyard at the base of the building, and Iman and Gerald helped Michel down from the horse as Michel clutched his wounded side and grumbled. Eve kept shushing him and calming him, anxious to have him resting again. They helped him up the flight of stairs and then directly to the bed once they entered the room. The room was sparse but had the necessities. A small hearth, one bed in the corner. A window and a table. She checked over Michel to see that several wounds had started leaking blood, and she felt a fever in his skin. She had no time to worry now, not until everything had settled. So, she set to work, boiling water for a medicinal broth and adding the necessary roots and herbs.

The men came in and out, bringing their supplies. Michel lay on the bed, blood seeping through his shirt, calling out orders. "Horses!" he insisted. "You have to board the horses!"

"Michel," said Eve. "The horses have been cared for—"

"We must make contact with the town officials and arrange guards while we are here."

"Michel—" she said, trying to calm him, as she finished her concoction and strained it into a cup.

"The wagon must be obscured and stripped of our affiliation."

"Michel—" she repeated.

"We will need towels," he called into the room.

Eve paused and looked at him. "Towels?" she repeated as the last of the men left to tend to her shopping list.

Michel looked back at her daftly. "You always want towels."

Eve stifled a laugh. "Perhaps I won't need any if you stop getting hurt so often." She came and sat beside him on the bed. "Michel," she said. "Do not worry, everything has been taken care of."

"What about..." He paused, as if he were unable to come up with something else to check.

"At the moment, we are safe." She sat beside him. "Now drink this."

He groaned. "Ugh, I hate these stinky things."

"Just hush and drink." She had to agree that it was quite pungent. "It will make you feel better."

He hoisted himself up with a grimace and took the cup. He drank while glaring at her. He pushed it away, half done. She pushed it back. "All of it," she said.

He complained again, but finished it.

"You will have a dreamless sleep now, my love," she said, touching his cheek.

His droopy eyes shot open. "Did you call me 'love'?" Suddenly, his arms were around her waist, tipping her toward him. She fell across his chest.

Startled by his reaction, she thought about it. "Yes," she said, suddenly breathless from being in his arms. The worry of getting him safe had eclipsed her desire to revel in the feelings of the night before, but now, it all came back, memories in her mind, in her body. She shifted to lean on him in a way that didn't put pressure on his injuries. "I suppose I did call you 'love.'" She ached being near him, his dark eyes locked on hers. Now was not the time, so she kissed his nose and adjusted his cushion. "Rest while I change your bandages."

Michel let her out of his arms and leaned back to watch her. He didn't speak anymore. He had that smug look on his face again. It made her purr for him inside her chest. She smiled, knowing they were both thinking of their night together. The broth would work quickly on him. It would soothe his fever and aid in healing his wounds. It would also put him to sleep, so she could tend to him without being harassed. She laughed to herself.

Eve removed his bandages and checked the large wound across his side, by now an angry red. It did, however, show signs of scabbing. His skin felt feverish. She worried that he had been far too active. They had ridden fast on the horses, and it had been harder on him than he led on. She covered the wound with a towel. *Ha*! she thought. He was right. She did use towels often. She returned to create a soothing poultice that would pull any new toxins from the wound.

Michel continued watching her. Every time she looked his way, his eyes were on her. She enjoyed caring for this man very much. She knew that he did not put his trust into others so easily, but he had completely submitted to her authority. The thought filled her with warmth.

By the time the poultice was ready, Michel's eyes had closed, and he was drifting into a light sleep. She placed the poultice across his wound, warning him that it would sting for a moment before cooling and creating a numbing sensation. He grimaced, and as he did, she leaned forward to kiss his lips before pulling back. When he closed his eyes for the evening, there was peace in his expression.

Chapter Thirty-Four

Over the next few days, Eve fell into a pattern. The modest room became a home in which she cared for Michel and played his nursemaid. Each morning, she would rise, check Michel's wounds, and make their tea and breakfast. She had become friends with the daughter of the landlord. They would go to the market together, where Eve would choose foods for the day and select the herbs, spices, and roots needed to help Michel recover. Then she would return, busy herself with tending, mending, cooking, and cleaning. She could not believe how fulfilling it all felt, this way of showing Michel her gratitude and affection.

Michel slept for much of the first few days, the fever slowly dissipating. He began staying awake for longer stretches. She liked very much when he was awake. He made her laugh. He made her ache, too. He asked her questions, wanted to know about her life, her family, everything. It still hurt to talk about the loved ones she left behind, the events that led her from the comfort of her family's herds to the safety of Michel's arms. She carefully skirted around information about who exactly her father was. She just enjoyed this moment too much to bring in any more conflict.

Then on the fourth day, when she returned from the market with her sack of vegetables and grains, she saw something very surprising.

Michel was on the floor doing pushups.

She almost dropped her turnips.

It thrilled her to see him getting stronger. It also thrilled her to see the muscles flexing in his back. A shudder ran up her spine along with a tingle down her thighs.

"Michel," she gasped. She slid to her knees next to him. "Are you hurting?" She could see the sweat shimmering on his skin.

He did three more quick lifts and turned to his side. "I feel great." He grinned at her. He still had the bandage on him, but the scab had formed well and did not bleed.

"Don't do too much," she said, her brow furrowed.

"I won't." He jumped up onto his feet. He looked at her and stumbled back, having overexerted himself.

"Ok, careful, love," she said. She caught him under the shoulder and helped him back to the bed. "It will take you a while to regain your strength."

"I like it when you call me that," he said, grinning like a wolf. "I have some strength left."

Sitting beside him, she breathed in his scent and looked at him. The nearness controlled her thoughts and her body. Of all the things they had talked about, they hadn't spoken of what had happened between them. Eve feared her body could not hold back once they spoke of those moments. They had been sharing a bed, too, but Michel's healing sleep had been deep, and though he would reach for her in the night, she stayed still enough not to wake and arouse him.

He pulled her to him, turning their bodies so they were face to face. She felt the firmness of his chest against her, his muscles unyielding. It caused her breasts to tingle and her breath to come more quickly.

His hands worked into the fabric of her dress to grip her and touch her skin. "Eve," he whispered, looking up at her. "That was your first time," he murmured. "I'm sorry that I was not at my best."

"You were perfect," she whispered, running her hand through his hair. "Everything was perfect. The way you touched me." She ran her hands across his chest, his hands still working up her legs. "The way you took me."

"What was your favorite part?" he asked, his hands encircling her thighs, reaching into her undergarments.

"How it hurt and then immediately felt good. When you put me on my back." She shifted to kiss him while opening her legs to get more of his touch. "The sounds you made when you climaxed. Everything."

Michel groaned. He pulled at her undergarment now. "Are you going to make me fight another man before I have you again?"

She laughed a *no* as her body urged for contact between her legs.

Michel came up on his knees and then moved above her. She felt his power and his presence grow until it filled the room, and there was only him. "Take your dress off," he instructed.

A jolt went through her at his command. She came up on her knees, too, as she reached to unlace the dress. In seconds, she was pulling it off with Michel's help.

His hands on her body caused her to feel weak. Michel held her steady as he pulled off the rest of her undergarments. Then his lips were on her neck and his hand between her thighs. She moved to feel the pressure of his fingers

"Michel," she said, unsure how she could make words. "You must go slow. For your own sake."

"I'll try," he murmured as he pressed a finger against her, causing Eve's hips to jerk, seeking him. "But you make it too difficult to go slow. You haven't even given me a chance to seduce you." He placed kisses along her jaw, teasing. "Because you've been the one seducing me this whole time."

It was this, he thought, this desire for Eve that had kept him alive. He wanted so much from her. He wanted to protect her, to help her, to save her. He wanted terrible things too—to make her gasp for air, to make her beg, to own her. He raged inside because, despite all the ways he wanted to contain her, he knew he couldn't outwit or manipulate her. He had lost himself to her.

He grinned, looking down into her green eyes, mottled like a storm. Here, he thought he could be in charge this way.

He reached into her hair and held her firmly with his free hand while his other one worked into her. He was shirtless, in nothing more than his breeches, allowing him to feel the heavy press of her breasts against his skin.

He held her, wanting to watch her pleasure as he continued using his fingers on her, hearing her sounds, letting her soak his hand.

When he felt her body starting to reach, to clench around him, he pulled back. "Not yet," he murmured. "Together."

Eve groaned and threw her arms around him, pulling him into a kiss.

Michel wanted to go slow, to tease her and keep her on edge all morning, but he felt his own desire spiraling. He took her and turned her to lie across the bed. He pulled his breeches off. Still on his knees, he opened her up, bending her knees and spreading her apart.

His eyes felt so full, he didn't know where to look. Her face—lips parted in desire, eyes storming—the fullness of her body, or her wet heat, deep pink and slick, waiting for him.

"You are made to be worshiped," he said, taking himself in his hand. He stroked his shaft once to spread his own eager wetness across. Then he balanced himself over her. Eve writhed, pulling at his arms. He breathed in, filling his lungs with her scent—currants and citrus—thick and raw with her desire. "I don't deserve to touch you, Eve," he said. "But that doesn't mean I will stop."

"Don't stop," she said, pulling him down for a kiss.

He took her lips and her tongue against his own, and he felt the desire fighting its hold inside him. Still gripping himself, he used the head of his cock to tease her outsides, letting their liquid desire combine.

"Michel," she demanded. "Hurry, now, don't make me wait."

Her words, her body...how could he make her wait? Somewhere, pain tugged at his side. Somewhere else, caution told him to go slow. With Eve writhing below him, though, he couldn't stop anything that was happening.

He pulled her legs open, and in one sharp thrust, they were joined.

He wanted to take a breath and assess her—if she felt ready, if it was too much—but Eve was a force below him, already locked on, pulling at him and jutting her hips to his. Michel could do nothing more than give in to her. He met her hips with his own as he moved inside her, slow and deep.

He struggled between wanting to allow the build, to let his affection reach out toward her, and wanting to exploit her body roughly, hurtling them both toward release. But his Siren wanted more, everything, all at once. When he pulled away to look at her, she jerked him back down. When he leaned in to nibble at her collarbone, she ripped at his hair and choked out his name. She pulled and scratched at him, her body begging, and so he drove into her, Eve having made the decision for him.

He felt her body teetering on completion. So was his, he realized, in absolute wonder. There had never been such a connection for him or a fury inside him. He rode her, giving her everything he could. He felt her body tightening even more for him, and he had no time to stall, to extend the experience. Somewhere in his brain, he knew the moment was coming that he had to pull away from her body, to let his release happen outside of her, but with Eve wrapped tightly around him, he could hardly bear it.

"Eve," he whispered, a weak plea. He wanted her to climax, and then he would spill outside of her, like he had done before, as he had always with every woman he'd been with. He felt the tightness, the pleasure of his orgasm gathering. He tried to pull away. Eve shrieked and held onto him tightly. She moved her hips against him, and he felt her body stiffening on a moan. He couldn't handle it. Suddenly, his face was in her hair, and he was nearly lifting her from the mattress, burying himself as deep as her body would let him. His own moan came full and primal, and he had no other thought in his head than this beautiful connection to this beautiful woman as he spent himself completely inside her.

Gasping for breath, he looked down at her. Eve's eyes sparkled back at him, and she had her own look of shock on her face. She smiled, reaching toward his lips, devouring him with kisses. Michel took each one, smiling as he did, whispering her name, praising the heavens for letting him keep her safe, all as he continued moving inside her, drawing out each of their sensations until the last moment.

Chapter Thirty-Five

Thus began the happiest time in Eve's life. Her day was filled with nothing but Michel. Household chores, trips to the marketplace, Michel. The flooding pull of want he had awakened inside of her. Eve hardly knew what had happened to her. She was completely overcome by desire for this man. When he was near, when she had his scent in her nose, it changed how she acted. It turned her into a crazy person, and the only antidote was to have more and more and more of him.

She knew him so much better now. This strong, tall, steadfast man who would fight for her, who would attend to whatever she needed, was completely dependent on her. She loved it. She loved the way she controlled him, but he, at the same time, completely overpowered her. It seemed that all along she had been looking for a place that her adult self could call home, and in Michel she found exactly where she belonged.

Meanwhile, Michel grew stronger, a relief to the both of them. At first, their lovemaking was all he could manage, and once they were finished, he would be spent, asleep for hours, until he woke up and wanted her again. It delighted Eve. Never had she indulged in such pleasure of the body before, and Michel did things to her she never knew could feel so wonderful. Every touch and caress from him was a new story he wrote into her skin, and she quivered just thinking about how he touched her.

They began taking trips together to the market. They cloaked themselves and did not stay out long. Back home, they would eat together. Chat. Play cards. She made him drink stinky teas that he hated. She borrowed books from their landlord and read aloud on treatises of war, history, and bawdy stories of bards and maids. It didn't matter what she read, or what she cooked, or mended, or anything else that she did. She would always end up in his arms, her body begging him to touch her.

It was three weeks that they were caught in this happy routine that Eve never wanted to end. As long as she didn't think of the chaos littered behind them, everything was perfect in their little home, their lives complete. What a gift to be given these days—the thought lived inside her. That is, until one day, she noticed the twinges in her lower stomach. At first, she thought it was signaling that she would need her female supplies. When that day didn't come, she realized that she had not had one full cycle since she and Michel had been together in that way. As the gentle tugs and pulls in her belly continued, she began to understand what had happened. She was not stupid. She had known it was a possibility, but she didn't know it would happen quite so fast. She certainly didn't think it would happen before she knew what was happening next.

However it came about, it seemed as though Michel's mark on her would be permanent.

Michel felt strong again. He could move. He could lift. He could work. He'd been exercising in the small courtyard outside their room, training with his sword once more. He felt his muscles regaining their strength. Soon, he would be ready to travel.

He'd also been exercising with Eve. His body came alive, he knew, because he wanted her. Only her. It felt like his flesh and muscles couldn't wait to heal, just so he didn't miss a moment with her. And she was *voracious*. He did all he could to keep up with her and give her what she needed. *Dieu merci*—thank *God*—he had started regaining his strength because he felt he could be consumed completely by her at any moment, worn down to bones. He could certainly think of worse things.

That afternoon, he worked with the landlord and his son-in-law, building a porch in the courtyard. They had been working since morning. Michel took it slow, careful not to pull on his wound. He liked both men— the landlord, kind-hearted and smart, and his son-in-law, a friendly sort.

Michel pounded a nail and looked up to see Eve, standing at the window, her worried eyes on him. He grinned, feeling warmth grow inside him that rivaled the heat from the sun. He had never felt so coddled and cared for in his life. He had never known this happiness before.

He slammed a nail home and then gave her a wink. He cared about nothing else—not his title, not his kingdom, not his reputation. Eve held his only objective: to get her home, to get her safe. He would have to return to Chevalerie with no trade, with *less* trade in fact. He would have to face up to his family—he, who had always spouted that he knew his purpose and wouldn't be swayed by some beauty. But now. *Wow.* He had never expected it.

It was time to make things official.

Many hours later, Michel felt himself waking up cozy in bed. He had been to the baths, had dinner with Eve and the landlord's family, and then he must have fallen right asleep, his muscles heavy with exhaustion from the day of work. In his sleepy daze, he turned to reach for Eve, but she was not in bed. Suddenly, he startled awake, hearing what sounded like her tears coming from across the room.

"Eve," he whispered. He leapt out of bed. She was leaning on the table with her back to him, her head dropped. He came to her and wrapped his arms around her body, pressing his chest to her back. "What's wrong? Are you crying?"

"No," she whimpered.

"Yes, you are." He held her and nuzzled his lips into her hair. "What's happened?"

"Michel." She did not turn but continued to speak to him. "Are you sincere when you say you will take me to France? Do you still have any designs to get rid of me?"

Michel laughed. "How can you ask me that?"

"Or is it sex?" she asked. "Am I here because you like to have sex with me?"

At the mention, his body became immediately ready. "Sex with you clouds my brain," he murmured, his hands already roaming. He loved the way the night shift slid over her skin as he touched her.

Eve groaned as she pressed back into him. "Is this all you want?" she asked, now breathless.

Suddenly, Michel understood that Eve wasn't so much worried about his plans but more worried about his feelings. He grinned. She must have noticed the change in his demeanor because now she turned to look at him with anger in her expression. "Why do you smile? Do you think I am joking?"

He held himself around her. "Do you not know my feelings for you by now?"

"You have never told me much about your feelings." She turned away again with a huff. But her body stayed soft in his arms.

He moved his hands and pulled at the fabric of her shift, bringing it over her head, leaving just her drawers to cover her lower half. "How could you not know?" he said softly, his hands running across her bare breasts and back down over her body. "You know basically everything else about me." He tangled his fingers in her undergarment. "Listen to me now," he insisted, "and I will try to tell you how I feel about you." He kissed a trail down her spine and then reached to tilt her chin toward the window. "Do you see the stars outside?"

"Yes," she whispered, her breath catching as she as he began to move against her. She directed her gaze toward the stars.

"I'm jealous of the stars, Eve," he said. "I'm jealous they get to watch you while I'm asleep." He pressed himself against her bottom and kissed the back of her neck. His hand came up her front, and he took her breast against his palm. He heard a breath escape her lips.

"What else?" she asked.

He smiled, enjoying her reactions. "Do you feel the warmth from the fire?"

"Yes," she whispered.

"I'm jealous that it can touch your skin even when you are across the room," he rasped, against her ear.

"More things," she said. "Tell me more."

"Hmmm," he said, thinking, pressing himself into her, dizzy with her. "I'm jealous of every smile you've given to anyone else. Every laugh you've ever had that wasn't my doing." He leaned back, suddenly frenzied, his hands gripping at her undergarment. "That this fabric is touching you where I want to be touching you," he growled. He couldn't get it off fast enough. "Help me get this off."

"Yes." She pushed them down and leaned back into him, groaning as she did.

There it was, the absolute panic to take her, to get inside of her. He ran his hands up her legs, over her ass, across her torso, her breasts, her hair, and her throat. He wanted to touch her everywhere, all at once. He lifted one of her legs, resting her knee up on the table, spreading her open. He had to have her.

Eve, up on her toes, caught herself. She gasped his name and reached back for him. Michel held her while he situated himself, and in a moment, he penetrated deep into her. He clenched his jaw at the pleasure of it, the heat inside her body, the connection between them, the tension holding them together. It was an out-of-control torrent that took him over like an avalanche each time he was close to her.

He thrust inside, feeling her wetness coat him, and he did it again. He knew her body well enough by now to know if he held himself inside her too long, she would orgasm immediately. Sometimes he would let her. Sometimes he wouldn't. Now he wouldn't, he thought, fingers digging into her hips. He wanted to control her body and her pleasure. He wanted to make her say she was his.

Eve cried out as he set an aggressive pace, causing the table to drag loudly as he drove into her. Michel held her, one hand digging into her hip to hold her in place, and the other wrapped around her torso to keep her skin against his. He kissed the back of her neck and buried his face in her hair. Even inside her, he never, never, could get enough.

Eve hadn't been crying because she worried about his desire, Michel knew. He had wanted to ask her this when he had risen to the honor of his position, when he had gotten her home to Chevalerie and safe, when he had a chance to fix everything that had fallen apart. Not when he was recovering and deserted, having bungled every deal he had attempted. He felt the words. He couldn't hold them back any longer. His strain for her wouldn't let him. He stood tall and held her hips, changing his angle and quickening his pace, a sudden rush of emotion causing his head to swim.

"Marry me, Siren." He said it as a command, but he'd plead if he had to.

He felt the surprise stiffen her body. He thrust roughly, nearly lifting her off the floor, turning her into liquid once more. He leaned forward, running his hand over her hip and down between her legs, his fingers parting her skin as he stroked her there. He spoke in her ear, "Say yes."

Eve whimpered and stuttered a moment. She struggled to steady herself, even though he held her solidly. She arched into him, her head back, gasping his name.

"Say yes," he repeated. He used firm pressure with his fingers between her legs while he beat into her from the back.

"Yes," she gasped, her hands gripping the edges of the table.

He grinned and bit her neck, lowering his voice to a tease. "Yes, you'll marry me, or yes, you want to come?"

"*Yes*, I'll marry you." She choked out a laugh. "Yes, to both."

The tension snapped like a rubber band inside him. He leaned forward, pushing her down against the table. He ground down on her clitoris and slammed into her until her body stiffened on a scream, causing his own body to implode as he, once again, lost himself inside her. He couldn't help it, but surely, one more time wouldn't matter.

Eve slumped across the table, and Michel collapsed over her. He felt his breathing align with hers as their hearts slowed together. He kissed her neck and down her spine. He had never felt so happy.

When she spoke, he realized that with her, his happiness had no limit.

"I love you, Michel," she gasped. "I love you."

Chapter Thirty-Six

The next morning, Michel calculated it was the twenty-second day of their solitude. Michel lay lazily, happy in bed, propped on his elbow, watching Eve in a pretty lavender day dress that she had bought in town as she moved around the hearth. Michel enjoyed watching the way the dress cinched at her waist and flowed down her hips as she brewed tea and put together a breakfast of fruit and nuts. Every time she looked back at him, she smiled.

"You look very pleased with yourself this morning," Eve joked. She looked down, grinding herbs with a mortar and pestle.

"I am pleased every morning that I wake and get to watch you."

"Michel—" she began.

"What?" he said. "Do you suddenly not want to talk about my feelings anymore?" he teased. "You were so interested last night."

"I know that," she grumbled, shooting him an annoyed look.

She turned her face down, and for a second, Michel saw a flash of emotion, like what he had witnessed last night. He realized that they had made love, sworn themselves to each other, and fallen asleep in each other's arms, but he never discovered what had made her cry. "Eve," he said. "Come here."

She looked at him, exasperated. "Michel, if we start now, I will never get the breakfast served."

"No, not for that," he laughed. "Please?" He held out his hand to her.

Eve gave him a warning look before dusting her hands off on her skirt. She came over and slid in next to him in bed. Outside, Michel could hear the sounds of the early morning city. Shouting, clanging, the noise of the marketplace. All of that faded as he focused on Eve.

They had learned each other's bodies over the last weeks—they fit so comfortably together now. She leaned her head on the pillow and looked up to him, waiting for him to continue.

"Eve," he said. Being this close to her always became a problem. Despite his best intentions, he stopped thinking when she looked up to him. He felt a growl deep in his chest. He wanted to take her. Right away. He felt himself grab onto her waist. But she grabbed his hand.

"Michel," she said in a warning tone.

"Sorry, I know." He laughed again. He shook his head to refocus. "What made you cry?"

She blinked. "What—"

"Last night," he said. "You cried. Why?" He touched her cheek. "You miss your family? Or have I done something?"

"I miss my family, yes. But it wasn't that." Her smile reassured him. "And no," she continued, "you have not done anything to upset me."

"Then why?" Outside of their room, Michel heard the clamoring shouts of men, but the noise could not distract him from her words.

"There is a part of me..." She looked up to him. "*Was* a part of me," she corrected. "That worried...that didn't know your intentions with me." She bit her lip. "You'd sworn to take me to France. I always believed you would. What would happen when we got there?"

Michel wrapped his arms around her, grinning. "How could you not know my feelings?" he teased. "I've done nothing but worship you."

"My body, yes." Her twinkling eyes teased him back. "Michel," she said. "You've still never told me you love me."

"Of course, I—" he halted. Hadn't he? He'd been in love with her since perhaps the first moment he saw her. Had he truly never said it aloud?

The noises of the marketplace continued to swirl in through the window, but the space between him and Eve stayed silent. He blinked away the confusion and looked in her waiting eyes. "I love you," he said, gathering her close. "I can't believe I made you wonder." He began dotting kisses across her jawbone. "I have felt it for so long, I guess I just never told you."

"I surmised as much." She chuckled. "I am happy to hear it, though." She put her hands on his cheeks. "Say it to me often."

He kissed her neck, his hands running down her back. The cacophony outside blurred as he prepared to lose himself in her entirely.

She held him off, pushing back enough to look at him. "Michel," she said. "I do want to tell you something, though."

"I don't care what it is," he said, wondering how quickly he could get out of his pants. "As long as you are mine."

But he didn't get to hear what it was she wanted to say.

The nagging noises from outside suddenly hit a peak as the door to their small apartment crashed open. Michel and Eve shot up in the bed as uniformed men poured into their space. Michel, up in a flash, leapt in front of her, ready to take each of them apart. He cataloged his space. His sword was within reach, but he would need luck to get it. He didn't know who they were or what they wanted. He wouldn't let them take Eve, that much he did know.

"Back up," Michel shouted. "You may not enter," he blustered.

The men—six, eight, twelve of them pouring into their space—ignored him and advanced before splitting into two lines. An older man, decorated in the same symbol as the rest but clearly the one in charge, cut their ranks, entering the room.

"Enebish," said the man, bowing to her and looking right through Michel.

"*Sain baina uu*, Khuyag," Eve greeted him in Mongolian. Michel felt her hand on his back in a warning as she came out from behind Michel to bow her head to the man.

As she did, she gave Michel a look that told him to stay down. He trusted her direction, but remained tense, understanding nothing more than that Eve did not feel threatened by this ambush.

"We have searched the sky and sea for you, my lady," the man said to her, continuing in Mongolian.

"You have found me safe and unharmed," she affirmed. Michel heard her voice free of emotion, though he could see the tension in her body.

He then gave a menacing look to Michel, which Michel responded to with his own protective posture. "Has this man given you trouble?" Khuyag asked.

"No, Khuyag. He is a warrior. Call off your dogs." She indicated to the soldiers in the room. Then she flipped into that Mongolian dialect Michel did not understand. Their voices stayed neutral at first, but then they seemed to argue. Her voice rose as she indicated toward Michel this time. Michel couldn't keep up. He knew she'd become upset. He could tell she was arguing on his behalf, but for what, he didn't know.

Finally, Eve clicked her tongue. Then she turned back to Michel.

Her eyes were full of sadness and regret, but otherwise she remained stoic. "Michel," she directed in French, he assumed to keep the others from understanding. "These men are going to take you prisoner, and we'll be returning to my home. Do not fight them, they are my kin." She took a breath, her posture straight, her voice holding none of the warmth he'd grown used to. "My father wants you, but you're going to have to trust me that I won't let anything harm you." Then, before he could respond, she turned and exited the room, the leader Khuyag following her.

"Eve!" he called. He didn't understand. "Eve!" he yelled again, but he lost track of her in the confusion, the soldiers swallowing him up.

As one man went to bind his arms, Michel came out of his shock. "Who are you?" he demanded, resisting this capture. "Where's Eve?" His eyes swung around, looking for her. "Is she safe?"

No one responded or acknowledged his words. He tried to pull away, but he didn't fight. Eve had told him not to.

"Do you know who I am?" Michel ranted at them, his frustration having nowhere to go.

The two guards who secured his hands ignored him while the older man reappeared among them. He cocked his head to look at Michel, and Michel saw the same mottled eyes as Eve. He raised his eyebrows. "Do you know who she is?"

Michel lost all fight. His body slumped and his heart sank. Because seeing this, he realized that, no, he did not.

Eve was once again surrounded by the markings of her family and she felt she was protected, completely safe now. No one would harm her. No one would even say a bad word in her direction.

But she was devastated to leave the life she had just decided to have with Michel.

She took the steps down to the courtyard, which had been filled with men from her homeland. They parted so Eve could pass. She went through the stonework arch, which led into the marketplace. Instinctively, she had grabbed her shawl, and now she started to pull it over her head. But she stopped, seeing her family's markings around, letting the shawl drop around her shoulders.

Khuyag joined, standing by her side.

"When will we depart?" she asked.

"Immediately," Khuyag said. "My lady, *Gonji*." He paused to touch her arm, tenderness in his voice. "Are you sure you are well?"

"Of course, Khuyag," she said. She knew he must have questions about her situation, about Michel, but it would be improper to ask. Instead, she turned to him. "How did you find us?" She corrected herself. "Me," she said. "How did you find me?"

"We searched every town, every village, and then we went further." He gave her a small smile. "You are quite good at hiding."

The people in the market had stopped their milling transactions to watch her family's symbolic *Tamga* markings, branded into the leathers of the soldiers and horses filling the streets. Behind her, the men mobilized. She thought she heard Michel's voice. She felt his pain and confusion despite being separated.

Khuyag continued, "We knew Ganbold hunted you. We were able to track him. Learned that you traveled with a French party." He folded his arms. "We discovered his death in Kashgar. From there, we were directed here."

Renault, she thought. A coward.

She looked down. "I was afraid I would bring war if I returned home," she said, her voice small. "I ran from the tribe, but I feared coming home would mean everyone would fight. I did not want that."

"The ancestors decide when we go to war," he consoled. "It is not up to us to try to change their will."

A soldier approached, telling them the apartment had been cleared.

"Is there anything you wish to retrieve before we leave?" Khuyag asked her.

"Yes," she said, thinking of the things she would gather. Michel's sword and dagger, and other things that had become important. She hoped she would have the chance to return the items to him. But she didn't move yet. She put her hand on Khuyag's arm. "I ask you again. Allow the Frenchman, Michel, to remain here. He has no fault in this."

"Like I said, *Gonji*, it is not my decision. Your father said when we found you to bring anyone you were with back as well."

"What does he want with him?"

"I do not claim to understand the Khan's will. You must speak with him."

Eve looked back toward the apartment, but she did not see him. "He's not a criminal, Khuyag. Don't treat him as such," she said, a sudden sob coming out of her. "He protected me."

"My dear," Khuyag said. He put his arm around her. "I would do my best to hide that emotion. Your father won't take to such affection."

"I am aware," she said, the sob disappearing as quickly as it had descended.

Chapter Thirty-Seven

Michel had been in a closed oxcart for several days as the party traveled well into territory he had never seen. The wooden cart had slatted gaps that allowed him to watch the terrain as they moved. He had enough space that he could sit up without hunching, but it was not comfortable by any means. He alternated between staring at the landscape and then exercising himself to exhaustion in his only bid to stay healthy and sane. His wound had healed over by now, but it still pulled on him, making him wince with certain movements.

The party moved with an efficiency and speed he had never experienced, switching out horses to continue a fast pace and stopping only for moments to relieve themselves or to sleep for a few hours each night. Michel quickly became confused about how long they had traveled. He thought maybe five days by now, but he really wasn't sure. He hadn't spoken with Eve. Occasionally, he spotted her among the thirty or so men and the sea of horses as she rode alongside the man called Khuyag. Only Khuyag had come to look in on him and speak a little with him. The man would slip him dried beef and sugared fruit to eat and mare's milk to drink. A blanket to protect him from the wind. He assured Michel that Eve was safe.

Michel thought always of Eve, awake or dreaming.

At present, he felt the party slow for the first time in hours. He'd been doing pushups, but at the change of pace, he rolled to peer out the slats of his prison. Ahead, he saw yurts scattered across deep green pastures filled with herd after herd of goats and sheep. Beyond, rolled naked blue-gray mountains. The air had been growing thinner on this journey, and the low-hanging clouds, mixing with the smoke from the yurts' chimneys, confirmed the high elevation. Michel changed his position to look ahead where he could see large imperial buildings with golden roofs tipped up at the edges, and one very large palace that seemed like it could be from his own home. The dread that had curtained him the further they had gone into new land continued to deepen. The whole time he'd been with her, from the moment he plucked her out of Merv, to the moment he'd finally told her he loved her, he had thought he'd been protecting an exceptional woman from men who aimed to harm her. Hearing the bits of conversation he could make out, seeing this military procession, and just opening his damn eyes to the reality of Eve's life, he'd realized that no, he hadn't saved a tribal woman. Michel had kidnapped a princess.

He rolled to his back, placing his hands on his chest, trying to catch his breath in the thin, smoky air. The blue of the sky seemed darker here. The colors everywhere were more vivid. He knew he was never meant to see this land. The tribes were notoriously insular and did not trade with or even permit Westerners far beyond Kashgar. Trade, his position, his reputation, none of it mattered anymore. The questions he had since the moment their little home had been invaded still ratcheted his brain: why did she keep all this from him? Even more crushing, he wondered if any of it, anything between them, had been real.

Eve could outthink him. Had all of this been a ploy just for her to get away? Were they holed up together in Carth just so she could bide her time until she was found by her people, since he hadn't gotten her to France fast enough? Their fledgling engagement, the care she gave him, the *sex*...was everything done to distract him long enough for her to alert her people to her whereabouts? And Ganbold...had she tricked Michel into fighting her enemy despite knowing it would destroy his livelihood?

He was mad at himself for falling in love so stupidly. How did it happen? He, of all people, should not have let this happen. He, of all people, should not have let himself be manipulated by a beautiful woman. An intriguing woman. A woman to whom he could never measure up. He shook his head. He never stood a chance against her.

But in his heart, if he thought about it, he didn't believe it had been an act. It couldn't have been.

He just needed to see her again. To speak with her and look into her eyes. To understand if the way she looked at him had changed now that she no longer needed him.

They moved through the valley and into the town. Michel watched with an idiot's awe as the buildings became even larger and more opulent up close. Every person they passed stood reverently by and bowed at the procession. A lifetime of meeting kings and queens and nobles had not prepared him for this. Her family, her identity, it was all beyond him.

He rolled his head to the side and looked out as they passed the colorful buildings. Over the rumbling of the horses, he heard men shouting in a dialect he could not understand. Eve was right. Everyone was right. He knew nothing. Outside, he felt the wind pick up. He closed his eyes, letting the movement of the cart lull him. He knew he would have no peace when he arrived.

Was he to be killed? He didn't know.

It didn't matter. If he could never see her again, none of it mattered.

She was home.

The procession went right to the steps of the palace. Eve patted the mare she had been riding and dismounted. The high stone walls blocked the sun, and she stood in the shade as the wind howled her return, evidence that her welcome would bring strife. She took in the thin air, needing two full breaths to feel full. She smelled the sweet yellow poppy scent. She felt an unbridled excitement to see her family again, but at the same time, the sadness of what she had to leave felt almost too much to bear. She worried for Michel—his body, his heart. She had kept away, afraid that showing him care and affection would rouse suspicion of their relationship. She did not want that to reach her father's ears before she had a chance to weave her story.

Khuyag came around to hold her arm. She realized she had frozen in front of the high southern-facing doors. Inside, she could see the long-pillared room that led to her father's high-backed chair, where he presided over meetings of the people. The juniper incense of her home reached out to welcome her, but she just wanted to turn and run back to Michel.

"Let's go, *Gonji*," Khuyag coaxed her through the entrance. "It won't be so bad."

At once, they marched down the corridor to her father's study. There was no pause, no softness to her arrival. They traveled through the high hallways that were at once both French and Mongolian with a staccato rhythm to their feet. They climbed the stone steps to the second level. Through the open windows, she saw the family yurts in the valley. Eve knew she would have to speak very carefully to spare Michel's life, giving her father the information he needed while avoiding the details of their relationship.

The soldiers believed Michel had kidnapped her. She said nothing, did nothing to dissuade their rumors, because to look desperate right now would only cause damage. The small directive she gave to Khuyag to treat Michel well, she knew, would be enough to keep Michel safe on their journey. It would be more difficult with her father. Having Michel to blame for her going missing and the death of the warriors would be the easiest solution in her father's eyes, one that would avoid a war. Michel was not tribal, and nothing outweighed the wellness of the tribes.

Her father was not cruel, however. Eve felt confident she could express that Michel had helped her and deserved more than to be executed for the fault of others.

Her affection for Michel, however, he would not accept.

Too foreign, too far, even though they had French blood. Her father would never allow such a match. Her marriage, her union, would still be needed to heal the tribes. To her father, Michel and her feelings for him were expendable.

She did not believe their feelings were expendable, but her priority was to save Michel's life by convincing her father to release him. Ill-timed emotions had no place now.

Khuyag rapped on the door. Eve prepared herself, and in seconds, the door swung open, and she saw her father—the solid, brilliant man she loved. He gripped her shoulders and ran his eyes over her face. She knew he was searching for any pain she carried.

"Are you well?" he asked.

"Yes, father," she replied.

At seeing him here once more, when she never thought she'd be again, a knotted ball of relief suddenly unspooled inside her. Tears came up and overflowed. Her father hugged her as though she were his young princess once more, the one who would cry her heart out to him at the unfairness of childhood things. It was always the case. Her strength would dissolve at the sight of her father, all her pain rising to the surface, waiting for him to soothe it.

"Eve," he said once her shuddering sobs had subsided. "I am so sorry you had to face this all alone."

"For most of my time away, I have been protected." She chose her words carefully. She pulled back to look at him, to show him she was strong once more.

"Darling, I need to know everything that has transpired. Take a moment to compose, but we must discuss it all soon. I don't want to rush you, but it is imperative that I take action. Timicin is here, and I must make a declaration."

"Timicin is *here*?" she asked, anxiety knotting her up once more.

"The eyes of the tribes are on us, my darling."

"I can speak with you now, Father," she said. "I do not need any time." She hoped matching him with urgency could work in her favor.

He bowed his head to her. "I am proud of you, Daughter. I see your strength and your spirit have not diminished. I admire you as always. Whatever you have been through," he said, taking her hands in his, "I know it has not been easy."

"It's been a trial," she said with a conceding smile.

He dismissed Khuyag and closed the door before bringing Eve to the cushioned seats.

"Come," he said. "Sit." He guided her to a chair. "Start at the beginning, when you were taken from our land." He paused, putting his hand over hers. "Do not leave out any details." He gave her a knowing look. "Eve, I implore you."

Eve nodded to her father. Calculating, she took a deep breath. She began her story.

Chapter Thirty-Eight

That evening, Michel sat alone on a stone bench with his head hanging between his knees in a dark cell. There was a high, open cutout in the stone, and streaks of moonlight were coming into the space. He still wore the same clothes he had been wearing when they had been captured. He'd been given a blanket when he was left in the cell, which he had draped over his shoulders.

He had looked for escape every step of the way. Michel had lived a life where his future title gave him enough backing to avoid many situations. His skills with his sword and his ability to outthink opponents avoided the rest. This far east, though, nobody cared. He was no one. He had nothing. He meant nothing.

He felt hopeless. He tried to talk his way out of the cell, but the guards ignored him. Maybe they didn't even understand him, and his skills with the language were as bad as Eve had said they were. He had tested his weight against the bars. They were more solid than him. He had no sword, no horse, no coin, no connections.

Worst of all, he had lost Eve.

He watched the moonlight change patterns across the floor as the minutes and hours drifted by. He did not have the will to lift his head. He only stared at the ground. At some point, he believed he ate something. At some other point, he drank. His body did not complain in those ways, but he hadn't paid enough attention to remember. He had nothing to do or occupy him other than the tortured memories of Eve and the lights of his small prison slowly stretching across the floor.

He closed his eyes and imagined what it felt like to hold her warm body against his once more. To listen to her laugh. To feel her hair between his fingers.

As the night passed, he must have dozed off with those thoughts in his head because a scrape of metal startled him awake. He heard fast footsteps coming toward him. He knew immediately that they were hers before she came into view. He jumped up and was at the door to his cell before she arrived.

"Eve!" he whispered, up on the balls of his feet. He didn't know if there was danger, but he could see the panic on her face. His sword, belt, and boots were in her hands. She fumbled momentarily with a key, then popped the door open with a clang. She pushed it in, and he grabbed at her, greedily wanting her in his arms, caring about nothing else. "Are you safe? Are you okay?"

"Michel," she urged. "You must get dressed, and you must leave. Right now. I had the guard called away. We don't have long."

"But...Eve," he said, filling his arms with her body, his nose with her scent.

"No, you will be killed if you stay here." Her voice was stern, but he heard the remorse around its edges.

"Come with me," he begged.

"I *can't*," she said, fighting back emotion.

"We will go to France, like we planned," he said, pulling on her arms. His voice, supplicant, frantic.

"Michel, if I leave now, it will be worse." She brought her hands up to her face, shaking her head at whatever outcome she feared. "So much worse for you."

"If I don't have you, Eve," he insisted, still trying to contain her, hold onto her somehow, "nothing matters."

"Put your gear on," she demanded. "Right now." She pulled him off her, pushed him back.

"Eve—" He reached for her again.

"No, you must trust me. You have to leave."

He paused and looked at her. His fingers brushed her chin and tilted her head up to him. He read her expression and the words she wasn't saying. "Your father won't accept me as your husband?" He asked finally.

"Absolutely not." Then her voice broke. "I tried."

"What do you mean, 'you tried'?"

"He is too old-fashioned, distrustful of the West. He would never let me go. Besides..." She shook her head. "He would never accept the relationship we've had."

"Let me speak to him." He was desperate, pleading with her.

"You have no value to him," Eve asserted. "He will not give me to you."

"I do have value," he said, indignant. "I have a city. I have Provence and France behind me."

"Michel, you don't understand your position here. Titles, cities, they're of no importance. I could barely convince him not to have you killed before dinner."

Michel just stared at her. "I protected you. I fought for you. Eve," he begged. "I love you."

She shook her head. "You must understand when I say I have a duty to my tribe just as you do to your people. Everything happened—my kidnapping, the murders—because I was selfish and refused to do what was expected of me. I abused my privilege because I wanted life to bend to my desires." She pulled in a breath. "The ancestors brought me home. Now I must pay my penance to my people."

"What does that even mean?" he asked, trying to get her to look at him.

"It means I have to stay, and Michel, it means you must leave, because you will be executed if you stay. And I cannot see that happen and have your death on my conscience too."

An uncontrollable surge of tears came upon her then, and she had her face in her hands. Michel took her in his arms against his chest, as he had before, letting her cry as much as she needed.

When her shudders slowed, he asked, "Is this truly what you want?"

She nodded. "It's not what I want, but it is what has to happen."

Michel watched her for a long moment, doing his best to trace every emotion that went through her eyes. "Alright," he said, taking in a deep breath through his nose. He backed away from her and sat to pull on his boots. "I will go."

He felt himself closing off to the cruelty of the world. He dressed quickly, feeling rage battle hopelessness in his chest. He placed his sword. He pulled on his jacket. She gave him a cloak to help conceal himself until he was in territory that would protect him once more.

"A guide and a horse are waiting outside to help get you to the river. The guide has basic supplies for you. Beyond there, you will be on your own, but you can follow roads and markings to help you get back to Carth." Then she paused. "Michel, I want you to know this doesn't change my feelings for you. I wanted all those things. I truly did." She shook her head. "It is just impossible now."

Michel nodded, unable to say anything else.

He pulled her close. He kissed her. One last time. He felt wetness on her cheeks or it could have been his own.

Then he sniffed and wiped his hand across his face. "Okay," was all he could say.

They worked together to finish getting him strapped into his belt. For a second, he felt the care and attention that she had given him before. It made his heart ache with a pain he knew would consume him. She hovered her hand above his wound but turned quickly back to his belt. Terrible feelings of loss rolled through him, but he decided to deal with it later. Right now, he had to hurry so she could get back to safety. He stepped into the hall, careful to make minimal sound. She followed him.

They stood for a moment, looking at each other. He took as much of their limited time as he could to memorize her beautiful features, the ones that had caused him to act in a way he had never known himself to act.

"Alright," he said. He touched her cheek. "Goodbye, Eve."

"Goodbye, Michel," she replied.

He moved in and gave her a quick kiss on the lips. Then he turned and ran down the hallway and through the door that she had left open for him into the cool night.

She stood there, watching the empty space where he had been, still feeling the imprint of his lips on hers. Part of her couldn't believe he was gone. He had been everything to her over the last months: her enemy, her savior, her patient, her lover, nearly her husband. Now he, along with a life she had wanted so badly, had disappeared.

She had told her father of her marriage to Bataar and how the girl had killed him. How Eve had run, thinking it was the best way to avoid conflict. How she had found a Frenchman whom she convinced to bring her with him to France.

Her father agreed to protect the girl. Together, Eve and her father wove a story in which Ganbold killed Bataar, jealous of his new bride, while Eve escaped.

Now, my flower, if you wish to do your duty to the tribes, a marriage to Bataar's brother would be ideal.

Father, I want to heal the tribes. I want to do my duty...would you allow an alliance with France?

You mean the Frenchman?

He is a good man. A noble.

There are better men for you. Men in Timicin's tribe.

I care for him.

Has he coerced you, darling daughter?

No father, he is a good man. Strong and loyal.

He did not bring you home. He did not seek out your family. If he truly cared for you, if he were truly noble, he would have insisted.

Father, I concealed my identity. He did not know I was the daughter of the Golden Khan.

Would your family love you less if we were shepherds? He had asked, and Eve knew his mind about Michel had been made up.

She had grown up learning never to make excuses for her actions, to do what was right by the tribes, to control her emotions or be disregarded. But if she thought anything would change her father's mind, if anything could convince him to let her marry Michel, she would have done it, damn the expectations. She could continue to argue, beg, and plead, perhaps. She could point out the hypocrisy of Bataar stealing her and Michel protecting her, but her father was traditional and couldn't see through his culture, and though he loved her, he would want a solution that would appease the tribes.

Regardless, she did not know how much time she had before her body gave away her pregnancy. Her sisters-in-law always seemed to be fat with child days after it was announced. Eve thought for a moment she could claim it had been Bataar, but the timing did not line up, and even if the math was dismissed, a baby would come along that did not look like it had a tribal father. No, Michel would not be safe if she turned up pregnant. Her father, a fair, strong, brilliant Khan, was still a protective, conservative, volatile father who would have nothing to stop him from killing the man who had compromised his daughter.

It was the only option, then, to send Michel away, before the depth of their relationship was suspected, before Michel had to endure tribunals, before he suffered any more damage to his own life, so he could salvage some of his own legacy. There were too many complications and too many ways Michel could still be blamed or harmed. Her father, though he conceded not to immediately execute Michel for the crimes of others, insisted Michel remain imprisoned until he had a chance to mitigate expectations of the il-khans. That would take time. Eve did not have time.

When she had left her father's war room earlier that day, she had never felt more despondent, seeing all the ways she had caused harm. She knew, at least, what she would do about Michel, and that gave her something to focus on. She had made quick arrangements with a local guide who agreed to get Michel to the end of the mountain steppes, where he could have some autonomy and safety once more. She had secured a horse, clothing, and things he would need for survival. She retrieved his sword and weapons. She would get him out, she had decided, because that was the only way to protect him.

Now she stood where he had just been, silent tears streaming down her face.

It was early the next morning that Michel's escape had been discovered. A guard had rushed in alongside Khuyag, who had broken the news to her father. Eve had spent the morning hovering around waiting for the news. When they discovered the empty cell with no prisoner, her father turned to her with disapproving eyes. In all her life, this was truly the first moment she had ever felt his disapproval. She also knew it would get worse in the coming months as her pregnancy became evident. Then her father was moving, gone, like she knew he would be, launching a search and throwing himself into political handlings.

She took her only breath of relief then. She knew that Michel should have had enough distance to be safe. If he stayed smart, he could avoid trouble and get himself home. She had done everything she could for him. Now, he would be on his own.

Chapter Thirty-Nine

It had been one week since she had said goodbye to Michel. From the moment she knew he had escaped, Eve had gone to her bed. She did not wish to leave it. Ever. Her brothers had come to her one by one. Her grandmother sat with her, saying nothing as she stroked Eve's hair. Her sisters-in-law trickled in. Eve would just dismiss them all, roll over, and sleep some more. Her father had tried to talk to her. Thankfully, he did not press the issue, mumbling that Timicin would wait as long as he had to. Everyone was afraid of her now, afraid of what she had been through, afraid of learning the reasons she was so depressed. Her father did not share any of her story with the family. It stayed between them, he had said, for as long as she wanted.

The one thing she did was mentally track where Michel could be. She knew how far he could travel each day. She estimated that he should have reached Carth by now and gone past it. It renewed her sadness as she thought of him alone in that city where their commitment had been fully forged. It didn't matter. She would never truly know where he was or if he was safe. It was just something to occupy her mind rather than letting her heart miss him. One thing she did know was that he had not been captured by her family's guards. She would hear if that had happened.

As she lay in her bed, she felt the star of happiness travel further and further from her. She felt her body changing, too. On top of her despondency, she had reached the point of having a hard time keeping food inside her, her stomach heaving at the thought of eating. It made everything seem impossible. All she could do was sip milk tea or bone broth and continue to sleep.

It was on the seventh day of her solitude that her mother demanded she get out of bed.

The knock came softly. When Eve did not answer, her mother entered her room anyway. Eve looked at her and then closed her eyes once more.

"Come, daughter," her mother said. "You must rise now."

"Mother, I do not feel well," Eve said, dismissing her, turning over.

"It is time to feel better." Her mother hummed as she opened the curtains to let the morning sun into the room.

Eve loved her mother dearly, but they were so different. Her mother was simple and allowed all her decisions to be made by her husband. She never had an independent thought in her head, whereas Eve had nothing but independent thoughts. Even being there in Eve's room, demanding Eve get out of bed, was at her father's insistence.

Her mother pulled the covers off Eve. Eve shrieked and grumbled at this attack and tried to pull them back onto her. Her mother didn't allow it.

"Up." Her mother took Eve's hands and pulled her to sitting. Then she led her daughter to the chair at the vanity. She sat behind Eve and began brushing through Eve's hair. Eve stayed silent, watching the woman in the mirror. They looked very much alike, despite her mother's dark coloring and Eve's light hair. Eve, for a second, wondered if her child would have her light hair or look more like Michel. Her eyes stung with pain at the thought.

Her mother did not seem to notice. She spoke. "Was it your intention?"

"Was what my intention?" Eve replied flatly.

"To become pregnant?" she said. She continued humming softly.

Eve blinked, "I'm not, I did not..."

"Enebish," her mother said. "You were my seventh child. I know what pregnancy looks like. I saw it on you the moment you arrived."

"But—"

"Answer my question, were you hoping to become pregnant?"

"No," Eve replied, shaking her head. "Why would I try to become pregnant?"

"To secure a proposal?" her mother hummed.

She dropped her head to her arms, which rested on the surface of the vanity. "No, I was not hoping to become pregnant. But..." She took a breath. "Our union was not unwelcome."

"My beautiful daughter," her mother said. She rubbed her hand down Eve's back. "I am sorry I did not prepare you to avoid this."

Eve stared at her mother in the mirror. Her mother continued brushing through Eve's hair, detached from her words, still humming. Her mother had never once spoken to her about such things, and Eve was shocked to hear that she would have ever had this conversation with this woman.

"Does father know?" Eve asked, feeling a spike of shame run through her.

"Of the pregnancy?" Her mother laughed. "He never knows until I tell him." She traced her fingers across Eve's scalp, separating her hair into sections. "He suspects your feelings for the man are greater than you expressed. But, no, he does not know of anything more." She took a section of hair and placed it over Eve's shoulder. "Have you fallen in love?"

Eve couldn't help it, and suddenly tears wet her face like a summer storm. Her mother put her arms around Eve's shoulders and held her tightly. "My sweet girl."

"Do you think Father will send me away?"

"Of course not. He will not stop loving you, dear child. He will just need time." She pulled back and resumed her work on Eve's hair. "Did you help the man escape?"

Eve nodded.

Her mother's persistently happy eyes turned down. "I am so sorry it did not work out for you. Love is a wonderful thing."

Eve let the tears fall freely from her eyes. "What will Father do when he finds out I am pregnant?"

"You know what he will do. He will attack the world."

"He expects me to marry someone in Timicin's tribe," Eve said softly. "How can I do so?" She heaved a great sob at the thought.

"He will not force you to marry. He hasn't done so before. He won't do so now."

"Then we must go to war."

"Oh, *war*," her mother humphed. "I'm so tired of hearing that word. These men go to war fifteen times a day. It is all for show."

"But Ganbold and Bataar..."

"Both deserved what they got." Her mother nodded to punctuate the claim. "They all know it's true. Timicin needs to bring some consolation back to his tribe so he doesn't look like a fool. Your father can figure that out without having to send you," she snipped. "He can just as easily send the goats."

The goats, Eve thought. If only she'd had more time. But it was far too late. "Mother," Eve said, "I don't think I've ever heard you talk of father like this. Or speak your mind so fluently."

"It is true, I am not like you, my Enebish. I don't always use words." She smiled. "But I do know how to control my husband." She set down the brush and squeezed Eve's shoulders. "Now, your hair is smooth. Bathe. Get dressed. Start to act like a woman of pride once more. Your father has brooded in his room as long as you have. I would like some sunshine in my life again. My daughter is safe with a new life inside her." She kissed the top of Eve's head. "There are many things to celebrate."

"When should I tell him that I am with child?"

"Wait longer. We must be sure that your man has had time to escape. You don't want your father to get his hands on him now." She smoothed her hands down Eve's shoulders. "I know it was hard, but sending him away was the right thing to do."

"Yes," she agreed. "I believe so." She put her hands on her lower belly and, for the first time, she felt more than just sadness. Her mother's words had affected her. She had lost the man she would always love, but she had gained something wonderful. And hearing her mother's consolation—that her father in time would come around—she was able to see new beginnings.

It didn't take away from the terrible loss she felt over Michel, though.

Chapter Forty

Once her mother left her room, Eve pushed herself to wash and dress for the first time since she had gone into bed a week ago. She sat in warm water and let the maids use fancy soaps and oils on her. She undid her hair and washed it, then arranged it back and up in the traditional braids. She wore one of her silk deel gowns—a royal blue with a high golden sash—and beaded shoes. It all felt very strange to be putting her old life back on when nothing about her was the same anymore. Her mother was right. She had to begin living again. If not for herself, for the new life inside her.

She ventured out of her room. The attendants showed their affection through smiles and offers of sweets. She made her way to the front sitting room, where she sat near the high window that overlooked the steppes and the fields of wheat, barley, and oats meticulously plotted. Her mother sent her a special tea to help soothe her stomach. She sipped it, but still did not feel up to more adventurous snacks.

She looked out the window, across the open market and the buildings of the city surrounding the large stupa monastery, with high white walls that formed bulbs on the top. The view was something she'd always known and never thought to leave. Now, she wondered what it would be like to look on the green forests and blue-green seas her grandmother had always spoken about. But that was not to be. And so, she acknowledged the beauty in her home, and she appreciated the fact that she could witness it once more.

She turned from the window and picked up a small book on philosophy that she had enjoyed just a few months before. She sat to read, tucking her legs under her on the couch. Just when she started to sink into it, the wives of her two middle brothers came into the room. They wore full traditional dressings and dripped with curiosity. Eve loved her sisters-in-law, but she had never much wanted to engage in the social games they played with each other. Each proud women in their own right and good to her brothers. Eve had long ago accepted them, each taking one of her brothers and pushing Eve further down the line of importance in her own family. Still, it didn't mean she always preferred their company.

They came in on the sweet smell of incense and gardens and sat across from her, all elegant, colorful deels and intricate hair. "Oh, sweet flower," said the elder of the two, "you have journeyed through such hardships."

"Yes," the other insisted, "tell us everything."

Eve closed her book, knowing her short moment of peace had come to an end. "Perhaps another time," she said with a defeated smile. "I am still adjusting to being home."

"You do not want to upset elder sister," the younger of the two retorted. Her tone was light, but Eve recognized this trick to force her into compliance. "You should do as she asks," the woman pressed.

"You are right. I don't mean to disobey," Eve said, her mischievous nature coming back. "It is just a difficult story to tell."

"You may tell us," elder sister said with an eager nod.

"You know I was snatched right from the fields," Eve began. "I was simply tending the goats for my morning chores when I was swept onto the back of the horse." Eve shook her head and looked down. "It was terrible to know I was being stolen by a young tribe that does not afford its women the same rights."

"Oh, how truly awful," said younger sister as she brought her hands to her face.

"And, yes," Eve said, opening her eyes wide with drama. "I was forced to marry. But I escaped!"

"Yes, but how did you escape?" asked elder sister. Both women leaned in.

"You see..." began Eve. She realized this was the heart of the question. They wanted to know if the rumors were true. If she had, in fact, killed the man who had been her husband. "As we walked to the marriage hut, there was a sudden flash of light."

"A flash of light?" elder sister asked.

"Where did the light come from?" asked younger sister.

"I had to shield my eyes," exclaimed Eve, "from the brilliance of it. It could have blinded me for sure!"

"Yes, yes, what was the source?" elder sister pressed. The two of them leaned forward.

"I felt the heat cooking my skin. I thought the sun had struck us all down, the sky punishing us all! I did not know!" Eve cried. "I squinted my eyes enough to look, and that is when I saw..." Eve paused for effect. She raised her hands, "The dragon!" she hissed.

"A real dragon?" questioned the younger woman. Elder sister rolled her eyes and folded her arms in a huff.

"Yes, indeed," Eve said, turning very serious, still teasing the one sister-in-law who wasn't completely convinced the story was untrue. "Now, if you will excuse me, I must go take my medicine."

"What for?" elder sister pried, her interest piqued once more.

"You see, if you are too close to a dragon, you will slowly turn to gold, unless you take daily medicine."

At that point, she jumped up to escape the women. She heard the two sisters-in-law complaining about her imagination as she left. Eve scampered down the hallway, feeling the first mischievous giggle she had felt in a long time.

As she made her escape, a jarring noise came from somewhere outside. Clangs of swords and shouts of men. Twisted struggles and booted feet scraping across the dirt. Eve turned toward the stadium, where her father would be if there were complications. She came to the railing that overlooked the rectangular throne room. Her father sat poised on his seat at the far end, facing the high open doors. Her brothers lined the walk up to him, as they did for any confrontation of consequence. Eve hung over the balcony. From this position, she could see outside the front of the palace. The guards shouted at each other as they came from their posts. Then she heard noise from inside as a rush of attendants flurried by behind her.

"What is happening? What is happening?" she called as they whizzed by and down the steps to the first floor. Unease gripped her core. She feared terrible news. Were they being attacked? Had Timicin decided to defy the ancestors and finally wage a war because she had not already agreed to marry one of his men? Or, and this thought twisted and made her want to vomit, was she about to see Michel's body?

Her father looked like he might burst into flames at any moment as he prepared for whatever was coming through that door. Her brothers flexed into their fighting positions, prepared to defend their father and tribe.

Her two sisters-in-law peeked in from the door behind her. Eve saw the one bite her nails and the other scold her for doing so.

For one second, the noise halted, and the silence blanketed the great hall. Then her father bellowed, "Bring him in!"

They came into view: several guards, Khuyag, and Timicin.

Then she saw him—Michel—at the center, arms bound, struggling.

Emotions tangled through her, causing her limbs to shake. *At least*, she thought, *at least he was alive.*

"Father!" Eve shouted from the balcony into the open space, putting all the desperation she felt into her voice.

"Quiet!" he shouted back to her, without taking his eyes off the commotion at the far end of the hall.

The guards dragged Michel across the carpet runner as Michel tried to catch his balance, missing some steps and stumbling. He looked a mess, clothes in tatters, dirt smeared across his face and down his shirt. She didn't know why he was here or at whose behest. Her heart ached for him, but she held herself back to understand under what circumstances he had returned.

"Leave him," her father commanded the guards as he leaned forward in his seat. The guards backed away, leaving Michel in the center of the room, facing her father. Eve's heart felt like it would beat out of her chest.

Her father, on the other hand, smoldered in his seat, pure fire. "How have you come here?" her father boomed, now in French.

"I escaped the cell a week ago," Michel spoke back, his voice loud and firm despite his tattered looks. "I have spent that time in hiding, looking for a way into your palace. To have your audience."

Her father stirred in his seat, obviously not happy that Michel had evaded his security. Eve realized that, in the time that she had been mentally tracking his movements, he had never even left.

"You have my audience," her father thundered. "Why are you here?"

Michel stood tall with his head up, looking square at her father. He was taller than her brothers, but they were clad in their warrior attire, while Michel had none of his protection or weapons. Still, he stared at her father with that pride he always carried. For once, she appreciated his arrogance.

"Speak," her father commanded.

Michel stared at him. Everyone in the room stared at Michel.

"Speak!" her father repeated.

"I am here for your daughter." He stood proud, noble, unflinching.

"Excuse me?"

"I would like to marry your daughter," Michel called, his voice booming across the hall.

"I should kill you now," her father ground out. On a wink, her brothers had their swords at the ready. "You are nothing."

"I am not nothing," Michel insisted. "I will be the Duke of Chevalerie, an important social and political region in France. I offer trade, I offer allies. I offer a wonderful life for your daughter."

"My daughter has all and more. Who are you to think that you can give her something she does not have?" Her father smoldered. "You are nothing compared to her."

Michel dropped his head. "You are correct. Without your daughter, I am nothing."

A tense silence hovered, but her father spoke, softening. "I know that you helped her. For this, I did not block your escape."

Eve blinked. Had her father let him escape?

Her father continued. "You do not deserve her."

"I have done nothing wrong by her—"

"You did not bring her *home*," her father cut him off, coming up to stand. "You would have taken her to your country with no word, no care for her family or her customs. You used your position to take advantage of a woman who had no one there to protect her."

"I did not kidnap her," Michel yelled back. "That was your people. I found her," he corrected himself, "she found *me*, after she had already been taken from *your* fields."

Borjigin stepped off the dais. Eve could see the flames in his eyes, ready to engulf them all. She feared this version of her father, the one who was torn by many different rights and wrongs, the one most volatile.

"Father!" she called out again.

"Quiet!" he roared back without taking his eyes off Michel.

Eve shook, her hands gripping the banister. Michel could die by his words.

Her father took a breath. Then he began, his words careful and even. "I respect that you have come here to try to speak with me. However, I cannot let you go again, boy. You have solved many problems for me by coming back." He turned to his eldest son, Dzhambul. "Now," he instructed.

Her brother pulled his sword and took quick steps toward Michel without hesitation. Michel took his stance, but he had no weapons. Eve knew he would fight, but he had no way of winning. Eve could shout for Dzhambul to stop, for her father to call them off, for Michel to run, but she knew that none of those things would save him. So, instead, she said the one thing that was sure to get a reaction.

"I'm pregnant!" she shouted down to the floor.

That froze everyone in place.

"You're *what*?" Her father yelled, finally looking up at her.

Eve hung over the balcony and locked eyes with Michel for the first time since he had arrived. "You're pregnant?" Michel called up to her.

"Yes," she said, nodding furiously, wiping sudden tears from her cheeks.

Michel stared, and despite the chaos between them, he breathed in and smiled and grabbed at his heart...just seconds before her youngest brother caught him with a left hook right across the chin.

"Oh!" Eve shouted and ran down the stairs as the floor erupted into a brawl. Three of her brothers had jumped onto Michel at the news. Dzhambul still stood with his sword drawn, but he had let it fall to the side as he leaned against a column and waited for his turn. Her other two brothers circled the pack, looking for an opening.

Her father stood at his chair, staring at Eve. She didn't look at him. She couldn't deal with the shame of finding herself pregnant or any disapproval right now. She only cared about Michel. She wanted to honor her tribe. She cared about doing what was right, but she didn't have the strength to turn Michel away again. She took the steps of the staircase as fast as she could.

In the center, Michel ducked and threw a punch at her brother, Yul. The youngest brother jumped on Michel's back, and Michel slung him off, while the other took a swing, which Michel evaded, only to be nailed in the stomach by Esen. Michel stumbled back and sucked in a breath, ready to take on the next attack.

"Stop!" she commanded, running up to them, wedging herself between them and Michel. "Stop!"

The men hesitated and they backed away from each other. They sniffed and wiped sweat and blood from their faces.

Michel stood in the same spot, now beaten, a black eye forming, a gash on his cheek, and a swollen lip. But his expression held joy. His eyes sparkled.

"How long have you known?" he said, reaching for her hands.

"A few weeks," she said, brimming with happiness, struggling to contain it. "Before we were separated."

He breathed in, and she saw him trying to control his own emotions. "Is that what you were about to tell me in Carth?"

She nodded and smiled. "Yes."

Michel grinned, too, and she couldn't hold back anymore. He had come for her, to face her father. Nothing mattered anymore, only to be with him again. Everything else would have to work out, because she saw her future unfurling before her and it was once again joyous. She threw her arms around Michel. He held her for a moment, then Michel sank to his knees in front of her and hugged her around her legs.

She huddled over him, her hands reaching down to wrap around him. She closed her eyes to take this moment to forget about everything else. There was just Michel. And his body and his arms around her. It was just the two of them. The three of them.

Until she heard her father.

"Stop this instant!" he yelled.

Michel looked up to her. The happiness unraveled as reality came in once again.

"Face me, boy," her father demanded, now standing himself.

Eve gripped Michel, not wanting to let him go, but Michel stood and pulled back. He turned to her father.

Eve wasn't sure what was coming, anxiety wrapping around her.

Her father approached Michel until he was inches away. Michel was taller than her father, but her father was a figure who could intimidate anyone of any size. Still, Michel held his own and clenched his jaw as he waited to be addressed.

He stared at Michel but addressed Eve. "Eve, when you mentioned this match to me, you did not express that you had already chosen this man. I believed you to be in shock, an affection to him because you were traumatized by the situation. I see now that is not the case."

Eve dropped her head, not used to disappointing her father.

"I don't know if you are a good man." He spoke now to Michel. "My daughter seems to believe so. I am inclined to trust her." He nodded. "And if the ancestors have blessed you with a child, it is not my place to interfere."

Eve felt strings of hope wrap around her heart.

"*If* I allow you to marry my daughter, my *only* daughter," her father continued, his eyes hot on Michel, "to take her from her home, do you promise to spend your life in her service?"

"Without a doubt," Michel declared without hesitation. "Nothing will ever change that."

"Because I will have no problem bringing war to your doorstep if I ever feel that she is not being taken care of."

"She will be my greatest concern, always. And..." He paused. Michel choked up, his voice cracked, and he had to stop to clear his throat. "And any children we have, too."

Her father pressed his lips and nodded.

Eve jumped forward then and took Michel's hand. He turned to her, and she saw in his face what she already knew in her heart: that, yes, he would spend his life worshiping her and protecting her and the family they would build together. She reached forward to hug him again.

Then her father barked once more, causing them both to jump. "No touching," he boomed. Then his voice softened. "Not until the wedding."

Eve bit her lip to contain the wonderful emotions set free inside of her. She smiled at Michel and stepped back to let him go.

Only because she would get to have him once more—and now for the rest of their lives.

Chapter Forty-One

From there, Michel and her father went into a locked room alone and did not come out. Eve was not allowed in, though it seemed every other advisor her father ever had was summoned at some point. Khuyag came and went. Each brother was called in. Timicin entered the room and stayed for hours. She heard bursts of yelling from behind the door throughout the day, but she never knew from whom.

Eve stayed perched outside the door. For a while, she paced. Then she sat. Then she stood by the window. Each time the door opened, she waited for news, like an expectant father. She received nothing more than stern looks from those coming and going. Her mother brought her broth and fruit to nibble on. Her sisters-in-law, all five of them this time, like a flock of geese, came to look at her, asking questions she couldn't answer. *What are they discussing? Why aren't you allowed in? Did you* really *see a dragon*? The time ticked by, and the sun traveled through the sky. It was not like her father to leave her out of things that mattered to her. Plus, she had input that could help this alliance be forged. But now, *now,* she wasn't invited while these men planned her future?

Finally, after hours and hours, the door opened. Her father stood there and asked her to come in. By now, she was *pissed.*

She rose and walked toward him in a halo of fire. Her father's expression went from sternness to surprise when he saw her, then to amusement as she glared at him while entering the room.

Michel, molded over a chair, perked up to smile at her, but his expression turned anxious when he saw her scowl.

Her father sat at the table, Michel stayed in the chair to his right, and Eve sat across from the two men. She folded her arms.

"So," she bit out. "What have you two intellects decided will be my fate?"

Michel opened his mouth to speak, then shut it. He looked from her to her father.

Her father sighed with irritation. "Michel has told me many things this afternoon," he began. "Many things that you did not tell me about the journey you have been on." He paused and breathed in a long breath through his nose. "I believe..." He paused. "I believe this will be a suitable match."

"Oh, really?" Eve said sarcastically, her arms folded.

"Eve," Michel began. "We didn't mean to exclude you. There were politics to discuss. How to handle Timicin."

"Do you not trust my input on politics? You don't know this tribe better than I."

"No, I—" stammered Michel. "Of course not."

"Enough." Her father waved his hand. "I needed my head to be clear. If you were here, emotions would be too high."

"Father, I am more than capable of controlling my emotions—"

He stood up and struck his chest with a closed fist. "*My* emotions, Enebish."

Eve shut her mouth.

Her father took in another controlling breath. "It is all done. Everything has been decided."

"What of the tribe of Timicin?" she pressed.

Michel scooted forward on his chair. "Eve, we will trade with him," he said, his voice hoarse from the hours of negotiations. "Timicin's tribe does business with the Chinese and other markets I've never had access to. It will give me enough that the loss of Renault and Kashgar will not destroy my business here."

"The trade will bring riches to Timicin," her father interjected. "He is satisfied."

"The girl?" Eve asked.

"As far as Timicin knows, it was Ganbold who killed Bataar." Borjigin nodded. "This was all a game played by the ancestors. Let them know the truth and no others."

"Well," she said, throwing her hands up in resignation. "That just leaves me."

"Eve," Michel said. He reached out to take her hand, but when her father grunted, he pulled his hands back. "We will be wed in the morning. Your father has agreed."

"No," Eve said.

"No?" Michel asked.

"No?!" her father bellowed as he slammed his hands on the desk, fuming once more.

Eve stood up too to match her father's gaze. "We are traveling to Chevalerie," she announced, fuming just as much. "I wish first to be accepted by my future in-laws."

"Who is traveling?" asked Michel.

"All of us," she asserted, still matching stares at her father. She could tell by his expression that he would concede without further argument. "My parents, my brothers, the whole damn family."

Her father sat back down in his chair and folded his arms.

"And Father," she said. "Prepare to bring the cashmere with us."

"The cashmere?" he repeated.

"Yes," she said, "All of it. Empty every storehouse and set the craftsmen to make more. I want every bolt, every string, every fiber coming with us."

"Where is this coming from?" he asked. He indicated toward Michel. "We spoke nothing of cashmere."

"Because he needs to bring home more than beads and barley from Timicin. Or my new family, my new people, will be persecuted." She stuck a finger toward Michel, who jumped when she did.

"I would have to discuss this with the il-khans." Her father hesitated.

Eve stomped out of the room and then returned with the orange-bound book in her hand. She tossed it onto her father's desk. "In there, you will find every agreeable merchant between here and the Mediterranean. Every transaction that can justify this level of trade. You have all you need to convince anyone that this will be a prosperous market for both the horde and my new home.”

“We aren’t prepared to initiate this level of trade...” he trailed off.

“Figure it out, Father, like you have just figured out the rest of my life.” Then she turned back to Michel. “I hope your little kingdom can handle our army,” she yelled as she slammed out of the room.

As she left, she had caught the look of shock on Michel’s face. But it wasn’t until she got down the hall that she heard the booming laughter of her father.

Later that night, there came a knock on her door. She knew that knock. It was the knock of a man who knew that her pride had been bruised and that she had been taking too much from this life. A knock she had heard many times growing up—whenever she was criticized for being too bold, knowing too much, or for being too demanding. The knock of her father.

She had been sitting in her chair by the window, staring out across the land that she had grown up in. She rose and called for him to enter.

“Eve.” He approached her with a heavy grumbling sigh. “You are wearing on my patience.”

“What Father? Have I offended you by taking an active role in my life?” She said the bold words, but her countenance could not back them up. She collapsed once more in the chair. Despite everything, she felt defeated.

“Did I not concede to everything you asked for?” he asked, voice terse.

“Yes,” she said. She dropped her head into her hands. “Thank you.” The words muffled in her hands.

Borjigin chuckled and sat beside her. “What troubles you, my Enebish?”

“Father, I am so sorry to put you through this. This pregnancy. I am terribly ashamed.”

“Ahh, yes.” He put his feet up on the table and leaned back. “That is not ideal.” He paused. “I certainly didn’t expect your marriage to come about like this. But I suppose...” He sighed. “There are worse things.”

She looked up at him, surprised he was not more upset.

“Do you know what Michel and I talked about today?” he asked.

"You talked affiliations. Alliances. How to navigate the marriage politically with the other tribes—"

"Yes, of course. I am not in a position to take a betrothal for you lightly. Our family has always had an obligation to the horde. You know that." He nodded. "But that wasn't what Michel and I spent our time on."

She looked at him.

"I needed to know what happened to you and how everything transpired. You gave me very little information. I needed to know how you suffered. You are my daughter. I failed to protect you." He sat up straight, placing his feet on the ground once more. "You have always had a problem telling the whole story."

"I was just trying to protect everyone," she said, a humbled softness to her voice.

"Yes, my flower, but if you don't allow anyone to see the full picture, you are not protecting anyone. Including yourself."

She looked down. "I am beginning to realize that."

Her father continued. "You did not tell me how Bataar treated you or abused his wives. How you were forced into exile. How Michel kept you safe."

"I was worried that if I spoke of Michel too fondly, you would be more suspicious of our relationship. I didn't want anyone to discover the pregnancy until he was far away."

"Again, these are times when you must trust in the counsel of the people around you. That was too heavy a decision to make on your own, and in an instant at that." He leaned forward to take her hands. "Enebish, you are impulsive. What have I always taught you? Think before you step, and what have you always done? Step before you think. If you want to lead, darling, you cannot do it on your own."

"I understand." She squeezed his hands, then let them go. "Father," she continued, realizing she was not yet finished with her demands. "It cannot be allowed anymore—wife-stealing."

"It is not *allowed*," he began.

"Yes, but it happens." She looked at him sharply. "It is terrible and degrading and brutal. Our culture is too beautiful to turn our heads when such a thing takes place."

"It has always been a complication among the young tribes. I truly haven't seen the face of it so close."

"It happens," she shook her head, thinking of the trauma of the girl, "to those poor girls without the support that I have. Their families can't do anything to help them." She gave him a weak smile. "And would you love me any less if you were a shepherd and not the Khan?"

He closed his eyes and stroked down his beard with a heavy sigh. "I'm sorry that it took happening to you to make me take notice," he said. "I will ensure it is punished. And that the women who have fallen victim are given protection."

"Thank you, Father," she said. She trusted him. He would make it right.

Her father shifted and cleared his throat. "Now back to Michel," he said, a grumble to his voice.

She looked to see his expression turn stern once more, causing worry to unravel inside her.

"I don't hate him," he conceded.

"No?" she gave a small grin.

"He never once mentioned cashmere," Borjigin continued, softer. "I didn't know anything about how he was trying to secure a line."

"I never said we produced it." She shrugged.

"We have thousands of goats roaming the steppes. He would have to be a horse's ass not to figure it out." He gave a small laugh. "I asked him, after you left, why he didn't bring it up. He said he didn't want any more complications. He only cared about becoming your husband."

"Why did you agree, Father?" Eve asked, looking up at him. "To let us marry?"

He just gave a far-off smile. He put his elbows on his knees and leaned forward. "I have entertained you through books, languages, history, philosophy, politics, studies in the cities, and debates with important leaders. But never once, Enebish, have I had to deal with you falling in love. You never cared for marriage, never showed any interest in any man that I saw." His expression was gentle as he spoke. "I would be a cruel and unwise man to deny this union."

"Thank you for trusting me." She sighed. "I should have just spoken to you outright."

"Darling, think before you step." He reached forward to take her hand.

"You helped the man escape before you let me see the full picture. Don't let pride stop you from asking for what you need. You will be a duchess, far away, and you won't have my counsel. You are smart enough to put your trust into the right people."

"I know, Father." She folded her hands, very much humbled.

"He adores you," Borjigin grunted.

"Yes." She couldn't help grinning—of this she was sure. "He does."

"Perhaps don't be so harsh on him," he said with amusement.

"Perhaps," she said, mirroring the amusement that was on her father's face.

Chapter Forty-Two

Over the next few days, Michel had the chance to get to know Eve's family, and it was a hell of an experience. Since the moment that Michel left his future father-in-law's study, he had not been permitted to see Eve. Not during the day, during dinner, or at night. He didn't know if her father commanded as such or if she was still enraged about how the marriage arrangements were handled. Michel didn't get to ask. Instead, he met what seemed like hundreds of aunts and uncles, cousins, nieces, and nephews, all who gave him suspicious glares behind warm smiles and warned him to treat their Eve well or the ancestors would haunt his days and nights.

And then there were her brothers.

Dzhambul, Esen, Tarkhan, Chuluun, Batuhan, and Yul, each terrifying testaments to the strength needed to thrive in this land. To be fair, his first interaction with them had been when he was almost beheaded at their father's feet. Now that they weren't trying to rip off his arms and beat him to death with his own bones, as Eve had once told him they would, Michel could see how much they cared for their sister. Not allowed to sleep in the palace, Michel stayed in the yurt of Yul, the only one still not married. Yul spoke to him and tolerated him more than the others, though still not that much.

With the brothers, he had learned to make yogurt, harvest barley, and shear the goats. He had sparred with them, learning new techniques. He listened to their deep, textured singing. He learned to weave the cashmere threads. And the *cashmere*. He felt so stupid dragging Eve around looking for someone who had a few hanks to trade when her family had thousands of spools just sitting around in their storehouses. Ridiculous. He must have looked like such a fool to her. But she saved his ass, in the end. He would return to France like a hero.

On the second night of his stay, Michel sat at the fire pit with the brothers and their families. The oldest brother, Dzhambul, the one who had drawn his sword to kill Michel when he re-entered the palace, came to sit near Michel. Seventeen years older than Eve, he already had the presence of a strong, weathered man. He would one day lead the horde himself, a successor to a powerful man, just like Michel.

The familial yurts spread out in the camp while the family clustered around the central fire pit. The sun sat just above the edges of the mountains, but the perpetual gray mix of wispy clouds and smoke from the chimneys obscured it. Off to the side, Chuluun and Esen sparred. A scattering of children ran through the area, playing and stopping only when a mother grabbed them to clean their faces, or an uncle picked them up to throw them playfully out of their way. Movement and laughter, shouts and swords came from every angle. Michel sat, enjoying the warmth and ease of the family. Ironic, he thought, that these men were ready to kill him just the day before, and now he sat at their table, among them. He'd been ignorant of so many things, but what a gift to be able to experience the depth of her culture from this vantage point.

After a moment, Dzhambul spoke. Up until then, each brother had come to him and given him the same look. Angry acceptance. Tentative family. Dzhambul was the last to address him.

Dzhambul did not look at Michel directly while he spoke. "You fought bravely." Then he gave just a hint of a grin, under his thick, dark beard. "We were all surprised."

Michel gave a laugh at that. "I know I didn't look like much when I came in," he agreed. "I'd been hiding in alleyways, stealing food, trying to figure out how to get to your father."

"Yes," said Dzhambul. "You looked like you had already died three times when you entered the hall." He nodded his head as he poured tobacco into his pipe. "I mean, we were surprised you fought well because you are French. The French, westerners in general..." He glanced at Michel. "It is not always the strong who lead."

"We have had many fine leaders throughout history," Michel said. He didn't want to start a debate while he was still ingratiating himself, but he felt compelled to defend his country.

Dzhambul held his hand out to continue. "A khan may have many sons. In some tribes, from many wives. It is not the first son that inherits the title, like it is in your home. Borjigin, my father, was the youngest. But he was the fiercest. It is why he is the Khan now." He shifted, pressing the tobacco down. "The one who will make the best leader is chosen."

"I see what you are saying." In fact, it made a lot of things about Eve and their early interactions much clearer.

"You have brothers?" Dzhambul asked.

"Yes," Michel replied. "Two."

"Are you the one who should lead?"

Michel stretched his legs in front of him. "They are both good men. They could do it. Neither of them would want the responsibility, though." Michel continued. "I am the right one."

"That is why we were surprised." He gave a grunt of approval. "Eve deserves the best."

Michel folded his arms, glad he seemed to have passed that test. "Do you think Eve will adjust to being away from her family? I can see how close you all are."

"Eve will flourish in any land." Dzhambul took a deep inhale on his pipe. "If you want to know if she will be happy, I cannot say."

Michel nodded, wishing for a better answer.

"For that," Dzhambul continued, "you will need to speak with Grandmother." He stood up. "Let's go."

Moments later, they were walking the halls of the palace. Michel had not been back inside since he'd left Borjigin's chambers. He watched for Eve but also watched for her father, fearful of angering the man. Michel scurried behind Dzhambul like a mouse trying to escape the dinner table with a hunk of cheese.

Dzhambul led him through the high stone hallways to a room Michel immediately recognized as a library. Dark wood bookshelves ran floor to ceiling, stopping only for a large window that overlooked the countryside. At the other end was a large fireplace. The fire flickered softly as the sunset cast its last light in through the window. There, reading by the window, was Eve's Grandmother.

Dzhambul led him in and approached the woman. "Grandmother," he said. "I have someone here to see you."

She turned, and at first glance, Michel was transported home to his country. Other than the Mongolian deel that she wore and the bright colors braided into her hair, she would have fit in perfectly with any royal court from Chevalerie to Paris. She had high cheeks and a long nose, with completely white hair. Michel saw Eve's resemblance immediately in the woman's stature, her posture, and her features.

"Well, well, a *Frenchman*," she said in their native language. "It has been many years since I laid eyes on someone from my home." She moved to stand as she set her book on the table before her. *Descartes*, Michel noticed.

"No, please." Michel reached forward to take her hand. He kissed her hand and bowed his head to her.

She laughed, enjoying his display. "Please, child," she tittered. "Sit." She situated herself as Michel took the seat across from her. "I was wondering if Borjigin would ever let me meet you."

Dzhambul spoke in hesitant French. "I will leave you two to your conversation. My mouth is not for this language."

The woman reached up to squeeze Dzhambul's arm, from elbow to hand, in a gesture of affection. Then she turned her attention to Michel.

"I'm very happy to meet you," Michel said. "Eve has told me many things about the influence of her grandmother."

"I have had my influence on this great family as it has on me." She smiled warmly at Michel. "I take it you have questions for me?" She raised her brow. "Speak."

It was an interesting sensation for Michel. At once, he saw in this woman Eve, Eve's father, the brothers, but also Michel's own heritage. "I would love to ask you many things," he said. "First, I must ask if you believe Eve will be able to settle so far from her home."

"Have you asked Eve this question?"

Michel gave her a sheepish grin. "I am not allowed to speak with her at the moment."

"Ah, my Borjigin." She laughed. "He's such a grumpy old fart."

Michel enjoyed this woman's humor very much.

The elderly lady leaned back and closed her eyes. She smiled. "When I was a young woman, close to Eve's age, I, too, met a man from very far away. We had a connection that made our differences unimportant. I left everything to be his wife." She opened her eyes and looked at Michel. "I was more settled here than I ever was in France."

"I am glad for you," Michel said. He hesitated. He had more to ask.

"Tell me, Michel, what do you wish to say?"

He looked down. Then out the window. "I just hope that I have not forced any decisions on her by our circumstances."

The lady smiled. "I will tell you a secret," she said, leaning in with a note of mischief in her eyes, just as Michel had seen Eve do many times. "My first son. Borjigin's eldest brother. He was conceived months before we were married."

Michel cocked his head at this news.

"My husband, Naranbataar, was virtuous in many ways, but there was no waiting for wedding vows once we found each other." She chuckled.

Michel dropped his head in a laugh.

"When we arrived here at the Issyk Kul," she continued, "we said we were already married in France. Shortly after, we had a marriage ceremony here. Everyone thought it was just a ceremony, but it was our one true wedding. I was several months with child by then." She put her hand on his, weaving her knuckles into his. "Michel, it happens. It wouldn't have changed anything between my husband and me. It wouldn't have changed my desire to be his bride. That connection was there regardless of when the first child came to be." She looked at him solemnly. "Don't tell Borjigin this secret, though. He is too old-fashioned."

Michel smiled. "You have my word."

"You must know Eve well enough to know she wouldn't let circumstance dictate her life." The lady clicked her tongue. "She is too busy commanding everyone and everything around her." She chuckled again.

"Yes," he said with amusement, a deep sense of relief at hearing her opinion. "That is true."

"You just need a chance to speak with her again. She will set your mind at ease."

He nodded.

"I am happy, Grandson," she continued. "After nearly seventy years, there will be a piece of me returning to my homeland." She squeezed Michel's hands. "You just promise to bring my great-grandson back here for a visit."

"I promise," Michel agreed. He shifted before continuing, "I just can't promise the baby will be a boy."

"I had five sons. Eve was the first girl after six brothers. There are only a few princesses scattered throughout her cousins, and not one is a first child." She laughed. "You may be breaking some traditions, Michel, but not all of them."

Two more days and they were ready to move. Michel couldn't believe the absolute abundance of people coming. At one point in his life, he felt in command of a great army with a company of thirty, but he had never experienced anything like this. All of Eve's family: brothers, wives, and children. Only Grandmother and Dzhambul would stay, along with his wife and children. There were the attendants, advisors, and warriors, all to accompany Michel and his future bride back to Chevalerie. It made his life, the life he had promised Eve, seem so small.

He only wished he could better warn his parents. His mother would have a fit that she did not prepare for such venerable guests.

They would travel for about a month, using some of Michel's trade lines, opting for more direct routes when they could. Once they reached the Mediterranean Sea, they'd sail until arriving at the docks of Chevalerie.

It would be an adventure.

He saw Eve for the first time as they departed early in the morning. As she mounted the horse at the front of the procession near her parents, she smiled at him. Michel, stuck in the back of the line behind the brothers, with the attendants, almost fell off his horse from the thundering in his heart. Dressed in the traditional garments of a bride leaving for marriage, her beauty ensnared him as it always did. Grandmother was right. He needed contact with her, confirmation that she was happy. He would feel uneasy until he held her in his arms again. He hoped it wouldn't be their wedding day before he had the chance.

But he supposed the fact that she was there, and her royal house was on the move toward his home, was a good sign.

Many hours later, the sun had come up, traveled across the sky, and started setting again. Michel nearly collapsed off his horse from the pace when they finally stopped, but the rest of the family stayed at work until everything was settled. He blinked and saw a stew steaming over the fire, while the children ran and played.

Michel's focus, the whole day, had been looking for an opportunity to get Eve alone, though it seemed impossible. He finally got his chance when Eve's mother sent her down to the stream for water. Her father was occupied with several of the grandsons, and the brothers were with their own families. For the first time since she had helped him escape the cell weeks ago, he had a chance.

Michel acted stealthily. He knew he would just have a minute.

"Eve!" he whispered sharply, going after her. His boots skidded down the slope, taking large steps to get to her. She had knelt by the river, and when he came to her, he stumbled to his knees. He grabbed her hands so suddenly she dropped the bowl into the rushing water of the stream.

"Michel!" she laughed.

"Eve, *Eve*," he said. "I need to know, quickly, before you are pulled away..." He was suddenly out of breath. "I need to know if this is what you want."

"What?" she asked. "Going to France?"

"Not going to France." He smacked his hand against his chest. "Marrying me. Is this still what you want?"

"Michel," she said. She looked at him quizzically, then playfully, and suddenly he felt stupid for asking her.

"I just wanted to be sure..." he said, deflating. "We haven't spoken. You were so angry with me."

"Michel," she repeated, hands to his chest. "Of course I want to marry you."

"There was so much that you didn't tell me about yourself. About your family," he said. "I didn't know what was true anymore."

She looked down. "I'm sorry for the things I kept from you. I only thought I was protecting you." She touched his cheek. "I won't do that anymore," she said. "I want only what is best for you and me." She touched her stomach. "Our family."

Michel's whole body changed. There was relief inside him that muddled his thinking. Suddenly, he was pulling them both up to stand, and he had her in his arms. He kissed her with abandon, answering a debilitating hunger. Her arms went around him. Her sighs hung in the air. It had been far too long since he had touched her, had her scent in his nose. Then, despite knowing that he couldn't possibly manage, his brain scrambled for a way to get her alone. Her effect on him, maddening as always. Her fingers wove through his hair, pulling, urging him forward. Nothing mattered more than claiming this woman as his own and succumbing to her every will and desire.

Just as his hands began to move, he heard the deep bellow of her father.

"Hands off!" he shouted.

Eve pushed back instantly. Michel stood in a stupid daze, just as Borjigin picked up a rock and threw it at him.

"Ow!" he shouted when the rock hit him on the shoulder.

Borjigin picked up another rock and threw it. Michel ducked just in time to miss a headshot. "Okay, okay!" Michel called.

Eve brought her hands to her mouth in a laugh as she turned to fish her bowl out of the stream. Michel turned and darted away, narrowly missing another stone.

He'd needed to connect with her. Badly. But he could wait. As long as he knew she felt the same way.

At this point in his life, for the emperor and liege of the Chagatai horde, direct descendant of Genghis Khan, and the vector of control for the Western Mongolian tribes, there was not much that Borjigin could say was fun in his life. There were wonderful moments of pride in his family, victory in his tribe, and deep and consoling meditation. But *fun*? Not so much. However, for the weeks that they traveled—in which he reveled in the beauty, intelligence, and love of his family—Borjigin Khan, the Golden Khan, enjoyed torturing his future son-in-law quite a lot.

Ultimately, Borjigin believed it was a good match. During their conversation, he could feel how earnest and thoughtful the boy was. He would have a position of nobility. He would care for and adore his daughter. These things were agreeable.

He did not like that the boy had been intimate with her. That should have been saved for after the wedding. The pregnancy was not ideal. Borjigin himself had only ever been with his own lovely wife, and their wedding night was their first time together. Borjigin thought fondly back to those early days together and wished that Eve could have similar happy, carefree days as she discovered what it meant to be in a marriage. Eve would have to begin her marriage with responsibilities that should not come so soon.

In his deep meditation, Borjigin forgave the pregnancy. Their circumstances of falling in love were unique. In fact, keeping them apart now was nothing more than Borjigin's own ego. But he very much enjoyed throwing rocks at the boy whenever he got too close to his daughter. That was *fun*. And, Borjigin knew, he had great aim. At some point, he started purposely turning his attention away, allowing Michel to sneak to his daughter's side. It made him laugh every time he hit the unsuspecting future duke.

There was one moment, though, that Borjigin let them be. On the final boat trip across the Mediterranean, on a ship captained by Michel's brother, Serge, Eve had been violently seasick. Coupled with stormy waters and a baby in her belly, the poor girl was green for nearly the entire trip. At one point, Borjigin had truly lost track of the two of them. He knew nothing could be happening because Eve was too sick, but as he came down the stairs, he spied them through an open door. The scene did not make him look for the nearest thing to throw.

Michel sat on a bench with Eve's head in his lap. She had closed eyes and a green tint to her skin. Michel stroked her head, whispering to her. Borjigin couldn't hear what he was saying, but Eve was laughing, and the boy was smiling. Michel would say something, and she would laugh with closed eyes and a hand on her stomach. Then she would grimace, and Michel would soothe her and make her laugh once more. The feeling of warmth traveled through him.

As he stood there, spying on them, his wife passed. She peeked in through the crack in the door. "Leave them," she said, as she put a hand on her husband's shoulder. "They are doing nothing."

"I will," Borjigin replied. Then he put his arm around his wife's waist and went with her back down the hall.

As a father, he felt a swell of confidence that his beautiful daughter would be fully cared for in his absence.

Chapter Forty-Four

Duchess Laure was taking her tea on the balcony of her sitting room, overlooking the vast expanse of the city, when she saw the town erupt with energy. From atop the hill where her palace was situated, she could see the markings of a large troop, a very large troop, coming through the city and toward her palace. Below, she heard the clangs of swords, which often rang out in the morning as her daughter-in-law, Alex, held her swordsmanship class outside in the warm sun.

Her husband, Guillaume, the Duke of Chevalerie, was in his study with their youngest son, Philippe, and Cardinal Mazarin. They were going over territory maps and local disputes.

"Guillaume, Cardinal," she called into the room. "Come see this."

Several days ago, a cryptic message had arrived from Michel's own hand. He would be home soon. He would be traveling with some very important people. He requested the audience of the Cardinal. He did not give any more details, other than that he would explain everything in person and not to worry.

But Laure was a mother. Of course, she worried.

Guillaume came to stand by her side. The Cardinal and Philippe followed.

"That is more than we expected," snorted Philippe upon seeing the trail of people, carts, and horses.

"Michel said nothing of all this," said Guillaume.

"Are they aggressive?" asked the Cardinal.

"Don't worry," said Guillaume. "You are protected in my walls, Cardinal. Remain in the study until we determine the situation." Guillaume turned, Laure presumed, to go rally the guards.

"I'm going down with Alex," Philippe said tersely, his pace hastening as he went to his wife.

Laure hustled herself. Though she didn't want to assume the worst, Laure would need to organize the inside of the house. Down the back stairs, around the kitchen, with determined and practiced calmness, she found her head housekeeper. She caught her off to the side. "There is a large troupe approaching. We haven't determined their intent, but please alert the staff if we must lockdown."

"Yes, *madame*," Cosette said, and she was off.

Laure went down into the stables to notify the workers. Then she went to the front.

Guillaume had gathered the guards, and they stood at the ready behind him. Philippe stood beside him.

Laure remained behind the gates. She did not want to be of concern to her husband if things became suddenly dangerous.

She quickly saw, however, that it was indeed Michel at the front of the large group, and she felt relieved at seeing him safe. He looked...well, how did he look? Terrible, haggard, his hair grown out and messy. He looked handsome as he always did, but she could tell her son had been through trying days. Then, as she focused on more than just her son, she realized these were people from far away. Imperial, majestic.

"All is well!" Michel called out.

Guillaume, taking the cue from Michel, called the guards to relax their stance. Laure came out from behind the gates.

Michel dismounted his horse. The imperial man joined him, and together, they approached Guillaume.

"This is my father, the Duke of Chevalerie." Then Michel turned to his father, looking very serious. "Father, this is Borjigin Khan, the Golden Khan, of the Mongolian Chagatai Empire." Michel nodded toward the formidable man at his side. "With your consent, he will be my father-in-law."

That's when Laure saw the beautiful girl on her own horse come into view.

Oh my, Laure realized. *Oh my*! She held her hand to her chest. Laure watched with a breath held.

Guillaume looked from the man to Michel. Michel nodded. "He speaks French."

The man—truly golden, his hair, his skin—and his daughter matched the sunshine. They came before Guillaume. Guillaume extended his arms in the formal greeting. They gripped each other, elbows to hands.

"Forgive me for not speaking your native tongue," Guillaume said. "It has been some time for me." They released arms. "You have traveled far. Please be welcome at our home."

The men nodded at each other, and both began calling out orders to their sides. Then Michel took the girl's hand to help her down from the horse and led her to Laure.

Laure understood. It was not long ago that she teased Michel about how his life outlook and his rigidness would change once he fell in love. She would tease him more later, but now was not the time.

"Mother," Michel said. He reached forward and hugged her.

"I'm happy to see you, Son."

Michel pulled back. He turned to take the girl's hand. "Mother," he said pointedly. "This is Eve. We will be married." He paused to put one hand on the girl's belly. "And it will need to happen soon."

Laure's eyes widened, suddenly realizing her son had more challenges on this journey than he was used to. She felt the warmth between Michel and his future bride, the rightness of their union. Then the girl's father, Borjigin, shouted something at Michel in their native language. Michel grimaced and pulled back. The girl looked down with a laugh.

Indeed, Laure thought, keeping her amusement to herself, Michel, her most patient, rule-abiding, stoic son, had gotten into some trouble on this adventure. Good for him.

Borjigin came forward to speak. "I thank you for welcoming us. Before we can be family, I must insist that my impulsive daughter is assigned a chaperone."

"Father," she said sharply. "We have just arrived. Allow us a moment to breathe."

"No, Eve," he said. "You are still unmarried and shall be treated as such."

"Then mother can continue to stay with me," she said. "Do not start making demands of our new family."

"No," he said. Now he spoke to Guillaume. "I have not had the enjoyment of my wife in a month because she has slept by Eve's side."

Guillaume smiled and nodded his head.

Laure jumped in. "I'm sure we can find her a suitable chaperone. We have a staff and any one of the girls—"

"I want her," Borjigin said, pointing past the group of people. "I saw her with her sword as we entered."

Laure followed his hand and saw he was pointing at Alex, Philippe's wife. Alex was leaning against her sword as she stood next to Philippe.

"Me?" she croaked.

"Wait a second—" said Philippe.

"Please come here, my lady," Borjigin insisted.

Alex and Philippe exchanged a glance and she came forward. She stood before Borjigin.

"You are a woman who wields a sword?"

"Yes, I am," said Alex, straightening up at being addressed.

"You are the sister-in-law of Michel?"

She glanced at Michel. "Yes." She nodded. "I am."

He turned to Michel. "Would you feel safe having this woman chaperone Eve?"

Michel gave a grin. "I would indeed."

Borjigin turned back to Alex. "Then will you do my family the favor of guarding and protecting my daughter until she is wed?"

"I would be honored to do so," she said, bowing her head to the man and casting a smile to her new sister-in-law.

"Then you have my gratitude," he said, giving Alex a nod.

In an instant, movement came from every direction. There was much to do. The men would go behind closed doors to discuss legal arrangements. The women would have all the other arrangements to make. Laure would prepare her home. She would be planning a wedding. Alex would chaperone Eve. They would all be a family soon.

And then she was soon to be a grandmother!

No pauses, no more pleasantries. Michel followed his father and Borjigin to the study, where the Cardinal waited. They navigated introductions. Michel cared very little about the dealings at this point. Now that he was home, with the three men before him, it would be out of his hands. They would negotiate terms. Michel felt glad that he was able to bring the market home, that he could protect his family and city from an unfair tax and political unrest, though in the end, he had very little to do with it. Despite his planning, scheming, and reputation, it was Eve who had procured the deal, Borjigin who had accepted it, and Michel's father who would maintain it. Michel would just inherit the benefits, like everything else.

They entered his father's study and sat around the long wooden table where many missions had been planned. His father sat at his seat at the head, with Borjigin in his regal deel and golden features, to the right. Michel sat next to the Cardinal, an intense and very insistent man with a spindly mustache, dressed in fine silks. Aware that it was to appease this man that Michel had set out with such lofty goals in the first place, Michel was just too exhausted to be proud of bringing home such a fine offer for his country.

The negotiations went on and on. Michel answered specifics. He translated a few phrases that Borjigin did not understand. The orange book, the one Eve had kept meticulously updated—minus any crass drawings—passed between them multiple times.

At the final layer of negotiations, when the sun had begun to descend, and the attendants had been in to light candles and change out refreshments, the Cardinal spoke.

"The king will find this agreeable." The man had pleasure in his hollow features. He turned to Guillaume. "You, of course, will be the vector for France and will maintain the king's authority and oversight." Then he reached forward to shake Borjigin's hand.

Finally, Michel thought, it was done.

Borjigin, however, did not take the Cardinal's hand in agreement. "No," Borjigin said. "It will go through Michel." Borjigin turned to speak to

Guillaume. "I mean no disrespect to you, but I prefer to work directly with this one." He nodded toward Michel. "He will be my contact. My only contact. I will deal with him directly."

Michel's eyes darted from the Cardinal to Borjigin. He hadn't expected that.

The Cardinal, not used to being told *no*, spoke up. "Trade at this level is typically done through someone with a title, like the Duke here."

"I do not have a problem with this," said Guillaume. "Michel put the work into this commodity. It's his deal."

The Cardinal leaned back, in thought. "What of Renault? He refuses to work with Michel now. He is an important administrator on this route."

Guillaume threw up his hand. "Let Renault twist in the wind. He abandoned Michel." He nodded to Borjigin. "And my future daughter-in-law. When they were in need." Guillaume leaned forward, his elbows on the table. "He comes to ask *our* forgiveness, not the other way around. Besides," he continued, "this cashmere," he let out a whistle, "will more than make up for what is lost through Renault and Kashgar."

Borjigin spoke then. "Michel will be a Duke. My daughter will be the Duchess. Together, they know both ends of the agreement, both parties, and any commodities we trade. Eve will know the value of the cashmere. Michel will know how to manage the rest." He nodded. "It will be him or no one."

The Cardinal nodded. "Very well, if everyone is in agreement. Michel, we will rely on you."

Michel nodded, accepting the responsibility. Proud of the trust from these men. "Of course," he agreed, straightening his spine as he did. "I will do my best as always."

Handshakes were exchanged, signatures made, and negotiations completed.

A quarter of an hour later, Michel walked with Borjigin back to the great hall, where the attendants would take him to his room so he could prepare for dinner. Michel felt the silence between them, but it did not feel strained. He decided to speak to the man while he could. "I appreciate you putting your trust in me to run the trade."

Borjigin nodded.

Michel continued. "I recognize that it is Eve you wish to work with, but I will be the best liaison I can be to make that happen."

He was silent, and Michel thought that was the end of the conversation. Then Borjigin spoke. "I do want Eve involved. That was not why I said I wish to work with you, though. I believe you are a good businessman. A good leader."

Michel blinked back surprise that he didn't want the man to see. "I appreciate that, Khan."

"I am glad Eve has found you," Borjigin continued after a moment. "If I trust you with my daughter, it should be no surprise I will trust you with some cashmere."

"Thank you, Borjigin," he said, careful not to appear too pleased, careful to control his emotion. "I will do my best to make you proud."

Borjigin didn't say another word to him for the rest of the night. But he didn't throw any more rocks either.

Chapter Forty-Five

Eve liked her new sister-in-law, Alex, very much. She was sweet but not at all subservient. Eve wondered at her ability with the sword. She had never seen a woman warrior before, and Eve looked forward to watching her spar. She delighted at the mention that Alex and her husband, Philippe, often sparred with each other. What a way to get out frustrations, Eve mused.

They spent the day watching Eve's family set up their yurts around the palace. Alex showed her the Chevalerie gardens and all her favorite spots in the palace. The greenery was much different than her home. It was softer, smoother. The breeze on the hilltop did not attack her but rather brushed past in a hurry. From everything she saw, she already loved France. Philippe lingered around them, not seeming too happy about losing his wife to this assignment of chaperone, but Alex would calm him and send him away.

Her father's proclamation that she must have a chaperone, Eve knew, at this point was purely ornamental. He had to make his final stand and complete Eve's punishment for getting herself pregnant before marriage. He refused to drop the importance of it. But *oh,* how she had been humiliated in front of her new family members and at the palace where she would one day be the mistress. She had come all this way to be scolded by her father in front of an audience.

At the end of the day, Eve lay in bed in what would be her room until she and Michel were married. She had been bathed and dressed in her night clothes by excited maids, while Alex made her laugh with stories of Michel and his brothers. Now, Alex lay on the bed, still dressed, as she had not yet prepared for bed, telling Eve the story of how she and Philippe had come to marry. Eve enjoyed hearing that these brothers had a tradition of showing up with an unexpected bride.

"So, perhaps it was not a great surprise that Michel showed up with me?"

"Michel showing up with a bride is a surprise. He's always said he would only marry when it 'suited his position,'" she said in a mocking tone. Alex tucked her hands together under her chin. "Now we will wait for Serge to come off the seas with a bride. That will be the true miracle."

Eve felt warmth for all these new people. "I know Michel must be overwhelmed with all of this," she said. "He is so used to being in charge of everything."

"It is good for him to lose some of his control, especially to his wife," Alex continued. "Marriage is a constant battle to be on top." She grinned.

Eve smiled at her new friend. She was about to say how happy she was to have met Alex when she heard something like a grunt from outside and metal scraping against stone. Alex perked up and gave her a mischievous wink.

"What's that?" Eve asked.

Alex just leaned over and gave Eve a quick kiss on the cheek. "I pledged to your father I would protect you, but I think someone else can do it better, at least during the night." Then she hopped up to scurry to the window. She pulled the curtains aside.

Eve sat straight up. Suddenly, she saw Michel hoist himself through the window.

"Thank you, Alex," he said, running his hand up the back of his head. "I'm not as used to sneaking around this place as you and Philippe."

She snorted a laugh as he gave her a hug. "Anytime, Michel." She turned back to Eve. "Goodnight!" she called in a whisper as she scooted out of the window. Then, to someone outside, "I *am* being careful." Then again, "Philippe, just hold on."

Eve heard their laughter as it disappeared into the night.

Then she was alone, for the first time, with the man she would marry. Michel.

The emotion of it struck her like a horse whip. She looked at him, feeling her hands shake and her skin tingle. She wanted him so badly, and he had been so near, but utterly untouchable for so long.

"I only came here to be with you," he said. He held out his hands to prove his innocence. "We don't have to do anything."

"Are you insane?" She leapt out of bed and ran to him. She threw her hands around his neck and blanketed him with kisses.

"Are you sure?" he laughed. Even as he did, he pulled her closer to him. His hands squeezed into her hips, and she could feel his heat through the thin layer of her night clothes. "The wedding—" he trailed off.

"Please don't make me wait any longer," she whispered against his lips.

Then Michel grinned wickedly at her and picked her up. "Thank God."

He moved her to the bed and set her down gently, but Eve was up on her knees in an instant, pulling furiously on his shirt while he threw off as much as he could. He ran his fingers across her body. She tingled where his fingertips touched.

He pulled his shirt over his head, removed his belt, and his shoes. He dropped his pants, and they were both in only their undergarments. Then he came up on the bed behind her. He kneeled behind her, with his front against her back as he pulled her shift up over her head. She could feel the rigidity of his body, his muscles, the thick length of him. She had his spicy scent all around her, his warmth already penetrating. She wanted everything now, right now.

She turned to urge him forward. Michel held her in place. "Slowly," he coaxed.

She groaned and turned again to attack him.

"Slowly," he repeated, his hands firm on her.

She groaned but conceded to let him take his time and touch her.

With his hard body behind her, his hands on her front, he ran them over her thighs and up over her hips. He paused over her belly, which had only slightly expanded at this point. "It feels different," he said in awe. "It's firm."

"Yes, I know," she hurried her words. "Faster, Michel," she pleaded. "Now, take me now."

Michel just laughed softly in her ear and continued moving his hands up her body, using his touch to tease her—his breath in her ear, his lips on her neck. Eve could barely take it.

She threw her arms back around his neck, urging his hands onto her breasts. "Michel," she begged.

"Slowly," he replied in a whisper. Now she could hear his own voice becoming raspy. She hoped it meant he wouldn't make her wait too much longer.

He slipped his hands up her skin and gripped her breasts. The contact caused her to groan and fall back against him, pressing herself into his hands. She gasped for breath. So did he.

"Michel," she said, her legs weakening as she fell against him. "Please."

"Would you like me to hurry up?" he whispered against her ear, a tease in his voice.

"Yes, please." She swallowed. "Anything. Do something."

Then Michel moved around to face her. He grabbed her hips and lay her down across the bed. He gave her that wicked smile she loved so much. Eve reached for him with both her arms and legs, trying to pull him into her as fast as she could. He dropped his head and found her breast, sucking her nipple into his mouth as he made the other one pebble with his fingers. She arched into his touch. Then he switched the motion, trading mouth for hand, hand for mouth. Eve moved her hips up to feel him, wanting pressure between her legs. She felt like she might implode waiting for him.

She felt him grinning as he traveled down her navel, drawing circles with his tongue. She could do nothing more than wait.

Then his hands were on her undergarments, pulling them down. The cool air hit her, but it was quickly replaced by his warm, wet tongue, swiping right up her center.

Eve gripped the quilt and arched up off the bed.

"Easy," Michel chuckled. He touched his tongue against her, causing Eve to moan again.

Her mind had gone mute. There were only the sensations in her body causing her to twist and writhe beneath him. She bucked her hips up against him, only to be held down by his strong hands.

She wouldn't think again, couldn't, until she had this release. She had needed him, dreamed about him, cried because of him, fought for him in the time they had been apart, and now she needed to feel him. She reached into his hair, begging for relief.

Just as she was ready to crest the wave and explode into a thousand sunsets, she realized Michel had slowed, his kisses became too tender, his touch too soft.

She looked at him, and he gave her a lazy smile as he licked her wetness up. "Slowly," he drawled.

"Michel," she scolded, angry. "If you continue to tease me, I swear I will scream."

"No!" he laughed. "I'll be good." And he returned to her sweet spots.

This time, Eve felt his finger slide inside her. As he curled it into her, he took a heavy stroke with his tongue. It took just seconds of feeling all his attention on her, and Eve was back at the edge. Her breath caught, and she threw her head back. She felt the wave overtake her as Michel continued manipulating her until she had no order or control over her movements. The pleasure throbbed through her, centering on the places he touched her.

After she caught her breath, she found his eyes again as he kissed her thighs and stomach. He held her around the waist and nuzzled into her navel with a groan.

"Eve," he moaned. He looked up at her.

Her body still ached, wanting more, wanting all of him. But she calmed herself. They needed this moment of softness. "Yes, my love," she said, reaching down to caress his cheek.

Michel pulled himself up. He rested his hands on either side of her. They stared at each other. Eve could see he was working out things to say to her, but she knew what he felt.

"You thought you had lost me?" Eve said to him.

He put his forehead against her and nodded while he still held his body above her.

"You didn't think we would ever come together again," she continued.

"No," he breathed. "It terrified me. When you got me out of the cell, I hope you know, I never once thought to leave. I was there the whole time. I would have died trying to get back to you."

She reached her hands up and wrapped them around his neck. "I know that now," she said, resolutely. "I should never have sent you away."

"It scared me how quickly nothing else mattered to me. Only you." Then he smiled. "I hope I can still function now that I have you in my life."

"Michel," she murmured. She pulled him to her, letting her lips touch his, tasting herself on him. "We have it all to figure out, together."

He kissed her, their lips and tongues coming together past the slick layer her orgasm had left on him. She had never imagined sharing so much of herself with a man, but here she was. And she couldn't be happier.

That is, until her body couldn't take it any longer.

Suddenly, she slapped her arms down on the bed. "Now, Michel, please take me before I lose my mind."

He needed no more provocation. "Siren," he growled, drawing the word out between his teeth. He spread her legs apart and lined himself up against her. She angled toward him, wild with want. She almost couldn't stand it. She felt his stiff cock at the base of her, and then with a growl and a bite to her neck, he was fully inside her.

Eve groaned and fell back onto the pillows, her body arching up and her head going back, full with him. It felt different somehow. Her body had changed since the last time they were together. After the intensity of the last orgasm, she felt even more sensitive. When he finally pushed all the way in until her body wouldn't let him go any further, she knew if he stayed just a second longer, she would orgasm right there and then.

But Michel pulled back.

"*Michel*," she hissed.

"Greedy girl," he growled, and he did it again, repeating the same slow, agonizing movement.

Every nerve in her body reacted. She wrapped her legs around him. This time, when he was all the way in, she held him, wanting to orgasm, not wanting to wait.

"Slowly," he whispered, delighted, against her lips. He pulled out again, leaving Eve's body shuddering with wild want.

She groaned loudly, then threw her head back and laughed. She gave herself over. He had control of her now. He had found her. He had saved her. He had come to her and brought her home, and he would marry her soon. She'd let him have control.

Her surrender seemed to be all he wanted, and she saw his face change. His body moved quicker, his pace gave new intensity. He leaned in and kissed her. He held her lips while he moved into her again, joining them in the most delicious way. The friction unfurled inside her, and she felt her body doubling back and rebuilding. She would wait for him, let him take his time, knowing they belonged to each other.

"Yes, *yes*," she urged. She moaned loudly as his movements came more quickly.

"Eve." He grunted. "Quiet." He put his hand over her mouth.

She bit him.

"Ah!" he pulled back and shook his hand.

Eve laughed. He didn't have *complete* control over her.

"You're too much," he said before kissing her once more.

Michel's chest rumbled with sounds of pleasure, and she let only small gasps and moans escape her lips. Then Michel took one of her legs and threw it over his shoulder. He moved in her, deep and desperate. The new angle caused Eve to throw her head back. Michel moved forcefully, endlessly.

Eve clung to him. She arched forward, and on a wave of tension, she felt Michel's pleasure meeting hers. He gasped and grunted, and the tension caused her own orgasm to release, rocketing through her in a way that had her arching up off the bed. Her hips continued to move against him, her body still seeking contact. She kissed his shoulder and his neck as he relaxed on top of her.

As everything subsided, she became aware that they were kissing, slow and steady and calm. They were no longer running, she realized. They were there.

"Now," he said with a laugh as he rolled to the side, taking her with him. He ran his hand down her side and kissed her neck. "I just have to make sure your father doesn't catch me leaving your room in the morning."

"Indeed, Michel," she replied. "There won't be a rock big enough."

Chapter Forty-Six

One week later, Eve stood at the altar with Michel, a man who was minutes away from being her husband. He was dressed in the finery of his home—a dark blue jacket with gold accents, his dark hair brushed back, his eyes sparkling with happiness. Eve wore a white silk gown, slim-fitted—not too tight around the waist—cut in the French style, but with beautiful colored designs woven through by her mother and sisters-in-law. It was a perfect combination of all the things that were parts of her: her ancestry, who she had been, and who she would become. She couldn't wait for her future with Michel.

Thank goodness the day had finally come, though, because in the last week, her body had really begun to change. It would feel very good to be the wife, the pregnant wife, of the future Duke rather than the daughter who had gotten herself into trouble. Or the woman who had gotten herself kidnapped. Who cares if people ever figured out the math?

Behind her were two families. Her lavishly ornate mother and father, her brothers, sisters-in-law, nieces, and nephews. Their own guards, elders, and captains. On the other side sat Michel's family, simply elegant and regal. Michel's two brothers were there, along with her new friend Alex, who had her hands up to her chin as she grinned away through the ceremony. Her in-laws looked proud. Her parents, though they were as stoic as ever, did not hide their pleasure at the event. Eve felt the ancestors' approval, deep in her heart.

Then there was Michel. Her handsome, strong, wonderful man. A man who would protect her, who would exalt her, who would do anything he could for her. He had visited her every night in the last week, but tonight would be the first time they could be together with no one having to climb in and out of windows and without having to give him up to the sunrise. She felt so elated that she hardly heard the ceremony taking place. Everything had come together, the once unraveled threads of her life all finding their way into this perfect, beautiful pattern.

When the priest asked her to kiss her new husband, she did. Funny how their story had started with a very different wedding. This wedding, however, would be their true beginning.

Thank you for reading! Did you enjoy? Please add your review because nothing helps an author more and encourages readers to take a chance on a book than a review.

If you'd like a bonus scene to see how Michel and Eve are adjusting to being in Chevalerie after the wedding, you can grab it here or on Florence's website at www.florenceabliss.com. And don't miss more from Florence A. Bliss's *Swords of Chevalerie* series, coming soon.

Until then, discover THE LAIRD OF DUNCAIRN, by City Owl Author, Craig Comer. Turn the page for a sneak peek!

You can also sign up for the City Owl Press newsletter to receive notice of all book releases!

BY CRAIG COMER

SCOTLAND, 1882

Effie exposed her hand to the growling bear. Her fingers found Rorie's head and gave him a few soothing strokes behind the ears. A rumble came from deep in his gullet, as fierce as his wee body could muster. Frigid wind blasted them as they hid behind a large boulder atop the crown of Ben Nevis, the highest peak in the Highlands. A stranger had come to speak with her employer, Thomas Stevenson. Not an odd occurrence, but for a fortnight Rorie had groaned and whined, pawing for her attention as if disturbed by dark thoughts, trying to plead with her that something was amiss. And now that the stranger had come, Rorie's discomfort had turned into malice.

"If only I could peer into that head of yours and see what the fuss is about," she said, planting her hands firmly on her hips.

Rorie squatted on his haunches with a big huff, turning his head away. Though preferring the wild of the forest, he behaved himself around others when she asked. And only because it was she who asked. The bond had something to do with her Sithling blood, but Effie couldn't explain how it worked. It was as much a mystery to her as any of the uncanny bonds she'd made with woodland creatures, lazy housecats, and goofy hounds over the years. As much a mystery as why the queen and all the lords of London abhorred her kind, though she'd done nothing to warrant their wrath.

Rorie had been loyal to her ever since she'd convinced Stuart Graham to rescue him from a carnival the prior year, saving him from a brutal—and probably short—life of baiting. But he'd never acted so ill-tempered. Had the stranger come to take him away? Or was it she who should be fearful? By sight alone, the stranger wouldn't know her for a Sithling. Short of stature, with a young woman's curves and chestnut locks clipped about the shoulders, she lived her life amongst the Scots all but unnoticed, the truth of her mixed fey blood hidden.

Yet such reliance on appearance was a false safety.

Her hair whipped about her face, blinding her until she swept it back. The lodge of the Scottish Meteorological Society perched only a short distance away, a cozy, timbered house well-weathered from years of driving gales. Its chimney puffed white smoke, teasing her with thoughts of hot tea and honeyed biscuits. But that was where Mr. Stevenson had taken the stranger, and he'd instructed her not to return until he bade her. She blew into her hands for warmth, vexed by the riddle of the strange visitor, unable to contain her curiosity any longer.

"I'm going for a closer look," she said to Rorie. "Wait here." Hoarfrost crunched as she shifted her weight and slunk forward. The frozen dew crusted the fern and bracken around the lodge, radiating a cold that sank into her bones. Her olive-colored dress and drab woolen coat were serviceable enough, but they did little against the cutting winds atop the mountain, winds that drove in the damp air as if she wore nothing as all.

She understood why Mr. Stevenson wished her to hide. He was a man who believed in prudence. He would not jeopardize one of his great works, nor his reputation nor her safety, on the off chance a stranger would find her out. There were some who could recognize her fey nature if they stood close enough. The scientists of the day, many of whom had their pockets lined by London's coin, said fey blood corrupted the flesh, giving off an odor that some could smell. Catholics and Protestants alike said it was the sins of the fey that radiated a cloud of evil around them, allowing those pure of heart to perceive them. Other tales held that a fey's eyes glowed in the dark or that they would burst into flame if they touched iron. All of it seemed foolish to Effie. She drank her tea and let it pass the same way as anyone she'd ever met, regardless of their blood. How some knew her for a Sithling while most did not was as random as why some seeds took root and others wilted.

A whistle shrieked, drawing her attention. Next to the lodge, Mr. Stevenson's plans for a great observatory were coming to fruition. Steel beams braced half-raised walls as masons slathered on stone and concrete by the ton. The pipes of a steam crane shuddered, and a burst of gas exhaled as another beam was lifted into place, soaring thrice the height of a man to the workers waiting above. The construction was what had brought them to Ben Nevis, and Effie guessed the stranger would not have come if he weren't involved with the great project in some manner.

She stalked forward, half-crouched so the wind wouldn't stagger her, and reached the sill of one of the lodge's thick windows. Grabbing the smooth, lacquered wood for support, she peered through the glass into the lodge's main room. It held several tables of a dark and sturdy teak, and a stone hearth large enough for a royal estate.

The stranger stood with his back toward her. His coat and polished shoes bespoke a city, but not the odd leather cap with its flaps that clung tight around his ears. She didn't recognize the tartan on his trousers: blues, greens, and purples all jumbled together as if shouting at her. She recalled he'd driven his own steam carriage up the winding road, working the levers and knobs as if he were used to the task, an odd thing for a wealthy man.

"I will take your concerns into account, Mr. Crofter," said Stevenson. The window's frame had warped over the years, allowing her to hear him clearly. He stood by the hearth. A dark coat fit snugly around his stout frame, its wool threadbare from years of rugged service. His balding head held tufts of hair around the ears, yet they served to dignify his face rather than embarrass it.

"They are not just my concerns, Mr. Stevenson. They carry the weight of the Society. It is time to distance ourselves from such relations. Lord Granville will have his way, and you must choose where your loyalties lie— with the Society or with your fey friends."

Stevenson's face darkened. "We have pushed back these threats before and should not wilt so easily to tactics of hatemongering. Parliament has no grounds, and Lord Granville not enough allies."

A shadow moved from the corner of the room, and Stuart Graham's stocky frame came into view from where she crouched outside. The man's knee-length boots were coated in mud, a workman's badge he wore proudly, and his white locks curled in ringlets atop a face as cheery as it was round.

"Bah, let us speak plain, Mr. Crofter. You knew of Mr. Stevenson's associations before you funded the observatory. It was his name alone which brought in enough benefactors to ensure the completion of construction."

Mr. Crofter grunted. "Do you think any of these benefactors will stand against the threat of an Inquiry? No, Mr. Graham, they will scatter like rats." The stranger turned to Stevenson. "You will do as we ask, or we will sever ties and throw you to the wolves. One noted engineer is easily replaced by another. Now I bid you good day." He slapped his gloves together and strode for the door.

Effie recoiled. The news from London must be dire for Mr. Crofter to speak to Stevenson as he had. She crept to the front corner of the lodge and watched the small yard of trampled grass where the stranger's carriage sat. Graham emerged from the lodge's main door. He pulled a worn and battered watch from his pocket and studied it before casting his gaze to the skies. Mr. Crofter came out on Graham's heels, walking cane thumping the dirt as he ambled. The pair exchanged a cordial nod, similar to one shared by passing gentlemen in a city street. Effie didn't understand such manners. It was clear Graham was in a foul mood and Mr. Crofter the cause of it, but they pretended like nothing cross had occurred between them.

Rorie wasn't as polite. A low growl came from behind the boulder where she'd left him, and the bruin's head popped into view, teeth bared. She waved at him to stay back, but the noise had already drawn Mr. Crofter's attention. He peered at the boulder, his eyes growing wide. He muttered something, a scowl on his face, before clambering into the waiting steam carriage. Graham stood stiffly while the other man brought the boiler into action. The carriage's engine was a monster of steel and wood, with copper tubes lashed in a lattice across its flank and a charred snout thrusting upward from its roof. With a parting nod, Mr. Crofter threw open the valve, and the carriage sputtered forth with a burst of burnt coal perfuming the air. Only when the squeaking of the carriage's axles had faded down the mountain road did Graham turn to stare right at Effie.

As he beckoned her, brooding clouds rolled over the surrounding hills, darkening the sky. The wind gusted, flapping his leather coat about his legs. Neither were good omens. She stood and crossed to him, her cheeks flushed in embarrassment. He greeted her with a grin forced from pursed lips, and he spoke in a rushed manner, barely taking a breath.

"Och, lass," he said. "You took a risk. If my waistcoat weren't as round as an ox, ye'd surely been seen. It's like to piss down any moment. Let's get into the warmth before it does. Mr. Stevenson wants a word."

Effie nodded sheepishly as the steam crane's whistle shrilled again. Black smoke belched from its boiler, the engine fighting the strain of the wind. But she needn't watch the work progress to know the shape of the observatory. Its structure had long been affixed in her head from the drawings she'd rendered of the project. That was her place in the endeavor. Stevenson had discovered her talent for depicting his designs years before when she was just a lost girl sheltering under his protection. She'd sought him out after the death of her mother, the famous lighthouse engineer who designed edifices powered by stardust—the glowing azure silt, forged by Fey Craft, that burned hotter than oil and slower than coal. Her eyes grew glassy. The time was a blurred memory that still haunted her dreams. She'd come close to starvation and almost succumbed to exposure. Worse, she'd been captured and beaten by the queen's Sniffers, those who hunted fey, and only managed to escape by sheer luck. Yet none of those trials compared to the sorrow of isolation, the sense that all her warmth and cheer had fled. That she was alone, the last of her family, nearly the last of the Sithlings.

Alone and yet not alone. She glanced at the dark shadows of forest sprouting from the hills ranging beneath the peak of Ben Nevis. How many of the other fey races hid there watching them? Pixies and brownies, gnomes and hogboons all still dwelt within the Highlands. The remnants of a Seily Court existed, yet her mother had taught her to be as wary of it as of the Scots. She could count on a single hand the number of fey she'd ever met, and none were likely to take her in if the need arose. Such was the way for many Sithlings. Despite their appearance, they lived between races, not quite human and not quite fey. Their blood derived from a sect of the Daoine Sith interbred with the Votadini, an ancient human clan whose might had receded under an onslaught of Scoti tribesmen. What remained centuries later could claim neither as kinsfolk.

Effie followed the man she considered an uncle into the lodge. Heat from the hearth enveloped her the moment she stepped inside, soothing away the bite the cold wind had left. Laid out on one of the tables were Thomas Stevenson's plans of the observatory, his lines and notes as formal and stiff as he was. On another perched the casing for one of his famous screens, a protective box for meteorological instruments. Its sides were angled slats designed to keep moisture from the instruments contained within, allowing them to collect data for weeks on end unattended. Her own worktable rested in a corner. A collection of colored charcoals, neatly arranged within a tin, sat atop a rendering of the observatory. Her drawings always held more flora than the bleak locations Stevenson chose to build on, and the observatory was no exception. Ben Nevis' crown boasted none of the hearty pines and spring flowers her depiction held, but that never seemed to bother her employer.

Stevenson greeted her with a curt nod and gestured to a chair by the hearth. He didn't make her wait long, once settled. "Our caller was Mr. James Crofter, a noted engineer whose father worked with Thomas Telford on the Great Canal." Effie's lips tugged at a smile. To Stevenson, names were always linked to matters of accomplishment. His own noted a long family line of engineers. "He came to us in haste with news from the coast. Murder has been done in the village of Duncairn."

Effie started. If given a dozen guesses, it was not the news she'd expected to hear. She read Stevenson's face, but it remained a stone mask. "Was it someone you knew?"

"A fisherman," answered Graham, bringing her a cup of tea, "An Ewan Ross. His boat capsized in the Bay of Lunan."

She took the cup, piping hot and full of sugar the way she liked, and breathed in its sweetness.

"The importance is not whom but the how," said Stevenson. "Fishermen in the area swear a host of rabid seals tipped Mr. Ross' boat, accosting it in unison. Not normal behavior to say the least."

She stifled a laugh. The poor fisherman deserved better, but the image of a group of seals harassing his vessel, barking and slapping the water with their flippers, was comical to her. "Surely these fishermen are mistaken in what they saw, or perhaps Mr. Ross agitated the seals in some manner. Perhaps they were trying to help the man." She glanced between the two men, wondering if they were jesting with her. "Yet I fail to see how one could call it murder."

"That's what I did say," said Graham. "The Scottish folk are long known for tales of fancy. Any dark bed of kelp becomes the Kraken in their minds."

Stevenson cleared his throat. "Putting Mr. Ross aside, there is a second account Mr. Crofter related. A week ago, a young lass was accosted on the road to Montrose, just outside of Duncairn. She suffered woefully and is much delirious, but describes her attackers as hairy imps slight of stature, with sharp ears and wicked fangs. They battered her as she fled. She recovers now from a fractured skull and other wounds." Stepping to the table, Stevenson rested his fingertips on it. "Short, devilish imps with pointed ears. These creatures have a name. The Shetland folk call them trows."

"Bah, bollocks," spat Graham.

Effie blinked, taken aback by the certainty in Stevenson's gaze. "I had not believed trows real." Her cheeks flushed at the admission. Her knowledge of the fey races, and of Fey Craft, were scarce at best. Much that she knew had come from Stevenson.

"Real enough," said Stevenson, "though not seen in the Highlands for centuries. They are fell creatures not of the Seily Court."

She frowned. "I thought all fey were bound to the Seily Court, before the Leaving at least. The binding is what gave Fey Craft power in this world." That power had dwindled ever since the Daoine Sith abandoned Sidh Chailleann, their ancestral home.

"There are some fey the Seily Court cannot control. They form their own covenants, Unseily Courts they are called, though decades have gone since the last rumors of one's appearance."

"Oh," she said. She stared into her cup, feeling a bit lost. It seemed, every time matters of fey lore arose, she understood the least.

Graham read her expression. "Don't fret, lass. You still ken more of your blood than all of us together. Mr. Stevenson's just got more years of hearing tales than you." He winked. "Many more, by the top of his head."

She forced a smile. Graham often reminded her how young she still was. For all her curves, she was still recent to adulthood by human standards, let alone fey. Thinking on the accounts of Duncairn, she drew the simple connection. "You believe the two attacks are linked, and if these trow creatures did the one, then the seals were really—"

"Selkies," affirmed Stevenson.

"But that doesn't make any sense. Selkies are not wicked creatures. They shed their sealskins in favor of human form to lure men and women into loving them. They don't work in packs, nor accost fishermen at sea."

"I have never heard tale of such a thing either," said Stevenson. "Just the same, fey sightings have grown in past weeks across the Highlands, enough to reach the ears of Her Majesty's Fey Finders, and now with these attacks it is almost certain there will be an Inquiry."

Effie blanched. There hadn't been an Inquiry by the Sniffers in almost fifty years. Most in London called the fey hunters relics, the funds used to support them better used elsewhere. Yet as dire as the news was, it did not follow why Mr. Crofter had spoken of such immediate threats. There was more to the stranger's visit Stevenson wasn't telling her, something she hadn't overheard. She studied his face. Her foot tapped impatiently. Cheeks growing red, she forced herself to still and sip her tea. She could be more stubborn than a stone when it fancied her, but secrets foiled her patience. As much as anything else, curiosity had driven her into the world of man after the passing of her mother, the need to explore the enigma of their society. Yet even as a girl she had always quested after knowledge. Her mother had often scolded her, reminding her life wasn't a puzzle to be solved but a great riddle to be savored.

The lesson had rarely stuck.

She would need to pull the truth out of the man. "Rorie is in a foul temper," she said. "He wants to warn me of something, but I can't understand what. I thought it might be Mr. Crofter."

Graham traded a glance with Stevenson. "She's a woman more than twenty years grown. There's no sense as treating her like the girl she was."

Running a hand over his chin, Stevenson worked at the muscles of his jaw. "Parliament pushes for legislation to formally outlaw any association with the fey. That would include the use of Fey Craft—stardust, precisely—and the harboring of those with fey blood."

"Bah!" Graham cursed. "That kind of nonsense comes up every odd year. They'll make no ground with it. We've still friends enough in London."

Pain flashed in Stevenson's eyes. "That is not the worst of it, you well know, Mr. Graham." He turned to Effie. "The Society feels a sacrifice is in order, something to appease the crown and end talk of an Inquiry. They instructed I draw up a document listing the fey I am in contact with and hand it over to the crown."

Stevenson drew up his weight into a rigid posture, clasping his hands behind his back before speaking. "That is why Mr. Crofter came to us—to demand I betray dear friends."

Effie's blood ran cold, and she had to swallow hard to keep the tea in her stomach from surging upward. So that was it—the missing piece. To protect their investments, the Society wished to send her and Stevenson's other fey allies to the gallows. It was not strictly illegal to harbor pro-fey sympathies, but neither was it fashionable, and those who did often found themselves in prison or their fortunes waning. She sensed Rorie's seething hatred for Mr. Crofter and felt a fury of her own spring to life.

"Do they all know of me, then?" she asked.

"Not directly," answered Stevenson. "But they know I have enough involvement with the fey that I could perhaps influence the crown's good graces."

"You wouldn't!" Effie exclaimed.

"Of course not," Stevenson snapped. He turned from her to cool his temper, yet she thought nothing of his outburst. His benefactors had placed him in a horrible position. They would not let their investments fail; they had too much money at stake. Either he sacrificed the fey known to him, or they would find an engineer to run their projects who would. She had heard Mr. Crofter threaten as much, she now understood.

"It's a fool plan," spat Graham. "I should've skinned the man alive for suggesting such a cowardly thing. The Fey Finders would hang the fey and still seek an Inquiry in Duncairn. Better if this observatory falls to ruin."

Stevenson shook his head. "The Society will not allow that. But they do underestimate the devastation of an Inquiry; they see only what it would mean in London. Her Majesty's Fey Finders care naught whether a fey is good or fell, peaceful or sinister of purpose. Their aim is to demonstrate their own worth. Without check, they'll scour the coast and put to the question all they find, as they did during the Potato Famines a few decades ago. They'll use the Inquiry as a grand stage and propel these legislations through. From there, their wrath would spiral out of control." He pressed his palms against the table, though it appeared he would rather knock it over. "We cannot let that happen. We must strive to show the world that fey and human can coexist."

"What will you do?" Effie asked, eager to hear his thoughts. Part of what drew her to Stevenson was his work, always seeking to blend science with nature. He was a pure naturalist who used stardust to power his famous lighthouses, promoted harmony with the fey, and sought to canonize their lore.

"We must sap the hatemongers of their advantage," said Stevenson. "I will stall them as best I can, but we must find the true motive and intent of these attacks before their Inquiry can come to bear. If the truth is known, there's a chance the Fey Finders will find no allies north of Edinburgh. The Scots have no fondness for London's authority."

Effie considered his words. She had no stomach for politics. Large crowds and public debate went against every fiber of her nature. But that did not mean she would wither away like some English violet. She could not let innocent fey fall victim to such a scheme as the Society planned. If Stevenson meant to unravel the truth of the attacks rather than appease his benefactors, it would take all his resources to hinder their enemies in Parliament, leaving nothing for Duncairn.

So to there she must go.

She rose, her mind settled. "If an Unseily Court exists in Duncairn, we must know of it before the Inquiry. It may be our best chance of gaining leverage, and our only chance to forestall Mr. Crofter's designs." Her words were heavy, but she stiffened her back against them. "I will go there and uncover the truth of the matter."

"What!" Graham barked. "You can't mean to go near that village. The queen's bastards will be crawling over it before the fortnight is through."

Effie swallowed to keep her voice from trembling. "There is danger, but to do nothing is to guarantee more fey will suffer." She faced Graham. "I can do nothing here to help; my presence might even bring greater danger if Mr. Crofter returns."

"You can do less against an Unseily Court!"

"If one exists," she reminded him. She tried to keep herself steady despite the knot forming in her gut. Graham and Stevenson had risked their lives and the fortunes of their families to let her in and give her a sheltered life. She would not balk at doing the same for them. "You are both needed here. At the least you cannot be seen in Duncairn. The scandal would link your names to whatever judgment the Inquiry handed down."

"There are others," huffed Graham. "I ken a man near Montrose who often trades with the fishermen of Duncairn." His tone was more tired than she had ever heard. "He knows much of the fey and has befriended a few in the area. I would have him handle this."

"If you could reach him," said Stevenson. "The man is a drunkard and hasn't responded to your missives in weeks."

"I'll speak with the fishermen and the girl's family," said Effie, "and if an Unseily Court exists, we will throw them to your benefactors and limit the crown's hand. It is the least either party deserves. Please, Mr. Graham, I must do something to protect the lives of the fey. I will not run and hide when I can offer aid instead."

"Bah!" Graham stammered, but his shoulders sagged in defeat. He spun on a heel and stormed out, slamming the door behind him.

The cold gust that rushed in made Effie shiver. She smoothed her coat and stepped closer to the hearth. Stevenson's face fell as blank as unmarked parchment, and he bent to scour over the observatory's designs. Effie knew Stevenson well enough to leave him be. Silent brooding was his nature, and she didn't take offense. To others it might seem he didn't care, but she knew he cared perhaps too much.

"Mr. Graham left his coat," she said. "I'll go after him."

She found Graham watching as the workmen set the observatory's giant lens in place. It was a moment they had planned for weeks. She knew a few of Graham's crew by name, but they all recognized her, giving her a cheery nod or word of greeting. Mr. Stevenson thought it a risk, yet she took that sentiment with a grain of salt. Where Stevenson placed prudence above mirth, Graham naturally exuded an honest warmth. He treated the crew like family and didn't employ a man he didn't trust.

"He should be seeing this." Graham had his arms folded across his chest. His cheeks and nose were rose-colored, as if he'd been nipping a few drams, but it was only from the wind.

"He has more pressing matters on his mind," said Effie, handing Graham his coat. She was not in a mood to speak in circles. "How dangerous are these creatures?"

Graham raised his eyebrow and stared at her askance. "If they're real? Dangerous enough you shouldn't go messing with them. It's a thick lad who pokes at a badger and doesn't expect to get bit."

"But you doubt trows exist?"

Graham stomped his boots for warmth. "I think Stevenson's nose has sniffed after funding for so long that it doesn't know a fart from a flower." Her eyes narrowed, and he held up a hand for her pardon. "This observatory is funded by landowners hoping its weather data will lead to better crop growing. They don't give a cuss about Acts of Parliament or the stars or the fey or any other bit of science that doesn't put more money in their pockets."

He pointed down the road. "That man, Crofter, is from Newcastle where the Hostmen lord over the coal trade for the entire empire. They aren't the type of men one should meddle with, and I wouldn't doubt the bugger is afoul of them."

"And Mr. Stevenson has been led down this path before." Effie finished Graham's thought. The affair with the lighthouse engineer, John Wigham, had left Stevenson accused of reckless slander, his name tarnished forever in the eyes of many in the scientific world.

"He's blinded by his own interests," said Graham.

"It is the fey's interest too," said Effie. "We are also his benefactors and have no other voice. The constabularies will not defend us. The magistrates of Edinburgh are bought and paid for by men who proclaim us the offspring of Black Donald." She stopped short of mentioning Graham's own interests, those of the French merchants who stocked his warehouses full of goods.

Graham gave her a cheery smile, but she saw the doubt and fear behind it. "We have enemies, lass. Too right. Some we know of, some we don't. I can't say as I understand what's going on myself, and that's what frightens me most. There's a strange feeling to this whole ordeal." The smile dropped from his face. "Robert Ramsey is a good man and no drunkard."

She rested a hand on his arm. "I will inquire after him."

He squirmed in frustration. "The tale of this Mr. Ross being killed by selkies is foolishness, and no doubt the other attack was carried out by some drunken rogue. The lass is just mistaken in what she saw or embellishing the tale for some reason." His skepticism made her love him more. It was the concern of a father not believing night had fallen, if only so his child could play in the sun a little longer.

"I've lived a happy life these past years, sheltered from those who would do me harm. That was your doing, yours and Mr. Stevenson's. It's time I repaid you the favor."

Graham's eyes grew moist. "Be careful, lass. The queen's appointed a new Fey Finder General, the man called Edmund Glover. I fear you know him, and he knows you."

Effie's stomach dropped to her toes. The name made her skin crawl. The last time she had heard it, she'd almost died.

Don't stop now. Keep reading with your copy of THE LAIRD OF DUNCAIRN, by City Owl Author, Craig Comer.

And sign up for Florence's newsletter to get all the news, giveaways, excerpts, and more!

Don't miss more from Florence A. Bliss's *Swords of Chevalerie* series, coming soon, and find out more at www.florenceabliss.com

Until then, discover THE LAIRD OF DUNCAIRN, by City Owl Author, Craig Comer!

A war is brewing between the worlds of fey and man . . . but only one can prevail. Find out which in this fantasy featuring nefarious plots, dashing knaves, and militant gnomes.

When Sir Walter Conrad discovers a new energy source, one that could topple nations and revolutionize society, the race to dominate its ownership begins.

But the excavation of this energy will have dire consequences for both humans and fey. For an ancient enemy stirs, awakened by Sir Walter's discovery.

Outcast half-fey Effie of Glen Coe is the empire's only hope at averting the oncoming disaster. But she finds herself embroiled in the conflict, investigating the eldritch evil spreading throughout the Highlands.

As she struggles against the greed of mighty lords and to escape the clutches of the queen's minions, her comfortable world is shattered.

Racing to thwart the growing menace, she realizes the only thing that can save them all is a truce no one wants.

Please sign up for the City Owl Press newsletter for chances to win special subscriber-only contests and giveaways as well as receiving information on upcoming releases and special excerpts.

All reviews are **welcome** and **appreciated**. Please consider leaving one on your favorite social media and book buying sites.

Acknowledgments

So many people to thank for putting up with me.

Thank you to Nicole Op Den Bosch, my author business coach. You took confused me and gave me structure, a timeline, metrics, and a strategy. You are the most amazing cheerleader and your enthusiasm has helped me keep going, even when I wanted to burn down my computer. Your name may be difficult to spell, but you are worth every letter and then some.

Thank you Jessica Shearer, my editor. As I have said to you before, you are *mean* but you are *right*. You find the things I hope no one notices and make me make them work. You gave me deeper insight into the story, helped me find the authenticity of the characters, and were the catalyst for some of the most special moments in the book. This book and all my future awards for it wouldn't exist without you.

Thank you to my Writing Up Romance writer gal pals. Claudia Severin, you were a wonderful mentor throughout the process, and Kristina Knight, you always gave very clear insight to our submissions. Lisa, you always get the joke and laugh at the right moments in the story. Sherry, you are there with unending encouragement, contest info, and resources. Teresa, you never fail to come up with some crazy idea to fix a scene. Cece Trotter, you did a really fantastic edit for me and helped me make big decisions about the story. We have so much fun in our weekly meetings. I will be the first in line for each of your debuts.

Thank you Embry and Jess, for letting me text you over and over about how much I wrote that day and always responding with love. Thank you to Heather for just knowing everything about history and being my personal encyclopedia. Amanda and Mariah, you let me complain endlessly about how much I hate marketing. Thank you Mandie, for letting me go on and on about what a process this is. Thank you Kara for ideas that are great both in and out of the story (wink), and also Gary for all the support, even though it still is weird that you read my books.

Mom, you are just the best. Thank you for supporting me so aggressively. Like, really aggressively supportive. Like you're-kind-of-obsessed-with-me supportive. I love you so much. Thank you Dad for everything you do to keep our family running. Thank you Des, best sister in the world. Without you, I wouldn't be me. Gennaro, my husband, you gave me hours and hours of kid-free time to get this done. Don't worry, babe, now that the book is out, I'll have at least one free evening for you. And thanks to my kids, for giving mama I don't know how many "just five more minutes" of work time.

And of course, Mel! The beautiful woman who inspired Eve. Throughout our friendship, you've always been the cool one, the daring one, the fashionable one, the brave one, the one who knew how to put boys in their place, and the one who stood up for the both of us. How would I have survived without you? Thank you for being such a huge part of my life that you eventually invaded my creative psyche.

Finally, thank you to the City Owl Press team for guidance, community, and a place for this story to call home.

FLORENCE A. BLISS is an author from Las Vegas, NV who has a keen eye for writing love stories full of drama, heartache, humor, and enough passion to light the pages on fire. With an MFA in creative writing from UNLV, Florence loves to write across genres but has found her home in romance. She lives with her fancy Italian husband and two children. Together they love to travel, explore the ghost towns around Las Vegas, and roadtrip up and down the Pacific coast. (Luckily her husband takes great pictures so she doesn't have to.) Florence is an avid people watcher and strives to  understand why people do what they do, and she never tires of imagining the stories of what couples have had to overcome in order to come together.

www.florenceabliss.com

 instagram.com/florence.a.bliss

About the Publisher

City Owl Press is a cutting edge indie publishing company, bringing the world of romance and speculative fiction to discerning readers.

Escape Your World. Get Lost in Ours!

www.cityowlpress.com

facebook.com/CityOwlPress

x.com/cityowlpress

instagram.com/cityowlbooks

pinterest.com/cityowlpress

tiktok.com/@cityowlpress

www.ingramcontent.com/pod-product-compliance
Lightning Source LLC
Chambersburg PA
CBHW021145160726
47994CB00001B/86